T0384372

Acclaim for

ILLUMINARY

"In *Illuminary,* a group of intriguing characters must compete in a prestigious quest where they are not only up against mind-bending puzzles and cryptic challenges, but also the weight of societal scorn. Each riddle they solve–every obstacle they overcome–raises the stakes. Armed with intelligence, determination, and strength forged through adversity, Schroeder's characters are more than just competitors–they are symbols of hope. With every page turn, the suspense mounts, immersing readers in a race against time that demands intelligence, bravery, and faith. *Illuminary* is a delightful surprise that will stay with you long after the final page–simply a must-read."

–**Jill Williamson**, Christy Award-winning author of *By Darkness Hid*

"A competition becomes much more than a game when this charmingly mismatched team sets out on a deadly serious competitive quest. Here's an intriguing story, built on nuggets of spiritual wisdom, and it launches a new trilogy."

–**Kathy Tyers**, award-winning and best-selling author of two Star Wars© novels and the *Firebird* series

"An endearing cast of characters. A harrowing quest. And an enchanting story world that illuminates the imagination with wonder. Chawna Schroeder's latest innovative book will leave readers begging for more!"

–**Angela Bell**, author of *A Lady's Guide to Marvels and Misadventures*

"Enchanting characters, dangerous stakes, and an imaginative story world all create a dynamic tale. A series of puzzle-solving scenarios made me feel like I was in a delicious escape room with dear friends. It was a joy finding answers–both practical and philosophical–as I journeyed with the characters."

–**Sharon Hinck**, Christy and Carol award-winning author

"A fantastical tale of love, loyalty, and trust, *Illuminary* was a book I couldn't put down. I became attached to these characters so much that I rooted for them, wept with them, shared in their ultimate joy of victory and crushing blow of defeat. If you're looking to be swept away into a storyworld you won't want to leave, this is the book for you. Truly Chawna Schroeder at her finest."

—**MICHELLE GRIEP**, Christy Award–winning author

"Filled with rich world-building and powerful prose, Chawna Schroeder's *Illuminary* is just the beginning of what is certain to be a trilogy that captivates the hearts and minds of readers. The intricately woven threads of found family and fierce faith work together to create a stunning tapestry of a tale. The nods to a timeless children's classic are delightful, but make no mistake, this story is completely and uniquely its own."

—**SARA ELLA**, award-winning author of The Curious Realities, *Coral*, and the *Unblemished* trilogy

"Peppered with wisdom and wit, Chawna Schroeder's *Illuminary* is a gorgeously imagined fantasy transformation of *A Little Princess* which hits all the right notes of the beloved classic. With compelling characters, deep themes on every page, and stunning world-building throughout, *Illuminary* is a book you do not want to miss!"

—**J. J. FISCHER**, award-winning author of The Nightingale Trilogy

ILLUMINARY

Other Books by Chawna Schroeder

Beast

The Vault Between Spaces

ILLUMINARY

The Sceptre & the Stylus | Book 1

CHAWNA SCHROEDER

Illuminary

Published by Enclave Publishing, an imprint of Oasis Family Media, LLC

Carol Stream, Illinois, USA.
www.enclavepublishing.com

ISBN: 979-8-88605-190-2 (printed hardcover)
ISBN: 979-8-88605-191-9 (printed softcover)
ISBN: 979-8-88605-193-3 (ebook)

Cover design by Emilie Haney, www.EAHCreative.com
Typesetting by Jamie Foley, www.JamieFoley.com

Printed in the United States of America.

For My Sovereign Lord
Who sustained me through the night
And guided me by His radiant light
To put the creeping dark to flight.

The taunting voices in my ear–
You silenced every mocking fear,
Your words of truth to let me hear.

And when no words had I to say,
You filled, restored, and made a way,
Providing each and every day.

Now may this tale return to You
And bring You praise and glory true,
For this and more Your righteous due.

The Illuminary's Journey

A nomadic teen of ancient history,
An envied student of Victorian fiction
The inheritors of wealth and favor reduced to
Dire circumstances of undeserved servitude mocks
Beliefs and behavior and impossible hopes tried with
Passing years and worse situations show
Abused and forgotten but persevering on leads to
New prosperity of sudden exaltation gives
The restored status of favor and wealth revealed with
Generosity of a pretending princess,
Forgiving spirit of a dreaming ruler.

Beginnings

Once upon a time . . .

Isn't that how a good story should begin? Set at a specific time in a specific place, where specific people live and do specific things? Yet before any of that happens, there is darkness, a void without form or shape or light. A place of infinite possibility both for good and for evil, for nothing that will be made has yet been made. All that exists is the creator and possibility and the hush of anticipation, as all that is not waits to be.

Then words come, and possibility becomes reality, ideas taking on substance and thoughts manifesting as tangible. Word made incarnate. A wonder inexplicable.

Is it any surprise, then, that the sounds formed by our tongues and the symbols joined together on the page carry in them the power of

Life

and

Death?

1

Birthfest doldrums were a real affliction.

Many laughed them off as a literary device, dreamt up by keshel awful novelists to create easy suspense. Others attributed them to the overwrought drama of the fainting female seeking to draw more attention to herself. The reality was much simpler. Sometimes celebratory occasions carried so much weight that they burdened a person's spirit with the musts and oughts of the day, and especially with the expectations of how one should feel, wringing out all joy.

I rested my hand atop a ribboned box, light spilling across my dressing table from the nearby window. But its warmth did nothing to disperse my emotional cloudiness. Yes, birthfest doldrums were real, for what other explanation could there be for the drizzle of melancholy dampening my spirits on a day that sparkled with sunshine?

My maid turned from fluffing the pillows, my earlier attempt to make my own bed having failed to meet Rivka's precise standards. Her usual maroon pavadai sattai had been replaced by a multicolored one, and the cascading colors of the cap-sleeved blouse and cone skirt stood out in festive contrast to the buttercream sheets. "Is something wrong, Sibah Yosarai?"

"Just feeling dreary today, Rivka. That's all."

"On your birthfest–and your twentieth one at that? Whatever for?"

Whatever, indeed? I had all I could ask for and more, as my bedchamber attested. The circular room was adorned with every luxury wealth could afford without turning the place gaudy, from gauzy curtains embroidered with real gold thread and seed pearls to the whimsical flower garden painted upon the plaster walls by my mother before my birth. And if I discovered anything more I could desire, I needed only to ask, for *lack* and *need* were words with which I had no personal acquaintance. A strangely depressing thought, that.

"Ah, I know what you're missing." Rivka returned to pillow-fluffing, her eyes crinkling at the corners, accentuating her impish looks.

She was baiting me. I knew that. I bit anyway. "Pray, do tell, what grand light has vanished from the heavens of my life to cast a shadow across my birthfest?"

"Hasib Bane could not come today."

I snorted, completely unladylike, but such an outlandish suggestion could warrant no other response. "Yes, that peacock's absence shall be mourned with all the grief of a lost wart."

Rivka paused from smoothing the coverlet, head tilted thoughtfully. "They say a poultice of cidapple and orleen is very good for removing warts." Then she refocused on me. "Do you wish me to inform Hasib Bane of your sentiment the next time he visits?"

"If you do, I'll– I'll– I'll demote you to field hand."

"Understood, sibah." She bobbed her head in respectful acquiescence–an acquiescence marred by the merriment glinting in her eyes. Because she knew full well I'd never follow through on such a threat. Which was why many of my sphere discouraged such familiarity with menials. It made them insubordinate, they said. Twaddle, I said.

Turning to my wardrobe, I withdrew a rose-colored dress made of layers upon layers of gauzy fabric, created for my birthfest.

Rivka abandoned her arranging. "Allow me."

"I'm quite able to dress myself, Rivka."

"You would deny me this privilege, today of all days?"

"Especially today, because I'm no longer a child to be coddled."

Rivka grasped the dress a moment longer, the stubborn tilt of her head revealing her inner struggle. Then she let go. "As you wish." She returned to her organization of the room, straightening pictures and shaking out curtains.

A retraction of my statement leapt to my lips. I choked it back. It was high time we both acknowledged I was no longer a child and therefore ought not rely on others as much as I did. Starting with this dress.

I tugged and twisted, pulled and pushed, grunted and groaned. How could pliable fabric be this uncooperative? It defied me at every turn, but after many contortions, I prevailed, though with far less satisfaction than anticipated.

With the first battle won, I sat at my dressing table. Time to conquer my black mane. Except, no matter what I did, the wild locks refused to be tamed. Should I leave them loose? But that made my face seem narrow and my eyes too big.

"Even the strongest cannot do everything." Rivka's reflection materialized in the mirror, her black eyes holding no censure, only sympathy. "Nor do the wisest know all things."

My hands dropped to my lap. "Would you arrange my hair, Rivka?"

"It would be my pleasure." Her smile could have illuminated the whole room without the sun's aid. How did she find such delight in serving me day after day? Surely, to anyone else, it would be absolutely maddening.

Which caused tears to sting my eyes afresh. "Have I told you what a blessing you are?"

"Every day."

"I mean it."

Rivka met my mirrored gaze with . . . tenderness? Affection? Pity? I couldn't quite decipher it. "I know."

She placed the final hairpin as a knock sounded. While she checked on the visitor, I examined my reflection. Almond-shaped eyes were set into olive skin, but my chin was too square to be delicate, giving it a perpetual jut of defiance. As for my hair, Rivka had twisted it in a way that framed–rather than swallowed–my face, in perfect replication of my mother's self-portrait from her twentieth birthfest. I fingered the small oil painting on the corner of the dressing table, a knot swelling in my throat. *Oh, Ima, I wish you were here to help me celebrate.*

"You look very much like her." Rivka reappeared in the mirror, startling me. She, like every menial I knew, walked with the soundless tread of velvet feet. "I have no doubt she would be very proud of the woman you have become, if you would permit me to say so, sibah." Like a watercolor wash of the palest pink, her words spread across the page of my heart.

Such words from any other menial would be considered fawning due to the difference in our spheres. Not Rivka. She preferred to speak her mind or say nothing at all. How would I ever replace her when she passed her crossover assessment? For despite her doubts, she would pass and leave behind the menial sphere to become an elite like me, pursuing her dream of being a stylist, helping others look their best.

I returned the portrait to its place of honor. "Since when have you sought my permission to speak your mind?"

"Whenever I speak bold words that are too late to retract."

"Then it isn't permission you seek, now is it?"

"Permission may be given for actions already past." She

sifted through my jewelry box, searching for the perfect accents to my dress.

"And if I refuse?"

"Then it's good I spoke first and asked permission second, for truth unspoken is worse than a lie."

A familiar argument, one for which I had never found a suitable retort. Instead I fastened my gold hoop earrings and slipped on my bangles. "Who was at the door?"

"Lascar. Your father awaits your arrival in the gazebo."

"You thought to tell me this just now?"

"It is your birthfest, sibah, and beauty anticipated is beauty appreciated." She secured the clasp of my gold-and-pink topaz necklace. "According to a Mounce tradition, wearing pink topaz on one's birthfest will bring true love in the year to come."

True love? Of all the subjects to leap to! Not that Rivka was being intentionally evasive. Because, for all her outward orderliness, Rivka's mind switched rails somewhat at random. "It is good I'm not superstitious, or you would be searching for a different necklace. I can ill afford a romance this year."

"If you say so, sibah." She retreated. "Now let's see the whole together."

I rose and, at her prompting, spun in place, arms outstretched.

"Faster."

I shook my head but did as she asked.

"Faster."

I twirled, my full skirt flaring and bangles jangling, feeling so like my five-year-old self that a smile couldn't be contained by the time I stopped from dizziness.

"I knew you were in there. Now go and enjoy yourself." She shooed me toward the door.

I picked up the ribboned box from my dressing table and headed into the airy hall, the far side open to the entryway. As I descended the grand staircase, my hand glided along the polished banister. Maybe later tonight, after everyone was abed, I could sneak out and slide down one last time, a final goodbye to childhood.

But not now. Avi was waiting. I pattered through the covered breezeway, its shade making the summer humidity bearable while allowing the fragrance of the gardens to freely waft through. I greeted menials by name and accepted their birthfest blessings with a nod, until I reached a small courtyard where a nursemaid scolded two young girls.

"Is something the matter, Hezzy?"

Face reddening, the woman crossed her hands to the opposite shoulder and bowed. "Sibah Yosarai, the blessing of Sustainer be upon you on this, the happiest of days. May the bloom of youth never fade from your countenance, nor the light of life dim in your eyes."

The children followed her lead. "Many blessings, Sibah Yosarai!"

"My gratitude to you all, but if this is to be the happiest of days, I must dispel the clouds of gloom overshadowing you three." After setting my box on a stone bench, I knelt before the girls, flouncing out my skirt. Rivka would thoroughly scold me, twentieth birthfest or not, if I spoiled the beautiful fabric.

Hezzy stood behind the two girls. "There is no need to trouble yourself, sibah–"

"I didn't steal it." The younger girl, face tear-streaked, hugged a simple doll to her chest.

The older girl jutted her chin. "That doll is mine."

"You threw her out!"

"I did not–"

"Girls!" Hezzy tapped them on the shoulders before bowing apologetically to me. "Forgive us for marring your day with such petty squabbles, sibah."

"There is nothing to forgive, for there is nothing petty about the matter of theft or the accusation thereof . . . is there, girls?"

The younger's shoulders caved around the doll she hugged, while the elder glared at the ground.

Hezzy nudged them. "She asked you a question."

"No, sibah," they responded in unison.

I studied the two girls. The older, Ayah, had been born on our estate. Her parents, having served in difficult houses, indulged their daughter's whims as much as their position permitted. As a result, Ayah sometimes bullied the other menials' children. Still, her parents would never permit her to discard a lavish gift like a doll.

Nidhi and her family arrived less than two months ago, acquired from a tyrant of an elite master who'd nearly starved them. Even now, Nidhi was too much bone and not enough flesh. After such deprivation, she could be tempted to take what was not hers, since the other children had much.

How do I find the truth, Sustainer?

My hands tingled. "May I see the doll?"

Nidhi relinquished the toy to me.

The tingling in my hands increased as I examined the doll, which had suffered severe maltreatment, boasting both stains and rips mended with tiny uneven stitches.

As my finger traced a repaired seam, a flash struck.

I am the doll sitting on a chair as Ayah pours me tea. She spills some on my arms.

Ayah and I hunt tigers among the bushes. My dress snags and rips.

Ayah sets me on the ground as she reads. She is called away for afternoon lessons. She leaves me on the ground, and a summer storm mires me in mud.

I sit on a shelf, one arm hanging limply, torn at the shoulder. Ayah and her mother argue.

> *Ayah says she needs a new doll. Her mother refuses. Ayah needs to care for what she has.*
>
> *It is night. Ayah carries me through a darkened hall to the trash bin by the kitchens. I'm dumped inside.*
>
> *Light pierces the darkness of the bin. Nidhi envelops me in a hug.*

With a sharp intake of air like breaking the surface of water, I blinked the world into focus. The flash hadn't lasted more than three seconds, but being yanked in and out of reality had never become comfortable in the twelve years since the visions began.

Knowing my blankness during a flash could be disturbing, I offered the girls a wobbly smile. Ayah squirmed impatiently, while Nidhi's eyes were round, never having seen one of my "spells," as my father called them. The elchan gifting unnerved many, especially since many priests of the kodesh sphere claimed the elchan no longer existed. Therefore, Avi allowed people to believe I suffered from a rare disease that caused seizures.

Which meant I couldn't render judgment based on the flash, not without either revealing my gift or sounding arbitrary. The first was not permitted, and the second was unacceptable. After all, I was the daughter of Hasib Caleph Patican, the fairest-minded judge in all of Indel. To render arbitrary judgment would be a travesty on par with murder, for it was the death of justice.

How, then, do I render justice, Sustainer?

I fingered the doll's uneven repair. Ayah couldn't mend anything. Nidhi was the daughter of a seamstress. That made this Nidhi's handiwork, which she would hate to see destroyed.

A story from the Writings of the Scribes about Indel's wisest chancellor came to mind. Would the same tactic work here?

"Would you please fetch me some scissors, Hezzy? Since their testimony has not revealed who is telling truth and who is lying, it seems just to give each girl a half."

Ayah jutted her chin. "Your judgment is most wise."

"No!" Nidhi took a step forward, then flinched as if expecting me to hit her for her objection. "Please, sibah, don't." Her whimpered words quavered, like a script written with an unsteady hand.

It nearly undid my resolve to follow through with this ruse, and I clenched my teeth. Some elites deserved to be stripped of their strata solely based on the mistreatment of their menials, for inspiring such fear in one this young . . .

The right to revenge is Mine; repayment will come in due time.

The words of Sustainer, as recorded in the Last Declarations of Eshom the Gatherer. I forced out my frustration with an exhale. She needed gentleness, not anger. "If I'm not to divide her, Nidhi, what am I to do?"

The little girl bit a trembling lip. I held my breath. Her next words would determine everything.

She scrubbed an arm over her face. "Give her to Ayah."

Good girl. "She's yours." I placed the doll into her arms.

The smirk left Ayah's face. "But–" She clamped her mouth shut. It was not proper for a menial to question an elite.

Yet it was fair to answer. "Only someone who did not care about the doll would willingly condemn it to destruction. If Nidhi had stolen the doll, she would have considered half better than none. However, it was you, not her, who condemned it. Why would you do that–unless you had already thrown it away?"

Ayah's mouth gaped as Hezzy said, "A wise ruling, sibah, befitting Hasib Patican himself."

"Indeed it was," said a man at my back.

The girls shrank against Hezzy as all three bowed. My father appeared from the shadows of the covered breezeway, his head almost brushing the low arch. The movement caused the metallic embroidery on a new midthigh vest to shimmer with dozens of colors. At his side, Dowser sported a wide, doggy grin and a plaid bow tied around his neck, his golden fur brushed to a gleam. Apparently, the menials had decided both of them also needed new attire on this festive occasion.

"Avi." I rose, shaking my skirts free of debris and wrinkles.

"My little illuminary." My father planted a kiss on my forehead. "I see you're bringing light into darkness and making the unseen seen again."

"But I didn't do anything." I stooped to scratch Dowser's ear, his stubby legs keeping him close to the ground, and was rewarded with a lick on the chin.

"Being an illuminary is not something you do, Yosi. It is something you are. Nonetheless, I'm pleased to see that not only do you grow more beautiful every year but also wiser."

His praise flooded my cheeks with warmth. "If I have cultivated any fruit of wisdom, it's because an even wiser man planted an abundance of seeds over the course of many years." I retrieved my box from the bench of the now-deserted courtyard.

"A wiser man? Should I be concerned another vies for my Yosi's affections?" He tucked my hand into the crook of his arm.

"I promise, Avi, when another man finds his way through the maze of my heart, you shall be the first to know." Something that would not happen anytime soon, for though streaks of white adorned his dark hair and goatee, my father remained the most handsome man I knew, in addition to being the kindest and wisest. As we strolled along the shaded path, Dowser faithfully shadowing us, a cool breeze brought the chortling of a kooka bird mixed with laughter and music from the fields beyond. With a sigh, I rested my head against Avi's broad shoulder.

"For someone celebrating her twentieth birthfest, that has the odd timbre of one feeling forlorn."

I shouldn't ask again, but the question surfaced anyway. "Must I go to the capital next month?"

"I know you question my decision, but you need to trust me concerning this."

"I'm trying, but I simply see no advantage in taking the Strata Exam in Kolchan rather than here. Hasib Kells will apprentice me regardless; I'm certain of it." Kolchan was a noisy, bustling, crowded city–everything opposite of my quiet country life. How could studying in a place of constant distraction be better than my focused work here?

"Your mother trained there, and you know what came of that."

It would be impossible not to. She may have died shortly after my birth, but even now Jasmene Patican was regarded as one of the greatest artists of a nation that prized artistry above all else. A weighty legacy, which was why my father insisted I be well-educated in all fields. He wanted me to have other options. But, in the end, my heart was set on becoming an artist, albeit one degree removed from my mother's painting. I wanted to become an illuminator.

My father leaned toward me. "Besides, Kolchan is home to the Scriptorium Grande, where the original Writings are stored."

"For a man reputed as fair, you employ tactics most unfair."

"But that is your dream, is it not? To create an illuminated script based on the originals?"

"Dreams can change."

"A cat may shed its fur, but its stripes remain the same." My father knew me too well. "Besides, it's not as if we're still trapped in the era of horse and carriage. The rails do travel between here and there the last time I checked, and I am more than able to afford a visit every fortnight."

"Promise?"

"From the moon to the depths of the ocean." Avi turned to me. "But more importantly, Sustainer will always be with you, ready to help, no matter what you face, whether the problem is big or small. All you have to do is ask. It's no bother to Him. Do you understand?"

My uncertainty must have shown, for his hands cupped my face. "So strong, so fragile." He rested his forehead against mine. "Effulgence, be her fuel, be her light."

His simple prayer tightened my throat, stirring up a strange mix of yearning, envy, and trepidation.

Avi straightened. "Now, no more talk of departures and separations, or letting tomorrow's gloom overshadow today's joy." He guided me to the table in the center of a gazebo arranged with a pyramid of packages encircled with my favorite foods, far more than I could eat in a week, much less in a day.

"Please say this is not all for me."

"I suppose Muri may have been a bit zealous." Avi palmed a sweet cake of shredded carsnip and offered it to Dowser. Then my father wondered why the furry scamp stayed closer than a shadow to him. "But as she would tell you, 'A celebration without food is no celebration at all, and our girl celebrates her twentieth birthfest but once.'"

I stifled a laugh at his imitation of our high-strung cook and stood on my tiptoes to plant a kiss on his cheek, then extended to him the package I carried.

While tradition dictated that the parents were to be honored with a gift on every birthfest, I had applied special care to this year's present.

Avi opened the box. "Is this . . .?"

"Ima's poem, illuminated from the original." An original that Avi kept locked away. It had taken some conniving–and a bit of bribery–to obtain it. "You're not upset I borrowed it?"

"I should be, but in light of the purpose, I cannot be." He

held the framed picture so we both might read the poem Ima gave Avi at their wedding gala. Its wraparound style, where the beginning word of each line both finished the previous thought and started a new one, was meant to convey a marriage's continuity in the midst of constant change.

Love is
Fragrance wafting
Hope carrying
Through troubled times unyielding
Faithfulness offering
Joy defying
Hardship forging
Iron love.

Among the words, a blooming vine grew from flames of fire. In the background, a pair of doves flew above tumultuous waves, caught in a shaft of light piercing the sky's stormy clouds. The custom silver frame, which I bartered from one of our craftsmen, edged the whole piece with interlinking hearts.

My father brushed a finger over a tiny egg nested among the vines and letters. A small detail, one I hadn't been sure he'd notice, but one I was loath to omit. "This is what she imagined when she wrote the words?" he asked.

"There were a few elements I couldn't include, but yes, that is most of it."

"The blessing of Sustainer upon you for the honor you have brought to your mother and me." Emotion roughened the traditional acceptance like uneven brushstrokes. "You have given a piece of your mother back to me. My deepest gratitude, Yosarai."

He kissed the crown of my head. Every moment of work from the past six months had been worth it.

"And since we harvest what we plant . . ." He retrieved the

topmost present from the table's stack, shooing Dowser away from the food. The scamp flopped on the ground, resting his head between his forepaws, his golden eyes staring up at us woefully.

No doubt Avi would soon give into his plea, but until then I returned my attention to the package he gave me. The size and shape indicated a book. Now, every handcrafted work he acquired for me was a precious treasure, but what set this one apart that he'd break the tradition of gifts after the meal? I withdrew a leather-bound volume from its pouch.

The cover bore the simple title *Illuminary.* No author's name. No adornment or other artistic work. Plain, unpretentious, and . . . I gasped. The front page bore the same beautiful penmanship I'd studied for the past six months.

Birthfest Blessings
upon my beautiful Yosarai, now full-grown.
May Sustainer's Light spill from your heart,
illuminating the lives of those all around you.
From my heart to yours, Ima

"H-how is this possible?" My mother had been gone for nearly nineteen years.

"She worked on this throughout the pregnancy, and almost feverishly after your birth. Almost as if she knew . . ." He broke off as emotion filled his eyes, then he cleared his throat. "She wanted you to have it today."

I turned the page. The cream paper had been covered in black-and-purple swirls with a single shaft of light cutting across them. In the middle were words in a lightning-like font, sharp enough to make me hesitant to touch them.

But the lure to glimpse my mother's mind was too strong. My finger, the tip stained with ink even on this auspicious day, moved across the smooth page, and within two letters everything transformed, as it did every time I touched the written word. Through my elchan gifting, my finger felt raised letters, which in reality had no texture, and a soft, lilting voice—my mother's thought-voice—spoke words I alone could hear.

Once upon a time . . .

My mind filled with images—the very ones my mother had imagined as she wrote these words. The glimpse evoked much of the same imagery as her painting: churning purple waves, edges razor-sharp. Swirls of black fog. A beam of white light piercing the chaos. The waves and fog separated, the waters calming. The light curled into the word *be*, then coiled around the fog and water, molding them, dispelling darkness, coloring them.

Is it any surprise, then, that the sounds formed by our tongues and the symbols joined together on the page carry in them the power of life and death?

With the final word, the artistic renderings transformed into a scene vividly real yet utterly surreal. I saw myself sitting on a stone bench in an unfamiliar garden courtyard, a fountain bubbling in the center. I wore a blue brocade anarkali with a full skirt and lace sleeves, the neckline edged in tiny pearls—a dress finished last week. At my feet sat a simple clay jar. My younger cousin, Jamarde, stood across from me in a stance unusually confrontational, though I sensed she wasn't alone. She thrust an uncapped flask into my hand. "Choose wisely, cousin, because it could mean the difference between life and death."

My hand wrenched from the page. With the physical connection broken, the scene fled my mind. Yet the images, the words, remained imprinted there, thick, heavy, bold . . . undecipherable. A warning written in smeared ink.

And the future that had seemed merely dismal but one bell ago, now loomed black and ominous.

Not again.

Xander dug his fingertips into his thigh, his sole concession to this latest threat. Perhaps he should be more concerned, but endless repetition could make anything wearisome–even attempts on one's life.

Instead of looking over his shoulder, Xander stared at the stony mountain filling the window of the sky gondola. The vehicle bounced once as it passed by another pole, the steel cable upon which the skondola hung drawing them ever nearer the station. Eight minutes, ten at most. Dare he hope the potential assassin would wait that long before attacking?

Across from him, Massard peered around an unfurled newspaper. Should he dismiss the unspoken concern? Except that would border on apathy, and that was one thing he could not afford to become, no matter how wearisome the attacks grew. Besides, his bodyguard had a knack for detecting subtleties no one else did. Xander tugged on the cuffs of his greatcoat. The code word for a suspicious person of low threat should be sufficient. "A crow is circling three skondolas behind us."

Massard shook his paper as he turned the page. "You're quite right, Your Highness, though his wings should be tiring after three bells of flapping about."

Three bells? Xander suppressed a groan. They'd been tailed for almost the entirety of this outing, then. And here he had been congratulating himself on finally concocting a plan that would avoid drawing notice. He should have stayed in his workshop, tinkering on the swan for Ellie's fifth birthfest.

His father should have never named him crown prince instead of his older half brother.

But what was done was done. He stretched out his long legs as much as the narrow space between the benches permitted, adopting a relaxed posture in case the crow was monitoring them with a scope. "I hear we need to detour past the mapmaker's." Code: What's the plan?

"You have a tight schedule. Allow me to take care of the package."

A wise course of action, but for once, he'd like to face the problem instead of letting others handle it. Like he did before it leaked that he, not Selucreh, had been named crown prince of Egdon. Would the attacks even end with his coronation, after the official mourning period for his father finished?

Xander clenched his gloves. His father was supposed to live a good many years more. At least long enough for Selucreh to reform and have the title returned to him. Xander never wanted to be king. Had never planned to be king. Never should have been considered for kingship. Not as the illegitimate son.

"Your Highness?" Massard frowned, newspaper folded beside him.

And there he went again, losing time as he'd frequently done since his father's death–minutes, even whole hours, slipping away, unaccounted for. Grief fog, the palace physicians called it, due to insufficient space to mourn. Proof that he was unsuited for the throne, Selucreh said. Whatever the cause, he could ill afford it now. "I beg your pardon, Massard. What did you say?"

"I asked if the plan met Your Highness's approval."

"Yes, with the normal reservations."

"Only a fool faces danger without need."

"So my options are fool or coward?"

"Cowardice is any act done from fear, including risk-taking due to the fear of criticism." Massard's dark eyes glittered with experience, vouched for by the pale scar running the length of the left side of his face. Experience Xander desperately lacked.

"Are you certain you don't want that advisor position?"

"I am where I can serve you best, Your Highness."

Xander pulled on his leather gloves and fingered the goggles resting against his cravat, but the light mist would render the goggles more hindrance than help. Once they reached the station, he'd need to dash to the steam carriage. Hopefully, the scarriage wouldn't be compromised too.

But as the skondola began its final descent, metal screeched against metal. The skondola jolted to a stop, stranding them high above jagged rocks and the steaming lake water of Thalassa.

Massard yanked him to the floor. There was a pop, and glass showered over them.

"Prepare for a hard landing." Massard shoved open the door and swung himself onto the roof.

Cool, humid air swirled in as Xander positioned the bench's cushions around him. What was his bodyguard planning now?

A muffled shot smacked the air. Beside him landed a ball, its fuse nearly gone. Was that the best they could do? Xander kicked it out the door. It exploded midair, shaking the skondola but doing no damage.

With a screech, the skondola edged forward, then gained speed. Far more speed than it should have, especially since none of the other skondalas moved. Wind slapped his face, and sparks flew by. A yellow canopy flashed in the distance–zephyr wings, perhaps? Hard to say, for the mountain swallowed him. Xander braced himself between the two bench seats. Impact in five, four, three–

Metal crunched as the skondola halted. His body did not, knocking all breath from his lungs.

By the time his senses revived, all was still and quiet. He shook his head. A stabbing pain ricocheted through his skull. A hard landing? Once again, Massard proved the master of understatement.

As if summoned by the thought, his bodyguard peered into

the skondola, hanging upside down of all things, his hair wild and eyes afire.

"I shall ignore the fact that you look like you enjoyed that, Massard." The throbbing localized, and a quick probe reddened his fingers–blood.

Massard's boots hit the floor, sending another surge of pain through Xander's head. "Your Highness?"

"I'm fine." Or he would be as soon as the floor quit teetering like the deck of a storm-tossed airship. He gripped the bent frame, the dash to the scarriage now impossible. He never did have the legs–or stomach–for long-distance skyfaring. "Was anyone else injured?"

"All were empty." Massard offered Xander his top hat to cover his head. The attack would be front page news. No need to add rumors of injury. It would worry his supporters and encourage his opponents.

At least no one else had been hurt, but it could have been otherwise. Next time, it might be otherwise. "Then I am walking out of here without help. For their sake." He gestured to the people gathered along the U-shaped trench that the skondolas glided around before returning to Ora Peak. The crowd pointed at the mangled, metallic mess of skondolas, heads bent in conversation.

Massard stepped onto the stone platform. "Please, make way for Crown Prince Xander Torris."

The crowd parted, someone calling out, "Is he all right?"

"All's well." Xander smiled as he followed Massard, though the ground didn't feel as solid as it ought. More like that gelatinous dessert Cook liked to make. Reaching the stationmaster, Xander cocked an arm across his waist and one behind his back in respect, then inclined his head. "I'm afraid I've made a mess of your station."

The stationmaster bowed deeply in return. "Skondolas can be replaced. You cannot be."

A supporter, which made this an improvement over the last incident. He'd endured a lecture for an entire quarter bell about royals doing "what they pleased with no respect for nobody's property." Even the memory worsened the throbbing of Xander's head.

"Thank you, but I insist all repairs be billed to the palace." The palace accountant would glower at that, but others would not suffer due to the damage he caused. If they had to sell every painting and rug to ensure that, so be it.

Massard spoke up. "Do you have a room where His Highness might wait for a constable?"

"Of course. This way." He led them into a small reception area with a few chairs, a table, and a rug. Not lavish but warm and clean, if a little threadbare. This out-of-way station's lighter traffic was why Xander had chosen it for this outing; he'd hoped to prevent an incident like this. He should ask the accountant to add a little extra above the cost of repairs.

After the stationmaster left, Massard inspected Xander's head. "Might need a stitch or two, but you'll live."

"Thanks for the assessment." Xander pressed his handkerchief to the wound.

"Then, with your permission, I would like to pursue the assassin."

"Go, though don't hope too much. I saw the canopy of some zypher wings as we raced away."

Massard bolted out of the room, leaving Xander in quiet but not at peace.

The attacks had become more dangerous, more innovative, and more frequent in the seven months since his father's death. Increasing protection, moving back from the university, limiting his excursions outside the palace . . . none of it had helped. No innocents had been seriously injured yet, but for how much longer? More drastic action was needed, especially since Massard returned without apprehending the assassin once again. After the constable's questioning and the requisite stitches, they returned to the palace. The gears of an idea began to mesh.

As expected, the queen awaited their arrival, her layered skirt swishing against the marbled floor of the foyer as she paced with all the worry that a mother alone could produce. Proving once again that, somehow, Queen Epolene had set aside the pain of her husband's betrayal to accept him as a son.

"Xander!" She took his face in her hands as if to assure herself he was well–then bopped him on the nose. "That's for scaring another decade off my life."

"Then I will give you this to restore it to you." He kissed her cheek. Despite all the difficulties of her life and position, his stepmum retained a beauty that time and white hair could not erode. Should he ever find a woman to wed with even half of her grace, he would be a blessed man indeed.

"What shall I ever do with you?"

"Keep loving me, a mess though I be." He surrendered his hat, gloves, goggles, and greatcoat to a liveried maid. "And perhaps listen to another half-cocked scheme?" The maid moved on to Massard, who waved her away.

His stepmum arched an eyebrow. "Not another plan to modernize the kitchen, I hope."

Xander forced a weak smile. He'd spent two days helping the staff scrape off burnt food after attempting to equip a table with steam heat to keep meals warm. "Nothing that innovative. Rather, I was contemplating alternative security measures. No new inventions involved."

She looked over at Massard. "Anything I ought to be concerned about?"

"His Highness has not spoken to me of his plans."

Xander fiddled with the chain of his pocket watch. Perhaps he should have consulted Massard first. "My ideas often seem odd, but if you'll hear me out . . ."

"It's not the oddity that concerns me, Xander. It's that the execution of those ideas is frequently accompanied by unintended consequences."

That was a gentle way of describing the many disasters over the years. The dinner party that went up in literal smoke. The flooding of the suite for the ambassador from Kossac one bell before her arrival. The near sinking of the midsummer Water Rose Festival. Catastrophe after catastrophe rolled through his mind. Perhaps he had been hasty in this.

She sighed. "But I suppose no harm can come from discussing your idea. However, let us find someplace more comfortable to talk."

"If you are sure you have the time."

"I always have time for my children. All three of you."

A lump rose in his throat. Did his half-siblings understand what a gem they had in her? Sometimes he wondered.

Massard entered the queen's private sitting room first, searching for threats or unwanted ears. A precaution that shouldn't exist, which started the gears of Xander's idea again. For if he wasn't safe even in the palace, where else in Egdon could he go?

His bodyguard motioned all was clear, and Xander escorted the queen inside, the thick rug muffling their tread. On the far side of the room, a waterfall cascaded outside the mullioned windows with a soft murmur. With sunlight, it would brighten the simply furnished room with rainbows, but with the day's typical clouds, a muted greyness dominated. Xander turned up a gas lamp while the queen settled in a wingback chair. Massard started to retreat, but Xander stopped him. "Please stay, for my idea concerns you as well."

"As you wish, Your Highness."

Queen Epolene's grey-green eyes studied him. Like Massard, she missed little.

Xander sat across from her. "By the grace of Sustainer alone has no one been killed. But for how much longer, especially with the attacks increasing?" He took a breath. "Therefore, I propose I remove myself from the equation."

"And what do you mean by that?" Her voice sharpened, a spring coiled tight.

"The easiest method would be to abdicate the throne to Selucreh. It should have been his anyway–"

"Stop, Xander. As your father and I told you four years ago, we love your brother very much and have high hopes for him. However, he sees the throne as a right, not a privilege, revealing his heart to be unready for such a responsibility. Kingship is a position of serving the people, not the people serving you."

"But how can I serve the people if my very presence jeopardizes them?"

"Once you're crowned and they realize what a good king you are, the opposition will taper off."

"And if it doesn't?"

"The ones behind this will err and be brought to justice."

The argument was an old one, dating back to the first week of attacks, but he had to try once more before he proposed his real plan. "Then if abdication is not an option, I must leave."

"Leave?" She fingered a diamond earbob, a favored gesture when puzzling over a problem. "You wish to retreat to the northern estate?"

"I wish to leave Egdon. Secretly. Alone." His tone firmed with the last word; it would be the point of greatest contention.

"You cannot be serious."

"Unless my adversaries have a longer reach than expected, my departure would hinder their attacks. However, traveling with a retinue of servants and guards would advertise my movements, which could endanger the people of another land. No king, council, or senate will thank me for such an action, and I have no wish to damage diplomatic relations. However, one cannot attack a target whose location is unknown."

"But you are also much more vulnerable alone."

Massard bowed to the queen. "Forgive my intrusion, Your Majesty, but may I suggest one change?" He looked to Xander for permission.

Xander nodded. If Massard had spotted a flaw or a hole, it was best Xander learned of it now.

"Let the prince travel with a trusted companion. This would provide more eyes to spot danger and someone to protect his back."

Xander rubbed his chin. "I would be amenable to that–if you're willing to be that companion, Massard."

"I'd be honored, Your Highness."

His stepmum rose and straightened an already level painting. "And when will you leave? To where? For how long?"

"As soon as possible," he told her. "Perhaps within a fortnight? For there will be stories to concoct, travel arrangements to be made, papers to be drawn up, at least if I wish to keep my departure secret."

His stepmum now rearranged the music boxes displayed on the side table below the painting.

He continued. "As for my return, I'd like to delay for as long as possible without incurring Parliament's wrath. Perhaps until just before the Winter Solstice?"

She stilled. "Five months. That is a long time to stay hidden, Xander."

Xander stepped up behind her, resting his hands on her shoulders. "Don't think of it as hiding, but as a retreat to prepare me for this mantle of leadership."

Her fingers caressed the back of the mechanical parrot he'd given his father when he was fourteen. "And space to grieve?"

His stepmum knew him well.

She sighed. "Your plan has many potential benefits, but you still haven't told me where you'll go."

Where, indeed? With his plan being less than three bells

old, he hadn't worked out all the logistics. Then the nearby painting caught his gaze with its lush, colorful landscape. A picture by a famous Indel painter, commissioned by the queen herself. It was rumored to be one of the last paintings the artist completed prior to her death nearly nineteen years ago. While Xander had never met the painter, the queen had maintained contact with the family. "How about Indel?"

She followed his gaze. "If you must go, I can think of no better place. Indel it is, with my blessing."

Xander's tension eased, but only for a moment. At last, he was doing something about the attacks instead of waiting for calamity to strike. But was he only exchanging one potential disaster for another of his own making?

CHANGE

All around us change occurs regularly. The sun rises, the sun sets. The moon waxes and wanes. Spring blossoms into summer, summer fades into fall, fall withers into winter, and winter births spring once again.

Why, then, do we fight change with such fierceness? What about it causes us to melt in fear or resist in stubbornness or oppose in anger? Even when a change is for the better, we embrace it like a cactus.

Is it because even a good change reminds us of the uncomfortable truths we do not wish to remember? That control is beyond our control . . . that more is unknown than known . . . that even a good life is not a perfect one?

Thus, with weaknesses exposed and limitations revealed, we stand on the edge of an eroding cliff. Will we plunge to our deaths, clawing at the crumbling rocks of what was? Or shall we leap into the wind of possibility, trusting Sustainer to lift us upon wings?

2

If change was good, why did this feel wrong?

My ink-stained fingertips skimmed the battered top of my art desk, its barren surface foreign. Gone were the half-finished illustrations, loose papers, open reference books, scattered pens and brushes, blotting paper, ink bottles, and other tools of my trade. Stored away to await my return. Another stark reminder I was departing for Kolchan today.

I sat back on my stool, staring at the purple flowers bobbing outside the atelier's window. By the time I returned at Winter Solstice, those blossoms would be gone, the vines faded to their rusty winter foliage. Expected and needed change, providing the earth time to rest and rejuvenate. Why couldn't I see this trip the same way?

My thoughts refused to reason the question through, so I drew out a clean paper and a leadstick and let my fingers do the thinking.

With a few bold strokes, the word *change* nearly filled the page, the letters thick, angular . . . crushing. A small figure–a girl–peeped out from between the legs of the *h*, as if hiding from something. More partial figures appeared, huge compared to the girl–a pointing finger, a laughing mouth, a giant pair of eyes peering down its nose. Then came the path snaking among the base of the letters with various obstacles, like fences and pits, along the way. Finally, in the background, dark storm clouds built. No wonder the girl didn't want to come out of her hiding place.

"You forgot something."

I started at Avi's voice. "Have you finished with your unexpected guests already? I didn't hear you come in."

"Your mother was the same way. When she was creating, an airship could have crashed into the house, and she would have never known." He held out a hand. "May I?"

I relinquished my leadstick, and he bent over my sketch. After a minute, he shifted the paper back to me. He'd added a crude stick figure between the legs of the *h*. In one hand, the figure held up a lantern. His other hand was held out in invitation to the girl. And although simplistic compared to the rest of the sketch, those few additional lines altered the mood of the entire picture.

Avi laid the leadstick beside the paper. "No matter what you face, you never walk alone." Then he put his arm around my shoulders and drew me to him. "What will you miss most?"

A dozen answers crowded into my mind: Muri's orange-blossom muffins, curling up with a new book in the front of the fire, wandering the gardens while dew still hung heavy upon the leaves, chiding Avi when he walked in late–again–for dinner. Then my eyes closed, the breeze from the open window bringing the scent of late summer roses and karob, Avi's embrace warming me, everything quiet, peaceful. "This. Just this."

Avi's pocket watch chimed

Time to depart. To leave behind everything I knew and loved. I might not be facing this alone, but that didn't mean studying in Kolchan was an adventure to anticipate, as many of my peers thought it was. I'd visited the capital and my aunt's home enough to expect stiff formality, unrelenting scrutiny, and the extra social pressure of being constantly assessed, constantly judged . . . constantly found wanting.

But there was nothing to be done about it now. Change had arrived, whether I wanted it or not. We left my refuge, and I locked the atelier's door behind us. Just as when the space had belonged to my mother, this was the one room the menials weren't to touch unless I was present. I glanced around for Dowser, but surprisingly, my father's furry shadow was missing. Probably left in the kitchen so he wouldn't whine when we departed.

Sliding a hand into the crook of Avi's arm, I strolled with him toward the front of the house. "How was your surprise meeting?"

"Rather peculiar, with an unforeseen outcome."

"Is that so?"

"My visitors came with a delicate problem, and the result is they will be accompanying us to the capital."

I stopped. "You cannot be serious." We'd spent a month arranging schedules and choosing our favorite haunts to visit along the way to celebrate this new stage in my life, according to Avi.

"I'm afraid I am, Yosi." He patted my hand. "I know this isn't what we planned, but will you trust me?"

I swallowed the urge to demand his visitors find their own way to Kolchan. Avi would never change plans if it wasn't of the utmost importance. "If this is what is needed, then this is what is needed." I quirked a smile at him. "Though I do have a request."

"What might that be?"

"Whenever you are free to explain, you will not present it in summary fashion, like some court case, but you will dramatize the tale, complete with costumes and props, in a way worthy of an elite storyteller."

"Such a condition you ask of a poor country judge. Have

you forgotten your mother was the one with the artistic flair? But for you I shall give it my very best effort."

"And will love every minute of it." Despite my jab about court summaries, Avi's courtroom was known as one of the most engaging in Indel, as well as one of the fairest.

A menial opened the main doors, and warm air, more summer than autumn in its humidity, surrounded us as we descended the broad, marble stairs to the gravel drive, where a covered coach awaited us. Rivka was already there, sneaking carrots to our matching bays, while our driver checked the straps around our luggage. But it was the two strangers, standing in the waning shade of the coach, who captured my attention. My father's guests were foreigners? Because though both men wore traditional bandhgala suits of fitted pants and high-collared jackets, Indeli blood would have never permitted their pale complexions.

Perhaps it shouldn't have surprised me. Avi associated with a variety of people, including citizens from the other six Realms. Even so, Egdonians rarely ventured this far south.

The taller of the two men was about the same height as my father. But while Avi had the softness of a man who spent his time behind a desk, the foreigner was muscular, as befitting someone from the athletic or labor strata. His most notable feature, however, was the jagged scar cutting through the left side of his face, giving him a fierceness I would not want to cross.

The scarred man spoke to his chestnut-haired companion, who was shorter by a few finger widths. He turned. My eyebrows rose. This second man carried refinement to the same extent his companion bore ferocity. Indeed, with a few pointers, he could pass as a politico, having the strong bearing derived from carrying the mantle of authority, even if that mantle rested uneasily upon his shoulders. As for his face, it would have been handsome if not for the deep weariness–and wariness–lining his countenance, the look of one fighting a losing war.

"Yosi, I would like you to meet Hasib Mascad"–Avi gestured to the scarred man–"and Hasib Saunders. Hasibs, may I present my daughter, Yosarai Patican."

"A pleasure, Sibah Patican." Hasib Mascad presented his forearm in traditional greeting. "We humbly beg your pardon for our intrusion."

Interesting. Hasib Saunders wore the mantle of authority, yet Hasib Mascad spoke as if in charge. I placed my arm below Mascad's, acknowledging his superior position as Avi's guest. He lowered his forearm, not beside mine as was customary, but under it, claiming me as *his* superior. Odd. "Please," I said, "call me Yosi, and do not concern yourselves further. Plans must be held in the loosest of grips, and if we are willing to embrace the winds of change, we might soar to even greater heights than before." Echoes of my mother's words. Perhaps I ought to reread her wisdom again at the first opportunity.

Hasib Mascad inclined his head. "You speak wisdom, but we appreciate your generosity nonetheless."

"Gratitude accepted."

"We should be on our way." Avi waved to the coach, Rivka and the driver now both seated on the elevated bench at the front.

Hasib Saunders slid onto the back bench, causing me to veer toward the middle one. My father arrested my approach. "I know it's unconventional, but would you sit with Hasib Saunders? I have some business to finish with Hasib Mascad."

I stifled a groan. We would reach the station at Werec in a quarter bell. If riding fifteen minutes with a stranger would free the six-hour ride north from tiresome business discussions, it would be worth the sacrifice. "As you wish, Avi."

I settled beside Hasib Saunders, while Avi and Mascad took the seat in front of me. They bent their heads together, the crunch of wheels swallowing their voices. It should have been me sitting beside my father, engaged in quiet conversation. Instead, I was tasked with entertaining a stranger about whom I knew nothing more than a name.

My companion shifted in his seat. "I feel I ought to echo Mascad and extend apologies for our interference. If we had known of our inopportune timing, we would have delayed our arrival." His voice molded sounds into a smooth stream, suggesting a precise but intricate script that flowed across the page. Quite the contrast to the block letters conjured by the gravelly tone of his companion.

I angled toward him with what I hoped was a reassuring smile. "It's not as if you interrupted some grand occasion."

"Pardon my contrariness, sibah, but time with those you love is always a grand occasion. Or ought to be, for time is short and fleeting." He turned, posture rigid.

Less than two minutes into conversation and I'd already offended Avi's guest. The coach jostled through a rutted part of the road, adding to my discomfort. So much for being a proper Indeli hostess. Had I learned nothing from my lessons in the social arts? "It appears it's my turn to beg pardon, hasib, for my upsetting words."

He remained statuesque for a dozen hoof beats, then relaxed slightly. "Do not blame yourself, for the problem lies with me. The matter of family is tender for me."

My mind added a wash of blue behind his articulate words. Had he lost someone recently? My gaze slipped to Avi. Here I was pouting I wouldn't have time alone with him, but at least he was here and traveling with me. *Sustainer, forgive my selfish callousness.* I took a slow, deep breath, the remnants of my resentment ebbing. "Is this your first trip to Indel?"

"Not my first, but it has been many years since my last visit."

My mind sharpened the edges of his script. Even with losing their earlier terseness, his words still carried a clipped edge. Definitely Egdonian, though there was a refinement to his accent the northern merchants lacked. I mentally added some small flourishes to the words. "A visit with good memories, I hope."

"Good ones indeed."

"I'm glad to hear that." Now what ought I to ask next? Avi indicated a delicate problem prompted their visit, which meant the usual inquiries into their visit's purpose would be unwelcome. "Is there anything special you hope to do while here?"

"I . . . hadn't considered it."

"Then perhaps we ought to discuss some possibilities as we travel north. Kolchan has much to offer, especially with the Ingathering Festival in less than eight weeks. If your visit extends that long, you should participate in the festivities, as Kolchan will be at the peak of gaiety."

My companion raised an eyebrow. "Are you sure a foreigner would be welcomed at such an important religious festival?"

He knew of the Ingathering's religious roots? Yet he did not question whether he would find the festival entertaining, but whether he would be welcomed. Was he a seeker–or even a follower of Effulgence? "Rest assured, all are welcome. In fact, merchants travel from all Seven Realms to participate in the street fair in the fortnight preceding."

"And the festival itself?"

"Few foreigners attend the ceremonies, though that seems due to lack of interest rather than prohibition. I hear Kolchan's Ingathering has all the drama and pageantry of a night at the Teardrop Theatre."

"You've never been?"

"Not to Kolchan's. I've always celebrated here in the Cashirsa Province in order to participate in our Quest." At his blank look, I added, "As part of the reenactment of the Ingathering story, coteries of six compete in a series of trials for three days to gain the privilege of presenting the water jar in that province's final ceremony." Emotion welled up inside of me as the coach passed through a shaded portion of the road. For the first time in a decade, I wouldn't be participating in the Quest. "Meanwhile, I would personally recommend a visit to the Arboretum Capital, if possible. It should be in its full glory right now and is unrivaled for its beauty anywhere in the Seven Realms, I am told. Allot sufficient time to wander the grounds, however, for it's meant to be experienced and absorbed, not viewed like some carnival sideshow."

"I do believe I detect a note of passion in your voice, sibah." He relaxed a little more, revealing he was younger than I'd first thought–probably no more than five years older than me.

"I admit I'm a quintessential Indeli in that way, believing life is meant to be experienced, not survived. That things ought to be beautiful as well as practical. And that, indeed, beauty itself has value."

Curiosity tilted his head, like a sparrow determining whether I was trustworthy. "Still, we are to be good stewards of both time and resources, are we not? Does it not seem wasteful to spend these things on lavish displays and costly artifices when many need bread to eat? Should we not focus on improving our fellow man's position?"

A common indictment against the Indeli culture, and one not without grounds, as demonstrated by the many garish displays of the elite at the cost of their menials' welfare. "Something does not need to be expensive or lavish to be beautiful. Moreover, cannot time and money be spent to an unnecessary extreme in any pursuit? For example, is it not also detrimental to endlessly change an invention, making needless but incompatible improvements, forcing people to buy the newest deviation, though the simpler one they already possessed worked just as well?"

"Art does not put bread in a man's mouth nor ease the toil of life."

"Someone must build the artifices and paint the murals, tend the gardens and write the books; and when they have accomplished that work, they have something in which they might take pride. Is it better to earn a wage for a meaningless task or to receive money for no work at all?" I paused long enough for the questions to penetrate, but not for him to rebut. "As for the toil of life, art might not simplify their labor, but it can ease the burden of work, refreshing the soul and invigorating the mind, bringing encouragement, inspiration, and motivation for one's life. Is that not as important as any gadget to ease a task or to improve a process?"

Hasib Saunders rubbed a hand across his clean-shaven chin. "Your father said you were enrolling at the Academy. What course of study will you be pursuing, may I ask?"

"A little of everything, per Avi's request, but I hope to qualify for an illuminator's apprenticeship."

"Not politics?"

I nearly snorted as I steadied myself against a particularly sharp lurch of the coach. "Avi has trained me well in logic and debate, but my emotions control my tongue more than they ought."

"Better too much passion than none at all, for a fire can be tempered and tamed, but how do you stir up a blaze when there's no flame to stoke?"

I glanced at him. A man who did not condemn my outspoken passion? That was a rarity. And misguided. "A generous thought, hasib, but I'm afraid no flame is better than too much, for the lack of fire might be uncomfortable, but it's rarely destructive."

"Cannot a man freeze to death as easily as burn? Moreover, you speak as if all destruction is bad, though the destruction of a log is needed for a fire, and the destruction of a weed for the flourishing of a garden. And do not your own fire-lilacs require burning to produce their flowers?"

I opened my mouth to counter his logic and found no retort. "Perhaps you should be the one pursuing politics, hasib."

His expression shuttered, as if my compliment had insulted him. "I believe we have reached the station."

Was I so inept that I couldn't converse for one quarter bell without causing offense? How, then, would I ever survive the Academy? *Focus on something else.* Thankfully, the coach rolled to a stop, drawing my attention outside.

The rail station wasn't elaborate, as was expected for a village the size of Werec, but the five arches supporting the roof over the open-air platform created a pleasant symmetry with the outer columns covered in flowering vines and the interior ones painted with a complementary palette. Of course, the crowning piece was the central pillar, painted by my mother before she became famous. It was almost as if Ima were here to see me off too.

Despite our tight schedule, Hasib Mascad alone left the coach. He strolled the entire length and breadth of the platform, then approached the circular desk surrounding the central column. Words were exchanged; he nodded at my father. What *was* this delicate matter these foreigners were navigating? Their furtive behavior could suggest something criminal, except my father would never condone such a thing. He prized justice too much . . . unless that was the problem? Would Avi break the law to obtain justice?

After I alighted, my father tucked my hand into his elbow. "What troubles my little illuminary?"

Should I say nothing? Except the question would plague me until I asked. "Pardon me if I tamper with a bee's hive, but I must know something before we travel farther. The delicate matter of these men–it doesn't entail anything illegal, does it?" I held my breath, trusting my father to speak the truth.

"Rest your mind, Yosi. We're doing nothing illegal or unethical. The secrecy is protective, nothing more."

The assurance I was hoping for. Why, then, did I not feel reassured? "Would you ever break the law?"

Avi stroked his goatee as he watched his guests. "I cannot say I never would, for the laws created by men are flawed like their creators. Yet the Writings of the Scribes also declare all governments, even the flawed kind, exist by Sustainer's providence, and therefore to defy the government and its laws is paramount to defying Sustainer Himself."

"That sounds like we ought to never break the law."

"Not never, but rarely, and only when the purpose surpasses possible punishment for breaking it. For you cannot assume you shall escape punishment because you disobey for the right reasons. Rather, you must count the cost and determine if the purpose outweighs the punishment."

"It sounds as if you've considered this conundrum before."

"As one sworn to uphold the laws of the land and as a follower of Effulgence, I've had to think about it often. Yes, we enjoy much freedom now, but it has not always been that way, and it won't always stay that way. I've had to consider my course of action should the Council pass laws contrary to our beliefs." He paused to direct a rail runner concerning our luggage. After the runner hurried on his way, Avi refocused on me. "You still looked troubled."

"If the matter is this important, why have you not spoken of it before?"

"Are you sure I haven't? Consider Kimchi and the mushrooms."

It took a second before the incident surfaced in my memory. We had an elite chef preparing an important dinner when one of our kitchen menials, Kimchi, recognized a delivery of wild mushrooms as poisonous. She tried to warn the chef, but the chef refused to listen, causing Kimchi to deliberately throw the mushrooms away–an act of defiance that could have cost Kimchi her stratum, if not her life. When Avi investigated the matter, he told Kimchi she was responsible for the cost of the very expensive mushrooms, the equivalent of an extra hour of labor for the next six months. Kimchi responded she would destroy the entire batch again, even if it cost her twice that much.

"That's why you believed she told the truth, isn't it?"

He nodded. "She felt the cost was worth it, and that belief prevented the illness of many, if not their deaths."

"Considering what it could have cost her, she was very brave."

"She'd tell you that, despite her bold words, her middles were nothing but melted butter."

Typical Kimchi. "That might be, but she was still very courageous. I hope if I ever have to make a similar choice, I will be as brave."

The rail whistled the first ten notes of "Onward We Go," warning of departure. Avi helped me mount the narrow steps of the rail car. Yet, though I had done this hundreds of times before, it somehow felt different, more removed, even unfamiliar.

What else had I overlooked concerning my father?

Yosarai Patican was too perceptive.

Xander had guarded his answers on the way to the station, but small flickers in her expression intimated he'd revealed more than intended. Not that Sibah Yosarai had pried. On the contrary. She'd exercised great discretion. But if he could not manage the small talk of a country judge's daughter, how would he ever navigate the cutthroat politics of Parliament?

The landscape rolled by the window of the rail carriage, its leisurely pace only elongating the hours before him. Five more bells to avoid any more conversational missteps while he and Massard shared the Paticans' private rail compartment. But he had survived one bell thus far. Surely, he could survive five more until they reached Kolchan and they all went their separate ways. Sibah Yosarai's studies at the Academy would occupy her, while he and Massard would be busy posing as . . . something–he did not know what yet. Those details hadn't been finalized. Whatever guise they settled on, there would be no need to further their acquaintance with the sibah.

Behind his eyes throbbed a headache, which intensified with the dawning awareness that four pairs of eyes stared at him. What had he missed now? He shifted on the cushioned bench he shared with Massard, facing the two Paticans and their menial. Rena? Rabah? Something with an *R*. He cleared his throat; if only he could clear his mind as easily. "I gather I have missed a vital question."

"You might say that," Massard said dryly, a subtle reprimand for not paying attention.

"It was not of much import." The rounded tones of the sibah's accent gave her voice a rolling timbre. "But if you will allow me a different inquiry of a more personal nature, may I ask when you last ate?"

"Breakfast, of course."

Massard snorted. "If a cup of tea and a slice of toast constitutes breakfast."

Xander glared at his bodyguard.

"You must be famished," said Sibah Yosarai. "Avi, with your permission, I should like to ring for refreshments."

Xander tensed. "There's no need–"

"Of course there is need. Travel can become wearisome without proper nourishment. In fact, I've been negligent not to have suggested it sooner. Avi?"

"Some refreshment is a wonderful suggestion, Yosi. I could use a little something myself."

"Then it's settled." Sibah Yosarai reached around her menial to a bell pull near the door.

A moment later, the door of their private compartment slid open, and a rail menial dressed in spotless white linen bowed to them. "How may I be of service, hasibs, sibah?" Sibah, singular, as if the Paticans' menial was not there.

"I have discovered our guests are in need of a light repast, Hab Nehi." The rail menial's name rolled off her tongue without hesitation, as if it were the most natural thing in the world–which it wasn't. Most Indeli families of his acquaintance could barely remember the names of their own menials, much less those who weren't. "If it isn't too much trouble, I would like some tea and one of your sampler trays."

"For you, it is never too much trouble." The warmth infused into the required response seemed genuine. "For how many am I to prepare?"

"All five of us, if you please."

She meant for her maid to dine with them? It was odd enough that the menial rode with them instead of in the menial carriages farther back. For menials and elites to dine together–he'd never witnessed such a thing.

"It will be as you wish." Hab Nehi backed out and closed the door just as a ten-note whistle announced their departure from another station.

At least the meal would provide a diversion from the rail's tedious pace. Maybe under different circumstances their progress would be mesmerizing, for they traveled fast enough that the landscape never became boring, but leisurely enough that it never blurred together into an unmemorable smear of color. Today, however, speed trumped aesthetics. The sooner they reached the capital, the better. As he stared out the window, he could feel her gaze upon him.

"Is something wrong?" Sibah Yosarai indicated his drumming fingers.

He stilled their movement. "Not at all. I am simply unaccustomed to how . . ." *Slow* sounded insulting. "How different your rail is."

There it was again–a flicker in her brown eyes that indicated she'd heard what he hadn't said. "Have you looked down, hasib?"

Down? Xander pressed his forehead to the window. The ground blurred into a brown-grey streak, exactly as would be expected at typical rail speeds. Indeed, now that he concentrated, he could feel the rail constantly deviating its speed, slowing when buildings and trees pressed closer, accelerating when farther away. The leisurely pace was an optical illusion created by precise velocities and the deft cultivation of the landscape. As a result, a field of bobbing flowers melted into rolling pastureland dotted with red-and-white cows, and then gave way to a moderate lake of placid blue.

"And does not such a relaxing view, such beauty, improve your condition?"

The reference to their earlier debate drew his eyes from the landscape outside to the young woman across from him. Such confident determination. Something he was woefully lacking. "You present a strong case, one worth further consideration."

A light tap sounded on the door. The rail menial rolled a narrow cart between the benches. Draped with an embroidered tablecloth of purple and gold, the cart boasted a stack of painted porcelain plates with matching teacups and sterling silver utensils at one end, a steaming teapot, creamer, sugar, and honey at the other. Between, three tiers of the so-called light repast exhibited scones, finger sandwiches, sweet and savory tarts.

After setting the cart's brake, the menial reached for the teapot and cups, but Sibah Yosarai dismissed him. "Thank you, Hab Nehi, but I shall serve. Please present my compliments to

Siv Pom and all who helped. It looks almost too pretty to eat, and I suspect it will taste even more delightful than it appears."

"As you wish, sibah."

She poured the tea and served the food, first to Massard and himself, then to her father and her menial.

Massard sampled his food, then gave Xander a slight nod, approving the food as safe for consumption. Even here, an entire country away, they could not be certain he was free from danger. Xander's appetite faded.

Sibah Yosarai paused in stirring honey and cream into her tea. "Does the food not agree with you, hasib?"

"On the contrary; it looks delicious." He nibbled at a finger sandwich, but he might as well have been eating sand wrapped in paper for all the taste it had. Concerns over poison had a way of depleting taste.

Massard leaned forward. "You must pardon Saunders. He can be quite the grumpy moonbear when he must travel farther than a couple of days."

Xander refrained from rolling his eyes.

But Massard knew. "It's true. You'd rather be in your shop."

"What can I say? Automatons don't give unwanted advice."

"You're an inventor?" Sibah Yosarai's eyes brightened.

"More of a tinkerer." He had hoped to become more, even studying engineering at the university, until his father informed him he was being named successor.

Massard balanced a scone on the edge of his saucer. "My cousin is far too modest."

Cousin? Xander choked on a bite of food. They looked nothing alike in frame or coloring.

But Massard wasn't done. "He is a wonder at all things mechanical, with some of his inventions even presented to King Rion."

Sibah Yosarai's eyes rounded. "You've already had inventions accepted by kings?"

The misleading statement had him tugging at his high collar. Yes, as a twelve-year-old, he'd given his father a clock–one that didn't keep time–and then two years later, the lopsided mechanical parrot, but neither truly qualified as "inventions accepted by kings." "I have, though it's not the achievement you suppose. I, ah, had some connections."

"Too modest, as I said." Massard lifted his teacup. "But his inventions lack beauty. That's why I brought him on this trading trip, that he might learn some of your country's artistry."

Nuts and bolts! What kind of cover story was that? Besides an impossible one, that is. For he'd never convince people he was a mechanical "wonder," an inventor for kings. If Selucreh were here, he'd be howling with laughter. *"Inventions accepted by kings? You don't have sufficient spine to present one long enough to be accepted."* Xander glanced at the judge, but his placid face revealed no indication of whether he'd aided Massard in concocting this wild story.

"As you can tell, he hasn't embraced the idea."

"Because, as you can tell, my cousin can be quite assertive." He shot Massard a look, which his bodyguard avoided with a request for more tea.

"Is the thought of studying art that distressing to you, Hasib Saunders?" asked Sibah Yosarai.

"It is not the art itself that concerns me, but the expectations. Many presume I will do grand things upon my return."

"And many others would be glad to see you fail?"

Xander startled at her insight.

She offered him a wan smile. "The problem of expectations is not isolated to a particular people, sphere, stratum, or job, hasib, but is a common burden faced by many." She arose, resting her cup and saucer onto the edge of the cart. "If you will excuse me, I need to freshen up." She left the compartment.

The menial made eye contact with the judge, who nodded

his permission to the unspoken request. She also departed, leaving the three men alone.

Xander slumped back, his headache reasserting itself. If he couldn't manage this, how would he ever convince the people, much less Parliament, his ascension to the throne wasn't a colossal mistake? That *he* wasn't a mistake? Especially when he himself suspected the whole thing was one giant blunder, a disaster waiting to happen.

"What do you think?"

Xander refocused on the judge. "About what?"

"Yosi."

The question he was always asked after meeting a young lady considered a suitable match. Normally, he would choose some complimentary but disinterested answer, but here it seemed superfluous. "I'm not in the market."

Judge Patican chuckled. "Good thing, because neither is she. She's adamantly opposed to a match with anyone in politics."

Xander's hackles rose despite his declaration of not being in the market. "Is that so?"

"She finds politicians to be egotistical word-benders with no sense of humor and little appreciation for the simple things in life." He held up a forestalling hand. "Her words, not mine, and they are not without justification, are they?"

Too many examples presented themselves among the Egdonian parlies he knew to disagree. He shifted toward Massard. "Art? That is the best you could concoct?"

"Can you think of a better reason for being in Indel, Your Highness? And which enemy would search for you among sculptures and paintbrushes?"

Massard's logic was indisputable but grating. "Did you consider anything else?"

"Several other ideas were considered," answered the judge, "but I encouraged the adoption of this one, not without personal reasons, I confess."

"Color me intrigued."

"Yosi is strong, intelligent, and gifted–yet untried and naïve. I was hoping you would watch over her. Though she'll be staying with family, my sister-in-law isn't known for warmth and maternal instincts. Casualties of a difficult marriage and early widowhood, unfortunately. Yosi, I suspect, will need a friendly face."

That proposition was as appealing as counting threads on a screw. "You remember I am a hunted man, who endangers anyone associated with me?"

"That only strengthens my argument. Since she's my daughter, that relationship places her in danger she knows nothing about, and therefore, does not know to watch for . . . unless you prefer I tell her the truth?"

Although the judge had every right to be protective of his daughter, the either-or choice boxed Xander into a corner he did not like.

"I beg your pardon, Your Highness," Massard said, "but most men would not consider spending time with a beautiful young lady a hardship."

Most beautiful young ladies were not as perceptive as Yosarai Patican. "And if she gets the wrong idea?"

"She's too focused on her aspirations," said Judge Patican, "to her benefit or detriment, I haven't decided. However, I'll explain to Yosi your visits are a favor to me, while the study of art will provide a logical reason for your paths to cross."

Xander fingered the edge of his saucer. Perhaps it would be safer to tell the truth and then disappear into the masses of the capital. "This will add to your burden as well, Massard, for in protecting me you will also end up protecting another. Is this truly the safest path?"

"A rope of three strands does not break easily, Your Highness. You have considered the liability of Sibah Patican but have not weighed her potential as an asset. The sibah is quite perceptive, and her native eyes would notice dangers we may overlook as foreigners."

The judge nodded his agreement. "I could ask that she notify you or Massard if she notices anything odd. No further explanation needed."

Xander eyed the two men. "How much time did you spend on our story–and how much on devising these answers?"

"Only what was necessary on each subject," said Massard.

"Ah, you *did* plot these arguments ahead of time."

The judge smiled. "Guilty as charged, though I cannot pretend any remorse. For I admit when I received the queen's letter, it seemed an answer to my prayer, ordained by Sustainer Himself."

There was no arguing with that, especially with their auspicious arrival on the very day Yosarai left for the capital. A day later and their paths would not have crossed. "Considering all you've risked for us, I promise to watch over Sibah Yosarai."

May he not see the day he rued those words.

He was not there.

The informant's report yet hung in the air. It taunted me. Mocked me. Even after my men removed the weasel from my office, the words dredged up the ghost of insufficiency to judge me and find me wanting. Again.

I slammed my cup down, sloshing tea into the saucer. I was not at fault. My subordinates were the incompetent ones. They let the crown prince slip through their fingers. They failed to follow his trail.

No more. I had tolerated their mistakes long enough. If they couldn't locate the prince, I would uncover the pretender's plans myself. I had worked too hard for any other outcome.

I rang a bell, and my butler appeared. "Prepare the scarriage. I have an appointment at the palace."

A perpetual sensory cacophony.

If I had to describe the Kolchan station as succinctly as possible, those would be the words I would choose. Because the moment I exited the rail carriage, the hubbub assaulted my senses, each sensation vying for attention. People, animals, and luggage created eddies of color around the pillared archways. Floral perfumes were salted with sun-baked stone and flesh. Endless chatter was punctuated with clatterings and bangings and hawking vendors and three strains of music. In view of such chaos, my preference for my quiet, orderly home should not mystify as many as it did.

"Are we ready?" Avi presented me his hand.

Clutching it with more force than necessary, I descended the steep steps to the platform where I raised my gaze to his face, to misty eyes and a wobbly smile. I blinked back my tears. This separation may have been his idea, but it would be as hard on him as on me. Perhaps harder.

Rivka hurried off to oversee our luggage's transfer to the hired coach, but Avi steered me toward Saunders and Mascad, standing along a quieter edge of the station.

"We are about to depart for my sister-in-law's home. Is there anything else you need before we leave, hasibs?" he asked. "You know how to reach the Banyans?"

My head reared back. They were staying a short walk from my aunt's.

"We appreciate your concern, but we have all we need." Mascad turned to me. "But perhaps once we have settled, you can show my cousin the many beautiful aspects of your capital. Convince him art is a worthy endeavor."

Saunders was right. His cousin could be quite assertive.

But Saunders bowed to me, one arm behind his back, the other across his waist. "I would be most appreciative of any time you can spare me, Sibah Yosarai, though I understand your studies at the Academy must take precedence."

The Egdonian bow prodded at me, as if I had seen Saunders before, in a half-forgotten memory or a half-remembered dream. An impossibility, of course, for we just met. "I'm sure something could be arranged. However, since we are headed the same direction, would you like to share our coach?"

Mascad looked at Saunders, as if consulting him. As if Mascad were only the spokesman for the pair and Saunders the true authority. Which made no sense if Saunders was here at his cousin's behest. "A most generous offer, sibah," replied Mascad, "one we must respectfully decline. It has been many years since my cousin has visited, and I intend to take a circuitous route through the city to reacquaint him with it."

"Then I wish you a pleasant tour." At least that would give me one bell alone with Avi and perhaps a chance to ask about Ima's book, for the vision at the end of the first page was not an anomaly.

"Let us not detain you any longer, then. Good evenfall, hasibs." My father nodded to the men, and we wound our way to the street. Rivka was already perched atop our hired coach, the driver awaiting our arrival.

My father gathered my hands in his. "I am extremely proud of you, Yosi. This day could not have been easy for you. I know how much you were looking forward to our memory tour, but you handled yourself with grace and generosity."

His words erased any smudges of frustration at the intrusion. Avi was proud of me, and I could ask for nothing more. As we settled in, I snuggled closer to his side.

"Yosarai . . ."

At the gravity of his voice, big drops of black ink splattered across the page of my renewed contentment. I cleared my throat. "Yes, Avi?"

"You do know I love you? And that what I do, I do because of that love?"

The ink spread, staining all it touched. "But of course."

Avi brushed my cheek. "Why was I blessed to have such a daughter as you? Surely there are men more worthy than I."

"If there is one, he must live far away, for I have not heard of such a man." Something in his expression gave me pause. "What is wrong, Avi?"

"The coming months will be difficult for you."

I pondered his words. They carried the weight of truth, but a weight shy of the full truth. "What are you not telling me?"

"I've asked Hasib Saunders to watch over you."

"You what?" I sat upright.

"It's a big city, Yosi. Many here will not seek your best interests."

My jaw tightened. "I am not a naïve little girl needing a nursemaid to protect me, Avi. Though I suppose I ought be thankful that is your only intention."

His goatee twitched. "You could do worse. Much worse."

"Avi!" Fire flooded my face.

He held up his hands, palms out. "Only teasing, my little illuminary. I know neither of you are ready for such things."

"Good, or I would have to remind you of your last attempt at matchmaking."

"Lascar and Muri are happily married." His eyes crinkled at the corners.

"After they nearly tore each other apart. They only learned to work together in order to end your awful attempts to force them together."

"That sounds successful to me."

I didn't bother suppressing my snort.

"However, it is not your protection alone about which I am concerned." The stroke of his words thickened from renewed seriousness. "I made the request as much for his benefit as for yours."

The coach crossed into a building's shadow, and a chill pricked my skin. "How so?"

"Hasib Saunders is a stranger in an unfamiliar land. Dangers a native would notice, he will miss."

I stared at the passing buildings. Their white walls gleamed golden in this final hour of sunlight, even as shadows added contrasting splashes of ebony. Shadows that could conceal those who lurked within them. My words from the rail resurfaced. *And many others would be glad to see you fail?* "His competition," I said aloud. "Some would see harm befall him."

"I cannot confirm or deny your suspicions."

I may not have hit the bull's eye, but I'd struck the target. "Do not worry, Avi. I shall be the model of prudence while in Kolchan." If allowing a stranger to shadow my movements would set Avi's mind at ease, I would tolerate it for his sake. Which left only one other concern. "Does he know about my gift?"

Avi shook his head. "I gave him the usual explanation, but even if he discovered the truth, I doubt you'd have any trouble with him."

Oh, to have his confidence! While most dismissed the elchan as a myth or religious allegory, some elites would gladly exploit the gifted, while a corrupt segment of the kodesh saw us as a threat to be destroyed. Exploitation, destruction, or secrecy–those were my options. But secrecy, while protective, was also isolating.

That raised the question that had hovered since my birthfest. If I didn't ask now, another chance may not present itself until Winter Solstice. "Avi, was Ima elchan-gifted too?"

A deep stillness settled upon him that defied the jostling of the coach. "You saw something in her book."

I locked my hands together. What if he insisted I tell him what I'd seen?

Avi rested a hand on my arm. "Yes, she was a heart seer, like you. She didn't talk much about it, though she often had flashes when working on her art. From what I understood, they usually revealed a future decision with far-reaching implications."

That meant, sometime in the future, I would be forced to make a decision on which someone's life depended. A haze of sickly yellow green tinted the world.

"Yosi." Solemnity weighted Avi's voice. "I don't know what you saw, but do not try to predict your decision. Sometimes the obvious choice is not the right one. Jasmene warned me of this. Once, I was convinced I knew otherwise, and I almost made a disastrous decision that would have ended a man's life. By Sustainer's grace, an interruption prevented me from acting on that predetermined course, and that extra time revealed details I'd overlooked, leading to the opposite conclusion."

"I am to prepare by not preparing?"

"Your mother would have told you, although prediction and preparation begin and end in the same place, it is what you do in the middle that makes the difference."

"Can anything be done to avert that point of decision?"

"You mean stop the vision from happening?" Avi stroked his goatee. "I suppose you could, in theory. In reality, I suspect the answer is no. Although Sustainer leaves us free to make our own decisions, He knows our choices before we make them and therefore knows where those choices will lead us. Either way, I have never known any of her visions to have failed."

Not the answer I was hoping for. *Sustainer, I don't want anyone's life to depend on me!* A pointless prayer, if what Avi said was true, but I couldn't help uttering it nonetheless, hoping this time Avi was wrong.

Our coach stopped, truncating further conversation or prayer. We were here. Before us stood a blocky, flat-top house that mirrored the lavish uniformity of the surrounding neighborhood. Where some middle-stratum neighborhoods delighted in uniqueness, adding metal scrollwork or cascading vines or vibrant murals according to preference, this particular area lacked all such charm. It was as if the owners employed the same craftsmen to do the same work. Indeed, the only thing that distinguished this house from those surrounding it was the severe lacquered look of the over-polished door, accentuated by the glow of the orbed lamp hanging above it. My aunt's home. My home for the next several months. "I hate it."

"Hate what, Yosi?"

Heat swept through my cheeks. I hadn't meant to speak the sentiment aloud, but I could not retract it now. "That." My sweeping gesture encompassed the whole street. "Sustainer meant beauty to be an expression of our individuality, our uniqueness, a way to share with others what brings us joy and hope. To use it to flaunt one's wealth or prove one's stratum . . . it seems so wrong."

"It is a twisting of Sustainer's original intent, but don't judge too harshly. It's easy to maintain your uniqueness when all admire and applaud you. However, when pressure abounds to conform or else be despised, rejected, isolated, cast out–that is the true test of character."

I winced.

"Wealth, high stratum, education, talent. Sustainer has gifted you many wonderful privileges, Yosi, and you need not feel shame or guilt over those privileges. The key is to remember they are gifts, things to be enjoyed and shared freely with others, not clenched and hoarded." Avi stood. "But we shouldn't keep your aunt waiting. She probably has dinner ready."

At Avi's firm knock, a starched butler opened the door,

his black linens looking stifling in their stiffness. This was not the same man who'd greeted us on our last visit. It shouldn't surprise me; my aunt changed menials like some changed fashions. Nonetheless, it always startled me to be greeted by a different face every two or three visits.

"The sibah gadolah has been expecting you. Please follow me." The man guided us through the tiled hall to a winding staircase at the center of the building.

"And what is your name?"

The butler startled. "Ebon, sibah."

"Ebon." I mentally calligraphied the name, thick in the middle, fading along the edges. "That's a good strong name, with an edge of mystery. Which, of course, suits a butler, don't you think? For you always see more than you tell."

That brought up one corner of the man's mouth. "Yes, sibah."

"I will do my best to remember, but please forgive me should it escape to the black cavern of memory, and I must ask for it again."

The man began to respond but then stiffened into starched formality.

My aunt had arrived. I knew it before I turned because all her menials responded the same way whenever she entered a room. Sure enough, Dodah Mirina descended the central spiral staircase, all spine and dominance. A necessity to keep order in her classroom, Avi said, but would it hurt to smile? The stretching of her thin lips from side to side never quite qualified.

"Brother, I'm happy to see you have safely arrived." Her words were as ramrod as her posture. She might teach social graces to the younger students at the Academy, but sometimes it seemed like she forgot grace entailed more than perfect posture and strict adherence to custom.

Avi met her proffered arm as an equal. "As am I."

Then she turned to me, the stiff silk of her straight lehenga skirt rustling, and I placed my arm below hers as her subordinate.

"Niece, you grow lovelier with each passing year. I'm sure your beauty will be the talk of the Academy."

"You are generous with your words, Dodah Mirina, but I am sure I'll only be a simple country wildflower among a plethora of cultivated roses, lilies, and orchids."

Dodah Mirina's smile stretched wider, still devoid of any warmth. "Modest too, no doubt due to your excellent parenting, brother."

"I would like to think that, though I suspect it has less to do with me and more with Sustainer's grace."

"Quite. Butler, you may go." She ascended the stairs. "I have a light dinner laid out for us on the roof. Nothing as fancy as your regular fare, I'm sure, but after a long day of travel, it should be refreshing."

I reached for the polished banister, then recoiled. Hands left smudges, a maid told me once, and unattended the oil would darken the wood.

The rooftop garden was as I remembered. Oil lamps gleamed in the darkening twilight, strategically placed among regimented flower boxes. On my right, the city glittered upon the hillside like a scattering of diamonds, while on the left, the setting sun painted the valley in reds and oranges.

In the middle of the roof, an embroidered cloth covered a low table, with silver candelabras and fine bone china upon it. Plump cushions of scarlet and purple provided comfortable places to sit. I had never ascertained if this was truly how my aunt's family dined or if it reflected an attempt to impress us.

From a nearby bench, Lavidah rose with a languid grace that insinuated our arrival was merely an interruption to be tolerated. Though my cousin and I were the same age, her heavy makeup and revealing drape of her sari added an air of bored sophistication to her dark beauty.

Jamarde, on the other hand, rushed to embrace me. "You're here!" A couple of years younger, Jamarde lacked the grace and refined beauty of her sister, her face considered too round and eyes too narrow behind her wire spectacles. While Lavidah was a script with too many flourishes, Jamarde's letters would be easily legible, with soft, welcoming curves.

Dodah Mirina cleared her throat.

Jamarde flinched and angled away from her mother. "Welcome, cousin." She offered me the traditional greeting of equals.

I winked at her, then turned to Lavidah.

She placed her forearm side by side against mine, acknowledging me as her equal, and yet her arm was slightly elevated, as if to assert dominance. "Welcome, cousin. I expect it shall be a great diversion to have you here, and I hope your time with us defies all expectations."

As did I, though our expectations were likely realms apart.

Dodah Mirina motioned us toward the table. She, of course, took the head as hostess and seated Avi at the place of honor at the other end. Lavidah stepped toward her mother's right hand.

My aunt stopped her with a disapproving glare before giving me a tight-lipped smile. "Please, have a seat here, niece."

"I thank you for the honor, Dodah Mirina, but if it pleases you, I would like to sit beside my father."

"If that is what you wish."

I sank onto the cushion at my father's right with Jamarde to my right. My aunt might be disapproving and Lavidah disdainful, but I was not alone. Jamarde was here. Rivka, too, with Saunders and Mascad just down the street. Nor would all my time be spent at my aunt's. Surely I'd make other acquaintances and maybe even a friend or two at the Academy.

Menials emerged from shadows at some unseen signal and unveiled plates of food with a flourish. Blue-fin bisque? Such a dish was a treat at home, and the capital was twice as far from the coast as we were. The courses that followed were no less extravagant: northern pear salad, purple potato mash and candied onions, center-cut beef, and for dessert, iced coconut cream drizzled with a red sauce made of Egdonian bubble berries.

My father laid his napkin beside the bowl. "As always, Mirina, you have served a meal suitable for the chancellor himself."

"You are overgenerous with your praise, brother, but I thank you nonetheless. I wanted only the best for you and your daughter."

"You certainly accomplished that." Avi patted his stomach. "I may not have to eat again until I reach home. I'm glad Yosi will be in such good hands during her time at the Academy." Avi extended to my aunt a folded cheque.

Her eyes widened at the amount written thereupon, even as a gleam lit them. "This is far too much."

"Nothing is too much where my illuminary is concerned."

"Truly, I cannot accept this." Yet Dodah Mirina made no effort to return the cheque. She was protesting because Indeli tradition dictated two declines before accepting a generous gift.

"Not only do I insist you accept this, but also the additional cheques that will arrive here every month of Yosi's stay, since you are caring for her in my absence."

My aunt tucked the cheque into a pouch attached to her chatelaine. "I accept, but my niece is always welcome here. She is my sister's daughter, after all."

A sister she'd hated because of her success.

My father made a move as if to stand. "Now, if you'll excuse us, I think Yosi and I ought to trade our fare-thee-wells this evening as I must leave early tomorrow."

"Please, stay and enjoy." Dodah Mirina arose, Lavidah and Jamarde following suit. "I've household matters to oversee, and the girls have their studies. May you have a pleasant evenfall and enjoy the deep sleep of refreshment. Come, girls." My cousins followed her downstairs.

I wandered to a bench along the eastern edge of the roof where I could be wrapped in half shadows, away from the orb lamps swaying in the evening breeze.

Avi took a seat beside me. He was here now, but he wouldn't be tomorrow. I propped my arms against the top of the wall. To the north, strings of colored lanterns illuminated the Arboretum Capital, while lamps painted a welcoming aura around the Chancellor's Palace and the Teardrop Theatre. Nearby, the black bulk with no illumination marked the Academy.

"The teachers are strict but fair. As long as you work hard, you'll do fine."

He was probably correct, but nothing about this felt right. Everything in me wanted to hide from the world's impossible expectations and withering disdain. Never good enough because I found difficult what others found easy, terrified by what others considered benign. However, whether I wanted it or not, I could not linger in my father's shadow any longer.

"And before we know it," continued Avi, "Winter Solstice will arrive, and we'll be on a rail for home."

I swallowed the lump in my throat. "That's assuming you listen to Muri's fussing and don't land yourself in a sickbed from malnutrition."

He chuckled. "I'll make you a deal. I promise to eat three meals a day and all of my vegetables if you promise to have some fun instead of moping in your room."

"I never mope."

"I never sneak snacks to Dowser under the table."

We glared at each other in mock indignation before smiles resurfaced. "I suppose I occasionally mope–just a little."

"And I suppose I occasionally slip Dowser a treat–but only when he asks for it."

"Which never happens, does it?"

"Almost never."

My smile faded, and a hole from Avi's coming absence gaped within my heart. What would I do, how would I cope, when death made that separation more permanent? *Please, Sustainer, don't take him for a good many years.*

Avi caught my eye. "'Night may water the earth with tears . . .'" he prompted.

"'But flowers of joy will spring forth at the rising of the sun,'" I responded automatically, a tear wending its way down my cheek. My voice choked. "Still, the night looks so long, so black, Avi."

"Oh, Yosi . . ." My father gathered me into his arms.

Though I felt their strength and assurance, they couldn't fill the hollowness inside, a void left by a stolen treasure. No doubt a stronger or braver person would embrace the emptiness, see it as full of possibility. But it only reminded me of everything I was losing.

Avi stroked my head, rocking me slightly as if I were a little girl again in need of comfort. "Even the longest, blackest night without stars or moons must end. The morning will come, though it may seem to tarry, and it is worth waiting for. Keep your eyes on the horizon, Yosi. The light will return because Sustainer Himself is light."

His words soaked into me. *Morning will come. Keep your eyes on the horizon.* I couldn't do that looking over my shoulder. With a shuddering breath, I did the hardest thing I'd ever done. I withdrew from his embrace. It was time to let Avi go and stand on my own.

Expectations

Hopes. Dreams. Desires. Ideas about what should be and what the future ought to hold.

None of these things are bad in themselves. Properly used, they can motivate us to stay the course through rugged mountain terrain and barren, sun-scorched deserts. Improperly, though, they weigh us down, like a load of bricks strapped to our backs, making arduous the easiest of journeys through the most pleasant of places. Is it any wonder, then, that so many struggle to travel well the journey Sustainer sets before them?

For milestones were meant to be passed, not carried.

3

Beginnings, by their very nature, implied an end.

Sitting on my bedroom's small balcony, I pulled a blanket tighter against the morning chill. Tatters of grey fog twined around the buildings, the noise of the early morning bustle muffled, a city in hiding. Yes, today marked a fresh start in a new place, but what was I losing in exchange?

"Oh my." The utterance called me from my musings to Rivka, halted inside the bedroom doorway, staring at my war-torn bed, sheets and blankets wadded up at its foot, pillows scattered on the floor. Pressing lips together, she arranged my bed with her usual rapid precision, for as she often admonished me, no one can be comfortable living in a mess. "I see it is a two-cup day, sibah."

I stifled a yawn. "Maybe even a three-cupper."

"I shall make sure the cook has a full pot ready." She opened the wardrobe containing the dresses she'd unpacked yestereve and withdrew my turquoise dress. "An oceanspray orchid is one of the most beautiful flowers of Waibean. And one of the most poisonous." She exchanged the dress for a royal purple anarkali with pale pink roses and thick vines embroidered all over the flouncy skirt and fitted bodice. Not the fanciest I owned, but one that announced my wealthy stratum.

I could already imagine the green tendrils of envy twining

through the other students' accounts of the day, accentuated with red sparks of anger. "I was thinking something a bit less . . . ostentatious."

"Perhaps you're right. People often show their true colors to one they consider inferior." She exchanged the gown for a butter-yellow tunic dress with wide sleeves and a scalloped hem. No beading. No embroidering. No yards of fabric. The most ornate piece was the wide, colorful sash that would give the dress shape.

Surely the simpler selection would help me blend in, declare me a non-threat. I shook my head. Who was I fooling? As a final-year transfer, I was practically announcing I could compete with the best of the best without passing through the same strict training. The worst kind of threat.

In keeping with the dress, Rivka chose modest jewelry, basic cosmetics, and a hairstyle simple enough I could have done it, maybe to create the illusion I had. Yet, upon finishing, one corner of her mouth edged up. "You wished not to be ostentatious, but outward simplicity cannot hide your inward radiance, sibah. You will be seen whether you wish it or not."

I rolled my eyes. "Perhaps I should borrow one of your dresses, then. I doubt anyone would notice me if I were a menial."

"I'm not certain about that, which would be worse by far, since the elite despise being overshadowed by those who serve them. Yes, thank Sustainer for making you an elite and not a menial."

What an odd reason to be grateful for my sphere, but before I could respond, a knock sounded.

Jamarde entered the room. She wore a faded blue sari that did nothing for either her figure or her complexion. "Good morning, is my cousin–oh." Her stubby nose wrinkled, her eyes squinching behind her spectacles.

"Today I'm your simple country cousin who qualified for

the Academy by dumb luck." More wishful thinking. The Academy trained only the brightest and wealthiest of Indel, and no amount of luck could obtain admittance. My cousins could attend solely because Dodah Mirina taught there. "You, on the other hand . . ." I tapped my finger against my lips at the lopsided hairstyle Jamarde obviously *had* done herself. "Such potential. Rivka?"

"If the sibah is willing." Rivka waved toward a stool.

Jamarde scuffed her feet. "If Lavidah sees, she will think she can demand the same service."

"Then we'll keep her from seeing." I pulled a veil from a trunk. "Later, Rivka can teach you to do it, so Lavidah can demand nothing."

Jamarde sat gingerly, as if fearing the collapse of the stool beneath her, but she allowed Rivka to undo her hair. "I'm glad you are staying with us, Yosi. I'm sure my studies will go better with you here. I mean, if you're not too busy."

"If I'm too busy to help, then I am too busy." Now there was a possibility I'd not considered. Perhaps my time in Kolchan was meant more for others than it was for me. "Actually, I was hoping for a trade."

"You were?" Jamarde sat straighter as Rivka modified her cosmetics.

"Rivka has been preparing for a crossover assessment, and while she's ready for the knowledge and skills portions, social graces have proven elusive."

"She's welcome to practice on me, and"–her face lit up–"I know a couple of other girls who might also help in exchange for some extra tutoring."

"Consider it done."

"Done indeed." Rivka extended a hand mirror to Jamarde.

Her mouth formed a small circle. "I look . . ."

"Beautiful," I announced. "Even prettier than Lavidah, in

my opinion. Now, shall Rivka bring up our breakfasts? That way we won't risk Lavidah glimpsing you before we're ready."

Jamarde plucked at an invisible speck on her skirt.

"It'd be an ideal time for Rivka to practice her social graces."

"I suppose," she hesitantly agreed.

While Rivka fetched the food, I rearranged the furniture for our breakfast. Something bothered my cousin, but what? Not a single possibility suggested itself. Hence my failure to teach Rivka the social graces. I created awkward situations flawlessly and excelled at aggravating the problem when attempting to rectify it. Maybe a change of subject would help? "Have you any advice about attending the Academy?"

"Besides not attend?"

I set a vase of flowers to the side. "Avi won't permit it."

"He told you no?" Her words arched upward in genuine surprise as we carried a low table to the center of the room.

"He does occasionally." A blush heated my face. Why had so many blessings graced my life? Material wealth. Social stratum. Avi's love and care. Did my aunt ever hug her daughters? Not a single instance came to mind, though Dodah Mirina might reserve such intimate actions for private settings. I settled on a pillow at the table. "Now, do you have any advice? I'm beyond my depth, and Lavidah . . ." I censored myself. "Lavidah will be too busy to provide guidance."

"You mean she would feed you to the tigers?"

"Maybe that too." We exchanged a smile born from shared understanding, and Jamarde relaxed some.

"Beware of any girl associated with my sister or any friendliness from them. Actually, regard any friendliness with suspicion. Few things are as they seem, and sabotage is not unusual. A leading contender was even poisoned a couple of years ago before the Exam."

"Poisoned?"

"Enough to make her sick so that she failed to reach the top five placements. They never discovered who or how, though rumors spoke of poison-laced scones left as a gift."

Another reason why I didn't want to come. Not because of the tough academics, but because of the social labyrinth created by the competition. In order to become a politico, you had to earn the Exam's highest placement in one of the outer provinces or one of the top five in Duyah, the province where Kolchan was located. Only politicos could train as a counselor or marry one, for the spouses had to be as intelligent and as well-educated as the counselors themselves due to the social functions of the job. Of course, not all top placements became counselors or married one, but the prestige of the politico made those top placements coveted. "Where did Lavidah place on the last practice test?"

"Fifth."

"That means if I place in the top five . . ."

"She won't, which makes her the most dangerous of all."

Nothing like living with a keg of gunpowder and a lit fuse. Would it be terrible if I lowered my scores, just a little? After all, the politico stratum held no appeal for me. An apprenticeship with Hasib Kells, Kolchan's chief illuminator, and access to the Writings in the Scriptorium–those were my goals. Maybe after the final practice test revealed my current standing in Duyah, I could explain to Avi why not doing my best might actually be best.

Rivka bustled in with a covered tray. "I hope you don't mind, sibahs, but I took the liberty of making your food the same as mine, as Zibbah would not hear of providing three fancy breakfasts." She revealed a stack of plain dishes, a pot of tea, and a bowl of steaming nut porridge.

Jamarde released what seemed like a sigh of relief. I sniffed the air. "I suspect this will satisfy better than some fluffy pastry."

"Though Zibbah's pastries are flaky scrumptiousness, especially when she uses the milk of rose almonds," Jamarde said. “But then everything she makes is delicious. At least, when she is free to cook as she pleases.”

My cousin’s words were off-centered again, but now wasn’t the time to probe. I waved at Rivka. “Would you do the honor of serving?”

“Me?” Rivka froze.

“That was why we were breakfasting here, was it not?” Jamarde pushed her spectacles higher. “Therefore, the proper response would be, ‘I would consider it an honor, Sibah Yosarai.’ As an elite, you will be asked to do a great many unexpected things. The key is to handle everything–even rejection–with grace and poise, treating other elites as equals.” She nodded at me to begin again.

“Rivka, would you serve?”

“I am honored by your request, Sibah Yosarai, but I believe Sibah Jamarde,” Rivka glanced at my cousin, who gave her a reassuring nod, “would perform that honor with greater poise and grace as befitting the task.”

Jamarde’s smile mirrored my own grin. “You give me too much credit. Please, I insist you have the honor.”

“You are most gracious and . . . and . . .” Rivka floundered.

I opened my mouth, but Jamarde held up a finger.

“And in view of such generosity, how can I not accept such an honor?” Rivka glanced between us, and at our nods of approval, she relaxed into her role as hostess, pouring tea and serving breakfast with the grace and poise I’d struggled to elicit. Jamarde would make a natural teacher, whatever field she pursued.

When we finished breakfast, Rivka’s posture eased. “Maybe I ought to stay a menial. Less headache.”

Jamarde laughed, the amber glints in her brown eyes sparkling for the first time since my arrival. “It only seems easier because it’s familiar.” A clock chimed. “But the Academy waits for no one. I'll meet you downstairs, Yosi." She gathered the borrowed veil and left to collect her books.

I rechecked my own bag; Rivka had everything in perfect order, of course. "Was it me, or was there more behind this morning's porridge than your being a menial?"

Lightning flashed through Rivka's dark eyes. "Let's say the sibah gadolah feels the younger Sibah Chiman enjoys her meals too well and restricts the young sibah's diet to that of a gutter rat. The cook permitted the porridge because I promised the sibah gadolah would be none the wiser."

Jamarde wasn't as slender as either Lavidah or me, but that was because she resembled her deceased father. A well-tailored dress would better her appearance more than such a drastic change in diet. "I see a conversation with my aunt and Avi is in order."

"Pardon me for speaking, but I would not do that."

I arched my brow.

"The sibah must live with her mother after you leave. Such interference could stoke the embers of resentment."

Something Rivka would know firsthand. I had glimpsed once the scars upon her back, received from the elite she served before Avi acquired her as my maid. I deflated. "I will say nothing. But that does not mean we must do nothing, does it?"

A sly smile quirked Rivka's lips. "As always, I am ready to serve." She then opened the door and bowed. "Meanwhile, may Sustainer's blessing be upon you all the day."

May it be indeed.

Slipping the strap of my school bag over my shoulder, I reached the spiral staircase at the same time as Jamarde, veil now fixed over her head. She motioned for me to descend first. I reached the main foyer just as Lavidah left the dining room.

Lavidah's dark hair was artfully braided and arranged to soften the sharp angles of her face, while her off-the-shoulder dress accentuated her form in all the right ways, its coppery color highlighting the warm tones of her skin. My cousin was truly beautiful. But then again, so was a sand cobra.

Lavidah displayed a thin-lipped smile reminiscent of her mother. "Behind the clock, are we? Unfortunately, we can't afford any delays, as it is your first day. Perhaps a menial could fetch you a piece of fruit to eat on the way."

"Thank you for your concern, Lavidah, but as it happens, I'm not hungry right now."

Jamarde stifled a laugh behind me, drawing Lavidah's attention.

"Now that's one of the most sensible things I've seen you wear, sister. Perhaps we ought to purchase a whole set for your wardrobe."

"It does grant her an air of intrigue, doesn't it? I hear many men are attracted to a woman of mystery."

"You can't believe all you hear." Lavidah turned in a swirl of skirt and disdain.

We followed her to the small day coach my aunt owned, where I settled on the rear-facing bench opposite my cousins. Thankfully, my aunt had already been delivered to the school. One less critical gaze to endure.

Soon, the boxy homes of their middle-stratum neighborhood were exchanged for fenced estates bearing fancy crests, with an imposing white marble building towering over them all. The Academy of the Seven Arts, glowering down the long green nose of a lawn, as if daring whoever drew near to prove their worthiness to walk its hallowed halls.

The coach circled a drive of crushed pink shells and stopped before the massive bronze doors cast with the symbols of the Seven Arts: a paintbrush for creativity, a pen for language, a scroll for intellect, a teacup for social graces, a sword for physical skills, an open hand for virtue, and a flame for religion. I pressed a hand to my roiling stomach. Maybe I should have forgone breakfast.

A menial in the Academy's liveried greens opened the door, and Lavidah descended with all the pride of a politico. I followed, then came to a standstill, unable to move.

"It helps if you breathe." Laughter infused Jamarde's voice as she stowed the veil in her school bag.

"I think my lungs have forgotten how."

"Then when you faint from insufficient oxygen, please do it with grace and poise."

The echo of her instructions to Rivka drew a chuckle out of me. Tension eased from my body. Everything would be fine. I would be fine. Avi wouldn't have sent me here otherwise.

Inside, Jamarde provided directions to my lecture room, since Lavidah had conveniently disappeared, and soon I was navigating breezeways covered in mosaics, gardens heavy with the perfume of late-summer roses, and a hall adorned with intricate tapestries alternating with full-size portraits of prior Academy heads, all of whom challenged my presence here.

The lecture room itself was not large–perhaps the size of a formal dining hall, set with short rows of tables facing the desk near where I entered. Twenty or so other students gathered in tight clusters throughout. Within seconds, all turned my way, elbowing and whispering with not-so-covert glances. A few even stared openly, despite the rules of polite society. I schooled my features into pleasant but detached friendliness. Lavidah walked toward me with three other girls, as if to greet me, then turned her back as she and her companions sat in the front row, filling it. The message to the other students was clear: *Don't talk to the new girl; she's not worth your time.* The message to me was equally clear: *You can't compete here.*

My ink-stained fingers tightened around the strap of my bag, but I held on to my smile and walked toward an empty seat farther back. One of the boys dropped into it and stretched out long legs, blocking access to the rest of the row.

"This chair is empty." A lone girl in a tasteful but simple

sari of pale teal beckoned me forward, her every movement conveying grace. Lavidah was stunning in an eye-catching way, but this girl had a gentle beauty, easily overlooked yet worthy of a second glance.

Something tugged on my memory–a sense of familiarity I couldn't quite place. I was certain we had never met. Why, then, did I recognize her? Ima's book. I'd seen her in one of the visions there, wearing that exact dress.

"I'm Estelle Assah." As she greeted me, her long braid swished into view. Instead of being dark from root to tip, the color graduated from black to auburn to red to strawberry blonde before lightening almost to white at the very tip. A Mouncite-Indeli. That explained her unusual name, but how had a mixer ended up at the Academy?

That mystery would have to wait, as our classmates watched for my reaction to the social pariah of the room. Half of me wanted to ignore Estelle to avoid further exclusion. The other half wanted to embrace her in scandalous defiance. Both reactions were based on others' opinions. If my classmates dictated this simple gesture, would I be any better than my aunt's neighbors about whom I had complained yestereve? All deserved to be treated graciously, according to the Scribes. I extended my arm beneath hers, treating her as my superior. "Yosarai Patican."

Estelle shifted her arm to the space beside mine. "'A welcome and a smile / this is the best of style.'"

"You know 'The Bard of Miseno'?"

"At last, someone with sensible taste in literature!"

We smiled at each other, but then the teacher took her place at the front of the room, preventing further conversation. As I settled into my seat, our simple exchange already loomed large in memory, like an embellished capital letter marking the beginning of a new chapter.

"Yosarai Patican," called the teacher.

I stood. "I am Yosarai Patican, sibah gadolah." I raised my arm, then froze, a void in my mind where the detached bow of respect ought to reside. I had practiced it enough; why couldn't I remember?

The teacher's eyebrows arched toward her greying hairline. I had to do something–either admit I couldn't remember or extend some sort of greeting. The latter sounded like the better option. I crossed my arms over my chest in the traditional greeting of a menial to an elite, replacing the deep waist bow with a dip of the head.

Snickers and whispers circulated through the room. "Must be low stratum."

"Obviously, look at her clothes."

"A menial's greeting? How degrading!"

"Must be from a former menial family, and they admitted her from pity."

Lavidah smirked.

Less than a quarter bell into my first day and I had already disgraced Avi. My cheeks flamed. What was done could not be reversed, however, and I stood my ground, awaiting the teacher's rebuke.

The teacher rapped her knuckles against her desk. "Order."

The snickers and whispers died, though smirks remained.

"Sibah Patican, come forward."

Could offering the wrong greeting get me expelled? Anything seemed possible. I refused to glance at Lavidah as I passed the front row.

"Why did you give me the greeting of a menial to an elite, Sibah Patican?"

I clasped my hands together. "I couldn't remember the proper bow, sibah gadolah. Therefore, I modified a menial-elite greeting, which permitted me to greet you at a distance with the respect a teacher deserves, for am I not here to follow your instructions, much as a menial follows the instructions of an elite?"

"Hmm. Interesting." Circling me, she eyed my dress, my hair, my posture, every inch of my being. Maybe Rivka's more lavish dress would have been the better selection. I hadn't considered what the teachers would think.

"You're nervous."

I inclined my head in acknowledgment.

"Why did you select this dress? Do you not know your attire forms much of a person's first impression?"

"Indeed, sibah gadolah, which is why I selected this dress." Should I say more? I didn't want to sound defensive.

Just one eyebrow arched this time. "Please, go on."

"I am a final-year transfer to the Academy. This is a rare occurrence, as the Academy has high standards and will not cosset its students. Those who have reached this level have achieved it through hard work. To be accepted this late is a high honor." The other students shifted in their seats. *Make your point, Yosi.* "Therefore, to wear a dress more lavish seemed both dishonoring and arrogant. Dishonoring because such attire would declare I see this placement as something I'm entitled to, and arrogant because it would declare I'm equal to the students who have diligently worked through the Academy."

The teacher studied me a moment, then faced the class. "Hasibs, sibahs, let Yosarai Patican serve as an example for you today."

I stiffened.

"An example of how everyone should have acted but failed to."

My head snapped up as the room fell still, smirks fading.

"Where Sibah Patican has conducted herself with the grace, humility, and respect becoming one of the highest strata, the behavior of the rest of you has been demeaning, ungracious, and even boorish."

Was she looking at Lavidah? Whether she was or wasn't, my cousin was seething. If her anger was that fierce against me, what was it doing to her own soul within which it burned?

"Let this stand as proof that Sibah Patican has earned her place among your ranks and deserves to be treated as your equal in every way." The teacher turned to address me. "Your quick thinking, Sibah Patican, is a credit to your training and should serve you well. However, remember the Academy is first an institution of learning, and you should ask about what you do not know. For a detached bow of respect, place your forearms together in the same way as if greeting nearby, with your right arm representing your position. Then, bow either your head or your body, depending on the level of respect required. Now you may return to your seat."

I swallowed. Of course that was the correct bow. How had I forgotten something that basic? "Yes, sibah gadolah, thank you. I will remember." At least the teacher didn't seem upset at my lapse. However, as thirty pairs of eyes tracked me, tension coiled around me like a river python.

Because, with the teacher's praise, I'd vaulted from an insignificant nobody to the chief threat to be eliminated.

Outwardly, Lavidah kept her face neutral.

Inwardly, she fumed.

How did her cousin manage it? No matter what she did, no matter what she said, somehow she always manipulated the situation to her favor.

It took all of her control not to spit at her cousin's feet as she passed by. Instead, Lavidah fixed her gaze on the teacher, schooling her features into the expected contrition. Never mind her cousin should be the one doing penitence, not her.

It was hard enough to withstand the berating when she failed. Was she now to pay for her cousin's crimes as well?

It wasn't fair.

But when it came to her cousin—the favored one, the gifted one, the beloved one—fairness did not exist. Her very presence at the Academy proved that, and no doubt she would waltz her way into the top five on the Exam too.

Stealing everything Lavidah wanted, everything she had worked so hard to obtain.

Stealing her last chance to earn her mother's approval.

Her hands clenched under the table. No, this time she would prevail. She must.

Otherwise, there would be nothing left to live for.

Boredom was a sullen companion. It sulked in the corner, refusing to converse apart from an occasional snide comment, and it shuttered the room against any cheery thought. Gloom and doom were the only games it knew. Games Xander had no desire to play. But what else was he to do? He'd unpacked his trunk yestereve, after their arrival in Kolchan. He'd finished arranging the furniture in the rented flat hours ago. He had no bills to review for Parliament, no royal duties to attend to, no workshop to tinker in. He didn't even have Massard to goad into conversation or a rematch of Man & Machine, for his bodyguard had departed on "business," leaving Xander completely alone for the first time in . . . days? Weeks? No, it had to be months.

He wandered onto the narrow balcony of their flat. He finally had the time he'd craved—and no idea how to use it. "Sustainer, what am I to do?" He couldn't spend his days hiding in a room like a scuttlefish in its underwater grotto. Especially if he were a mechanical wonder seeking to improve his artistry. At least playing that role would give him something to do.

After sketching a coded picture of his plans for Massard, he slung a bag of supplies over his shoulder and headed down to the street. Should he hail a coach? While few Egdonians were aware he had traveled to Indel, and not even his family knew his precise whereabouts, it was best not to underestimate his enemies. An unfamiliar driver could easily whisk him away to an unknown destination. Walking was the better choice.

Now which way to go? Aimless wandering often led to hopelessly lost, but Sibah Yosarai was supposed to be staying nearby. Perhaps he should discover exactly how near.

The mid-afternoon heat, warmer than an Egdonian summer day, slowed his steps. Xander tugged a sketchbook from his bag. If he were a tinkerer in search of inspiration, he'd find inspiration starting with the buildings in front of him. Even if the shutters were impractically small and the landscaping was developed in such a way that there was no efficient way to water it, he would find one unique combination or one eye-catching detail for each place.

Jotting notes as he walked, he eventually reached the street where Sibah Chiman lived, according to the directions from Judge Patican. Odd how uniform the houses were here. More like Egdon than Indel. He nearly bypassed the house, noteworthy only for its lack of flowers and a door nearly black in its darkness. Not foreboding, but not warm and welcoming either. He stowed his sketchpad and crossed the street for the walk back to his flat. At least he'd accomplished one thing today, and maybe Massard would be there by the time he returned.

The clop of horse hooves stayed his departure, and a day coach of modest means stopped at the Chiman residence.

The first person to alight was a young woman with a veil over her head. She hurried inside without waiting for the other passengers. The next lady was tall, elegant, and sharp, about Yosarai's age. She was beautiful, the kind of woman who would attract his older half brother, but the rigidity of her spine gave an air of brittleness, as if she would snap at the slightest provocation. Which emphasized the soft grace of the third, Yosarai Patican herself.

Xander moved forward to greet her, then halted. Today would have been her first day at the Academy. This was probably not the best time.

"Hasib Saunders? What brings you here?"

Spotted. He approached her. "Nothing more than boredom, I'm afraid. My . . . cousin was out on business. I thought a walk would refresh me, so I took up the challenge of locating your lodgings to see if you were as near as indicated."

"Obviously you succeeded. Would you like to come in for tea?"

"A most gracious offer, Sibah Yosarai, but I have no wish to intrude."

"Please, call me Yosi"–she lowered her voice–"and please intrude, if you will. I love spending time with Jamarde, but Lavidah–let's say outsiders sweeten her temper."

He held up a hand. "You need to say no more. My half brother is the same way, and since I'm quite the soft heart for damsels in distress . . ."

"I am in your debt more than you can imagine." She led him into the house, cooler than the outdoors by several degrees. How did the Indelis do that? He saw no device to cool the air the way steam heated the buildings at home.

"How have you found your first day in Kolchan?" She handed a book bag to her maid, who had been waiting in the hall for her.

"Unusually quiet." He dismissed the maid's request to take his bag too. "And today was your first day at the Academy, was it not? How did you fare?"

"I fared."

Her lack of explanation said enough. "You have my condolences."

She summoned the butler. "Hab Ebon, would it be possible to set another place for tea? I met a friend of my father's on the street and have asked him to join us."

The butler's eyes flashed with alarm. Something worried him about carrying out Yosi's orders, yet no well-trained menial would dare refuse an elite.

Xander cleared his throat. "Actually, I hoped you would join me for a stroll, sibah, if that would be amenable to you."

Confusion wrinkled her brow, then her eyes widened. She pasted on an overbright smile. "What a lovely idea! I've been sitting all day, and exercise would go far to clear my mind." She dipped her head to the butler. "Never mind, Ebon. Let my aunt know I'm out with a family friend but will be back in time for dinner, should she inquire."

The butler relaxed as he bowed. "As you wish, sibah."

The moment he disappeared, she briefly closed her eyes. "I thank you for your discreet handling of that. Unfortunately, now it appears I must rescind my invitation to tea–"

He interrupted by cocking his elbow. "Would you do me the honor?"

A slow smile curled her lips. "I would love to."

"Leaving so soon, cousin?" The second lady from the coach emerged from the foyer's shadows. Somehow, she managed to peer down her nose at him, though he stood a head taller.

Yosi performed the introduction. "Hasib Saunders, please meet my cousin, Sibah Lavidah Chiman. Lavidah, this is Hasib Saunders, inventor for the Egdonian king."

At the word *king*, the cousin morphed into coy sweetness. "The king? How exciting. Did you know King Rion quite well?"

"As well as one can know a king, I suppose," he answered politely. "I was fortunate to spend many an afternoon discussing my ideas and designs with him." A lump rose in his throat as memories of doing just that with his father flooded his mind.

Sibah Chiman's fingers fluttered to her throat. "Pardon me for my callousness. I hadn't considered how the death of King Rion might remain a fresh loss for you." She gazed demurely up at him.

"No offense taken, sibah. My grief comes and goes, triggered by the oddest of things."

"Then allow me to provide you a pleasant diversion. Perhaps a stroll through our fair streets on this pleasant afternoon?"

"I was about to do just that with–"

"Excellent. I know all the best places to go." Sibah Chiman tugged him out the door, pulling him away from Yosi. He shot her an apologetic look as she trailed them outside. He should correct Yosi's cousin, but how to clarify without being rude?

"What would you like to see?" continued Sibah Chiman. "One of our famed sculpture gardens is up that way, or there's the open-air Musician's Forum. Ooh, I know! The Lower Market! Just the place to wander." She threw a haughty glance back at Yosi, following in their wake. "If you're coming, do keep up, cousin."

Xander stepped closer to Sibah Chiman, but he clenched his jaw as she interpreted that as an invitation to cling more tightly to him. "Please join us, Sibah Patican. There's plenty of space for us to walk three abreast."

Yosi took his free arm. "You are most gracious, hasib."

"Nothing gracious about it. Allowing one of you to go unescorted would be not only ill-mannered, but I'd also be a fool for missing the chance to have two beautiful ladies at my side."

A blush deepened the color in Yosi's cheeks as Sibah Chiman batted her eyelashes in a manner reminiscent of the court debutantes. Apparently, some feminine wiles were learned in every culture. Best to find a safer topic and quickly.

"Since I'm a stranger to your fair city, what other places would you suggest I see while I'm here?"

"Oh, are you planning to stay awhile, hasib?" asked Sibah Chiman.

He berated himself for mentioning it. "The exact length of our stay is unknown."

"Our?"

"I'm here with my cousin, who is conducting business in the city."

"How exciting."

It wasn't, but he should be thanking Sustainer. Not exciting meant no one was trying to kill him.

"What is Egdon like?" Yosi's voice padded into his mind, as warm as the sun on his face.

"And the court," inserted the cousin breathlessly, "what is that like?"

He lifted a shoulder. "Court is court. Beautiful women parading the latest fashions as stuffed-shirt men pretend not to notice them, all the while sipping champagne, eating fancied-up crackers, and exchanging empty pleasantries between spins around the dance floor."

Yosi seemed to stifle a laugh, but Sibah Chiman tugged on his arm. "Come now. Do be serious, hasib."

He was being serious, but obviously she'd never believe that. "Most days it's a humdrum affair, comprised of lengthy debates and protracted negotiations with an occasional party to interrupt the tedium. The royal family is a bit reclusive and wields far less control over the Parliament than most people think, despite the monarch's permanent seat therein." He turned to Yosi. "As for Egdon itself, I suppose many Indelis would find our collection of mountain islands and misty weather quite drab, lacking the colorful pageantry of your sunny days and vibrant landscapes. But our land has a quiet charm of its own. There are waterfalls everywhere, and on the days when the wind sweeps away the clouds, the mountains sparkle. In midsummer, when the water roses open their blossoms, thousands of them in pink, white, and yellow, gently undulating on the water–it's breathtaking."

"I thought art and beauty had no practical use." One corner of her smile quirked upward.

She was determined to win this argument. Xander didn't know if that amused him or impressed him. "On the contrary. I said I wasn't sure if they were worth expending time and resources to cultivate."

"Touché."

They entered a narrower street with shops shaded by colorful canopies. Sellers called out to shoppers navigating the broad, short steps that matched the gentle incline. Push carts and other small vehicles clattered up and down a central ramp, bringing with them the scents of flowers, warm bread, and wood shavings. Quite the idyllic place.

And the perfect setting for an ambush.

Sibah Chiman frowned at his abrupt stop. "Is something wrong, hasib?"

"I'm afraid I have become quite disoriented, and the hour is later than I realized. You sibahs will want tea soon."

"Don't worry, hasib. I know where we are and have the perfect spot for tea." Sibah Chiman strolled into the market, obviously expecting him to chase after her as propriety would demand.

But his feet were bolted to the street. So many places to hide. So many shadows and blind spots. So many people, every one of them a potential assassin, every one a potential victim. Just like when he toured the Hypoyan Stoa. Even with six additional guards, they missed the attacker mingling among the shoppers. If he had chosen a weapon more deadly than a smoker that day . . . As it was, a dozen people suffered various minor injuries in the chaos that followed, from bruised ribs to bloody noses.

Yosi nudged him. "Lavidah can care for herself if you are ready to return."

Except to turn back when there was no real threat would be true cowardice. "While I have no doubt about Sibah Chiman's capability, it would be improper to abandon her." Still, his feet refused to move.

"If you are determined, then I'll be your eyes and ears, for I know this market well."

Did she understand what she was proposing? Perhaps seeking her out hadn't been the wisest move. "We've already lost sight of your cousin. Do you know where she has gone?"

"Unfortunately, I suspect I do. Are you ready?"

He nodded. He had to face situations like this if he ever hoped to rule well. People and crowds accompanied the job.

Yosi pulled him forward. "This would be a good place for you to explore later, when you're not chasing down a female."

"Is that what we're doing? Chasing down a female?" Why had he decided that venturing out without Massard was a good idea? He'd never be able to discern friend from foe, assassin from bystander in this crowd.

"What would you call it?"

"Seeking to reunite our separated party?" A surge of lightheadedness crashed into him. "Why do you think this place worth my further exploration?"

"Look around you. What do you see?"

"People shopping for trinkets, I suppose." At least, he was trying to assume that was all they were doing.

"Look again. Before you spreads a ready-made study in art. Consider the colors, the textures, the forms. Some of them pleasant, some of them jarring, all intriguing."

"I would think the gardens or a gallery would be a more effective teaching tool," he said.

"They are indeed effective, but they show you only the best. Here, you see it all. What works"–she gestured to a display of stacked fruit–"and what does not." She waved at a canopy of green and purple. "What makes something garish rather than elegant, what is intricate versus overwhelming. All art, no matter how imaginary or creative or abstract, in some way reflects this, reflects life. We cannot truly create out of nothing, like Sustainer. We merely take what we see, what we experience, what we feel, and rearrange the pieces into a new form or unique combination. Your best classroom, then, is this; this is art in seed form."

"Are you still trying to sell me on the value of art?"

"Is it working yet?"

"Maybe."

She laughed. "Then perhaps we ought to take a detour."

"But your cousin . . ."

"Has already found another to flirt with."

Xander followed her gaze. Across the street at the fenced courtyard of an expensive-looking café, Sibah Chiman bent toward a man at a table for two. Selucreh was right; women sought him out because of his connection to the crown and that alone.

"Hasib Saunders?"

"It's nothing, I assure you."

"Nothing doesn't elicit the expression that crossed your face."

"Your cousin merely struck a well-deserved blow to my pride, confirming what another once told me."

"I wouldn't let Lavidah be the proof of anything. Her actions speak more of her character than yours."

Yosi might be right, but what if her cousin had found the company of a predator rather than a friend? "Do you know the man with whom she dines?"

"I believe it's one of the apprentice counselors. Therefore, she should be fine, and we ought to be moving on. This place isn't very friendly to outsiders."

What did that mean? "Nonetheless, I was escorting her." Xander strode toward the main door of the establishment.

"Hasib, that is truly not a good idea."

A bulky man blocked his path, arms of a miner across a barrel of a chest. The imposing stance was reminiscent of Massard in intimidation mode.

Xander lifted his chin. "Pardon me, I need–"

"We don't serve your kind here. Indelis only."

"What?" Xander stared at the man. Were his ears malfunctioning?

"Your kind are not welcome."

Yosi drew him backward. "Come, hasib."

Her whispered words triggered a snort from the Massard evil twin. "He is not a hasib. He's a lava slug, and you, sibah, ought to be mortified to be seen in his presence. You are a dishonor to your father's household."

Nearby, Sibah Chiman lifted a teacup, a smirk playing across her lips, as if enjoying a parlor amusement. That was what Yosi had been trying to warn him of. The whole thing was a trap–a way to humiliate him and publicly smear Yosi's reputation.

The evil twin wasn't done. "Only a trollop would dare to be seen with the likes of him. Unless that is what you are?"

Yosi stiffened. Xander's hands clenched. He ought to strike that leering grin off the man's face. Or better, blacken the man's eyes so he couldn't see anything at all. He took a step forward. But he'd never bested Massard in a fight, even when his bodyguard had restrained himself. This man's narrowed eyes spoke of a willingness to do him bodily harm, no matter how flimsy the excuse.

Xander pivoted. "Come, Sibah *Patican*. This establishment must be meant for the low stratum, unfit for the daughter of

Indel's most famed artist." He felt the cousin's smoldering glare searing into his back.

Once they were out of sight of the café, Xander breathed easier. Relations between Egdon and Indel were strained, but he'd never encountered such open hostility. A hostility they would have never shown if they'd known who he was. Perhaps this trip would unlock unexpected doors, provide the opportunity to see beyond polite casings to the inner workings hidden from him due to his status.

"I must ask a thousand pardons for what happened back there." By the gentle pressure of her hand on his arm, Yosi steered him into a quiet street.

"Since you tried to warn me, it should be me begging you for pardon."

"It's difficult to fault chivalry."

She thought him chivalrous? He peeked at her, but she was nodding to another passerby. A far cry from the batting eyes and coy smile of the last young lady who called him chivalrous, an obvious flattery meant to curry royal favor. Yosi knew nothing of his real position and therefore had nothing to curry. Would that change if she knew the truth?

"Ah, here we are." She faced a shop on the quiet street, a good pace off the main thoroughfare.

Though *shop* might be the wrong description, for no wares were displayed, no colorful canopy flapped in the breeze, no elaborate sign invited them in. There wasn't even a door. Instead, the stone wall before him was overhung with at least three different varieties of flowering creepers, bright red-and-green leaves mixing with purple-and-yellow blossoms. In two places, the creepers were tied back to reveal stained glass windows. "Where is here, may I ask?"

"You'll see." Yosi drew aside a swath of creepers to reveal an arched tunnel of three or four paces long, ending at a metal door overlaid with gears of every size and shape.

"Mysterious."

"The artist is a bit of a reclusive eccentric. His clientele demands he stay near, but he hates crowds and the bustle of the city." She beckoned him through the curtain of green. "He has done all he can to avoid unwanted interruptions and distractions."

"How did you come to know him?"

"He was a friend of Ima's. Avi has been bringing me here to visit ever since I was a child."

The door lacked a handle, but the placement of the gears suggested they were more than decorative, if he could find a way to turn them. "How do we get in?"

"Like this." Yosi pulled a crank from a well-concealed pocket and fitted it to a shaft on the door. The gears indeed turned, and to his right, boards folded up, their painted illusion so magnificent that, in the dim light, he'd mistaken it for a real stone wall.

Yosi returned the crank and walked into the open doorway. "Drom? It's Yosi!"

Xander followed her up narrow stairs and gaped at the sight awaiting him. Rows of cubed shelving stretched before him, each with a mechanical wonder in various states of production. Flowers and animals, rail carriages and airships. There was even one that looked like a nest of flames.

"That's one of my favorites." She touched a button.

The flames parted and a phoenix, trilling a beautiful melody, soared up and circled the nest, then was consumed by the fire once more.

"Astounding," he breathed. "The man must be a genius."

"Y-you l-like it?" Around a shelf poked a head topped with spiky hair that graduated from copper to red. A child? No, a half-size man, with a pair of goggles perched atop his head.

"There you are, Drom." Yosi dropped to her knees and gave the man a hug, as if there was nothing unusual about the stout man, a Mouncite at that, based on the hair color. “I would like you to meet a fellow inventor and a friend of mine, Hasib Saunders. Saunders, Drom Hadas.”

Xander shifted his weight. Should he lower himself to his knees like Yosi to greet the man—or would that be considered insulting? Maybe he should stoop instead.

The fellow grabbed a ladder resting against a shelf and swung himself up, perching at eye level. “H-hasib S-saunders. Y-Yosi’s f-friends are always w-welcome.”

“I am most honored, Hasib Hadas.”

“D-drom.” His green eyes sparkled. “Y-you invent t-too?”

“More like tinker. Nothing I have done begins to compare to what I see here.”

Yosi scrutinized a half-finished oliphant, its gears still exposed. “Hasib Saunders is here to study the craft and improve his art.”

“Hmm.” Drom stroked his goatee. “Your h-hand?”

Xander extended it.

Drom lowered the goggles over his eyes and inspected every inch of Xander’s hand. “I s-see.”

It took all his willpower not to jerk away. The man might be deficient in height and manners, but he lacked nothing in the mind. The wonders around him attested to that.

The man hopped to the floor. “B-be here at eight b-bells.” He disappeared behind a table stacked with gears and tools.

“What?” He looked after the man in bewilderment.

Yosi came up beside him. “I think he just offered you a job.”

“A job?”

“Or apprenticeship. Hard to say with Drom.”

“But . . .”

“You said you were here to learn. Can you name a better person to teach you? Or a safer location to while away your hours?”

"Hardly." But he, the crown prince of Egdon, an Indeli apprentice?

"Do you think such a job beneath you?"

Xander stiffened. "To learn from such a master would be a privilege."

"Then you'd better be here by the morning's eighth bell. Drom is a stickler about punctuality."

An apprenticeship. The days that stood idle only a couple of bells ago now hummed with possibilities. But to what end?

The sun warmed my face as I left the shadow of the Academy. Never had I spent this much time indoors, even during the dead of winter. Classes, study, tutoring, more studying–one could endure the confines of buildings for only so long.

And the barbs of Lavidah's tongue.

Three civil sentences had been all she'd managed toward me since our outing with Saunders over a week ago, and today Jamarde was visiting a friend. An entire coach ride alone with Lavidah was not exactly appealing. I paused beside the coach. "Hab Yordan, I will not be riding back with you today as I wish to visit the Lower Market."

The driver frowned. "Alone, sibah?"

"I'm meeting a friend." The term rolled off my tongue with unexpected ease. How was it, after one rail ride, an afternoon outing, and two brief encounters on the street, I already considered Saunders a friend? Yet the golden hue that the afternoon acquired at the thought of spending more time with him confirmed I did consider him a friend.

"I beg your pardon, sibah, but it is neither safe nor proper for you to walk that far without an escort. Allow me to drive you to Lower Market Street, at least."

I bit my lip. Less than a quarter bell. Surely I could withstand Lavidah that long. “Very well. Lower Market.” I climbed into the coach.

A minute later, Lavidah settled into her seat opposite me, covering her nose with a handkerchief, as if I’d uncapped a bottle of knusk ink. While that dye created a warm orange-pink color, it carried a horrid stink. Perhaps if I said nothing, she would say nothing as well.

Coach wheels crunched down the shell drive. Lavidah opened a window. “Cousin, you must sever your association with that mixer. You are casting a bad reflection upon the entire family.”

No need to guess whom she meant. Estelle was the sole student in our class who wasn’t full-blooded Indeli. What association she referred to was less clear. We exchanged a greeting each morning and a farewell each afternoon, and when teachers paired us, I never objected. But that was the extent of our interactions.

“They say she was accepted into the Academy only because her mother was”–she cleared her throat–“*friendly* with the director.”

Her innuendo dripped with red, and I wedged my tongue between my teeth. Control under siege was the sign of true discipline. Wasn’t that how the Scribes’ proverb went?

“They also say she’s like her mother.” Lavidah’s voice lowered, words coiling into a more serpentine form than usual. “That’s the true reason she is ranked first. Because of favors paid to the proctors.”

Was there any truth to that? An acquaintance of less than a fortnight didn’t provide much to judge by. Though, considering the source, the information was likely unreliable. The coach slowed.

Lavidah peered outside. “Why are we stopping?”

“I asked him to.” I alighted. Almost free . . .

Lavidah scooted to the open window. "By the way, they say that's why you like the mixer. Your father promised you would provide the same."

I froze. Slander of me or the other girls I could tolerate. But to drag Avi's name through the mud . . . I whirled around. The coach was already rolling away. Lavidah fluttered her fingers at me.

Of all the stupid, cruel . . . I hitched up my skirts and fled for Drom's shop. I shouldn't let it bother me. Lavidah was mostly hot air, and she probably started half the gossip around the Academy. But as I raced upstairs, the world blurred. "Drom? Drom!"

"Drom isn't here at the moment." Saunders rounded the corner of a shelf, the oil-splotched apron incongruous with the finely woven kurta beneath. "What happened?"

"Nothing." I spun away, frantically wiping away my tears, trying to stem the flow.

"That is not the look of nothing."

I dug for a handkerchief from my school bag. This was what came of letting Lavidah irritate me. I made a fool of myself.

"You look in dire need of a piping hot cup of tea and a listening ear." Saunders guided me toward Drom's workbench before I could find the handkerchief.

Saunders presented me his.

"Thank you." I blotted my face, as much to cool my flaming cheeks as to wipe my eyes. Why must I cry when I become angry?

Taking two cups and saucers from a shelf, he placed them upon the flatbed carriage of a miniature rail and sent it puffing around the room to the tea station Drom had mechanized. The familiar clank of gears and hum of the warming kettle calmed me, and I sniffled as the tears ebbed.

"Now what rakish rogue must I sally forth and pound some decency into for reducing a fair maiden to tears?"

"I assure you, hasib, my distress is due to nothing that dire."

"Then perhaps you ought to recount your tale of woe so I might determine how best to rectify the situation, whether that be retribution or revenge."

I hid a growing smile behind the handkerchief. He might be a tinkerer, but he could craft a well-oiled turn of phrase. "My cousin merely spoke meaningless words."

"Not very meaningless if they produced tears."

"That was all it was. Truly. Tittle-tattle that means nothing and has no grounding, spoken to provoke and goad. Today she succeeded."

The rail whistled its arrival and stopped where its journey began, the two cups now full of tea. Saunders added cream and honey to mine. He had remembered how I took my tea from our rail ride? I accepted the cup, a biscuit nestled along the edge of the saucer, and sipped the tea, burning my tongue.

"Drom likes his tea scalding." Saunders settled on a stool across from me.

"I remember now." I blew on the steaming liquid. "But I didn't come here to elicit your sympathy. At least, not that kind."

"Then what kind were you hoping for?"

"I was hoping Drom would let you accompany me on a walk. Avi warned me not to wander the city unaccompanied, but it is such a beautiful day, and it seems a waste to spend it all indoors."

"I can ask when he returns with his niece from the Academy."

"His niece attends the Academy?" Might I have another ally there? Although I knew Drom's niece lived with him, I'd never met her. I swallowed a bite of biscuit. "Do you know her name?"

"I'm afraid I don't. I could make some inquiries, if you wish."

"Don't trouble yourself. I know Drom will introduce us if I ask." Something I should have requested long ago, apparently. "How are you enjoying your work for him?"

"It has been an adjustment, but he is a good man and a skilled craftsman. I thought the wonder of this"–he lifted his cup toward the shelves of automatons–"would diminish after a few days. Instead, I find myself in greater awe than before." He rubbed the back of his neck. "It has proven I am nothing more than a tinkerer."

"You must underestimate your skill, especially if you had inventions accepted by King Rion."

His expression shuttered, like that first day when I mentioned politics. "As I stated before, that's not the achievement it sounds like." He set his teacup on the miniature rail and returned to sorting gears.

Did he doubt his abilities that much? I placed my cup beside his, searching for something to encourage him. "Even if what you say is true, you'll improve with time."

His hand tightened around a gear. "Unfortunately, time is the one thing I lack, and even if it were otherwise, I would never be comparable to Drom." His words took on dagger points.

"Hasib, don't wish yourself away in your admiration for another. If Sustainer had meant you to be Drom, then He would have made you Drom. He meant you to be you, to be Saunders. So be Saunders, not Drom. Nor anyone else."

He fingered the gear, then dropped it into the appropriate container. "That sounds like something my father would have told me." His script softened back into its normal form. "Thank you." He placed his hand over the one I rested on the table.

I opened my mouth to accept his gratitude, but a flash pulled me under before I could speak a word.

> *I am entering a stone room laid with a thick rug and lined with shelves filled with books. Between shelves, a mullioned window overlooks a vast stretch of platinum water, out of which juts a jagged mountain, mist encircling its peak.*
>
> *I approach an intricately carved desk. There waits a dignified man who radiates control,*

dressed in a smoking jacket of jade green and black pants with white pinstripes. A woman of soft grace stands nearby in a purple dressing gown, the skirt cutting away to reveal matching pants beneath.

I greet the man with a handshake and the woman with a kiss. "Father, Mum. Demaus said you wished to speak with me." The voice belongs to Saunders.

"Indeed, we did. Please sit, son." His father motioned to a wing-backed chair, which I took. "After a long discussion, your stepmum and I have come to a decision. We would like to name you the successor to the throne."

With a gasp, I resurfaced. Successor to the throne? The man, the woman–they were King Rion and Queen Epolene.

"Sibah Yosi?" Saunders's voice sounded far away.

Not Saunders. Xander. *Prince* Xander. I swayed, lightheaded.

"What's wrong?" He guided me to a stool.

"Just one of my spells." I choked back a *Your Highness*. How had I missed it before? The way he spoke, moved, carried himself–it all reflected his royal status. "I believe Avi mentioned them to you?"

Concern lined his expression. "What can I do to help?"

"Grant me a moment to reorient myself."

He hesitated, then busied himself with the remainders of our tea. I pressed a hand to my head. Prince Xander. Did Avi know? Surely he must. Why didn't he tell me? Or at least drop a hint. Inventor to the king? He *was* the king, or would be soon. What was he doing in Indel, posing as a merchant's cousin this close to his coronation?

And many others would be glad to see you fail.

Avi's veiled warnings sharpened into perfect clarity. Someone was trying to kill the prince. I scanned the shop. Everything normal, nothing amiss. Something I should have been more aware of before this. Was that why the vision had been sent? To remind me to watch for danger? And if so, what did that say of the danger? For nothing living had ever triggered the elchan before. Or if this was a new development in my gift, would I now have to be careful of whom I touched and how?

Xander returned to my side. "Feeling better?"

"Some. It was an intense spell."

"Need we seek out a doctor?"

"A doctor can do nothing for me. However, I ought to let you resume your work."

"What about that walk?"

My fingers dug into the fabric of my skirt. "I'm afraid I must now beg off from that. My spell has left me unsteady. I think it best if I return home to rest." I stood and, thankfully, my legs held. Time to leave, before my tongue betrayed my newfound knowledge. "Thank you for the tea."

"You're d-departing before your h-hello?" Drom rounded the workbench.

His familiar voice arrested my flight. "You're back." I stooped to give him my customary hug.

He gripped my shoulders, holding me at arm's length. "You've b-been crying." His gaze shot toward Saunders—or rather, Xander.

I shook my head. "Lavidah."

"Ah." This was not the first time I'd fled to his shop due to my cousin.

Xander tugged at the strings of his work apron. "Sibah Yosarai said she isn't feeling well. May I accompany her home? I'll be glad to arrive early and stay late tomorrow to account for the time."

I edged away. "That isn't necessary. I can hail a coach—"

"S-Saunders may go w-with you. I would p-prefer it, in f-fact."

"My flat is that direction," Xander reminded me. "So it is no trouble."

How to argue that? "Very well."

After leaving a message with Drom for Mascad, should he come looking, Xander hailed us a coach. I slumped upon my seat. What a not-splendid day this was becoming.

Xander settled beside me instead of across as I'd anticipated. "How are you feeling?"

"Improving. Mostly a minor headache now." I edged away, lest accidental contact trigger another flash. "As would be expected after a cry."

"My half sister complains of the same."

"Half sister?" Of course, Princess Patra was his half sister. He was Prince Xander, the *illegitimate* son of King Rion. "Pardon. I didn't mean to pry."

"You weren't prying, you were asking a logical question. My mother died when I was six."

A common maid, if my memory served me right, killed by the winter plague that year. Heartbreak enough for any child, but then to be thrust into the foreign world of the royal court, riddled with political intrigue and malicious gossip that followed him around–no wonder the mantle of power rested uneasily upon his shoulders. "My condolences," I murmured. "That must have been difficult."

"More than you can imagine." His grey eyes reflected fragments of blue, as if grief had embedded itself there. "But my stepmum has a very big heart, and she made room for me along with her own two children."

My estimation of the Egdonian royal family rose. Most politicos would have secreted away an illegitimate far from themselves, if they acknowledged them at all. Xander spoke as if King Rion and his family had not only acknowledged him, but also accepted him as one of their own. “She sounds like an extraordinary woman.”

“I think you would like her if you met her, and I’m sure she would like to meet you too.”

A sweet thought. Perhaps after I took the Exam, Avi and I could arrange a visit, if Xander wasn’t too busy with his new duties as king. It would certainly be a pleasure to see Xander in the world he loved. And though I would probably be eager to return to my quiet world of illuminating manuscripts by the visit’s end, I could endure the court politics and intense scrutiny for a few days.

Nonetheless, the thought of navigating the Egdonian court tightened my stomach. A new topic of conversation was in order. A poster in a shop window caught my eye. Its border of water pouring from clay jars announced its subject as clearly as the words I couldn’t read. “Have you considered attending the Ingathering? It’s only six weeks away.”

“Perhaps. Will you be competing this year?”

“In the Kolchan Quest? Absolutely not.”

“But I thought you always participated.”

“In Cashirsa. Where the Quest is a friendly competition.”

“What makes the one here different?”

“The winner’s reward. In addition to the privilege of participating in the final ceremony, each member of the winning coterie is awarded a sizable purse and a medallion that grants one request, as long as it doesn’t violate the dictates of Sustainer or the Council.”

“I imagine that would intensify the competition.”

“Indeed.” Headlines about various “accidents” from past Quests flashed through my mind. A suspicious coach crash. Sudden illness blamed on bad meat. A minor explosion due to an equipment malfunction.

“Still, it seems a shame to break tradition due to some ungracious losers.”

My hand clenched the strap of my school bag. Such a statement revealed the breadth of his ignorance. "Shame or not, the reality is I have no one to compete with, even if I wished to. Lavidah already has a team, as do most of the other students at the Academy." Not that any would have me. Nearly every day, a note appeared among my things or a remark was made within my hearing of the terrible accidents that would befall if an outsider like me competed. "I don't know many others in Kolchan, not enough to form the required coterie of six."

"What about Drom's niece? I gather she doesn't have many friends and may welcome such an invitation. And don't you have a younger cousin? There's also your maid."

A Mouncite? A menial? Had Xander forgotten how entrenched the social lines were in Indel? Or was it a continued misconception that the Quest was some lighthearted game?

Xander plunged on, misinterpreting my head shake. "Mascad and I would also lend you aid, and there, you have a team of six."

"Assuming all would agree, and assuming foreigners and menials are even permitted to participate." I raised a hand to forestall additional protest. "I appreciate your thoughtfulness, but I think it best if I focus on my studies this year."

"You won't reconsider?"

"Without a qualified team and a reason better than tradition, there is nothing to consider." Especially now that I dared not spend too much time with him, lest I reveal I knew more than I should.

The past three weeks working for Drom had been an exercise in humility.

Sweeping floors, filling oil cans, doing inventory, updating the books, sharpening tools, tracking down parts–half of which Drom identified by a name different than Xander did–these were his responsibilities. Reduced from a prince who had overseen his own workshop since he was twelve to a glorified errand boy and janitor.

But every time a complaint welled up, he swallowed it. This was better than being confined to his rooms in the Banyans, as Massard threatened after Xander's unplanned excursion that first day. After his bodyguard met Drom, the two reached some silent agreement, and Massard had uttered no word of protest since. At least the routine provided some stability for Xander to find his footing.

His pocket watch chimed the fifth bell of noonpast. Another week of work over.

"F-five m-minutes late." Drom didn't look up from his project. "Y-you n-need a n-new watch."

Of course he did. This one hadn't worked right since Selucreh smashed it. Xander kept trying to fix it, but it was a lost cause. "This one suits me." He removed the apron Drom lent him, though his clothing still seemed to acquire at least one grease stain by each day's end. Today he'd smeared some across his right thigh, *under* the apron.

Xander paused at the end of the table, where Drom peered at minute gears through magnifying goggles. Without glancing away, he exchanged tools, a flawless switch of partners in this dance between the human and the mechanical, breath and heartbeat and clicking gears melding together to create a fluid rhythm–

"P-problem?"

Xander jerked to attention. He was supposed to be leaving. "Do you require anything before I depart?"

Drom merely flicked his hand in dismissal, focused on the gears he was testing. They must not have moved correctly because he tightened the miniscule screw an eighth of a turn–an amount Xander would have once considered inconsequential. No more.

He headed toward the stairs.

"W-wages, Saunders."

Rusted cogs and threadless screws. He had been caught again. After working the books, he'd realized Drom couldn't afford him. The shop was technically sound, but three large, unpaid invoices for some unspecified project, plus the Academy's exorbitant tuition, left little to keep the pair clothed and fed. Several major bills were outstanding as a result. "I wish you'd reconsider. Learning from a master such as yourself is compensation enough."

Drom pushed his goggles onto his head. "D-do you e-eat?"

"Yes."

"D-do you live s-somewhere?"

"Of course."

"Ob-obviously you h-have clothing."

Xander pressed his lips together.

"These th-things aren't f-free."

"My cousin's income is more than sufficient–"

"A m-man is worth his h-hire. Or are you no l-longer interested in w-working for me?"

Confound the man! Drom had him in a box, and from the glint in his green eyes, he knew it too. He could always quit, but he'd never get another opportunity to work with such a master. Surely there was another option aside from draining the man's meager reserves.

Drom lowered his goggles back over his eyes. "D-do you have a s-sketchbook?"

"Of course."

"B-bring it after Shabbah."

"Yes, hasib." Xander's spirits rose as he headed for the exit. Maybe his patience had paid off. Maybe he would get to–

"S-Saunders, w-wages."

Biting back a sigh, Xander returned for the envelope of money he didn't deserve. It wasn't as if he could continue the work. His university aspirations to become an inventor died the same day his father did.

When Xander reached for the envelope, Drom laid his screwdriver on top of his hand. Suddenly, the goggles made Drom's eyes penetrating rather than oversized, as if they allowed Drom to see into things–see into him.

"People make mistakes. Sustainer does not." Drom returned to his work as if he had said nothing remarkable. Maybe the words themselves were unremarkable, ordinary gears of common metals. Yet Drom had meshed them together precisely, without a single stutter. Xander slid the envelope into his pocket and left the shop, the words circling his mind with the consistency of clockworks but failing to strike the bell of understanding.

A glitch he would have to fix later, for in the alcove downstairs paced Massard. Massard rarely ever paced. "Something wrong?"

Ignoring the question, Massard swept away the vines, and they advanced into a cloudy day. It almost felt like home. "Work was interesting. Yours?"

"Normal. Swept the floor. Filled the oil cans. Fixed tea. Sorted parts. Drom did ask me to bring my sketchbook after Shabbah. I hope that means some tinkering is in my near future."

Massard nodded in all the right places, but his eyes roamed restlessly as they skirted the Lower Market.

"What made work interesting for you today?" Xander asked. Massard said little about what he did, except that he regularly met with people whom Xander presumed to be real.

Massard thrust a folded paper at him. "This mean anything to you?"

At first glance, it appeared to be a mathematical equation or a formula with its string of numbers, letters, and symbols. As he skimmed it, his mind started calculations, flagging errors and nonsensical notations. "It looks like gibberish."

"Are you sure?"

"Of course. See here." He pointed at the paper. "You would never place a superscript three after an equal sign."

"I see." But his eyes flicked away so quickly. Did he see?

"Where did you get this?"

"One of my people intercepted it." Massard halted, his hand shifting toward his hidden pistol.

Xander scanned the street. Had another crow managed to trace his whereabouts, or was it something more dangerous? People walked by–two couples, a trio, a dozen loners. A wagon and two coaches rumbled past them. A stray cat darted between buildings. Normal activity. Nothing alarming. At least to him. No matter how hard he tried, he never saw half the things Massard did.

Massard lowered his hand without drawing his weapon. Whatever had unnerved him must have passed. "It was headed for Egdon."

"Why would someone send gibberish across the border?" Xander stared at the paper. "Wait a moment. You think this is a coded message." A code implied a pattern. Patterns were detectable. A numerical four appeared often, and hadn't he read somewhere the most common letter was–he shook his head. What was he thinking? He was no code breaker, and Massard knew those who were. He merely wanted Xander's university training to verify what he already suspected: the formula wasn't real. He tried to give the paper back to Massard.

His bodyguard ignored it. "I've already passed it on."

Coded message it was, then. "What do you think it means?" Had someone discovered his presence here?

"It might mean nothing."

Or everything. There were too many variables, and they were making his head hurt. "This was a bad idea, wasn't it?"

"What was a bad idea, hasib?" asked a female voice.

Xander yanked his head up; Yosarai and her maid were approaching. Stuffing the coded message into his money pouch, he extended an Indeli greeting as he glared at Massard, who lifted one shoulder. It wasn't his fault Xander became oblivious to everything else when he was trying to solve a puzzle. "Just a minor problem concerning home. What brings you out on this refreshing afternoon?"

Yosi lifted her arm, a basket hanging from it. "Shopping. The cook wanted extra olives and onions for dinner."

"Don't menials usually attend to such? No offense to you, Siv Rivka."

"I needed some fresh air before returning to my studies."

From the look on Rivka's face, the cousin must be troubling Yosi again. "Would you like some company?" Then he remembered the insults from their last excursion into the Lower Market. "Unless you think that will cause trouble?"

Her eyes flashed. "If it does, it is of no concern to me. I'd be delighted to have your company."

Massard offered his arm to Rivka. "Would you do me the honor?"

She retreated a step. "It wouldn't be proper, hasib."

He waited.

"I'm a menial."

He didn't retract his arm. Yosi looked as if she might speak, but Xander forestalled her. Massard was more than capable of handling her maid.

"They might think you're his menial." Rivka motioned to Xander. It would not be an inaccurate assumption, as technically Massard was his servant.

"I don't mind." Massard's voice softened. "Unless you do?"

Rivka lifted her chin. "Any sibah or siv would be fortunate to have you at her side, no matter your sphere or strata." She took his arm, then calmly regarded Xander and Yosi. "What are you waiting for? Zibbah needs that food."

They set off at a brisk pace, Rivka's chatter filling the air. That would be good for Massard. For once, he had something to think about besides Xander's safety.

They entered the Lower Market, busy with last-minute shoppers, though less crowded than at midday. They strolled at a leisurely pace that invited conversation, yet an appropriate topic eluded Xander. Massard's paper, heavy in his pocket, was taboo. Inquiries into Yosi's studies or her family's welfare seemed likely to cause pain. Drom and the shop felt self-serving. They could talk about the weather, but even there he was on uncertain ground. Indel's tropical climate differed greatly from Egdon's blustery one. He sighed inwardly. Another reason Selucreh was better suited for the throne; he never lacked for words.

"A keshel in exchange for your musings." Yosi guided him through a knot of shoppers filling most of the lane.

"I fear they aren't worth even that much. I was merely contemplating what a poor conversationalist I am." They entered a street dominated by food merchants, their windows and stands displaying bread, cheese, fruits, and vegetables, many of which Xander could not name. Scents swirled in the air, a tantalizing reminder that he'd neglected the midday meal. He'd been too busy to concern himself with food.

"An unwillingness to converse with meaningless words is not exactly a reprehensible trait."

"Maybe not for most, but in my line of work it is nearly an unpardonable deficit, a sign of a deeply flawed character." And he ought to have kept with silence. What use did an inventor have for a silver tongue? "When does your father next visit?"

"Tonight." She handed him a sticky bun she'd purchased. "I know it has been only three weeks, but it has felt like half of forever."

"I'm sure your father is as eager to see you." He bit into the warm bread, lightly sweetened with honey. Did the judge know how his daughter idolized him? And pity to any man who set out to win her heart with such long-established competition!

They stopped at a stand where Rivka picked through a pile of onions as she filled Massard's ear with the many uses of the vegetable. Apparently, it could improve one's complexion. "Any special plans for your father's visit?"

"Not currently. We wish these visits to be simple and uncomplicated." She licked the remnants of her sticky bun from her fingers. "Perhaps you would like to join us for dinner tomorrow?"

Xander doubted the aunt would appreciate extra guests to feed, based on her butler's reaction to Yosi's invitation to tea, but he would like to send a letter to his stepmum, and all correspondence was to go through the judge. "I'll see if something might be arranged."

They reached the olive shop. This merchant was unyielding about his prices, yet Rivka displayed that same stubborn set of jaw Massard did when he refused to be moved. As they haggled, Xander studied a nearby poster outlining upcoming events for the Ingathering. The festival market. Special concerts at the Teardrop Theatre and Musician's Forum. An exhibit of Ingathering-themed art. The Quest. Yosi may have rejected his proposal, but the idea of participating in the Quest lingered. Once he became king, all such activities would be prohibited.

Yosi stepped to his side. "I don't think it wise, hasib. Participating in the Quest, that is."

"I checked the rules. The only eligibility requirements are age and a reputation free of criminal charges. There's nothing barring foreigners or menials from participating." He fingered Massard's paper. He might not even be in Indel by the time of the festival.

"Not all rules are written, nor all consequences spelled out."

She sighed. "Violations of written rules might be overlooked where unwritten ones have been defied."

Rivka finished her bartering, and they retraced their path through the Lower Market, passing the café Lavidah had lured them to. *Your kind are not welcome* apparently extended beyond eateries. "Your people truly hate mine, don't they?"

"*Hate* is a strong word, hasib."

"What would you call it?"

They walked several paces before she answered. "There are some here who truly hate yours, I admit, and their voices are very loud. Considering our peoples' history, can you blame them?"

"Therefore, it is fair for all to be punished for the crimes of a few?"

"Is it fair to condemn all for the hate of a few?"

What wasn't fair was that retort. Her people's hate wasn't the same as his frustration over their behavior. However, neither were they distantly related. His anger, left unchecked, could lead him down the same bitter road.

They merged with crowds hurrying home on the main thoroughfare, preventing further conversation until they reached the quieter neighborhood of Yosi's aunt. Their exchange must have also weighed on her mind, for she said, "No one likes to be the recipient of hate, and hate directed at one person is often transferred to any associates. Thus to answer your original question, no, I don't believe most of my people hate yours. I think they fear the power of those who do."

"Yet here you are, walking in public with me." A thought pierced Xander. "Is that why you introduced me to Drom, to hide me away?"

"Not at all." She quickened their pace. "I introduced you to Drom because I thought his workshop might be something familiar in an unfamiliar place."

He touched his broken pocket watch. A logical explanation,

but one that sidestepped the real question. "Are you afraid of being seen with me?"

She pushed a lock of hair behind her ear. "I can't say I feel afraid, at least not about that. Perhaps I feel protected by Avi's stratum and reputation."

"Or maybe you are more fearless than you give yourself credit for."

"I am many things, hasib, but fearless is not one of them. Left to myself I would never gain an injury greater than a paper cut from reading my books. No, bravery belongs to the heroes of history. I shall be nothing more than a footnote in the annals of time, if I am mentioned at all."

"I didn't think it was left to us to determine our place in history," Xander said. Never mind that's what most of his countrymen would contend. He'd seen too much and studied too much history to accept the belief that they controlled their own fate.

"What would you say determines our place?"

Xander weighed his words. While his belief in Sustainer wouldn't be mocked here as it was at home, many Indelis mistrusted any foreigner interested in what they saw as their God. "The pieces of an automaton do not choose their role. Rather, every gear, spring, and screw is placed by the inventor as he sees fit, to fulfill the role he has determined. If this is true for the simple automaton, why should the complex workings of history be any different?"

She glanced at him. "Some would say that's quite fatalistic."

"Only if you see the Inventor as a heartless tyrant forcing His desires upon the gears."

"How else can He guarantee they fulfill the role He has predetermined for them?"

Xander smiled at the echo of a discussion he'd had with his father, and he offered her the answer his father gave him then. "By caring for each piece so well that He knows it completely–every strength, every weakness, every flaw and quirk–and He can anticipate precisely how every piece will change, wear, react under stress, and integrate with every other piece."

Her brow furrowed. Did such an analogy, clear to him, not make sense to her? Or perhaps talking about Sustainer in such common terms was considered sacrilegious here.

They reached her aunt's home. "Thank you for your company this afternoon." Yosi offered him a brief bow. "It has been most . . . enlightening." She hurried inside, leaving him wondering if it really had been.

The prince obscured his trail well. I credited him that. Only someone with extensive connections and resources could uncover sufficient clues as to the whelp's whereabouts, and only someone immensely intelligent could piece those clues together.

Thank the Fates, I had both, even if my father, the blind fool, had been unable to see that. So many regrettable actions could have been avoided. But he would not, and when justice was finally served, it would be delivered with the compound interest of retribution.

I pulled off my gloves as I entered my office from my latest trip to the palace. My secretary waited for me, which was good. There was no time to delay. "The queen has requested I make a goodwill visit to reassure our allies nothing significant will change with the coronation. Therefore, I need you to set the appropriate meetings to discuss plans for my operations during my absence. Also, travel arrangements must be made."

"Very good, and whence will you be traveling?"

"Kossac, Mounce, and"–my lips twitched–"Indel."

"Your building is skewed, Sibah Patican."

My art teacher's critique could summarize my life. Something always off, nothing quite right, and any attempts to correct the problem only wore paper and patience thin. I'd spent over half the class trying to correct the building in question with as much success as I'd had finding my balance in Kolchan. "Yes, sibah gadolah. I see that."

"When something doesn't look right, but you don't know why, try changing your angle." She shifted my easel away from me.

The right edge of my building bowed out at the top. How had I missed that?

"Often in art, as in life, finding the right perspective is everything." She moved to the next student. "Nice shading, Hasib Grebe."

I glanced at the other student's work. The shading was nice, but improper proportions tilted his Everstar Tower precariously toward the viewer. Yet my teacher walked on to the next student, never saying a word about his skewed building.

I refocused on my leadstick sketch, erasing the crooked line with more force than necessary. But such treatment was my own fault. My first day at the Academy, the teacher had detained me after class, asking if I truly aspired to be an illuminator as my application listed. When I had said yes, she told me I had Ima's talent, but in order to teach me all she knew, she had to be more exacting without the appearance of preferential treatment. That meant she wouldn't praise my work in front of the class. A sound plan. At least, it had seemed that way at the time. Now I was less sure.

"Excellent detail, Sibah Chiman. Your debutante looks ready to waltz off the page. The dress is stunning, even better than the last one you drew. Your own design again?"

Lavidah nodded.

"You ought to consider pursuing fashion. I would gladly recommend you to Iris Tombay."

Iris Tombay? The leading fashionista of Kolchan? I craned my neck to glimpse Lavidah's drawing. A debutante descended the steps of the Chancellor's Palace, and the dress she wore was indeed stunning, unlike anything else I'd seen with its tiered skirt and layered sleeves. No wonder our teacher was willing to recommend her to Iris Tombay.

Lavidah finished sketching some lace along the neck. Was that wistfulness in her face? "I appreciate the offer, sibah gadolah, and I will . . . consider it." Her hesitation said her words were more politeness than anything else. She'd set her sights on becoming politico and nothing would deter her from that goal. But why? Originally, I'd thought money was the attraction, but an excellent fashionista was the third highest paid artist in Indel due to the constant demand.

Our teacher clapped her hands. "Excellent job today, class. You may pack your tools."

I stowed my leadsticks and eraser.

"In preparation for your next assignment, I would like you to collect skylines, noticing how earth and sky meet. Please prepare at least three sketches by the end of this week."

At our dismissal, I gathered my books and tools slowly, letting the others depart first. It didn't prevent the snide remarks, but this way I didn't hear them firsthand. I nodded to Estelle, who probably delayed for the same reason. "A pleasant evenfall be yours."

"The same to you."

Navigating the back corridors, I reached the circle drive, where my aunt's coach awaited. However, despite her significant lead, Lavidah was nowhere in sight. Jamarde was also absent. "Is all well, Hab Yordan?" I asked the driver. "Has any ill befallen my cousins?"

"No distress has come upon them. The sibah gadolah wished for them to return home with her."

Odd, but I wouldn't complain about a ride sans Lavidah's barbs. How best to use the reprieve? "Would you leave me at the Lower Market Street? I have an art project for school, and I have a friend there who can help me." A slight stretch of the truth, but Drom knew Kolchan better than I did. "If my aunt asks, I should return at about a half bell past five."

"As you wish, sibah."

Within minutes I was mounting the stairs to the shop, the details around me hazy, as if someone had laid a thin piece of tracing vellum over the world. I'd not visited since Lavidah sent me here in tears, now almost three weeks ago. The day my flash revealed Saunders was Xander, the Egdonian prince. Though we'd crossed paths since, unease pinched my stomach each time. How would I explain my knowledge of his true identity, should I misspeak? I couldn't keep avoiding him, not with Avi's request lingering in my mind, but the anxiety when I was with him suffocated.

I emerged from the shelves. There, behind the workbench, sat Xander, his back to me, his head bent over a ledger. With shirt sleeves rolled up and hands stained with grease, he fit into Drom's shop. A far cry from the images "Egdonian prince" brought to mind. Then again, how many politicos would deign to do a shopkeeper's books? Did Egdon know how blessed it was to have a leader with such a serving heart?

"The Servant Prince." Now there was a sketch worth doing. Much more intriguing and challenging than skylines. To capture both serving humility and royal dignity in the same subject . . . I edged sideways, searching for the lines to capture that contradiction. A floorboard squeaked under me.

Xander spun on his stool. "Sibah Yosarai, I didn't hear you come in."

I would not acknowledge my breach of etiquette. "You were rather intent on your work, with the expression of one at a Vardas Impasse."

"You may not be far wrong. The meeting of the two priests, neither of whom will turn right or left, seems an apt metaphor for what I've encountered with Hasib Drom."

The Egdonian prince knew Indeli fables? "Drom can be stubborn, but I've never known him to be unreasonably so."

"Depends on your definition of *unreasonable*." He tapped the book. "The shop is teetering on the edge of financial ruin."

His words jumbled into an incomprehensible pile. Drom was the most sought-after creator of automatons in Indel, if not in the Seven Realms. "Is business that bad?"

"Not particularly, but he has several large, outstanding invoices, which he refuses to let me collect, and his niece's Academy tuition is quite the burden. His debt was mounting before I arrived, and now . . ." He plowed his hand through his hair.

"You could forgo your wage."

"I've already tried. In multiple ways. I even sent a food basket, thinking to spare him some expense, and he gave it to a neighbor who 'needed it more.'" He capped the ink. "I may have no choice but to quit. Even that may be too little, too late."

This was my fault. I introduced Xander to Drom. In trying to help, I'd caused greater problems. Still, with all the resources Avi had, there must be a way to fix this, although we would have to be careful as to the means. "How long until the debts are due?"

Xander skimmed the ledger. "I would say three weeks, four at the most, just following the Ingathering."

A finalist's purse from the Quest would pay for a year of Academy training and then some. Surely it would be enough to clear Drom's debts. But did his niece have the necessary skills to final? "I'll talk to Avi the next time he is in Kolchan."

"T-talk about what, Yosi?" Drom waddled into the shop.

My heart skipped a beat. How much had he overheard? "Helping a friend of Saunders's, that's all." I gave him my customary hug. "But I came to see you today. I'm supposed to sketch skylines, and I thought you might know some unique vantage points."

Green fire sparked in Drom's eyes. "I know the p-perfect place. C-close up sh-shop."

"I can watch it," volunteered Xander.

"You're c-coming with us."

Xander glanced at a jumble of pieces on the workbench.

Drom folded his arms. "B-beauty feeds creativity, and rest r-replenishes ideas."

I adjusted the strap of my school bag. This would be the perfect opportunity for an introduction. "If we're making an outing of this, you ought to bring your niece, Drom. Hasib Saunders tells me she attends the Academy, and I would love to meet her."

A puzzled expression darted across his face. "Very w-well. We'll j-join you outside."

Xander locked up, and we walked into the autumnal sunshine. Warm enough to be pleasant, but with a chill around the edges, banishing summer's swelter to distant memory. How could anyone not consider this Indel's best season? Especially when coupled with the leaves' transformation. The commonplace greens now freely mingled with scarlet, topaz, and coral, with an occasional splash of plum and salmon, as if the plants were exchanging their simple day dresses for party frocks. Too bad our sketches had to be done with plain leadsticks instead of colored ones, for the grey shades could never do this season justice.

We rounded the building's corner. Xander halted, and no wonder. Drom stood before us, about a third taller than normal, causing his head to reach my shoulder. "Stilts and modified garments," I murmured to Xander.

Drom shook a finger. "T-trade s-secrets."

"Hardly, Oda," said a familiar voice as Drom's niece turned from locking the front door of their home under the shop.

"Estelle?" Idiocy should be my name. How had I failed to connect the shared Mouncite heritage? Sure, she was a mixer, whereas Drom was full-blooded Mouncite, but how many Mouncites, full or mixed, had access to the Academy's hallowed halls?

Drom beamed. "You have met. W-wonderful."

"Only because Sibah Estelle, in addition to being the most beautiful and intelligent person in my class, is also the most gracious and inviting."

Drom seemed to grow a couple of inches at my praise. "That's m-my Estelle."

"Sibah Yosarai is generous with her words, Oda. Do not let it swell your head."

"Yosi doesn't s-stretch the truth."

Estelle rolled her eyes even as a blush pleasantly pinked her lighter complexion. "It was already bad enough the way he bragged to every merchant and customer we met. Now there'll be no living with him."

I gave her a helpless shrug. Estelle did deserve the top position in every way. May Sustainer prevent anything befalling her that resulted in less.

We followed Drom through the streets, and after a quarter bell, he turned down a narrow alley. An odd direction to go. Perhaps this was a more direct route to our destination? Then

Drom faced the wall and inserted a key into a brick. Part of the wall slid inward and to one side.

Xander followed Drom, examining the door's workings. Estelle and I entered the darkened interior more slowly. After lighting an oil lamp, Drom shut the door, his lamp the sole illumination in a vast room filled with strange, lumpy shapes, all covered by heavy canvas tarps.

"'What mysteries in darkness lay / in yonder cavern, hid from day . . .'" breathed Estelle.

Mysteries indeed. I reached for the nearest canvas.

"Leave it." Drom's sharp command made me snatch my hand back.

"What is this place, Drom?" I tried to speak normally, but the enigmatic aura of the place faded my words to a faint imitation of themselves.

"S-storage." He strode down an aisle to a small platform at the far end of the room. He motioned us aboard and flipped a lever. The platform jerked and began to descend. That was odd. How did he expect us to sketch skylines from underground? When we stopped, Drom flipped another lever. Gears popped, and we rolled horizontally through a tunnel.

That sparked a round of questioning from Xander about the mechanics of our ride. I turned to Estelle. "Do you have any idea what this place is?"

"I suspect it is indeed storage, though for whom and why he has access, I don't know."

"But we're doing a simple art project for school. Why bring us here if it's such a secret?" The ride ended as I spoke, and my last words rang out.

The lamp's flame flickered in a draft. The reflected light added dimension to Drom's eyes—the eyes of one who knew more than he ought. "Sustainer will d-disclose as He s-sees fit." He unlocked another door-that-shouldn't-be-there, and we entered a circular room that stretched high enough that shadows masked the ceiling from sight. In the room's center, a low brick wall surrounded a large pool and waterwheel. "A-almost there." Drom led us up a ramp circling the room in an ever-tightening spiral.

Estelle trailed her hand along the plastered wall. "'Circling higher, ever higher, / the spiral to bid the water–'" She inhaled sharply. "It can't be."

It couldn't be what? The dark, cavernous space didn't appear to be anything special. Drom unlocked a third door, and into the musty room swirled late-afternoon sunshine and fresh air adorned with the bouquet of flowers and harvest. I exited onto a balcony circling the outside of the building. A vast manicured lawn stretched before me, its circle divided into wedges by dry channels radiating from the tower where I stood. I gasped. We were halfway up the Fountain Tower, where the Ingathering was held. A place the kodesh alone accessed, except for once a year, when the winners of the Quest and the chancellor were invited to the top for the final ceremony.

I backtracked. "We shouldn't be here. How do you . . .?" Words failed me.

Drom extracted a tool from a pouch. "S-someone must m-maintain. Wouldn't w-want a m-malfunction during the Ingathering."

He maintained the intricate system? Why would the kodesh hire an outsider–and a foreigner at that–instead of doing such things themselves?

"Don't want to lose the m-mystique. Even if I s-said something, no one would b-believe me."

Even knowing Drom as I did, I wouldn't have believed it myself.

Drom waved a hand at Estelle and me. "Sketch." He extended a tool to Xander. "Would you l-like to help?"

"I would be honored."

The men disappeared inside.

I settled hesitantly on one of the benches lining the balcony. When I'd asked for a unique vantage point, Drom had certainly delivered. The hilly cityscape arching above the wall encircling the lawn was not a common view.

After flipping open my sketchbook, I arced broad strokes across the page to capture the general form of the view. Nerves added an extra wobble to the lines. But there was nothing nervous about the scene before me. Strong walls. Solid buildings. Flat roofs pressing hard against the sky. My strokes became surer and quicker as the story of the landscape unfolded.

Estelle sighed. "Have you ever dreamt what it would be like to win the Kolchan Quest?"

It took me a moment to reorient to reality. "Which Indeli hasn't? It's one of the greatest honors bestowed." I added a couple of quick strokes to my page. "Have you ever participated?"

"No." She fingered the end of her braid. The very white end.

There's nothing barring foreigners from participating. "Do you want to?"

"Desire is inconsequential in this case."

Because no team in its right mind would include a mixer. A sunfire shikra soared past, its iridescent plumage glinting a fiery gold, and I added the large predator bird to my cityscape. Maybe we could– I stopped myself. It was too outrageous, too dangerous. For us both. I erased the shikra.

"How about you?" she asked. "Will you be competing in this year's Quest?"

"Me? Hardly."

"I would think you'd be a valuable asset."

"I'm afraid the only assets I possess are my parents' names and my father's wealth, neither of which have any value in the Quest." I deepened the shadows among the buildings in my sketch.

"Don't underestimate yourself."

"Oh, I'm not." I tipped my sketchbook. How to best capture

the few clouds lingering in the sky? "I have competed in the Quest at home every year since I was eligible and have never even reached the finals."

"One person a team does not make."

"But a team one person can break." I blinked back unexpected tears. This was neither the time nor place to indulge in self-pity. The opportunity to stand on the Fountain Tower would never come again, and it would insult Sustainer to waste this gift with tears.

"I have completed my city. I think I'll sketch the country skyline on the other side." Estelle stood, then hesitated. "I know we aren't well acquainted, so I hope you won't find me too forward, but thinking too little of oneself is an error as grievous as thinking too much of oneself, for both disregard the work of Sustainer and perpetuate the lie that all depends on you." With a nod, she walked around the curve of the tower, out of sight.

My fingers coiled around my leadstick. Not everything depended on me, but living in the shadow of unbounded prosperity carried weighty pressures and great uncertainties of its own. No one ever seemed to understand the constant uncertainty of whether success came because you achieved it or because of your familial name. The perpetual doubt of whether people spent time with you because you were pleasant company or because you were wealthy. Always worrying about what would happen if all the advantages vanished and you had nothing but your own two hands. Forever fearing the day Sustainer removed His blessings because you didn't appreciate them or use them enough, and the trial unmasked you as a sham because you'd never known sufficient trouble to develop real character. In the light of all that, how could I judge myself rightly?

"A keshel in exchange for your musings?" Xander relaxed against the doorframe, his shirtsleeves rolled up and hair tousled, looking the happiest and most relaxed I'd seen since we'd met.

"I fear they are not worth even that much."

He shook a finger at me. "That's my line. You're not allowed to steal it."

"Steal?" I pressed my hand to my throat. "I was merely borrowing it. You may have it back whenever it pleases you."

He laughed. "I shall remember that the next time Mum teases me about stealing one of her sayings. How does your sketching fare?"

I flipped my book closed. "Slowly. How are things proceeding inside?"

His face lit up. "The system is incredible! I have never considered using a mesh gear for a locking mechanism. As for the amstead system, its application of rotor pulleys is pure genius."

Xander could have been speaking a foreign language for all I understood, but the thrill of whatever he'd discovered added jaunty flourishes to the script of his words, outlined with an edge of golden wonder.

"I can think of at least three different applications, and that's without trying. Except when I get home . . ." The golden edge around his words faded to ash, flourishes flattening. Because when he returned home, he would be expected to fill the role of prince and then king, rather than inventor. Why had his parents burdened him with a position he didn't want, when his passion lay elsewhere?

Xander plopped down beside me on the bench. "Anyway, Drom said he didn't need further help, and I was to join you sibahs in sketching. Speaking of whom, where is Sibah Estelle?"

"She went to the other side to sketch the country skyline."

"More inspiration to discover." He opened his own sketchbook to a page filled with outlines.

"What are you working on?"

He covered his work. "I'll show you on the condition that I may see your sketching."

A fair request, but to show my unfinished work? Using my own blood for ink would be preferable. What if my sketch was terrible? Unsalvageable? Xander would be polite, of course. He was a prince, and princes were trained to be tactful. But even tact could not hide the curl of contempt his words could bear. Yet it would be much harder to hear those disappointed words coming from my teacher. At least if Xander thought it poor, I would have opportunity to sketch something else for my teacher. I reopened my book.

Xander only stared. He said not a word, uttered not a sound. He was just a blank page of a response.

A lump formed in my throat. If even Xander's princely training failed to find a tactful response . . . "You don't have to be polite." I swallowed, bracing for the worst. "You can tell me it's horrible."

"Horrible?" The word arched with surprise before flowing into a breath that curled with wonder. "That's not a skyline, it's–it's a story. Without words. Of the heavens trying to lovingly embrace the city while the city pushes it away."

My own page of thought emptied of words momentarily. He had seen the story I was trying to tell, even in this raw state. Seen meant exposed. Vulnerable. The words overlapped each other in an unsettling way. I shifted awkwardly and gestured toward his sketchbook. "Now it's your turn."

His skin warmed to a fiery hue. "It's nothing but a few diagrams of a project I'm designing, so don't expect much." He withdrew the arm covering his work.

I studied the drawings, trying to understand the sketches wedged between calculations and scribbled notes.

"Drom's phoenix was such an inspiration, I wanted to try something similar," he said, "and then I remembered the nesting dolls a Kossacan diplomat had given Mum. So I started with a box that would unfold to disclose an egg. Then that would crack open to reveal the bud of a water rose, and finally the rose would bloom to reveal a miniature couple waltzing."

"How very non-utilitarian of you. Is it for anyone special?"

"I was thinking perhaps as a gift for my future bride."

The words were delivered with his usual flowing precision, yet they landed upon my ears with the blunt force of a blockier script. I had never considered that Xander would have a girl at home. It was only natural, even expected, that a man with his looks, intelligence, compassion, and position would have someone waiting for him. Even Avi mentioned he wasn't available. "I'm sure she'll love it." I stood. "Time is passing quickly, and if I want to outline a different skyline, I need to do it now." I circled the tower to join Estelle. But my cadence was gone, my lines stiff, mechanical. A headache pulsed behind my eyes, and I welcomed Drom's announcement that it was time to leave.

We returned the way we came, exiting the warehouse as lamplighters passed by in the growing gloom. It seemed like every other street boasted a pair of soldiers. That was odd. But maybe it was the lateness of the hour; usually I was at my aunt's studying at this time.

Xander edged me nearer to Estelle. "Is it me, or are there extra patrols this evenfall?"

"It would not be surprising if there are," Estelle replied. "It's rumored the Spectre has crossed the border."

My breath caught. The Spectre? The Egdonian assassin so elusive that no one knew what he looked like? "Do they have a suspected target?"

Estelle shook her head. "No one seems to be sure, though a diplomatic delegation from Egdon did arrive yesterday. Some speculate the Spectre was following them. Others say Chancellor Serex or another politico is the target."

Speculations that made sense–if you didn't know the

crown prince of Egdon was hiding in Kolchan. Had someone discovered Xander's whereabouts?

His jaw was set. "Whoever the target, the outcome would be the same: war."

"You there." A pair of soldiers veered toward us.

No, not us. Toward Xander. He bowed to them. "May I help you, hasib letad, hasib dalem?"

That was impressive. He recognized their ranks by the colored cords looped at their shoulders. The senior ranking letad raised his eyebrows, mirroring my surprise, but didn't comment. He merely extended his hand. "Travel papers."

"I'm afraid I don't have them on my person."

"Then I must ask you to come with us." He gripped Xander's arm.

"Is that necessary?" I inserted myself between them. "Hasib Saunders is a family friend who has been visiting here for the past month."

Drom stepped forward. "I c-can verify S-Sibah Patican's words."

"You're Judge Patican's daughter?" The dalem leveled his gaze on me.

"I am."

The dalem faced his superior. "I come from their province. If a Patican is willing to vouch for him, you know their word is true."

The letad hesitated, then released Xander. "I'll overlook it this time, but keep your travel papers with you at all times from now on."

"I appreciate your leniency, hasib letad."

They marched on. I released a breath.

A half smile quirked his mouth. "No need for concern, sibah. I'm no threat."

"I'm more anxious about you being threatened."

"My papers will travel with me from now on."

I slowed as Drom and Estelle continued on ahead. "That's not what I meant." How to word this without revealing what I knew? "You indicated you have enemies. Enemies, I'm assuming, who would do you bodily harm, otherwise there would be no need for you to be here or for Avi to request I keep watch on your behalf. What if the Spectre is here for you?"

"That seems unlikely. Few people know I'm in Indel, and fewer still that I'm in Kolchan. Moreover, hiring the Spectre would take immense connections and wealth, even for a home job, much less one in another realm. I cannot believe removing a court inventor worth such an investment, do you?"

An inventor, no. But what about the crown prince?

"Besides, it'd be easier and cheaper to hire the Spectre for my return. No, I suspect the target is one of yours."

But what if the intent was more than to kill Xander? What if they wished to start a war as well?

We turned the corner and found Mascad stalking toward us, blackness billowing around him. Drom intercepted him, and after a whispered exchange, the roiling black softened to charcoal grey. He nodded once at Drom, then thrust papers at Xander.

Xander tucked them into an inside pocket. "I see you heard the news."

"A coach awaits us." The words were one shade from a growl.

I smiled. "Give thanks, Hasib Mascad, for no disasters struck today, and Hasib Saunders assures me there's no real danger to either of you."

That earned Xander unspoken daggers from his cousin. He merely lifted one shoulder, supplying neither explanation nor defense, before turning back to me. "Would you like to join us, Sibah Yosi?"

I hesitated. Did I dare impose on them? Darkness was descending rapidly. "I think it best if I avail myself of your generosity, thank you."

"Then we b-bid you a p-pleasant evenfall," said Drom.

"I'll see you at the Academy tomorrow," Estelle said to me. "Until then, 'May pleasant dreams be through the night / and strengthen joy with morning's light.'"

At their departure, we boarded the hired coach, and within minutes Xander was helping me alight in front of my aunt's, the lamp already lit above the door. I was much later than I'd intended, perhaps as late as a half bell past six.

The driver muttered something.

"Thank you for making the extra stop. And for your patience while I escort the sibah inside . . ." Xander extracted a few coins from a money pouch.

A folded paper fluttered to the ground. In the dim light and with his focus on the driver, Xander didn't seem to notice. I retrieved the paper just as Rivka rushed out.

"Sibah Yosi! Please come quickly. Your aunt has been calling for you for the past bell."

"For me?" I followed her inside, only to realize I still held Xander's note. I stashed it into my school bag to return to him later. "Did she say what for?"

"I do not know." She rubbed her arms–arms that were unblemished this morning but now were covered in angry red splotches starting to purple.

I stopped. "Rivka, did she hurt you?"

She tucked her arms behind her. "She awaits you in the front parlor."

"You didn't answer me. Did my aunt hurt you?"

"It's nothing, sibah."

"To hurt another is never nothing." Xander spoke from doorway.

Rivka merely bowed her head. "Pardon me for saying so, hasib, but Indel is not Egdon, and a few bruises are nothing when one's a menial."

"Which is why Egdon outlawed such a barbaric system." A growl shadowed Xander's words.

I fisted my hands. "Is it better to let your people starve on the street or languish in prisons and workhouses? Or how about your indentures? Are they truly treated any better?"

He stiffened, but Rivka edged between us. "This is not the time or place, sibah."

She was right. I knew she was, though I didn't want her to be.

Precious is a befitting word, its beauty outshining its silver setting.

Sometimes having the Scribes memorized could be bothersome. I blew out a deep breath. "I will–"

"Niece, I need to speak to you. Now." My aunt's imperial voice filled the hall as she stepped into the parlor's doorway. Constrained anger sharpened every angle of her body. What had I done to raise such ire? "Menials, back to your labors."

Did she just dismiss the future king of Egdon as a menial? I kept my face impassive and offered Xander an apologetic shrug before following my aunt into the parlor. It was the most intimidating room in the house, its rigid furniture anything but inviting.

In the corner, Jamarde sat on a hard-backed chair, eyes red and puffy behind tear-splattered glasses. Lavidah perched primly on a settee across from her sister, a smirk playing about her lips. What had happened in my absence?

My aunt thrust an envelope toward me. "I require an explanation."

I withdrew a single folded page, thick and cottony and edged with gold. Finest of the finest as far as stationery went. The note itself, in bold-stroke writing, outlined my crime as inducing impressionable young ladies to fraternize with those below their station and teaching them uncouth manners. The note was signed by a leading counselor, whose daughters I had been tutoring in exchange for help with Rivka's social graces training.

"What have you to say for yourself?" demanded Dodah Mirina.

I set the accusatory note aside. "I was unaware a fair exchange of services was considered a crime." I kept my voice even. Still, rebelliousness against such an unfair charge added a shadow of crimson to my words.

"Your father has coddled and spoiled you, accommodating every whim and fancy, but I cannot afford such indulgences here. You will abide by standard social norms, conducting yourself as befitting your stratum while treating others according to their strata."

The bruising on Rivka's arms flashed before my eyes. "If abiding by social norms means hurting those lesser than me, groveling before those greater than me, and shunning those different from me, I will not."

"Insolence." My aunt stalked toward me, hand rising. Surely she would not strike me, no matter how furious she was. Still, the way her dark eyes sparked in the flickering lamplight . . . A tendril of ice slivered through me. But if I backed down now, I would become like Jamarde, cowering in my aunt's shadow.

Dodah Mirina's hand clenched. "I suppose you think yourself fearless, making such bold claims. It takes no bravery when you have nothing to lose. Would you dare to be so audacious if it would cost you everything you hold dear?"

Her question stole my breath. She was right. I could defy her because I had wealth, stratum, and Avi's love. Would I dare to declare the same if I were a menial like Rivka? "Having never been tested in such a way, I cannot say, but should such a day ever come, I hope by Sustainer's grace, I would dare." Yet, even as the words passed my lips, my legs felt weak. If the mere threat of trouble shook me now, how would I withstand the pressure when real trials came?

My aunt huffed. "Continue on this rebellious path, niece, and you may well find the answer."

"But she threatened her, Massard, threatened her!" Xander paced the small living space of their rented flat. While it hadn't been proper, he had lingered with Rivka after Yosi had been whisked away. Something in the aunt's face unsettled him, and the resulting conversation confirmed the concern. He'd nearly charged into the room, but Rivka had shoved him out the door in a very un-menial way.

In the corner, Massard sharpened his boot knife, as he did every night. "Many threaten. Few act."

Xander flopped into a nearby chair. "Perhaps you're right, but it's infuriating to be so impotent." He had, after all, promised Yosi's father to look after her.

Massard examined his blade and, apparently satisfied, moved on to cleaning his pistol. "Then focus on the possible instead of the impossible."

Sound, reasonable advice. Yet he had precious little power as the crown prince of Egdon, and posing as an inventor and a merchant's cousin, he had fewer options still. What possibilities were even available to him?

Massard extended a thick book to Xander–the daily selections from the Writings of the Scribes. "I may not prescribe to Your Highness's beliefs, but I cannot deny they help you." Then Massard lit a taper and presented it to him. "I shall leave you to your meditations while I check on dinner."

Xander watched the flame, small, flickering, able to be snuffed out with a single breath. Yet that same flame, as weak as it seemed, could bring light and heat, destruction and purification. It could cause death or sustain life, all depending on how it was used. Approaching the side table with the lantern tree, he set aside his misgivings to recall the evening prayer.

"Sustainer, bring light into our darkness." He lit the lantern dangling from the eastern branch. "Set ablaze our hearts with Your truth"–he moved to the south-branch lamp–"in order that every realm near and far might behold Your Glory"–the wick of third one, hanging from the western branch, caught flame–"as we anticipate the purifying Fire-Yet-To-Come." Xander ignited the wick of the northern lantern, then hesitated before the final one atop the central trunk. The traditional words were "*we await Your Illumination.*" But here the Tipheret sect deviated. "Thank You for Effulgence." With all lamps alight, Xander blew out the taper, his gaze lingering on the dancing flames. *Please, Sustainer, illuminate what I ought to do.*

The personal prayer had almost become a part of the ritual, so often he'd uttered it over the past months. A search for clarity that had brought him here, where Sustainer first revealed Himself to His people. For though Effulgence's final words included a promise to be with His people wherever they were, some Tipherets claimed an extra awareness of Sustainer's presence in Indel. He didn't expect any grand revelations while here, but it would be nice to receive assurance that his ascension to the throne wouldn't be one of the worst mistakes in Egdonian history. Instead, Sustainer's silence continued.

Xander opened to the day's reading. With the time of the Ingathering near, the excerpt focused on accounts of the miraculous events that the festival celebrated: how Sustainer raised up Eshom the Gatherer to collect the Indelis from the other six realms, and how each realm refused to release the people unless an impossible task was completed. Xander's face burned as he read once again of his own royal ancestor's arrogant rejection of the Gatherer, how he suggested to the other realms the idea of the impossible requests, and how he demanded the Gatherer retrieve the Scroll of Galena, reputed to contain the inner workings of all things. But Sustainer provided the elchan, which enabled the completion of the six tasks–the very tasks that the Quest commemorated.

Xander's attention returned to the lantern tree. After Yosi's first refusal to participate, he'd researched the Quest further and discovered she had minimized the honor of winning the Kolchan Quest. The honors and freedoms accorded to finalists and winners during the following year were dizzying in their scope.

Massard returned with a covered tray. One look at Xander and he set it down unceremoniously. "What's the plan?"

"How do you feel about participating in the Quest?"

"I thought we wished to avoid attracting attention," said Massard.

"Yet whose attention would we truly draw? A few idle curiosity seekers? Even the newspapers will have naught to report but a name and description, and they will be more interested in talking about the prominent citizens participating than some foreign inventor and his merchant cousin. And those back in Egdon have no interest in some Indeli religious festival. Besides, this would be good for diplomatic relations, showing such respect for Indeli traditions."

"Spoken like one destined to be king." Massard sampled Xander's food before passing him a plate. "But how does this help the sibah?"

Between bites, Xander explained the rewards before concluding, "If such a visible status of honor won't protect Yosi from her aunt's schemes until after the Exam, I don't know what will."

"She will agree to do this Quest?"

And that was the gear locking the rest of the works. "She's convinced I would be a liability."

"Then show her the asset you are."

Xander chewed the thought with a piece of bread. Could it be that simple? If he could prove himself capable and provide her a list of reasons beyond tradition, maybe it would be possible to overcome her resistance.

He spent the rest of the evening enumerating the benefits of participating. The next day, during his breaks at the shop, he narrowed down that list to the strongest arguments. Drom watched him with curiosity but didn't intrude. Xander appreciated the discretion, but as the clocks in the shop chimed a half bell past three, he had to explain, at least in part. "It won't be necessary for you to fetch Sibah Estelle today."

"Oh?" Drom looked up from the oliphant he was finishing for the upcoming birthfest of a counselor's son.

"Mascad will be escorting her here, along with Sibah Yosarai and two others. I wish to ask them to compete in the upcoming Quest with Mascad and me."

Drom gazed at him, reflecting neither approval nor disapproval.

Xander cleared his throat. "I beg your pardon, hasib, if I have overstepped, and if you desire I not ask Sibah Estelle–"

Drom silenced him with a shake of his screwdriver. "A g-gear does not choose which s-song the music box p-plays."

Was that Drom's way of saying he had permission to ask? Before he could decide, Drom hopped down from his stool. "S-speaking of music boxes . . ." He retrieved the phoenix Yosi had shown him the first day at the shop. The very automaton he planned to purchase on behalf of "his cousin's customer." The price wouldn't cover all of Drom's debts, but it would at least eliminate two or three of the smaller ones.

Drom set it on the table before Xander.

"Is something wrong with this piece, hasib?"

"F-for you. T-to inspire."

"But the price–"

"Is irrelevant."

"I cannot accept such an expensive gift."

"C-cannot or will not?"

Rusted cogs. Parrying this man's arguments was proving more difficult than opposing all of Parliament. "While I find this piece inspiring, I have been eyeing it because my cousin received an unusual request from one of his customers, and I thought this might meet that request." His explanation sounded plausible, even logical, but Drom's eyes glinted, as if he knew what Xander was not saying.

"P-present my regrets to M-Mascad, but you n-need this. He d-does not."

Drom walked away, Xander's efforts to help the shopkeeper once again thwarted. He'd have to review the other automatons later, during a time Drom wasn't present. Maybe he could find a trinket his stepmum or half sister would like, though nothing would match the expense of the phoenix. He could commission something, but Drom would likely refuse full payment beforehand, and the purchase of additional supplies for the commission would add to the debt, not lessen it.

He became so fixated with solving this latest conundrum, he wasn't aware of anyone else's presence until a scuffing of feet drew his attention.

Yosi, Estelle, and Rivka stood nearby, Massard reclining against a shelf behind them. Xander greeted them as he rose, wiping his greasy hands on a rag as he tried to gauge the difficulty of the task before him. "Where is Sibah Chiman?"

Massard's jaw tightened. "The sibah was not permitted to join us."

Which meant her mother's threats of isolation had not been idle. "I regret to hear that, but I thank the rest of you for joining me."

"I admit," said Yosi, "curiosity is a powerful motivator. Your cousin only said you wished to speak to us."

Xander sighed inwardly. When Massard said Xander was in charge of explaining all, he meant all. "I apologize for the mystery." Now to decide the best course of action.

Forthrightness, probably. "I have heard about your upcoming Ingathering and Quest. I was hoping you sibahs, along with the younger Sibah Chiman, would do my cousin and me the honor of forming a coterie with us."

They looked at one another, then their gazes cast downward. The pendulum of favor was not swinging in his direction.

Estelle finally offered him an Egdonian curtsy. To placate him? "Hasib Saunders, I'm sure I speak for all when I say we feel honored by your request . . ."

"But it won't be possible for us to accept." Tension rippled across Yosi's face. "The Quest is based on the Seven Arts, with the tasks and trials designed to test thoroughly the abilities of each competitor in every art. The competition here in Duyah is quite fierce, and only those well-acquainted with the Seven Arts have any hope of completing the first six tasks in time to reach the finals, much less win the Quest."

Drom, listening nearby, snorted. "In short, f-foreigners don't know anything. Even if we've always l-lived here."

Yosi clasped her hands before her. "Please, hasib, do not be upset. It is nothing personal–"

"Nonetheless, you have dismissed us without even a chance to prove ourselves." Xander had to swing that pendulum back in his favor. "Have you ever considered our differences may not be a weakness, but a strength? While I may not be acquainted with Indel from the inside, I've had a long–and if I might add, personal–interest in your country. As a result, I am familiar with your country, your traditions, and your ways better from the *out*side."

Estelle fingered the tip of her braid. "You know, he might be correct. 'The eagle's eye, from up on high / shall better see the path to flee.'"

Xander seized that opening. "Test me. Let me demonstrate what I'm capable of, that you may make a fully informed decision."

Yosi inclined her head. "Very well, let us proceed with that now. Estelle, would you please test Hasib Mascad while Rivka and I examine Hasib Saunders?"

And the pendulum of favor slipped between his fingers. His royal studies and diplomatic relationships should enable him to meet whatever challenges Yosi meted out, but how far did Massard's knowledge extend? "I would be glad to undertake any task, but my cousin–"

"Would gladly do the same." Massard gave a formal Indeli bow of introduction to Estelle. "At your service, sibah."

"Oda, may we use the downstairs?"

Drom hopped off his stool. "This way."

As Massard followed Estelle, he glanced back at Rivka, something flashing in his eyes. Regret, perhaps?

But that was a puzzle to piece together later. He placed his left arm atop his right and bowed deeply at the waist. "Whenever you are ready." This should be no different than one of his tutor's oral tests. He hoped.

Yosi pulled a stool over to her maid. "Rivka, would you check his knowledge of our customs and history? Consider it practice for your crossover assessment."

"As you wish, sibah." Rivka seated herself, then centered her attention on Xander. "How many provinces does Indel have?"

"Seven–one for each of Eshom's helpers, plus Duyah, which is representative of Sustainer, not the Gatherer, as some believe."

And so it went. Geography, history, law, religion. When Rivka depleted her questions, Yosi assumed control, posing a series of increasingly difficult queries. He took longer and longer in answering.

"Why did Egdon request the Gatherer to obtain the Scroll of Galena?"

"Which reason do you seek: the Egdonian one or the Indeli one?"

Rivka blinked. "They are different?"

"Indeed, they are. The Egdonian history books–and the answer I've traditionally been trained to say–declare we sought the knowledge contained in Galena for the betterment of our people, which we did. The First Scroll of the Gatherer, however, reveals the motive of our heart. We desired to become as wise as any god and thereby no longer require a god." Xander bowed his head. "Sadly, many Egdonians ascribe to that belief today. We've become so enlightened, we feel we no longer need a divine crutch to survive. Many are blind to the reality that some things cannot be fixed by knowledge alone."

Instead of asking another question, Yosi pushed a table aside. "I've seen your sketching, so there's no need to test further the Art of Creativity. That means the Art of Social Graces is next." She pointed to a carousel. "Rivka, would you?"

Her maid twisted a key, and a light melody tripped across the air. An Indeli folk dance. One he had been taught, but which one? He closed his eyes, trying to feel the melody. *Step, step, step. Hop. Step, step, step. Hop. Skip, hop, skip, hop.* At least that was what his body said.

The tune finished its first round. Xander extended his forearm to Yosi. "Would you honor me with this dance, sibah?"

She placed her arm atop his. "The honor would be mine, hasib."

Together they promenaded across the floor. *Step, step, step, hop.* "Have I proven myself sufficient in knowledge?"

They broke apart as they turned, then joined together again. "Are you so insecure that you require an answer forthwith, hasib?"

"More curious, as I've never been tested by an Indeli."

"You make it sound like Indelis are a rare breed."

"In Egdon, you rather are."

They moved through a quick set of triplet steps, which required Xander's full attention, but when they returned to the promenade, he said, "You avoided my question, but I think I already know the answer."

"Oh?"

"If my knowledge were lacking, why ask me to dance?" He inclined his head toward her, the scent of orange blossoms and sunshine filling his nose. "Unless you were looking for a convenient excuse to dance with me?"

"It's not every day one has an opportunity to dance with a royal."

Xander stumbled over the next step.

"I mean, as an inventor to the king, you must be a very important part of the royal court and have attended many a ball and other such functions."

A smooth recovery, but a heavy weight sat in his stomach. Somehow she knew. A suspicion confirmed by her refusal to meet his eyes when they finished dancing. Had all her kindnesses, all her visits, all the time she'd spent with him, been nothing more than an indulgence of his title? "Siv Rivka, would you please check on the others' progress?"

Rivka cocked her head but did as he asked.

When she had left, he faced Yosi. "How did you find out?" he demanded. "Your father had explicit instructions–"

"Avi didn't tell me." She still refused to look at him.

"Then how?"

"You wouldn't believe me if I told you."

"Try me."

She picked up a tool from Drom's workbench, then put it down. "My spells–they're caused by the elchan. I'm a heart seer."

The legendary elchan. He pinched the bridge of his nose. "You want me to believe some mythical ability enabled you to see who I was?"

"I told you, you wouldn't believe me."

"Lies ought to be believable."

Yosi whirled on him. "If I were lying, my lie would have been believable. Or do you think so little of my intelligence, that I'd choose an outlandish lie no one would believe?"

"Perhaps in your intelligence you concocted the outlandish, knowing no one would disbelieve you because of its outlandishness."

"So I'm either stupid and a poor liar–a credit to my character and an insult to my intelligence–or brilliant and a skilled liar–a credit to my intelligence but an insult to my character? If those are my choices, I'd rather be stupid and a poor liar."

"Prove to me you're not lying."

She flailed her arms. "And just how am I supposed to do that?"

"Have one of your 'spells.'"

She gave an exasperated huff. "The elchan does not work that way. I can't turn it on or off like a switch. It shows up at random, whenever I touch an object present during a past event that Sustainer wants me to see."

That made little sense. What could she have touched that would have been present in his past? Only his pocket watch, and that had been tucked away. "As I recall, you weren't touching anything, unless you count the ground."

"You're right. I wasn't touching any*thing*."

He was baffled for a moment, then it dawned on him. "You accessed my memories?"

"I don't know. Possibly. I've never had anything but inanimate objects trigger the gift until that day." She rubbed her temples. "No, it wasn't a memory. I saw what you saw and heard what you heard, but the thoughts and feelings were mine. Still, I imagine it was a shock to hear yourself named successor to King Rion."

The memory flashed through Xander's mind, and shock did not begin to describe the moment. Terror of what they were asking. Pride they thought that well of him. Confusion about why they would name him successor. Anger at being asked to relinquish his plans to fulfill a role he was ill-suited for. He could still see his father sitting at his desk, his stepmum seated to the side, both wearing garments neither wore in public and therefore unfamiliar to anyone but the closest of family and servants. "What were my parents wearing that day?"

"Your father . . ." She closed her eyes. "A jade-green smoking jacket and black pants with white pinstripes. As for your mother," a faint smile appeared, "a lovely purple dressing gown, quite becoming with her fair complexion, though most Indelis would be aghast at any female wearing such fitted pants, much less the queen."

Xander gripped the edge of a shelf. The description matched, information she could have never known.

Unless she was a heart seer.

The elchan were real?

"Your Highness?"

Xander tightened his grip. "Please, call me Saunders here."

"Yes, of course. I understand."

Did she? Could she? One wrong word to the wrong person, and the nightmare would begin again. Could he trust her to keep his secret? Or should he leave before anything could happen? Drom's shop had become such a refuge, even in the short time he had been here. A place where he could be Saunders, inventor, engineer, university student, rather than Crown Prince Xander, heir to the Egdonian throne. But even the best refuges could morph into a trap.

"What are we going to do?" asked Yosi hesitantly.

"We?"

"I know your secret and you know mine," she said. "There is a reason I call them spells, not visions. The kodesh has relegated the elchan to the realm of symbolism and allegory.

How do you think people would react to someone claiming to be a literal elchan?"

Xander winced at the possible results of such news. One of the better outcomes would include being paraded around like a carnival sideshow while people begged for visions she couldn't produce. Or with the threat it would pose to the kodesh's power, they might try to make her disappear. Worst case, she could be executed for the practice of the Dark Arts. At least Massard and others protected him from his attackers. What did Yosi have apart from silence and anonymity?

Would you dare to be so audacious if it would cost you everything you hold dear? Was that how Yosi's aunt planned to execute her threat? By exposing her gifting?

Thus, the need to participate in the Quest. It wouldn't provide long-term indemnity, but the kodesh would have no desire for outlandish charges to mar the competition's reputation and would have them dismissed as the prattle of envy. Such self-preservation tactics were common in politics and religion alike, much to his disgust. However, in this case, it could work in Yosi's favor. "Have I shown myself worthy for the Quest?" he asked.

She seemed taken aback. "Why is this important, hasib?"

The motive of personal protection probably wouldn't sway her much, but she might consider competing for the sake of her friends. "I cannot help but see the many benefits our participation could bring, even if we advance no further than the finals. Sibah Estelle could repay her Academy tuition, allowing Drom to fulfill his debts. I could use my purse as an excuse not to take a wage. Siv Rivka could use it as proof to the crossover assessment board that she has sufficient funds to begin life as an elite. Your cousin could hire a private tutor. Besides"–he drew himself taller–"I'll never have another opportunity to participate, and this show of respect for Indeli traditions could benefit diplomatic relations between our countries."

There was a pause before Yosi spoke. "You have given this much thought. I will consider the matter further and give you an answer soon."

Xander caught the imaginary pendulum of favor in his hand. That wasn't a yes, not yet, but it was one click closer.

My strategy was bearing fruit. My men were in place. Several key opponents had been removed from the board. Yes, the prince's disappearance had proven a nuisance, but even this I could manipulate to my advantage. If I maneuvered the pieces right, I might even achieve two goals with one move.

I strode down the hall to my borrowed office, two Indeli bodyguards shadowing me. Another nuisance, but one easily dealt with. They were not as competent as I was told. But I, of all people, understood the necessity of maintaining appearances, and the rumors of the Spectre's presence in Kolchan required extra diligence to uphold that image. I smiled to myself. What lovely chaos would ensue if they knew the truth.

One guard entered the office ahead of me to verify no intruders lurked inside. He then waved me on, he and his companion stationing themselves outside my door. I laid aside my meeting notes and removed a list from a desk drawer. Ten names, seemingly unrelated, but all with a close personal connection with the Egdonian royal family.

Thus far, six of them were struck, subtle probes assuring me they knew nothing. Three had questions marks. These hid something, but whether those secrets pertained to the royal family remained to be seen. The tenth name was a last-minute addition, since the connection between the two families dated back a couple of decades and primarily through the dead king. But nearly forgotten alliances sometimes proved the most dangerous of all, and it would be just like the whelp to leverage an old friendship to accomplish what his father could not. What must not be. Therefore, for the sake of thoroughness, I'd added the name to my investigation.

This one, however, would require finesse, for little reason existed for an Egdonian delegate to call on a country judge of an outlying province. Thanks to the Fates, I had years of acquiring finesse.

One way or another, the meeting with Judge Caleph Patican would occur.

Decision paralysis gripped me. Registration for the Quest closed today, and if I didn't make a choice before evenfall, it would be made for me. Yet, like the endless knot favored by the Ferri illuminators, my mind circled the same path, ending where it began. I couldn't think or reason this through, much less study, as the open books spread across my bed testified.

I slapped them closed and thumped them into a stack, but the sharp movements failed to break the loop, my mind beginning the circuit anew. Xander's idea had merit, solving several problems at once. We needn't defy all odds and win the Quest. Acquiring a finalist's purse would be quite sufficient.

But thus far all my attempts to help had only worsened matters. I gulped down some tea, grimacing at the tepid liquid, as bitter as my failures. My introduction of Xander to Drom had only increased the financial strain on the shop. Jamarde had been under strict supervision since her mother learned of my tutoring. Rivka's assessment training apparently meant she had time to ready Lavidah as well as me each morning. How, then, could I know if participation in the Quest wouldn't hurt more than help?

It wasn't fair. It seemed an impossible choice, like that new parlor game, Heights & Depths. Not the lighthearted version Avi favored, where the choice was between a trip to the Waibean crystal caves or the snowy Kossacan ice forest, but the chilling style played by Lavidah and her cohorts, where the choice was between death by strangulation or by stabbing.

Of course, a stronger-minded person would stop dithering and make a decision, accepting whatever may come. But when the welfare of not only friends, but also of entire countries could be affected, such a cavalier approach seemed unthinkable. *Sustainer, what should I do?*

As I set my cup aside, the folded paper near my jewelry box caught my eye. The note Xander lost the day we returned from the Fountain Tower. I kept forgetting to return it. Well, today was as good as any, and I could inform Xander of my final decision, whatever that would be. I picked up the paper, my thumb brushing some of the writing inside.

Assassination.

The masculine thought-voice startled me, and I dropped the note. Assassination? As in to kill someone of import? Surely I had misunderstood.

I gingerly picked up the note by the corner and unfolded it. An equation. At least, that was what the string of numbers and symbols looked like, but why would someone writing an equation be thinking about assassination? I nibbled my lip. Reading this would violate all kinds of privacy, but if it pertained to murder, was not reading it the right course to take? I cautiously ran my fingers across the words. The thought-voice rang in my mind again.

Assassination.

Set.

For.

Ingathering.

After each word, letters were equated to the symbols on the page as the writer encrypted the chilling message. Whom was the message for? Whom was it from? Why did Xander have it? Did he know what it said?

Was he involved?

With trembling fingers, I placed the paper into my reticule and checked my watch. Still plenty of time to reach Drom's shop before Xander left, and with Lavidah and Dodah Mirina out shopping for a suitable wardrobe for the Quest, now would be the perfect opportunity.

I intercepted Rivka in the hall. "Are you available for an outing? I need to make a trip to Drom's."

A glint sparked in Rivka's eye. "Now I wonder why that might be."

I ignored the innuendo. An assassination was scheduled to occur during the Ingathering. That was more important than avoiding any other notions my unscheduled visit might suggest.

Once we were out of the house, I set a brisk pace for the Lower Market. Xander couldn't possibly be involved in an assassination plot. I'd seen firsthand how much the strain between our peoples upset him. Besides, Avi trusted him. Avi was rarely ever wrong about a person's character. More likely, this was a warning that Xander's location had been discovered and an assassination would be attempted during the Ingathering. So, why hadn't Xander left?

I turned into the Lower Market, and as I did, a shiver skittered down my spine. I whirled around. People coming, people going. None of them watching me.

Rivka touched my shoulder, concern wrinkling her brow. I gave her a tight smile and continued on, the sensation remaining. It was one I'd felt on numerous occasions over the past week. Was that menial lingering too long at the meat merchant? Was the agate seller more persistent than usual about showing us his wares, trying to stall us? Had that elite bumped into Rivka intentionally?

Stop it! No one was watching me. I was only experiencing the same nervousness everyone in the capital was feeling. The ongoing rumors about the Spectre, stoked by the increased military presence, had everyone on edge.

Shrugging off my jitters, I paused at a bakery where trays of fresh buns were being set out. I should bring a treat as an apology for reading the note. I picked out a dozen herb buns, then let Rivka haggle the vendor down to a reasonable price. A chill crawled across my back. I gritted my teeth. I would not keep looking around. It would only be the same scene as usual, with people coming, people going, browsing wares, bartering with merchants. I turned to a different vendor. Some fresh fruit would be a nice complement to the buns, and we could leave Drom and Estelle any leftovers.

My uneasiness intensified. I shifted my stance, focusing on the peripheral. There. A man who seemed out of place, though I struggled to determine why. His skin was lighter than a traditional Indeli, but the market attracted many foreigners and mixers, especially before the Ingathering. Was it his absorption with cloth that struck me as odd? He could be gift shopping for a wife or a daughter or even granddaughter.

Rivka returned the remainder of my money, which I stuffed into my reticule without checking what she'd spent.

"Something wrong, sibah?"

"I . . . don't know." The man didn't seem like a cutpurse; he was too finely dressed for that. Nonetheless, I tightened my hold on the reticule. "Stay close." I wended through the Lower Market on a circuitous route. The man didn't appear again. *Quit being paranoid, Yosi.* I took a deep breath and headed for Drom's.

But as I neared the shop, apprehension wound around me like the webbing around a spider's victim. I dropped my reticule. Bending to retrieve it, I peered past my arm. A man, who resembled the one from the market, walked past on the adjourning street. Coincidence? I forced my gait to maintain its original speed and approached Drom's from the back way. As soon as I cleared the corner, where we were beyond the man's sight, I yanked Rivka through the veil of vines and flattened us against the wall.

Rivka's eyes widened, and I pressed a finger to my lips. A moment later, the man paused in front of the shop, frowning. It was indeed the same man from the market. The ring on his middle finger was quite distinctive. Snow quartz was rare in Indel, as was any jewelry boasting a single large stone. Most preferred many stones in an artful arrangement, and when a single large gem was used, it was cut into a unique shape. A big blob of polished rock was not considered tasteful here.

After a minute or two, the man walked on.

"Was that man following us?" whispered Rivka.

I nodded. But who? And why? Had someone connected me to Xander and was now trying to find him through me?

"Sibah Yosarai? Siv Rivka?" Xander stood in the stairway's door. "Is–"

I made wild slashing motions with my hands to cut him off, fearing Xander's voice would be recognized if the man was nearby. I nodded toward the stairs.

When we reached the shop, I blurted, "I think I was being followed, and no, I don't know who or why."

He stiffened with a tension I knew too well. I felt it every time I poised my pen over a blank page, ready to illuminate but uncertain where to begin, fearing that whatever I started would be the wrong choice. I rested a hand on his arm and told him the same thing Avi always told me. "Just breathe."

Rivka peered out the window. "Here comes Hasib Mascad."

"I need to let him know what's happened," Xander said grimly. "Stay here. I'll be back momentarily."

Momentarily might have been a stretch. I took to pacing as the clock on Drom's wall clicked off a quarter bell. Nine hundred agonizing swings of the pendulum. Finally, the men returned.

After assuring us no one lurked in the immediate area, Mascad thoroughly questioned the two of us. Though Rivka and I answered as best we could, the information did little to sate him.

"I regret we could not be of more help, hasib, especially in light of this." I laid the encrypted message next to the bundles of food I'd bought from the market.

Xander stilled. "Where did you get this?" Suspicion created an ominous shadow behind his words.

I could not fault him for that. "It fell out of your money pouch the day you escorted me home from the Fountain Tower." I shifted my feet. "I, um, I know what it says."

"You broke the code?" Mascad's voice pitched upward.

"In a way." It had been bad enough explaining my gifting to Xander. Would I now have to explain it to his cousin as well? "It says an assassination is set for the Ingathering."

"Cheery sentiment." Xander folded the paper away. "I wonder who the target is. It would be nice to warn them."

I stared at him. Wasn't it obvious?

He shook his head. "There would be no reason to tie that specific event to me. I suspect it is someone prominently involved in the festival."

Mascad rubbed his scar with his finger. "Nonetheless, I suggest we take precautions."

"What did you have in mind?"

Mascad said nothing, only cocked an eyebrow.

Xander's jaw twitched. "I'm not going through that again."

"Then let's compete." The words were out of my mouth before I could think them through.

"In the Quest?" Excitement lit Rivka's face.

I nodded. While the Quest had its own inherent dangers, none of the competitors would have the specific goal of assassinating Xander.

"How would that help?" asked Mascad.

"When I said the competition was cutthroat, I meant it literally." I rubbed an arm, a chill creeping across my skin. "About two decades ago, a competitor had his throat slit. However, because of that, the coteries are now under constant surveillance during the entire Quest, and whenever they are not participating in a trial, they are sequestered in a walled mahal. It's said no location is more secure during the Ingathering except the Chancellor's Palace itself." I paused, but I had an obligation to clarify all the risks. "That said, suspicious accidents still occur, and your nationality will make you a natural target. But anyone from the outside must go through the Indeli military."

Xander jumped in. "That would increase our odds of catching any attacker and provide us someone to question should anyone try something. Which I still seriously doubt."

Mascad folded his arms, widening his stance. Xander locked eyes with him in what appeared to be a battle of wills. For a minute, it appeared Xander would lose, prince or no prince. Then Mascad dipped his chin in deference. "As you wish."

I straightened my shoulders. "Good. I'll register us as soon as we leave here." While I tried to sound genuinely enthusiastic, my stomach sank.

What kind of nightmare had I volunteered us for?

Fire in a hearth brings cozy warmth on a cold evenfall. Fire in a lantern illuminates our path at night. Fire in an oven prepares delicious food for our enjoyment. We like fire . . . when it is controlled and contained.

Yet a fire-lilac blooms only when it is burned, and gold must endure the flames to be refined. Diamonds form under pressure and heat.

So it must be for us. The time and place and way may vary, but each of us must pass through the flames. Only then can the imperfect be burned away, the good refined, and our true character revealed.

4

This evenfall, the Quest would commence.

My hands clutched the balcony's railing, the setting sun already painting Kolchan in golden hues. In less than two full bells, I would stand on a platform with Xander, Mascad, Estelle, Rivka, and Jamarde, in sight of the whole city, proclaiming our intention to compete. If all went well until then.

That remained a large *if*, however, even after over a week of clandestine preparations and secret practice sessions.

The autumnal air nipped at my skin, driving me back into my room, where Rivka was locking up my trunk, which was crammed with more clothing than I would need for a week. Beside my trunk sat a smaller one containing Jamarde's garments and a large bag, which Rivka insisted contained all she needed. Avi might tell me I ought to feel no shame over the privileges I possessed, but it was hard not to feel embarrassed when my privileges obviously exceeded those around me. I should have insisted Jamarde share my trunk, for how many gowns would I truly need for the three-day Quest?

Rivka extended to me my white wrist gloves. "All will be well."

Oh to have even half of my maid's confidence! Although I had the least to lose among the six of us, all the secrecy had stretched my body tauter than a canvas upon its frame. Even now, every move had to be calculated, every word measured. For although my aunt had given Jamarde more freedom since Avi's arrival in Kolchan, Lavidah would leverage any excuse–even her sister's disgrace–to prevent us from competing and thus increase her odds of winning.

A tap sounded at the door.

"One minute please." Rivka straightened my collar before casting a critical eye over the whole dress–the purple one with the roses she'd wanted me to wear my first day at the Academy. As I had then, I argued for something simpler, but Rivka, supported by Jamarde, insisted I needed to make a statement, for the sake of our coterie. "Are you ready?" she asked me.

I pressed a hand to my stomach, as if that would calm its fluttering. "No." But this was for a good cause–several good causes–chief among which was the protection of the Egdonian prince. Surely with such intentions, Sustainer would bless our endeavor.

Wouldn't He?

Rivka smiled at my honesty. "Don't forget to breathe." She shooed me out the door.

Avi was waiting for me, as confidently poised as ever. "Ah, there's my illuminary, as beautiful as a star in the heavens." After kissing my forehead, he said in a low voice, "No matter where you place, I am proud of you."

I startled. Avi knew?

He winked, then escorted me downstairs, where my aunt and cousins waited. "Good evenfall, sibahs. You all look charming this night. May I wish you well in the Quest, Lavidah? I am sure your coterie counts itself favored by Sustainer to have you."

"Thank you, Oda." Lavidah dipped her chin stiffly, though due to tension or a desire not to disturb her piled curls was hard to say.

A hall clock tolled six bells, Avi's pocket watch chiming in.

"I believe that is our cue for our departure. Shall we?" He ushered my aunt and cousins ahead of us, and we all boarded the grand coach Avi had rented for the occasion.

As we pulled away from the house, my gaze wandered to the upper windows. Even now, Rivka hauled our luggage downstairs so she would be ready when Estelle, Xander, and Mascad arrived. Everything depended on precise timing, and many things could go wrong between now and the announcement of the coteries.

Avi settled in his seat beside me, facing my aunt and cousins. "I procured a place for us along the east rope in front of the Fountain Tower. I knew you would want the best place to watch Lavidah during the ceremony, Mirina."

"How thoughtful of you." But though she directed her words toward Avi, she frowned at Lavidah, who dug through her reticule. "Is something wrong, daughter?"

"I seem to have misplaced my gloves. I think I left them on the foyer table." She clasped her bare hands together. "Please, may we go back for them?"

The world around me greyed, and the taste of ash filled my mouth. If we returned, she would find Rivka with our luggage. If she found Rivka, she'd know our intention and do all she could to ruin our plan. Yet if I protested, she would also realize something was afoot.

Dodah Mirina patted her eldest's arm. "But of course. You can't be without your gloves. Brother, if you would."

Avi signaled the driver to stop.

Lavidah's eyes narrowed on my face. I turned my head, struggling to keep my expression neutral. But that was hard when there seemed insufficient air in the coach. The greys around me deepened to slate, then charcoal.

The driver approached, the words of his inquiry smearing like wet ink. Then Lavidah tittered. "Silly me. Here are my gloves."

I released a slow breath, splashes of color reasserting themselves–the pink roses on my skirt, the cream lace edging Lavidah's hem, the black scuffs on Jamarde's turquoise shoes. One disaster averted, but how many more traps did we have to avoid?

Avi gave the driver instructions to continue on, and Lavidah folded her hands, now gloved, seemingly at ease. "I still find it difficult to believe you're not competing this year, cousin. It seems a shame to break with tradition. Didn't you know I would have gladly found you a coterie?"

I offered what I hoped was a demure smile because, behind my lips, my teeth were gritted.

Jamarde huffed from the other side of her mother. "Yosarai is well aware of Kolchan's reputation of cutthroat competition, sister."

I took my cue from her. "Indeed I am, and among such fierce competitors, what chance would I ever have of winning?" In that I spoke the truth, for I had no illusion of winning. "Even if you had found me a suitable coterie, I would have refused to join them." The chief reason being that I couldn't have trusted them due to their association with Lavidah.

Dodah Mirina's return smile patronized more than complimented. "A reasonable conclusion, niece. You are wise to abstain this year, as difficult as that must be."

"I will indeed miss participating in the Cashirsa Quest. It was always such a delightful challenge." More truth. I would miss my home province's Quest, for its simpler reward gave it a friendlier atmosphere.

"But I'm surprised at you." My aunt peered down her nose at Jamarde. "I thought you planned to compete this year."

Jamarde toyed with the fraying edge of the sash knotted at her hip. "My schoolmates had other plans."

"Maybe if you applied yourself like your sister, you would excel."

I forced even breaths through my nose, lest a scream or some other regrettable vocalization should escape. Jamarde was intelligent in her own right, and she didn't need to trample people underfoot to succeed.

Avi leaned forward to lay a hand on Jamarde's arm. "Sometimes the late bloomers produce the prettiest and best flowers."

My aunt sniffed. "I suppose time will tell, won't it?"

After reaching the outer wall surrounding the Fountain Tower, we alighted from the coach and joined the steady flow of people entering through the wide archways into the rapidly filling field beyond. It seemed the whole of Kolchan had turned out for the opening ceremony–rich, poor, old, young, elite, menial, kodesh, politico, Indeli, and foreigner. Almost anyone from anywhere could blend in here. Perhaps enabling Xander to participate had been unwise. Police officers were posted at every archway and soldiers patrolled the crowd, but a hundred spectators to each peacekeeper left wide margins for someone to slip in and launch an attack, especially if extraneous casualties were of no concern.

Lavidah left to join her coterie, her mother admonishing her to make us proud as she departed. The rest of us wended our way along paths outlined by lamps to our reserved place at the base of the Fountain Tower. There, a rope and a dozen paces separated us from the torch-lit platform, which had been erected for the evenfall ceremony. At least we wouldn't have to fight to reach it when our coterie was summoned.

My gaze drifted up to the shadowy balcony encircling the Tower's midpoint. Had I indeed sat there sketching only three weeks ago? The Tower had seemed daunting enough then. This evenfall, looking up at its full height, our plan seemed like folly. Utter madness.

A murmur rippled through the crowd as the leading priest of the kodesh appeared atop the Fountain Tower, bathed in golden lantern light against a purpling sky. At the raising of the gadohen's hands, the crowd quieted. "Open your ears and hear, people of Indel. Open your minds and remember, you who have been gathered from among the Realms. Listen and recall the mighty work of Sustainer."

"Teach us, that we might hear and remember," I responded with the rest of crowd, the ritual words solid, immovable. Trustworthy, like the One who gave us the Writings in the first place.

Then the gadohen began to read from the First Scroll of the Gatherer about the events surrounding the Ingathering. How Sustainer raised up Eshom the Gatherer to ask the Six Realms for the return of the Indeli people. How the Six Realms conspired together, telling Eshom they would release the Indelis in exchange for one simple gift each. Then they proceeded to ask for the impossible. Eshom, instead of refusing their ridiculous requests, insisted each realm provide him a helper for the work ahead. They supplied those they deemed the weakest of their realms: a simplewit, a cripple-legged boy, a blind woman, a wizened old man, a pregnant girl, a man without hearing or speech. With these, the Gatherer set out on his mission to complete the six impossible tasks.

The story was familiar, one I'd heard every year since I was young. Yet the words resonated deep within me, maybe because this year, more than any other, I identified with the overwhelming impossibility of the Quest. Would Sustainer answer a plea for success? He had answered the Gatherer's request, but I had hardly proven myself worthy of such divine intervention.

The gadohen set aside his book, more of the Ingathering story to be read later. "Many trials lay ahead. Who will answer Sustainer's call?"

"Come forth, noble Questers. Answer the call," responded the crowd.

Priests took their places at the stairs leading up to the temporary platform. I gripped the rope before me. It was almost time. Had Xander and the others arrived?

Avi wrapped an arm around my shoulders. "Be still, my little illuminary. Sustainer rules over all."

I leaned into his embrace and his words, which echoed one of my favorite songs of the Scribes. Once we joined the Quest, I'd have no further contact with Avi until the final ceremony was over.

The gadohen unrolled a parchment. "Will the Whirlwind Coterie answer the call?"

A group of six marched forward to the platform and responded, "We answer the call."

The priest beckoned them up.

Another coterie was called, and another group responded. The platform filled with people. Academy students formed two full coteries, with several scattered among various others. At least three groups boasted members of the politico.

"Will the Cobra Coterie answer the call?"

Lavidah approached with five others. Among them I recognized her apprentice counselor friend from the Lower Market, a sculptor who recently gained his first showing at Kolchan's prestigious Lubzen Gallery, and Counselor Ahman, a leading politico and advisor to Chancellor Serex. How had she earned a place on their team? "We answer the call."

My fingers numbed, despite the warm gloves encasing them. We would be favored by Sustainer indeed if our coterie completed the initial six tasks, much less completed them quickly enough to earn a place in the finals. Only the first six teams to complete all six tasks before evenfall the second day would advance.

"Will the Illuminary Coterie answer the call?"

Too late to retreat now. Xander and Mascad strode toward

the platform, Estelle and Rivka behind them. Jamarde and I ducked under the rope.

"Girls, what are you doing?" Indignation sharpened my aunt's script to a point that I was certain would draw blood if I touched it.

I tugged forward Avi's blessing, as if its soft, almost ethereal shape could form an invisible shield around us as we gathered at the foot of the platform. "We answer the call." We then mounted the stairs, Mascad escorting Rivka and Jamarde, while Estelle and I were accompanied by Xander.

Though the priests bowed with respect, raised eyebrows expressed everything from surprise to disdain. Behind us, whispers rippled through the crowd as they glimpsed our coterie of two young Indeli elites, two Egdonians, a mixer, and a menial.

I knew we were odd, but until that moment, I didn't realize how odd. We were the only team with a menial. The only team with a mixer. Only the second team to include a foreigner. As we passed by, the other Questers snickered and muttered crude-sounding words, which I blocked from inscribing upon my mental page. That was an ugliness I could do without. Suddenly, Jamarde lurched forward. A man sprang from among one of the other coteries and caught her. I glared at the Questers congratulating a smug-looking man whose foot had been inconveniently placed for my younger cousin.

"Are you fine, sibah?" A low, smooth voice drew my attention back to Jamarde. Counselor Ahman was my cousin's savior? Not exactly what I expected from a leading politico.

Jamarde bowed to the counselor, her hands clasped behind her back as appropriate for addressing a politico. "I'm well, sri, thanks to you."

"No gratitude necessary. Fierce competition need not be crude, am I not correct, hasibs?" He lifted his chin, his goatee pointing accusingly.

They shuffled their feet, the platform beneath them suddenly fascinating. “Indeed, sri.”

“I thought so.” Backing out of our way, he motioned us on. “I wish you well in the tasks ahead.”

As we took our place at the end of the platform, I snuck another look at Counselor Ahman. If he treated everyone with this kind of respect, no wonder Chancellor Serex valued his advice. Maybe being on the counselor’s coterie would be a good influence on Lavidah.

Two more coteries answered the call, and the rest of the ceremony passed in a blur. We all took an oath to compete in a way that would honor Sustainer. The priests passed out envelopes to each coterie. Then the gadohen pronounced a final blessing, and we were escorted to waiting coaches.

After a half bell’s ride, the coach drove through a guarded iron gate and stopped at the kodesh mahal, where we would lodge for the duration of the Quest. I tipped my head back, trying to absorb the five-story, stone-and-plaster building. Ropes of tinted lanterns painted the carved exterior a kaleidoscope of fragmented colors, and as we entered the foyer, arched windows framed hedges that promised an extensive garden beyond.

Our suite was on the fourth level and charming in its simplicity, with its tapestry-adorned walls and parquet floors. In the center of the common room, a low, round table was set with bowls of rice and vegetables, nuts, and fruits, while plump cushions around its edges invited us to sit and taste the earthy aromas filling the air. A quick perusal of the other doorways adjourning the common room revealed two bedrooms, each with four beds, with a washroom between.

Returning to the main door, Rivka and Mascad each reached for the luggage, their hands meeting as they grabbed the same bag. Rivka tugged on the strap. “Please, hasib, it’s not proper–”

“Propriety be hanged.”

I smothered a laugh at the stubborn angle of their heads, neither ceding ground to the other. Did I imagine it, or was that a gleam of appreciation in Mascad's eye? Appreciation or not, we would be here all night if we waited for them to resolve this. "For the duration of the Quest, we are equals here and more than capable of serving ourselves." I dragged my trunk toward a bedroom. The others followed, and soon we were seated around the table and filling our plates with food.

Jamarde took a bite of her rice and vegetables, and she rocked side to side in delight. "This is delicious. Just the right blend of curango, black tupperic, and . . ." Her eyes widened. "Is that garsala?"

"You could tell that in one bite?" Estelle stacked slices of crispy majica along the edge of her plate. "You must have quite the sensitive palate. Majica?"

Jamarde blushed. "Not particularly sensitive. I think I feel sorry for the sense of taste because few people heed it. And no, thank you. I can't eat majica. It turns my face all puffy and makes it hard to breathe."

I nodded in sympathy, having suffered even worse reactions to a common sleeping powder my aunt had provided on one visit. It had given Avi and Rivka quite the scare.

Jamarde reached for a yellow carsnip instead. "Now, what's our first trial?"

I opened the envelope.

In the House of Books have I
Treasure stored both low and high:
A box, a heart, a key
(The eye of insight, see!)
A Bear with Goat and Deer,
One cloaked, one masked, one clear.

"It's a riddle." I passed the paper to Estelle before scooping up my own vegetables and rice. Rich spiciness warmed my tongue. Jamarde was right. Garsala seasoned the dish, though it was so subtle I would have never detected it if she hadn't said something.

"'In the House of Books.' That sounds like the Scriptorium," said Estelle.

Jamarde sighed mournfully at her half-full plate, then set aside her napkin. "Then I suppose we must be going."

I shook my head. "The Scriptorium is closed by now, and I doubt the priests will be persuaded to open it for us."

"Shouldn't we at least try?" Xander lifted a bite of food to his mouth, then hesitated, his eyes flicking toward Mascad, who gave a subtle nod. Surely they weren't concerned with someone tampering with the food here, under the watchful eye of the Quest's guard?

Estelle passed the riddle along for the others to see. "I agree with Yosarai that venturing out tonight would be fruitless. Traditionally, the kodesh refuses entrance to any of their buildings after they retire, and I see no reason for it to change this year. 'As has been done, so it will be, / now to eternity . . .'"

Jamarde frowned at her empty goblet. "But doing nothing tonight seems fruitless too."

Xander refilled her cup. "Do you have a suggestion for how we might use our time tonight besides sleeping?"

Jamarde's spectacles emphasized her flustered look. "I–I'm not sure."

"Surely we can prepare somehow." Xander looked from person to person, inviting any of us to respond.

Warmth bubbled inside me at his skill and care. He observed a need and filled it without being asked. He legitimized my cousin's concerns instead of dismissing them. He noticed others' discomfort and sought out advice. Perhaps King Rion had been wiser than I had credited him in naming Xander the heir to the throne.

Estelle pointed to the riddle. "If we can solve that tonight, we should have little trouble completing the first task at the Scriptorium on the morrow."

"If only we knew what else we would encounter." Jamarde rearranged the fruit and nuts on her plate into an eye-catching pattern. "That would make planning easier."

"Except the starting tasks are randomized, and the kodesh alone knows the order." I scooped up my last bite of rice and vegetables. Tasty and filling fare, yet I could imagine Lavidah snubbing the meal's simplicity.

"Must not all coteries complete the same six tasks?" asked Xander. "If we know where the other teams are headed tonight, we will have an idea of our destinations the next two days."

Mascad tucked his napkin beside his plate. "And people speak much when they think no one hears."

"Or think no one important hears." Rivka's eyes took on their impish glint. "And menials trust menials." Leave it to my maid to turn her sphere into an advantage.

"I believe we have work to do." Mascad looked at Rivka, the conniving expressions on their faces as perfectly matched as their earlier stubbornness. Definitely not a pair I would want to provoke.

After they left on their spying expedition, Xander shoved aside his plate. "That leaves us to unravel the riddle and strategize for tomorrow."

"Apparently." Should I use my touch on the riddle? It might not reveal anything if the writer had no idea what the riddle meant. Or if the writer did know, would glimpsing that be cheating? I pushed the paper across the table. "Outside the reference to the House of Books, it's nonsense to me."

Estelle read through the riddle again before passing it along to Jamarde. "The animals could refer to the Scriptorium's Forest Room."

"Or to specific Scribes." Xander pointed to the bottom of the riddle. "Their names are capitalized."

"Or that could mean nothing. '"Left, left," the trickster cries. / "Which left?" said I.'" Estelle fingered her braid looped over her shoulder, its colorful graduations accentuated by her green dress; she'd made no attempt to hide her mixed heritage tonight. "Tricksters are a Kolchan Quest specialty, whether as a capricious person giving unclear advice or false clues threaded among genuine ones."

I suppressed a groan. "That means we must not only unravel the meaning of the riddle, but we must also determine which clues are the right ones."

Xander's lips quirked.

"What amuses you?"

"I don't mean to offend, but I was noticing again how much Indelis love art. Maybe ten people will see this slip of paper, yet hours must have been spent creating it, with its hand lettering and illuminations. Quite the extravagance."

Estelle and I exchanged glances. The artistry was for more than eye appeal. "You're brilliant," I said as Estelle and I scooted around the table to look at the note together.

"I'm glad you think that, but would you enlighten me as to what I'm brilliant about?"

I pointed to an X swirl. "*Box, heart, Goat,* and *Deer* have this flourish, almost like it's barring entrance."

"And look at the word *key,*" Estelle added. "It has a faded lace motif behind the first letter, as is used with illuminated capitals."

Jamarde crowded in behind us. "*Insight, Bear,* and *masked* have the same."

"When you sibahs have a moment to explain, I'm ready to listen." Xander popped some almonds into his mouth.

"The words aren't the only clues. The artwork contains some too." Which, as an illuminator, I should have realized.

"The things we see the most frequently are often the things we notice the least." Xander propped his elbows on the table. "Where does that leave us now?"

"Assuming the X flourish marks the trickster words, while the motifs reveal the correct clues, we are left with 'key insight Bear masked,'" said Estelle.

I tapped the word *Bear.* "The scroll of Naviv Dov, I suspect."

"Why Naviv Dov?" asked Jamarde.

"Dov means 'Bear' in ancient Indeli," replied Xander.

My mouth gaped. He knew ancient Indeli? Why would an Egdonian prince know that, unless–could the rumors about the Egdonian royal family being secret followers of Effulgence be true?

Xander rose to look at the riddle over our shoulders. "That does not explain the rest of the phrase."

I studied the four words. "The illumination of Naviv Dov's scroll is known for its odd imagery. Maybe we're looking for a key or mask?"

"Or information masked by a key." Jamarde pointed to the third and fourth lines. "See how the motif of key and insight are intertwined?"

"Good eye," said Estelle.

My cousin shrugged as if it were nothing. But when criticisms outnumbered compliments, the value of the latter only increased exponentially. Perhaps the Quest would provide other benefits, like bolstering my cousin's confidence. "It sounds like we have unraveled the riddle as far as possible until we can look at the actual manuscript." I tucked the clue back into its envelope. "If we each examine a section, it shouldn't take too long to scan."

"What time do we need to be at the Scriptorium then?" asked Xander.

"It officially opens at nine bells. But while the kodesh retires early, they also rise early. If we could find one before morning prayers, we might gain access by six bells." I laced my words with optimism, but a jagged motif of doubt formed under them. As early as morning prayers were, eight bells of waiting stretched before us. Eight hours during which the other coteries pursued their own tasks, while we lost any momentum we might have had at the evening's start.

How would we ever overcome such a deficit?

Humiliation burned hot under Lavidah's skin, turning all food to ash in her mouth. This evenfall ought to have been a night of celebration. The savoring of the successes to come. The anticipation of the freedom the winner's purse would bring, clearing all the debts she'd accumulated from maintaining appearances at the Academy, debts her mother knew nothing about–could know nothing about.

Instead, it was a night of dishonor and shame. All because her cousin had the audacity to mar the Quest with such a disreputable rabble. Menials. Mixers. Foreigners. Slandering their family's good name. Her good name. She had striven so hard to earn the right to be among those with whom she now competed. As usual, her cousin thought of no one but herself, didn't consider what effect her actions would have on others.

"I say, wasn't your sister on that team?" Disdain dripped from Apprentice Counselor Lev, seated across the table in their common room.

Lavidah crushed her napkin under the table. That was the worst part. Her cousin had manipulated her addlepated sister's admiration, involving her in this scandal. One might distance herself from a cousin, but not from a sister.

Counselor Ahman spoke up beside her. "I do not see how that signifies. It's not as if Sibah Chiman is her family's keeper, and her reaction indicates she was unaware of their intention to compete, much less with whom."

Lavidah accepted his defense with a dip of her chin. "You are quite correct, sri. If I'd known, I would have stopped their misguided plan. It's nothing less than a disgraceful mockery of our sacred customs, and it ought not to have been permitted."

Ahman smiled enigmatically. "I believe the kodesh was wise in permitting it."

Lavidah bit back a gasp, and the woman on her other side choked on her drink. "You cannot be serious, sri."

Ahman tipped his goblet toward her. "Are you feeling threatened by a team of misfits, Sibah Resha?"

She bristled. "Of course not."

"Then what harm can come from letting the misguided souls compete . . . and lose?"

Lavidah's lip curled. Ahman had a point. Her cousin's team would never final, much less win, and such a public humiliation was the lesson her cousin needed. "It might be quite the education, might it not?"

"Both here and beyond, I believe. So, no more slander. Every member of this coterie has proven worthy to be here, and in three days' time, the rest of Indel will know it too." He raised a glass. "To the Cobra Coterie."

Lavidah mirrored the gesture, responding with the rest of the group, "Cobra!" When she sipped her drink, it went down smoothly. This time, her cousin would be the one to reap the humiliation she'd sown.

We were late.

We had slumbered longer than intended, our request to be awakened early having been misplaced, and it didn't matter how

much we hurried, we lagged further behind as we encountered problem after problem. Lost hair ribbons. Insufficient wash water. A breakfast that was made twice because the first mysteriously went missing. A long interrogation by the soldiers protecting the mahal to verify we were truly about Quest business. A sleepy coachman who moved at the pace of a bogsnail and even now drove with the caution of a pebble tortoise. Never mind the lamplit streets were deserted at this predawn hour.

My fingers drummed against my leg as we crept through another empty intersection. "I think walking to the Scriptorium might have been faster."

"Agreed." Jamarde hid a yawn behind her hand, even her spectacles looking foggy with sleep. "What if we don't arrive before morning prayers?"

"After morning prayers is still earlier than nine bells," Estelle said, far too alert for the early hour. "'The early riser who must wait / will come before the one who's late.'"

The coach rumbled to a stop in front of wrought iron gates. The Sanctum. Were we here soon enough? Xander helped us alight, and I shivered in the cool air despite the capelet over my warmest dress. Perhaps arriving before morning prayers hadn't been the best idea. What if it irritated the priests? Before I could utter my reservations, Estelle rang the bell, its deep tone booming through the courtyard beyond. I winced. It was too late to stop her now.

A priest strolled toward the gate, the greyness of his morning robes giving him an eerie, wraithlike appearance in the semidarkness. "May I help you?"

Estelle spread her arms to the sides, open palms out, and bowed deeply at the waist to express we came in peace with nothing to hide. "A bright mornrise to you, Elder Reuven. We were hoping to procure entrance to the Scriptorium."

She knew one of the priests by name? That was not a connection I would have predicted, yet somehow it suited her.

"Ah, Sibah Assah." A small smile softened the man's stern visage. "Why am I not surprised it's your coterie who has come? However, morning prayers begin soon." His eyes roved over our group. "Perhaps you would like to join us . . . unless you're in too much of a hurry?"

I bit my lip. Why couldn't he simply let us into the Scriptorium? The task would require no more than five minutes.

Xander copied Estelle's greeting. "We would be honored, if you will have us."

"Those who seek find." Elder Reuven beckoned us inside and led us toward the Sanctum.

I turned to Xander and softened my voice. "Do you think this is wise?"

"Do you think it unwise to remember Sustainer before proceeding?"

I ducked my head, shame burning. There could be no arguing that, for did not the Writings of the Scribes remind repeatedly to hold Sustainer first of all? Yet here I had to be reminded of that truth by an outsider, whom I wasn't even sure shared my beliefs.

The priest guided us to a narrow balcony overlooking the Inner Sanctum. The vaulted room stretched out many paces to each side of us, its narrow length outlined by a double row of priests carrying candles. At the front of the room, before an arched window with a panoramic view of the city, stood a tall lantern tree, its lamps lit.

After Elder Reuven left us, I stole a peek at Xander. Though I couldn't see him well in the gloom hovering in these upper reaches, his mouth gaped slightly, like one overwhelmed by wonder or awe. When had all this become so familiar that I failed to remember the privilege of where I stood, of what we were about to do? Somehow the ritual that once delighted me as a child, with Avi guiding my hand as we lit the lamps together, had dulled to a daily duty. How disappointed Sustainer must be with me. Bounty upon bounty He bestowed upon me, and this was how I repaid Him. *Sustainer, forgive my distraction, my short memory, my loss of what is important. Use this time, indeed even the whole Quest, to realign my priorities and hold You as more important than all else.*

Almost as if in response to my prayer, voices swelled to fill the cavernous space from every direction with the opening notes of the morning psalm. I knelt on a pillow along the railing, the others beside me doing the same, as my lips formed the words to the song, though I gave them no voice for fear of spoiling the antiphonal music.

This day is Your day, Sustainer;
We praise You for Your gift.
For You have made it and formed it,
(We praise You for Your gift);
Reflecting Your lovingkindness,
We praise You for Your gift.
Therefore, it is Yours and Yours alone,
To do with it as You wish;
From You this day has come.
Yet into our hands for joy and use,
This day You have given us;
What should we do with it?
O let us return it to You,
(Your gift we now release);
That Your glory be its brightness,
Your gift we now release.
Sustainer of all, sustain us;
Your gift we now release.

As the final echoes faded, the gadohen walked up the center

aisle, a long-stemmed snuffer in hand, and ascended to the lantern tree, the horizon beyond rimmed in red.

"Sustainer, thank You for sustaining us safely through another dark night." He extinguished the first lantern. "Now disperse the darkness of our hearts"–the second lantern was doused–"with the rising sun of Your glory." Smoke curled upward from the third lantern, flame now gone. "Let the light of Your everlasting day flood our land." The fourth light disappeared, leaving one flickering flame. The snuffer hovered over the central flame. "We await Your Illumination." Every light in the room was extinguished, plunging us into deeper gloom and silence.

The sun would rise. It always did. Yet I waited with my full attention on the eastern window. *I await Your Illumination, I await Your Illum*–my breath caught. The sun peered over the horizon, stretching long rays of light into the sanctuary. *Thank You for sending Effulgence.*

The radiance grew stronger and brighter, warming the white stone to a golden hue, and voices once again rang out in familiar words of praise.

All praise be to Sustainer
Who gives us life, Who gives us light,
Who will illuminate our darkest night.
Shadows will flee, and darkness surely die.
Lift up your heads; salvation's nigh.
To Sustainer be all praise.

This time I joined in, my heart stretching, yearning, pleading with a longing I couldn't articulate. For as good as my life was, moments like these accentuated a hollowness deep within me, a desire for something more.

The final echo died, and the kodesh filed out. It was time

for us to go as well; the Quest waited on no one. Elder Reuven met us at the front gate.

Estelle bowed. "Thank you for encouraging us to attend. While I can't speak for the others, the time was the refreshment I needed, to remind me of what is important."

"Thank Sustainer Who brought you here at the right time. However, you were seeking entrance into the Scriptorium. Shall we?" He guided us across the street, and soon he left us standing in the Revival Gallery before the scroll of Naviv Dov.

For a moment, I stared at the parchment stretched out under glass. Some came to the Scriptorium to admire the vaulted ceilings with their ornate frescoes or to examine the elaborate paintings and tapestries or to study the floor's mosaics, so intricate that a magnifying glass was required to see all the details therein. For me, these were a pretty casing for the true gems of the Scriptorium: the scrolls and books.

We divided the scroll into three sections, with Mascad and Rivka taking the head, Jamarde and Estelle examining the middle, and Xander and me studying the tail. I pressed my fingertips to the glass case, my hands aching to touch the words that I might hear the author's voice, might glimpse what the writer saw that inspired the beauty unfurled before me. For every letter was formed with precision as the flourishes connected letters into words and interlocked word with word, sometimes to those beside each other, sometimes to those above and below. Shifts in coloration highlighted certain words and phrases. Delicate swirls adorned the edges, some of which were made out of more words. Pictures and symbols filled the margins, decorated transitions, and wove among the words themselves. No wasted strokes, each mark intentional and significant, subtly hinting at the text's full meaning.

"What enchants you so?" Xander murmured.

"The nuances, the precision, the layers–no matter how often I visit or how long I linger over a particular text, there's always more to discover. At Sustainer's direction alone could anything be this perfectly nuanced. It's simple enough that a first-year student can grasp its basic truth, but complex enough that a lifetime of study would never uncover all the layers contained within. An inexhaustible trove of treasure."

I felt more than saw Xander's furrowed brow. "Are you saying all these flourishes mean something? I thought just the words were important."

"On the contrary." I pursed my lips scanning for a simple example. "Look at this line: 'He shall come with humble majesty.' At first, it appears *He* means the previous man, King Bahrain, but see how *He* interlinks with *Light*? That shows *He* refers to the Light."

"That's how they know the prophecy refers to Effulgence!"

My gaze darted to him. Only Tipherets referred to Sustainer's Light as Effulgence.

Beside me, Estelle shifted. "Perhaps we can save the lecture for another time? We are on a deadline here."

Xander sighed. "She's right, but I would love to continue this conversation later."

"That truly would be my pleasure." I moved to the next section, hunting for anything tied to a key or a mask.

I found nothing. Neither did Xander, Mascad, Rivka, or Estelle. Were we looking in the wrong place? Perhaps the animals did refer to the Forest Room as Estelle first suggested. Then Jamarde, being the slowest reader, gasped. "I found it." She peered closer. "I think."

"That's more than the rest of us." I studied the place she indicated. None of the words were related to a key or a mask, and none of the surrounding imagery was either. Then I saw it. Not a key, but a keyhole formed from the negative space between intertwining flourishes.

Estelle positioned herself on Jamarde's other side. "I read that section three times and never saw that."

"But what does it mean?" asked Jamarde.

The flourishes connected the words *look* and *ahead*. "Could it be that simple?" I lifted my head, and the empty eyes of a ritual mask stared back at me. "A key insight masked." I turned to my cousin. "Jamarde, would you do the honors? After all, you were the one who found the keyhole."

After verifying no priests were around, Jamarde removed the mask. A pouch hung on the wall. It contained incense, a silver coin, and a paper with a date.

Elder Reuven entered the hall, pausing at the sight of the pouch in our hands. "I see you have found all you needed."

"Not everything, for we are easily mislead and confused." Estelle bowed to him. "Do you have any further wisdom of Sustainer to impart to us this day?"

The priest's eyebrows rose a notch. "I have naught but breadcrumbs to offer, but what I have I give: silver seeds sown, golden grain grown." He strolled into the next gallery.

Jamarde huffed. "More riddles."

"I would be suspicious of any information spoken plainly," said Estelle. "This *is* the Quest."

Voices echoed nearby. I prodded the group in the opposite direction. "Perhaps we ought to move our examination outside. It would not serve us to give other competitors potential direction."

Mascad took a defensive position between us and the voices. "Or tempt them to take what is not theirs."

"Follow me." I led our group to the main foyer via a narrow, little-used corridor. We met no one else and escaped into sunshine.

A priest approached with a box in hand. "Gift for the poor?"

Such collectors were common enough around public buildings overseen by the kodesh, but something about this one gave me pause. My eyes went to his right arm, but he didn't wear the gold band denoting a Quest official. A regular priest.

Was it coincidence we were approached for alms so soon after being instructed to sow silver?

Jamarde held out empty hands. "With regret, we have no money with us."

"That's not entirely true." I nodded to the pouch.

Xander cocked his head. "Won't we need that for the Quest?"

"We were told to sow silver. Can you think of a better way to do that?"

Estelle withdrew the coin from the pouch. "I agree with Yosarai. 'Fruit of the generous heart / sweetness shall always impart.'" After receiving confirmation from us all, she dropped the coin into the priest's box.

He bowed to us. "Sustainer's blessing be upon you and yours." He ambled down the street toward another group approaching the Scriptorium.

I couldn't help but wonder, had we "sown" our silver unwisely? Maybe I'd misunderstood what Elder Reuven meant. Too late now. I shook my head and glanced around for our coach.

Belatedly, I realized something flew toward my head.

"Watch out!"

Xander threw his arms around Yosi and Jamarde, pushing them backward, as several objects splattered at his feet. Rotten food, thrown by a few ragtag streeters. That was all. Not assassins. Not an enemy bent on harm. A few young boys who didn't know better. But his insides were coiled like an overwound spring. He ushered the girls away from their attackers, but then halted. Of the dozen vehicles lining the street, not a single one bore the crest of the Quest, the jar spouting six streams of water.

The streeters followed, still tossing food and insults. "Be gone, Quest blighters! Lava slugs! Half bloods!"

Something struck his back, sharp, hard, and definitely not rotten food.

Massard snarled.

Xander whirled, but his bodyguard already stalked toward the four boys, each clutching small stones. Their eyes widened, and three of them backed up at Massard's approach. The fourth, the smallest of the group, held his ground.

Xander had to give the lad credit. It took a lot of nerve to brave Massard in protection mode.

Massard held out his hand. "The rock."

The boy stuck out a quivering chin. "Why should I?"

Impressive. The child could be no more than seven years.

Massard stooped to look the boy in the eye. "Because these actions are beneath a fearless warrior like yourself."

The boy gaped at him, then the small body transformed, his thin shoulders straightening with pride. "You're right, hasib gadol." He relinquished the rock to Massard.

Massard took it in his right fist and touched that fist to his left shoulder. "It takes great strength to admit you're wrong. If a strong, fearless warrior like yourself should ever wish to work with other such warriors . . ." Massard whispered something in the boy's ear.

The boy gave him a serious nod. "I will think about it."

"I hope you do." Massard walked back and glanced around. "Our coach?"

After a quick questioning of the bystanders, they found it located around the corner, their driver snoring in the sunshine. They roused him and soon were headed across the city to the Everstar Tower, the location of a battle that occurred on the date listed on the pouch's paper.

Actually, Estelle informed them, the Everstar was one of two monuments to that particular battle, but according to the scouting report of Massard and Rivka yestereve, the coteries who went to the location nearest the Scriptorium returned empty-handed. Therefore, their group aimed for the Everstar, whose lantern burned continually upon the bluffs overlooking the Hallel, one of the six Aiyn Rivers.

The morning traffic mixed with Ingathering revelers, slowing their progress to a creep. Walking would have been faster, but Xander negated the suggestion. The streeters proved that, despite the coach's slowness, it provided protection.

Rivka opened a basket she'd acquired from the kitchen before their departure and gave each of them a cold meat pie. At the first bite, Xander savored the simple heartiness of onion, garlic, meat, and potato blended together. "Thank you, Rivka. That was just what I needed to face whatever task lies ahead."

Jamarde's eyes crinkled behind her spectacles. "Your words reveal how undervalued food is. When we're busy, we sometimes treat meals as an inconvenience, something to rush through so we might resume doing the significant and the necessary. However, Sustainer created us with this need to eat. Not once a month like a winged gator or once a week like an ocean sloth, but daily. Meals are meant to be more than the simple consumption of food, more than an interruption of important work. Indeed, I believe Sustainer intended the rhythm of meals to be an important part of our day–a sacred space, even. A time to rest and be refreshed. A time to celebrate Sustainer's bounty and to share that bounty with others. A time to fellowship, to encourage, to remember, to strengthen not just the body but the spirit as well." Her eyes widened, and she ducked her head. "I beg your pardon. I didn't mean to ramble."

"No pardon necessary," Xander said. "I have never considered food from that perspective."

She lifted her face. "You don't think I'm being silly or foolish?"

"On the contrary, your passion is quite refreshing."

"Then, if I wanted to open a teahouse, you don't think that would be beneath me?"

Yosi smiled at her cousin. "With your talent for flavors and your passion for what a meal ought to be, that sounds perfect. Besides, didn't you just say a meal can be a sacred space? How can such a thing be beneath you? That sounds like a high calling to me."

Jamarde returned her smile. "I suppose it does."

Rattling and creaking filled the coach as Rivka repacked the basket. Yosi looked out the window. "Shouldn't we have reached Everstar by now?"

"Indeed, we should have." Estelle frowned. "Yet it is no surprise we haven't, for if I'm not delusional, we are traveling in the wrong direction for Everstar. Do you think he misunderstood our instructions?"

Massard's face tightened. "No." With that, he signaled for the coach to stop and hopped out. Xander bent forward to catch the ensuing conversation, but the clatter of wagons and the noise of pedestrians dulled the words beyond distinguishing. Which was perhaps for the best, since Massard's voice had taken on that threatening rumble as the coachman's responses pitched higher and higher.

Soon Massard returned, resettling between Jamarde and Yosi. "There will be no further delays." The coach lurched into motion.

"Let me guess," said Xander. "One of the other coteries bribed him?"

"Or more."

"'Greed uplifts the hand to do / deeds unimagined hitherto.'" Estelle brushed invisible crumbs from her lap. "I suppose we ought to thank Sustainer we've not had worse interference thus far."

Rivka nodded her agreement. "When I fetched our basket this morning, the kitchen menials were whispering about how two coteries had already quit the Quest."

Xander drummed his fingers against his knee. He hoped he had not made a mistake, encouraging this venture. Maybe he should have heeded Yosi and been only a spectator.

The coach stopped. Time to face their next trial. Xander gazed up at the Everstar Tower perched atop the stair-step bluff. Even now, in broad daylight, its beacon shone, ever lit in memoriam of those who lost their lives here.

Estelle turned in a slow circle. "If my memory serves me right, there's a plaque in the garden with our date inscribed upon it." She led them down a short flight of stairs to the garden at the bluff's foot, overlooking River Hallel. But as they entered, the path branched out in three directions, hedges blocking their view of the rest of the garden.

Yosi looked at Estelle. "I don't suppose you remember where the plaque was?"

Estelle shook her head.

"Then we must divide up," Xander said. After their speculations of interference, staying together seemed wiser, but time demanded they maximize their resources.

"Every pair should have one person who knows the area." Yosi nudged her cousin toward him. "Jamarde, you and Saunders take the middle. Estelle and Rivka can scour the riverfront. Mascad and I will take the bluff."

They all agreed.

"Are you ready?" Jamarde stepped to his side.

"Certainly." They started off. "Do you know what we're looking for?"

"Not exactly."

"Then this should be quite the treasure hunt, shouldn't it?"

Flaming bushes and evergreen hedges lined their pebble path, broken up with clusters of yellow-and-purple flowers, somehow both orderly and wild at the same time. So uneconomical, unlike the gardens at home, where every space had to be used fully.

Jamarde paused to examine a sign by a bench. No date. "You turn everything into something good, don't you?"

A lump swelled in his throat. That was one of the things he'd always admired about his father. "Gratitude."

Jamarde had the grace not to probe. They walked in silence through the middle of the garden, stopping to examine any place a date might be inscribed. Nothing. What if no one could find the plaque? Maybe Estelle incorrectly remembered its location. Would they have to search the entire area? He scrutinized the towering sandstone bluff. That could take hours! When they reached a locked gate, though, they had no choice but to turn around.

They were halfway back to the entrance when a cry of pain rent the air, followed by a shout. "Let me go!" That sounded like Rivka.

He and Jamarde broke into a sprint. What kind of trouble had the girls run into? Xander lengthened his stride. If any real harm had come to them . . . *Sustainer, let them be fine!* Jamarde trailed behind him. Dare he leave her? But who knew what additional dangers lurked around the corner? He slackened his pace so she could catch up, and they reached the entrance as a trio of men barreled by. One saluted Xander. "Thanks for the help, Eghead." A scrap of paper flapped in his hand.

Xander barreled after him, but another cry for help ended his pursuit. That one sounded like Estelle. He redirected his course along the waterfront path, Jamarde huffing at his side. The hedge ended, providing a clear view of the bluff's edge, the fast-moving river rumbling below. Massard and Yosi raced toward them from the other end of the path. To his left, Estelle struggled against her sash. Someone had used it to bind her to a thorn bush, and several scratches marred her hands and arms. And Rivka–where was Rivka?

"What happened?" Xander fumbled with the knots binding Estelle. Did every thorn have to snag the fabric?

Her eyes flashed. "A bunch of ruffians stole our clue, bound me here, and dumped Rivka over there." She pointed to the fence along the bluff edge.

"Dumped?" Jamarde's voice pitched upward. Massard swore. Xander abandoned his attempt to help Estelle as they all bolted to the fence. Dark, rushing waters roiled below. Not a log or rock jutted out, nothing to grab onto. Did Yosi's maid know how to swim? Xander leaned over the top rail. Maybe he should just dive in here.

"Whenever you're done gawking, will you please find a way to get me back up there?"

At Rivka's voice, Xander's gaze plunged to a narrow ledge beneath them. Rivka glared up at him. She was fine. She wasn't drowning somewhere downstream, Effulgence be praised.

Massard started to climb over the fence, but Xander stopped him. It was too far down, and there wasn't sufficient ledge to support them both, even if the fickle sandstone could handle the weight of two. There had to be a safer way. His eyes traced the scene, his mind diagramming as he went. He shrugged out of the vest over his kurta. "Mascad, free Estelle and bring me the sash."

When he did, Xander threaded the sash through the armholes of his vest and knotted it. Then he tossed the vest to Rivka. "Put this on and be sure to button it." He glanced at his bodyguard. "Be ready to grab her." Then he, with the help of the others, pulled Rivka upward, hand over hand, edging her along the cliff face, knocking small rocks loose and sending them tumbling into the dark waters below.

Rivka's head cleared the bottom rung of the fence. Massard

swung her up and over onto solid land. "Are you well, sibah? Did they hurt you?"

Rivka snorted. "A jelly squid has more spine than they do."

"Aren't jelly squids invertebrates?" Xander accepted his vest from her and unknotted the sash.

"Exactly."

Laughing, Estelle retied her sash. "It took three of them to wrangle her over the edge, and she gave each of them a reminder of their efforts."

"That would explain the scratches." Xander finished buttoning his vest. "But you are sure you're both well?"

"Nothing that reaching the prize first won't cure," bit out Rivka.

Yosi examined Estelle's scratches. "Nothing looks deep, and the bleeding has stopped. Do you remember what the next clue said, or do we need to retrieve another one?"

"Dalem Mesoni." Estelle plucked a twig from her braid.

The name seemed familiar. "Do you mean Alef Mesoni?"

"He wasn't an alef then. The battle he won here is what started his rise through the ranks. The question is where do we find *Dalem* Mesoni, instead of Alef Mesoni?"

Jamarde's eyes squinched behind her spectacles. "Memorial Hall?"

"Good suggestion." Estelle led them out of the garden and toward a stairway that zigzagged up the bluff to the tower itself and the museum attached to its base.

A man wearing fine clothes inclined against a pillar, idly swinging an ebony-and-silver cane. "I pity those who take a long path when a shorter route is to be had."

Xander's gait hitched at the man's tone. Bored disinterest propelled the words, but an underlying hum spoke of a second engine–a taunt or perhaps a dare. Another swing of the cane caused a gold band to peek out from the folds of his puffy sleeve. A Quest official? He glanced at Yosi.

Trickster, she mouthed.

He had read about those when researching the Quest. Tricksters, despite their name, weren't bad. Just unpredictable. And potentially vengeful. Engage them at your own risk–and ignore them to your peril.

Which was the greater danger in this case? The man swung his cane from side to side, his face pleasantly neutral. No one had come to Rivka's or Estelle's aid when they were ambushed. Why would a trickster help them now? Xander ushered the girls by. As he did, derision curled the trickster's lips.

Xander turned his head. "It is a pity to waste time, hasib, but some lessons can be learned only through the long path, which will save much grief and even time in the end."

The trickster straightened, spinning his cane into the air before catching it, its tip pointed at Xander's chest, causing Massard to edge forward. "What would you know about long paths and time?"

A jab at his Egdonian heritage and his people's reputation for always being in a hurry. "Every inventor knows the first solution is rarely the right one."

The trickster dropped the cane back to his side. "Come, walk with me." He brushed past them without waiting to see if they would accept his invitation.

Was the trickster testing him–or delaying their group? Another coterie descended the stairs. He hurried after the trickster, who might mean them ill but, per the code of the Quest, would do them no bodily harm. The others must have thought the same, for they followed without a word of protest.

His cane swinging with pendulum precision, the trickster ambled back into the gardens, taking the middle path he and Jamarde had explored. "You have not asked where we are going nor why."

Xander matched the man's pace. "When I joined you, it was in the faith you had a purpose for this excursion."

"And if your faith is misplaced?"

"Then I will learn from my mistake, making this time well spent."

"Even if it costs you the Quest?" They reached the locked gate at the garden's end.

"Not all successes can be measured in prizes and ranking."

"Well-spoken, son of the northern waters, and the faith of even the least is not despised." He unlocked the gate and indicated they should enter.

A trap . . . or a shortcut? Hedges taller than a man lined both sides of the path, which curled out of sight after a dozen paces. Go forward or retreat?

He glanced at the others, who shrugged. This decision was his. But they had come this far, they might as well see it through. He proceeded down the narrow path that spiraled inward with no obvious exits. The path terminated in a circle of benches around a fire pit.

So much for a shortcut. Xander strode back the way they had come. If they hurried, they could regain lost time.

But as the gate came into view, it banged shut, the lock clicking into place.

"Wait!" Jamarde darted forward and rattled the door. "Let us out of here!"

The trickster twirled the key on his finger. "Why should I? What do you have to offer me?"

A punch to the nose was what he wanted to offer. Instead, he clasped his hands behind his back. "Give us a moment to confer."

"Sure, sure. Take as long as you like. It's not as if the way out is in, or the way up is down."

Xander herded them back to the spiral's center. He slumped onto a bench as Massard prowled the edges. Xander berated himself. He'd experienced firsthand the Indeli antagonism against his people, yet he'd chosen to naively believe that a trickster, of all people, would treat them fairly.

"What do we do now?" Jamarde perched beside him. "It's not like we have anything to give him. Not even one coin."

Xander's jaw tightened. "Bribes are what people do to banish their problems rather than face them. We're not doing that."

"Then what do you propose? We can't sit here until he decides to let us out."

"I could try talking to him," said Estelle.

"No, if anyone should talk to him, it ought to be me." Xander rose, his earlier adrenaline gone and their short night of sleep weighing on him. "As he said, it's not as if the way out is in, or the way up is down."

Rivka pivoted away from him. "What if it is?" She examined the cobblestones lining the edge of the circle. "Many elite mahals want their menials unseen. From the kitchen, a server would use an underground tunnel to reach a garden pavilion, and to leave a bedroom, a maid would exit through the inner room. You must go in to go out, and down to go up. Like this." Rivka stepped on a stone with a carved marking.

A low rumble mixed with a clanking of gears. Then part of the hedge slid backward to reveal an underground staircase, well-lit with lanterns.

Jamarde cheered. Massard rumbled, "Remarkable," making Rivka's eyes sparkle.

They descended to a damp tunnel, which led to a circular stairway that curved upward. Within minutes of Rivka's discovery, they emerged onto the Everstar's enclosed upper deck, panoramic vistas of Kolchan in every direction. Xander leaned against the rail. Below him, two coteries wandered among a row of statues, while a third waved away the trickster.

Yosi joined him. "Congratulations, hasib. Your answers must have pleased the trickster, for we have bypassed many troubles and reached the conclusion by a shorter way than following the written clues."

She thought he'd done well? "But I didn't solve the riddle. Rivka did. I'd been ready to return and grovel."

"You were ready to take responsibility for your actions. A great leader is not one who makes no mistakes. A great man owns his mistakes, even at the risk of losing reputation." She rested a hand atop his arm. "Like your father, perhaps?"

His throat tightened, memories washing over him. How small and alone he'd felt that first day he walked into the palace. Big. Intimidating. Nothing like the two-room flat he'd shared with his mother. It might have been small and smelled of mold from the steam heat that worked only part of the time, but it was home, and he wanted nothing more than to wake up in the bedroom with his mother banging the stove, trying to make it work long enough to cook breakfast.

But his mother would never wake him up again, and he was being told the king was his father. A man who could have thrown him out or made him disappear. That was what his grandfather would have done, and it was, he found out later, what many counseled his father to do. Instead, King Rion publicly made known his indiscretions and claimed Xander as his son, raising him in the palace with all the same rights and privileges as Selucreh. It created quite a stir, and some even called for his father's abdication.

"Yes, he was a great man, though I suspect many would disagree with me after his dalliances became public." Yet if he were such a great man, why did Sustainer take him at the height of his reign? Why did he appoint the son who could never fill his position half as well?

"He made the right decision, then and now," Yosi said quietly.

Jamarde approached them, holding aloft a brown-paper

bundle she had unearthed from somewhere in the room. "We ought to learn what our next task is."

Once everyone was gathered, Jamarde unwrapped the package. Inside rested a hand mirror, another silver coin, and an envelope containing a military summons to Fortress Duyah. Apparently having proven their mental prowess, they would now have to show their bodies equal to their minds.

Of all the Quest tasks, the test of physical skills inevitably led to my downfall. Avi had trained me in all sorts of weaponry, as a proper Indeli education demanded, of course, but I hadn't excelled in any of them. As we entered the walled compound where the best of the best trained, my stomach churned. What if my inadequacy held us back?

I changed into the training linens provided for us–a cream-colored, wraparound top and loose pants–and joined the others in the adjourning antechamber, my steps wobbly. *Breathe, just breathe. Everything will be fine.* The fabric of my top chafed my skin, much like my imagination against my nerves. How would they choose to test our physical prowess? Training drills? An obstacle course? A mock battle?

Mascad exited last from the changing room, and he advanced to the front-most spot rather than hovering in the back as had been his wont. Comfortable, confident, and eager for the challenge ahead. Everything I wasn't. Because, unlike me, he excelled in this area. During our secret practices throughout the eleven days between registration and the opening ceremony, he established himself as a master of every weapon, as one impromptu session proved. He stopped a three-sided attack with nothing more than a rug, an old horseshoe, and a pomerquat fruit. Not exactly merchant skills.

With all of us now assembled, we bypassed six closed doors to approach the stern woman standing at the far end of the room, her sky-blue linens of a military trainer a colorful contrast to the whitewashed walls and plank flooring. The sapphire cords on her shoulder announced her rank as dalem, while the gold armband marked her as a Quest official. "Welcome, Questers. You have heard the summons and answered. Now your prize lies before you." She placed her hand atop a wooden box on a table. "Are you worthy of such a prize?"

Now there was a question with no good answer. If we answered yes, we'd appear arrogant and boastful, thus proving ourselves unworthy. If we said no, then why should they give us the box?

Mascad bowed to the dalem. "Our worthiness is not for us to judge but for you to determine."

A hint of a smile graced the woman's lips. "Spoken with wisdom, and with wisdom comes opportunity. For this task, you will compete one-on-one with another coterie in six contests of skill. The coterie who scores the most points overall leaves with the box. The coterie who loses must compete against the next to arrive."

I swallowed hard. If I failed here, such a delay could well lose us the entire Quest, especially with three tasks remaining.

"Since you answered wisely, however," continued the dalem, "I shall reveal what awaits you. Today you will face knife throwing, hand-to-hand combat, archery, shooting, running, and climbing." She pointed to a closed door with each skill named. "Select your contest."

Most of the choices were obvious. Mascad was built for hand-to-hand combat. Rivka's years as a menial made her fleet-footed. Estelle held the Academy's record for knife throwing. Xander had proven able to hit almost any target with any gun we provided him during our pre-Quest group practices. But neither Jamarde nor I excelled at anything.

"What should we do?" My cousin twisted her hands, her nerves mirroring my own.

"We compete to the best of our ability, and we trust the others to do the same." I forced my voice to remain level, for my sake as much as for hers.

"And if that's not enough?"

"We will handle that problem when we have that problem to handle. Now, do you prefer archery or climbing?"

"You're letting me choose?"

"You've had fewer opportunities to train, and you'll perform better if you're comfortable with the choice."

Jamarde thought for a moment. "Would it be fine if I choose climbing?"

"Of course." I nodded at the appropriate door. "Do your best; that is all we ask." I advanced to the archery room, my own hands trembling. Which was in no way comforting, since I was a mediocre shot with steady hands.

Mascad, standing at the door to my left, tapped his head. "Fight smarter, not harder, sibah."

The dalem surveyed us. "Choices made?" At our assent, she declared, "You may enter."

The room beyond resembled a forest. Stuffed birds flew suspended from the ceiling. Animals hid among fake vegetation. A fabric mural draping the walls provided additional targets.

Fight smarter, not harder. That meant absorbing as many details as I could, for if I knew where to find my targets, I would have more time to aim. I wended my way to a central dais stocked with two bows and quivers of arrows. From the other side emerged another Quest official and a tall, strapping young man.

I stopped short, my hands shaking harder. I would be competing against Yonath, the best archer at the Academy. *Sustainer, please help?*

Reaching the dais first, Yonath had his guard strapped on

and long bow strung by the time I climbed the stairs. "We could make this very short, sibah. Cede the match to me. I'll even allot you forty points if you do."

That sounded too good to be true, which meant it probably was. "You're allowed to do that?"

"Indeed, he is." The official inserted herself between us. "In which case, he would be awarded sixty points, as a forfeit is one hundred points."

I pulled my string into place and plucked it once. Taut. Like me. I could accept Yonath's proposition. Forty points, guaranteed. Besting that score on my own merit was unlikely. Did that mean ceding was a way to fight smarter rather than harder? But I had told Jamarde to do her best; I could do nothing less. I straightened my shoulders. "I'll shoot."

Yonath shrugged. "Your loss."

"Perhaps"–I nocked my first arrow–"but I'm here to compete."

"In that case," said the official, "you have five minutes to shoot all ten animals I list. Five points will be given for every target hit and five points for the better shot. The first person to hit all ten animals will be awarded an additional ten points, while ten points will be deducted for any target you fail to hit within the allotted time."

They were the standard rules, nothing unusual. Giving the room one more sweeping glance, I nodded my understanding, knowing I had rejected my one escape from this task. Would my bravado now cost us everything?

Xander didn't know what he expected when he passed through his door, but an art exhibit wasn't it. At least, that was what the long, narrow room resembled with life-size portraits hung along the walls. However, the guns resting on tables before those paintings confirmed it was indeed a shooting gallery, not an art gallery.

Two men walked through an adjourning door, one wearing the blue training linens and a gold armband, the other dressed like Xander.

The competitor's face wrinkled in distaste. "Is this what the Quest attracts these days? Egdonian water roses?"

Biting back a retort, Xander extended his forearm to his competitor. The past weeks had proven the enmity between their two countries ran deeper than he'd realized, and if he was honest, this man would likely be treated with the same disdain if he joined Egdon's famed water games.

The competitor bumped his forearm against Xander's, his arm slightly elevated. Though the man was forced to acknowledge Xander as an equal, he considered himself superior.

Let him think that. Such cockiness had felled more than one competitor, even when the better sportsman.

His challenger eyed him. "You know we could make this much easier for both of us."

"How so?"

"We could declare a truce and split the forfeit in half. Fifty points for you and fifty for me." The suggestion stuttered, like gears that didn't quite mesh.

Which meant something else was afoot. "A generous offer, but one I must decline as it would rob me of the tale of how I competed against an Indeli marksman."

"Then I shall endeavor to make it a tale worth telling." The man's dark eyes glinted.

The official motioned Xander toward the first table on his right, while his competitor was positioned at the first table on the left. "On each table are two weapons. Whirlwind, you will use the weapon on the left. Illuminary, use the right-hand one.

You will work up one side of the room to the far end and return on the opposite side. You have one shot per target. Your goal is to hit the deadliest place on each painting. The deadlier shot will be awarded ten points. In the case of shots of equal value, each will be awarded five points. The first shooter to finish will receive ten extra points." He retreated toward the door. "Positions, please."

Xander flattened his hands on the table in the traditional manner and studied the weapon before him. A pocket revolver. Light, quick action, but with a tendency to fire to the left.

"Begin!"

He grabbed the gun and aimed. The painting dodged to the left. His eyes widened. A moving painting! What a clever way to–

A shot jarred him. Shoot now, analyze later. He aimed again and fired–just as the painting dodged, dropping his bullet an inch to the right of where he had intended. A deadly shot but not the deadliest.

Xander barreled through his second and third targets with ease, and he snatched up the musket at the end table facing the back wall. Aim. Fire . . . oomph! His opponent bumped into him, knocking him forward into the table. A dirty trick, but an ineffective one. The shot still pierced the painting exactly where Xander intended.

His competitor muttered something under his breath as Xander switched sides. At this rate, he should overtake the other man and gain that time bonus. He squeezed the trigger of the rifle. It clicked. *What the* . . . Xander tried again. Still nothing. A fifth shot sounded. Xander grabbed the other rifle. It fired properly. Must he check every weapon? He turned the corner to the first table along the left wall. Pepperboxes. Had these been switched too? He snatched up both weapons to try at the same time. He wasn't quite as good with his left hand, but the time saved was worth the risk. The left fired. Not his best shot, but equal to his opponent's.

Based on the pattern set, Xander grabbed the left howdah before the seventh painting. The pistol clicked, empty. He bit back an oath, swapping weapons. He fired and advanced to the final table. An eighth shot rang out. He'd lost the time bonus. All because of a couple of cheap tricks. Since there was no reason to hurry now, he checked each tranter. The right one was loaded, as it should be.

Xander raised the weapon and then paused, noticing the portrait itself for the first time since the trial began. A Sarmazon warrior, his opponent's shot in his heart. Except in real life, such a shot would never have penetrated. This breastplate might look like leather, but their armor was coated with tungstanium. These bullets would never penetrate that. The single, real chink in the armor was the underarm gap. He aimed there.

His competitor snorted, but behind him the official gave a slight head dip of respect. Too bad respect didn't earn him points. Xander flexed his fingers. That time bonus should have been his. A point that could be driven home quite nicely with a right hook to the jaw.

However, his father had taught him to conduct himself better than that.

As the official examined the portraits, Xander bowed to his competitor. "Excellent shooting, hasib."

The other narrowed his eyes, as if waiting for the backhanded insult.

But though the words cost him, Xander meant them. His opponent's tricks guaranteed he gained the time bonus, but with a little extra training–and a strong dose of humility–the man could well be one of the best in the Seven Realms. "Do you shoot competitively? If you don't, you ought to consider it."

The official returned. "That was some of the finest marksmanship I've ever seen in a single competition. Six out of the eight are ties. The deadliest shot for the first portrait belongs to Whirlwind, while the eighth's deadliest shot belongs to Illuminary."

"What?" The man's folded arms dropped to his sides. "But he missed the man's chest!"

"If that had been a real Sarmazon warrior, his armor would have stopped your bullet, little more than bruising him. Apparently your competitor was aware of that and hit one of the few vulnerable breaks in the armor."

His competitor swung around. "How in the Seven Realms could you have known that?"

Xander clasped his hands behind his back. "My people are deficient in many areas, but knowledge tends not to be one of them."

The man's hands fisted, but the official intervened. "Brawling could be grounds for forfeiture. Now let us join the others for the final scores."

Xander glanced around the gallery once more. Ingenious, really. Maybe when he returned home, he could design something similar for their military.

But had he made a fatal mistake here? While the shooting score was even, his competitor had finished first, which meant he had a ten point lead on Xander–a lead that would not exist if he had taken the forfeiture agreement. All because he naively believed this would be a fair fight, despite warnings and evidence to the contrary.

May Sustainer forgive his folly.

"Time!"

My arrow sank into the leopard hidden among the leaves of a nearby tree, and my shaking arms slacked. At least I had shot all ten animals in the time specified, thanks to my scrutiny upon entry. Most of Yonath's arrows had lodged in the more obvious but more difficult targets. While I had no expectations of winning, I didn't know if I scored more than the proffered forty. I surveyed the area, totaling scores until I reached the tiger from which Yonath's arrow protruded. My heart stopped. Had I misunderstood our target? For my arrow clipped the leg of a tiger-*spider*.

I glanced at the official, but her body language told me nothing as she led us out to the changing rooms. What other mistakes had I made? My fingers trembled as I pulled on my dress. Maybe I had been foolish to refuse Yonath's bargain.

I entered the antechamber at the same time as Yonath, who smirked at me. "You should have accepted my deal."

I lifted my chin to hide the fact I'd been wondering the same. "Perhaps, if scoring points had been my sole objective."

"What other objective could there be?"

What indeed? Then my eyes landed on Mascad at the far side of the room, and I knew what the reason was. "The ability to hold my head high because I competed to the best of my ability."

He snorted. "I should have known you'd be an idealist. You'll soon find out such thinking gets you nowhere. Not in the Quest, not in life."

Xander approached. "That's peculiar. I've always found idealists go the farthest of all, for they dare to stretch for heights the rest of us don't even realize are there." He guided me away before Yonath could retort. "How did it go?"

"Despite my bold words, I wonder if I should have accepted the forfeiture of forty points." We joined Mascad, Rivka, Estelle, and Jamarde, all in their normal attire, at the far side of the room.

"Fascinating strategy." Xander studied the other coterie gathering on the other side of the room. "It seems we were all presented varying degrees of the same. My opponent offered me a fifty-fifty split, with great pain to him."

Rivka's face flushed, her eyes ablaze. "At least your opponents made a reasonable deal."

Xander leaned closer to me. "Her opponent made the generous proposition of twenty points since she was just a menial."

I looked at my maid. "Please tell me you won."

"If they had wished to make the race a challenge, they should have added a full water bucket for each hand." Her eyes focused on some unseen point. "Did you know some Kossacan ladies practice walking with water jars on their heads to improve their postures?"

I had to laugh. "I'm glad at least one of us enjoyed some success."

"Did your contest not go well?" asked Estelle.

"I did the best I could, but I was facing Yonath."

She clicked her tongue in sympathy.

"How did the rest of you do?"

Xander's mouth flattened. "I was a naïve fool."

Before I could ask him to explain, the dalem broke away from the other officials. "I have your final results."

Both coteries stood at attention.

"Contest one: racing. Fifty points to Illuminary. Ten points to Whirlwind."

I grinned at Rivka. She didn't only win, she scorched the competition.

"Contest two: climbing. Seventy points to Whirlwind. Thirty to Illuminary."

As the other coterie cheered, Jamarde hung her head. I wrapped an arm around her shoulders. "Great job."

"I cost us our lead."

"Yet isn't that higher than your best score?"

She nodded.

"Then that's a win," said Estelle. But did the others score well enough to cover both our deficits?

"Contest three: hand-to-hand combat."

The room quieted again.

"Illuminary won two matches for forty points. Whirlwind won one match for twenty."

Xander spluttered. "You lost a match?"

Mascad shrugged a shoulder. "He was doing the best he could."

"You gave up points?" The inside of Jamarde's letters drained of their pigment.

But Rivka beamed at him. "I think that was quite noble of you."

Mascad didn't answer, but he seemed to grow taller at her praise.

"Noble indeed," I murmured, but I twisted my hands together. Did we possess enough margin for such gallant deeds?

"Contest four: knife-throwing. Illuminary, forty-nine points. Whirlwind, forty-six."

"I was a little off-balance," Estelle said to me.

"You still won the most points. We don't have to win by much."

"Contest five: archery."

My pulse pounded in my ears.

"Whirlwind, eighty points. Illuminary, sixty-five."

My breath caught. How had I managed that? That was twenty-five more points than I'd been offered, leaving us in the lead. My lungs expanded fully for the first time since entering the fortress.

Yonath stalked forward. "That's not possible. I should have had at least a hundred points!"

My gaze darted to the officials. Was he right? Had a mistake been made?

The archery official bowed to him. "Maybe if there had been eleven targets, hasib."

"Pardon me?"

"You shot a tiger and a spider but missed the tiger-spider. That gave you the better shot for nine targets, for ninety points, but by failing to hit a tiger-spider, you lost ten points. Your worthy opponent, on the other hand, hit all ten targets, and since you failed to hit a tiger-spider at all, she received the points as the better shot for that target. She also earned the time bonus for being the first, and in this case, the only archer to hit all named targets."

Jamarde was bouncing on her toes by the time the official finished. Yonath shrank back to his coterie. I had done it. *We* had done it. We would win.

"Contest six: shooting."

Xander fisted his hands. "You tried to warn me."

What?

"Whirlwind, fifty points. Illuminary, forty."

I blinked. We lost? Sure enough, at the final tally we were two points short. Less than the five points for a better shot. That was all I'd needed. To hit just one target better than Yonath. My throat tightened as Whirlwind cheered. How long would we have to wait for the next coterie?

"Hold on." The dalem held up her hand. "We have one final announcement. For these contests test one's skill, yes, but they also test the coteries' character. During this final contest, the official observed how the competitor from Whirlwind switched weapons on Illuminary."

So much tension electrified the room that any illustration of the scene would need to include tiny sparks floating in the air.

"Therefore, after consulting with the other officials, we have decided to issue a five-point penalty, making the final scores 274 for Illuminary, 271 for Whirlwind."

Shouts erupted from Whirlwind, but the dalem handed us

the box from the table. "Well done. You have shown yourselves worthy of this."

My muscles uncoiled. We wouldn't be trapped here. We wouldn't have to compete again. Xander bowed. "Thank you for finding us worthy."

We clustered around the box. The wood shone warmly, the carved scrollwork displaying rich layered hues. The lid was inlaid with squares of varying shades of brown–with one piece missing.

I traced the corner left empty. "A puzzler."

Suddenly, Mascad shoved past us, just in time to block a wild swing intended for Xander, who spun to the side.

The attacker snarled and threw a flurry of punches, but the Quest officials made no move to stop the brawl. Somebody needed to do something! But Mascad countered every strike with ease, shielding Xander with every move. Like a bodyguard. How had I missed the connection all this time? Of course, the crown prince would travel with a bodyguard.

The attacker crumpled to his knees, red-faced and panting, held in restraint by an arm hitched painfully high.

"No control of emotions, no control of body. Fighting with no control is worse than fighting blind." Mascad pushed the man away and shepherded us toward the exit. "Let's go."

"That's right, run while you can. Because this isn't over." The attacker coughed, still trying to regain his breath. "Do you hear? This isn't over you–"

The door muffled whatever foul names ensued.

I lagged behind to walk beside Mascad. "Thank you for what you did back there."

"I was doing my job."

"I know."

He glanced at me askance. Let him wonder if I knew as much as my words indicated.

Ahead of us, my maid rattled off some obscure fact about

Sarmazon training regimens. I chuckled. “Sometimes Rivka seems scattered, but I think that shows how intelligent she is. I can’t imagine how else she could maintain as many details as she does without losing a single one, while also being aware of connections no one else notices.”

Mascad’s gaze alighted upon my maid. “The man who cannot see her intelligence has none of his own.” His block-letter script, while as rough-edged as usual, carried a light halo around the edges this time. Now that would be an interesting development worth watching.

Reaching the coach, we settled into our seats, but Mascad remained outside, staring across the street. Had he spotted danger? I craned my neck for a better view. No, not danger. A flower woman was trying to sell half-wilted flowers to passersby hurrying home for the second night of the festival. Behind her, huddled against the building, was a little boy, his arm wrapped around a younger girl.

The others must have noticed too, for Rivka took out the remainders of our lunch from the basket, then glanced around, her hands full. The basket was not ours to give away.

I presented my caplet. “Perhaps she can cut it down for a coat for the little girl.”

That prompted the donation of Xander’s vest and Estelle’s sash, and soon the bundle of food and clothing had been prepared.

“Wait.” Jamarde pulled out the silver coin from our second task, then hesitated. “That is, if you don’t mind.”

“I can’t think of a better sowing.” Estelle passed the coin to my maid.

Rivka climbed out, touched Mascad’s arm, and together they walked to the flower woman. She tried to reject the gift, but Mascad persisted, and at last she exchanged a large bouquet of flowers for our bundle. Mascad then presented the flowers to Rivka with a deep Egdonian bow before they returned to us.

As the coach jolted into motion, Mascad released a deep breath. "My deepest gratitude to you all."

His words bled such raw and deep emotion, they demanded the respect of silent acceptance, a potent reminder that as much as we wished to final, some things were more important.

How could good fortune turn to ill fortune in the space of a bell?

The judge's presence in the capital for a religious festival provided the perfect opportunity to invite him to a dinner at the Chancellor's Palace without raising suspicions. I'd ask a few questions and mark him off my list.

But as his last question about my recent travels as a member of Parliment hung in the air, uneasiness mixed with the kerala fish in my stomach.

Is it common for parlies to frequent areas outside their districts?

A benign question–except, why would a country judge even know the obscure locations I'd listed, much less that they weren't in my district? I sipped my wine before bestowing a smile on him. "Not for all parlies, of course, but I feel an obligation to work for the benefit of the whole country, and how can I do that if I never visit places outside my district?"

"Quite true, and an example worth emulating. Maybe someday others will follow your lead."

I hoped not. The last thing I needed was some young idealist nosing around my district. I lifted my glass to him as if to affirm his words.

The judge's gaze snagged on my hand. "That is a unique ring. I don't think I've ever seen anything quite like it."

"A family heirloom. One of only a dozen that exist, I'm told.

Something about snow quartz being difficult to cut without it crumbling."

That piqued the interest of the politico on my other side, effectively moving the conversation into safer waters. Nonetheless, the judge's thoughtful gaze rested upon me several more times throughout the evening. Although I doubted he was involved with whatever secret agenda the prince was pursuing in Indel, the judge would need close watching.

For unearthing other's secrets aided me only as long as mine stayed buried.

How ought one measure success? Does it reside in who knows your name? Or in the number of people you influence? Perhaps success has a price attached, measured by the weight of gold or the expense of one's possessions. Or maybe it's something simpler–a position obtained, a skill acquired, a quality exceeded, a milestone reached.

And therein lays the conundrum. Success is all these things and none of them, slippery and malleable, able to be fashioned into any shape or form desired. Changeable. Unique. An ever-moving target.

So the question ought not to be, "What is success?" Rather, we each should ask, "What does Sustainer desire me to aim for?"

5

Xander stared at the tiles of the box's lid. The pattern was there somewhere. Like an idea he knew would work, but the design remained elusive. Usually, he would walk away for a few days–visit his half sister's family, take a boating trip, or, when desperate, make overdue social calls. Nothing like conversations about fashion and the latest bills to spark the imagination.

Xander rubbed his bleary eyes. He couldn't walk away this time. Not if they planned to reach the finals.

A door latch clicked. Yosi, a robe wrapped around her, watched him from the doorway of the girls' room.

He rolled out the knots that had worked themselves into his neck. "I thought you already had your shift."

"I could say the same about you."

"I couldn't sleep."

"That makes two of us." Yosi sat on a nearby pillow at the low table.

Following dinner, they decided they couldn't all handle the box at the same time, so they would take turns, each person working for a set amount of time while the others slept. After Xander completed the first shift, he roused Massard at the promised time. Nonetheless, a niggling that he had missed something chased away sleep.

The one time he'd dozed off, wooden tiles refused to stay where he put them, shifting back to their original places or bounding off the board completely. That left him to explain to Yosi why tiles were missing and that they needed to return to the fortress to earn another box, when Selucreh swooped in with an open box and walked off with Yosi on his arm. There was no sleeping after that nightmare. So, he'd relieved Jamarde of her shift early. The poor girl was half asleep anyway.

"Any progress?" asked Yosi.

Xander shook his head and pushed the box toward her. The key to the puzzle continued to elude him. If only he could figure out what he was overlooking, everything else would lock into place. Literally. He was certain of it.

Yosi's fingers rearranged a few tiles, paused, then moved them back to their original positions. He rubbed his eyes again. "I keep thinking I'm overlooking something."

She worked the open spot to the opposite corner. "Or perhaps we are asking the wrong question?" She upended the box, her fingers tracing the scrollwork.

"What question should we ask, then?"

"How we should be looking at the puzzle." She examined the box's other edges. "As my art teacher reminded me, sometimes finding the right perspective is everything." She lifted the box to eye level and squinted across the lid, as if looking for a message there.

"What's that?" Xander pointed at the bottom.

Yosi overturned the box. Four squares were carved into the corners, with another one etched in the center. Xander fingered an indent. That felt familiar, like . . . His mind clicked, and the solution diagrammed itself before him. Simple, obvious, genius. "I have it." He grabbed the pick from the nut bowl and pried from the lid the four brown pieces which matched the color of the bottom's wood.

"What are you doing?" asked Yosi, leaning nearer.

"Watch." He placed the four tiles in the bottom's indents, triggering a soft click. Part one down, one to go. He turned the box upright again, the lid now having five holes to match the five squares on the bottom. Xander's fingers flew, and sure enough, each time he opened a corner space, a tile-sized piece of wood sprang into place. With the four corners filled, Xander took a deep breath. If this didn't work, he didn't know what would. He cleared the center spot.

A fifth, spring-loaded tile popped up, locking the tiles in place, unlocking the lid.

Yosi clapped her hands together with a cheer.

Massard charged out of the bedroom, revolver in hand. From the girls' bedroom stumbled a yawning Estelle, a half-awake Rivka, and Jamarde, spectacles askew.

Xander grinned at his bodyguard. "That was a cry of victory, not threat, Massard."

"So I see, *Saunders*." Massard slid his gun away.

His alias rang overloud, a bell struck by a too-tight hammer. Oh, nuts and bolts. He'd used Massard's real name. Had any of the ladies noticed? They all clustered over the box as Yosi lifted the lid. Saved by sleep deprivation and distraction. He suppressed a yawn, then shook himself. "What task is next?"

Yosi set aside another silver coin and a set of eating utensils before holding up a gilded invitation. "Sibah Veli's."

Please, let his ears not be working right. Let fatigue be taking its toll. But the name on the invitation did not change. The name that gushed from the tongue of every ambassador and diplomat, whether from or to Indel. The name of Kolchan's most famous teahouse. Xander tottered to his feet. Puzzles he could solve. Mechanical problems he could fix. But how did one unravel the mysteries of Indeli customs?

Be still, my heart. Cease your striving, my soul. For Sustainer rules over all, and all will exalt Him in the end.

I repeated the Writings over and over, but my heart pounded as we approached Sibah Veli's. I had never dined here–none of us had–but one did not have to circulate long among Kolchan's elite to hear the stories. Of guests' barred entrance due to inappropriate attire despite reservations gained months in advance and at great cost. Of diners being expelled for using the wrong fork. Of menials being dismissed for serving tea two degrees too cold.

So for hours we fussed over our appearances. I scrubbed my fingers with five different soaps, trying to remove all remnants of ink. Rivka had Estelle, Jamarde, and me try on every outfit we'd packed to find the "perfect" dress. Hair was styled and re-styled and styled once more. By the time we climbed into our coach, it was late morning, and I was ready for a nap. Why would anyone want to become a politico and endure this every day? It was truly incomprehensible.

As the coach rumbled past the towering dense hedge that enclosed the entire property in mystery and exclusivity, silence gripped us all. *Be still, my heart.* I had never fainted or experienced vapors before, but my body considered the possibility now. *Cease your striving, my soul.* Across from me, Estelle held herself rigidly while Rivka's skin had paled to a sickly sheen. *Sustainer rules over all.* Not that I could blame my maid. If I felt this terrified as a well-trained elite, how much greater must the terror be for her as a menial? I wanted to say something to encourage her, but my tongue stuck to the roof of my mouth. *All will exalt Him in the end.*

Please, let it be so.

The coach stopped before the imposing front gate, and Jamarde gaped in wonder. We all did. This was Sibah Veli's, after all.

We alighted and approached the gate as two trios. The police patrolling the wall eyed us with disdain. Because we didn't belong here; I didn't belong here. Ahead of my trio, Xander strode forward with confidence, the one person who *did* belong here. He extended our invitation to the teahouse's gatekeeper. "I believe we are expected." Though his voice lacked the haughty overtones of many politicos, it rang with an authority that commanded obedience, the strokes of his words bold and firm.

The gatekeeper straightened. "Indeed you are, hasibs, sibahs." The keeper returned the invitation with a bow and opened the gate. "Enjoy your time."

"We intend to." Xander led us into the broad archway, glass mosaics beneath us, a thick hedge on either side, and a trellis above, its autumnal ivy surrounding us with golden light.

Reverent quiet curled among us like the flourish around an illuminated capital. We were entering another world separate from the one left behind. Or so it seemed as our path wound around almost the entire perimeter of the property. Eventually an archway released us to the area beyond, which resembled a lavish garden party more than a teahouse. For instead of the traditional tiered building with indoor and outdoor seating, a covered breezeway lined three of the edges, with adjoining patios set with intimate tables for two and three.

Beyond that, various gazeboes, each unique, connected to the breezeways with colorful paths of crushed shells, providing shelter for larger groups. In the very center was a round dancing floor, its pergola hung with flowering vines and lanterns for evening parties. A raised dais in the middle boasted a lone harpist, playing soft lyrical music that made the air shimmer.

A cream liveried menial guided us to a gazebo at the far

side, where an imposing woman in a lavish sari stood with rigid precision, a ruling matriarch with whom no one dared trifle. Even the white streaking her dark hair, pulled back into a severe bun, added no grandmotherly softness, but commanded respect for her greater years. "Welcome, Illuminary." She stacked her right arm atop her left and bowed.

I returned the greeting in coordination with the others, even as colors bled from the world around me. The invitation had been generic, and we'd volunteered no information. How had she known which coterie had arrived?

"I am Sibah Veli, and I welcome you to my teahouse. Come, let us dine." She gestured to the table set for seven behind her.

The owner of the teahouse was hosting us? My fingers clenched at the folds of my skirt. No fault would be overlooked, no quarter for error provided. *Be still, my heart. Be still. Please, be still.* I circled the table in search of my place card. I was seated beside Sibah Veli on the right side. Who, then, was acting as hostess?

Rivka froze at the head of the table, and Sibah Veli cocked her head. "Is something wrong, siv?"

They made my menial maid hostess? Dozens of details swarmed my mind, things we hadn't talked about, protocols and customs we'd failed to cover–things I'd never imagined her needing to know. How could we ever hope to complete this task unscathed?

Rivka drew a shaky breath. "I am merely surprised by the great honor bestowed upon me, sibah gadolah."

With Mascad's aid, Rivka lowered herself upon the fat cushion, then beckoned us with the formal words of invitation. "Do me the honor of joining me."

Mascad turned to Sibah Veli as she glided to her place of honor at Rivka's right. "May I?"

"You may." She lowered herself with such grace, it was as if she floated down upon a cloud of satin. My own descent, despite Mascad's aid, was more of a stutter-plop. Meanwhile, Xander aided Jamarde and Estelle before taking his seat at Rivka's left and across from Sibah Veli, where she would be able to spot the slightest faux pas.

Everyone looked toward Rivka. Her chin trembled. She didn't remember what to do next, and the slight sniff from Sibah Veli told me she was aware of it too.

Xander inclined his head to Rivka. "I believe we are all comfortably settled, siv, and you may ring for luncheon without concern."

Sustainer's blessing upon Xander for his not-so-subtle hint. But Rivka still hesitated–there was not one bell but four of increasing sizes. A protocol I hadn't bothered teaching her, as no one used multiple bells, save the wealthiest of homes for lavish dinner parties. I raised a hand to indicate the correct bell just as Sibah Veli turned toward me. I smoothed down an imaginary wrinkle in the tablecloth instead.

Estelle spoke up. "Those crystal bells are gorgeous! They look similar to the rose-glass ones the Gaddans used for their dinner parties to summon the menials."

Of course! While Rivka had never hosted a dinner party, she had served a few. She closed her eyes, then rang the second to the smallest bell. Menials appeared seemingly from nowhere, setting a salad before each of us.

As Xander placed a forkful of lettuce into his mouth, Sibah Veli smiled at him. "What brought you to Indel, hasib, if I may ask?"

He didn't dare talk with his mouth full, which would create an awkward pause while he chewed. I jumped in. "Sibah Chiman, would you pass me the salt bowl, if you please?"

"Of course."

My request provided Xander sufficient time to swallow. "I am here to study your beautiful art, sibah gadolah."

"As a hobby, I suppose."

Xander hesitated. Being a prince, that was all it could be, but he couldn't admit that. "I'm apprenticed to Hasib Drom Hadas. I can't imagine that seems much like a hobby."

Truthful, but challenging the assumption. An answer worthy of a politico, something I kept forgetting Xander was.

Sibah Veli raised an eyebrow. "Drom the Mouncite? I was unaware that reclusive tinkerer even took apprentices."

"Sibah Patican graciously provided me with an introduction, and he granted me work," Xander replied. "I assure you, no one was more surprised than I. That such a genius would have time or energy to apprentice anyone is astonishing. I hope Egdon will be blessed someday with a person possessing even half of Hasib Hadas's skill."

A well-worded response worthy of the chancellor himself. If she dared to insult Drom further, Indel would lose status in a foreigner's eyes. Not good manners.

Rivka rang the lowest bell. The salads were whisked away and replaced with cups of fruit soup. I filled a spoonful, then noticed Jamarde's hesitation. One glance at my bowl showed majica floated in the soup.

The matron bestowed a patronizing smile. "Does the soup not meet your expectation, Sibah Chiman?"

Jamarde shifted. "I am sure it tastes wonderful, sibah gadolah."

"Yet you do not eat."

Jamarde moistened her lips. The perfect defense wrote out itself, but I erased it before I could speak it, as that would be a breach of etiquette since I was not the one addressed. I swirled my spoon, cursing the rules.

"If my reluctance gave that impression, I beg your pardon." My cousin's every word was outlined with deliberateness. "It is not because I do not wish to eat it, but because I cannot."

Rivka intervened. "It is we who should be begging your

pardon, Sibah Chiman, for it was inconsiderate of us to serve what you cannot eat." She rang the third bell.

I hid a smile behind my napkin. Like a good hostess, Rivka took responsibility, but her words were a clear chastisement to the one who had set the menu. Sibah Veli inclined her head, acknowledging Rivka's handling of the situation.

A menial replaced my soup with the entrée of braised lamb and roasted vegetables. The plate tipped, food sliding into my lap.

The menial paled. "Oh, sibah, I beg your pardon. It was an accident. Please, forgive me." She tried to scoop the meat onto the plate and sop up the sauce.

Of all the stupid accidents. And after all the work we had done to prepare, my sari was an absolute mess of a disaster. We would have no choice but to–

Cease striving, my soul.

Be still.

I drew a breath. It was only an accident. She hadn't intended to dump food on me. Unless she'd been ordered to as part of the trial. Either way, I could hardly scold or blame her. I stilled her hands. "No harm has been done. Both my clothing and I can easily be cleaned."

"That might be, but clumsiness is unacceptable in an establishment such as this." Icicles clung to Sibah Veli's words. "Consider this your dismissal. Return to the kitchen and gather your things."

"Yes, sibah gadolah." The menial fled the garden on the verge of tears. I pursed my lips. Dismissal was both unnecessary and unfair.

"I beg your pardon, Sibah Patican," said Sibah Veli. "I can assure you it will never happen again."

I clenched my hands around my napkin. "We should not promise what we cannot keep."

"I beg your pardon?"

I dabbed at my ruined skirt. Was she trying to goad me into breaking social protocols because of my relationship with Rivka? *Sustainer, grant me Your wisdom.* "No matter how many precautions are taken or how much training is given, accidents happen. That is the nature of the world we live in."

"I suppose you feel I was too harsh."

I rubbed harder at the stain, which only made it worse. "I . . . feel we ought to extend the same grace we would wish to receive should our positions be reversed."

"You have plans to become a menial?"

"Of course not, sibah gadolah, but neither should I presume the privileges I have today will always be mine to enjoy."

She regarded me. "Are you saying wrongdoing ought not be punished?"

"Not at all." I leaned back to allow another menial to set a new entrée in front of me, using the extra time to formulate my words. "I'm merely saying intentional wrongdoing, wrongdoing due to negligence, and wrongdoing by accident should not be treated as the same crime."

Sibah Veli dabbed at her mouth with a napkin before tucking it under the edge of her plate, indicating her impending departure. Was that a good sign or a bad one? "Sibah Patican, your father's reputation as a judge of wisdom and fairness is well-known throughout Indel. I've never had the privilege of meeting him, but if your answers are representative of his character, then the reputation is well deserved." She rose, motioning for the rest of us to stay seated. "Please excuse me. I believe I have a wrong to rectify. Enjoy the rest of your meal."

She glided away in the same direction as the distraught menial. No one else loitered nearby, so we had the garden to ourselves.

"Is your dress very much ruined?" Jamarde asked.

I brushed away her concern. "It can be cleaned, but we will have to return to the mahal before the next task." Precious minutes lost, but there was nothing to be done for it now. I smiled at Rivka. "However, we couldn't have had a better hostess."

"Indeed," seconded Mascad. "Your actions would complement even a royal house."

Rivka reddened, then dipped her face. "You are generous in your praise, hasib."

We finished our entrées with companionable chatter. It was amazing how much better the meal tasted now. "No wonder the Writings of the Scribes say the porridge of friendship sates better than a feast among enemies."

Rivka reached for the final bell, then hesitated. "Maybe one of you should–"

"Absolutely not. You are the hostess, after all."

She sat a little straighter and rang the highest bell.

Sibah Veli herself appeared, carrying a smile and a lidded basket. "My commendations to you, noble Questers. You have conducted yourselves today with gentility, handling insult with grace, accusation with wisdom, hostility with kindness. May you find your reward sweet indeed." Then she retreated once again. Somehow we had passed the task. Sustainer truly did rule over all. May all exalt Him in the end.

We lifted the lid. Nestled among the individually wrapped candies and chocolates was a bag with another coin, a small jar containing a red spice, and six tickets. Xander pulled one out, then dropped it as if were molten rock.

I withdrew a second stubby strip and skimmed its fancy script. It was a ticket for the Teardrop Theatre. Not a terrifying place to visit, unless you were presenting a proposal to the entire Council there. My breath caught. The Teardrop Theatre stood at the center of Council Hall. That was the one place in Indel where Xander would most likely be recognized, especially with the visiting diplomats from Egdon wandering around. No wonder Xander blanched.

We would need to find a way to protect him. The question was how. Leaving him behind would probably disqualify us from the next task. Waiting for empty halls before summoning him could take more time than we had. I developed and discarded various plans during our departure from Sibah Veli's and our return to the mahal. Still no feasible idea presented itself.

Mascad unlocked the door to our room, then barked a sharp, "Stay!"

That was *not* how we had left our common room this morning. Furniture was overturned. A slashed pillow spilled its cottony insides across the floor. Scattered nuts mingled with shards of a broken vase and the crushed remains of the flowers Mascad had given Rivka. One of the tapestries hung shredded, and every ugly slur possible against Egdonians, Mouncites, mixers, and menials was scrawled across the walls.

Mascad prowled through the room, weapon in hand. Had he carried that gun the entire Quest? He poked around the mess briefly before disappearing into the bedrooms beyond. After several agonizing minutes, he returned, weapon out of sight once more. "All safe." He began righting furniture, and Rivka, never one to tolerate a mess, immediately pitched in.

Estelle headed for our bedroom, where its open door revealed strewn garments, as Jamarde examined the slurs. "We'll need something stronger than water. I'll see if we can get some cleaning supplies and maybe some extra help." She disappeared back into the hall.

I almost charged after her. We didn't have time for this. Even now precious minutes ticked away. Yet I still had to change, so what harm could come from letting them work? I started toward my room, but Xander lingered in the hall, staring at the disaster.

"Peace, Saunders. It's just some coterie wanting to frighten us and steal any rewards we left behind." Did he even hear me? I should have never agreed to participate in the Quest. I should have known something like this would happen. But time once spent cannot be regained. I touched his shoulder. A violent shudder shook his body, but he finally looked at me. "Why don't you check if anything is missing?" I suggested.

He shuffled toward his bedroom, his faithful bodyguard two paces behind him. I gathered strewn clothing on the way to my room. So much for the Quest's security. Persuading Xander to enter Council Hall would be nigh impossible now, and for good reason. Where were all those guards who were supposed to be protecting us?

Estelle nodded toward Xander's room as I entered. "Is he unwell?"

I dumped the clothing I'd gathered on a bed. "I think the mess resurrected bad memories."

"I'm sorry to hear that." Her chestnut eyes darkened with a compassion born of experience.

Experience I knew little about. My cheeks flushed as I sorted through the garments for a different dress to wear that hadn't been harmed by our saboteurs. My life wasn't perfect. I had problems and heartaches and headaches like anyone else. Nonetheless, those who said my life was blessed weren't wrong. Sustainer had protected me from the worst storms, and I didn't understand why. Why give me much when I had done nothing to deserve it while withholding it from those who did? Why shelter me from the pain, hurts, and problems others faced? Was I so weak, my faith in Him so tenuous, that normal troubles would destroy me? "How do you do it?"

Estelle took her pile of garments from those I'd sorted. "Do what?"

"I've heard the rumors, seen how others treat you, yet it never bothers you." I found the dress I was looking for. Thankfully, my luanchari, with its emerald top and floral scarlet bottom, was undamaged. A black sash completed the ensemble.

Estelle checked one of her saris for damage and, finding none, folded it away in her trunk.

Had I opened a wound? "I beg your pardon. I didn't mean to pry."

"No apology is necessary. My silence was due to uncertainty, not offense. For such things do bother me. Sometimes very much." She used a damp cloth to scrub away food splattered across a sleeve. "If it doesn't show, it's because reacting aggravates the problem."

"Yet you speak with no anger, malice, or bitterness."

"Only by Sustainer's grace and Drom's instruction, for when I first came to him, I knew how to function on little else than fury."

I pulled on the luanchari dress. "What changed?"

"I don't think any single thing changed, but several lessons cumulated over the years."

"Such as?"

"I needed Sustainer to give me His forgiveness to forgive those who hurt me, as my own supply was insufficient. I had to trust Sustainer's sovereignty; that this was part of His plan." A soft smile quirked her lips. "To ask why less and how more."

I wrinkled my nose as I folded away my soiled sari. "I like whys."

Estelle laughed. "So do I. But when I realized I was demanding that Sustainer explain the inexplicable and reveal a plan larger than I could comprehend, it became easier to bear."

Such wisdom. The kind that came only through pain and trials, and though I craved such wisdom, such circumstances would surely destroy me.

In the common room, Jamarde's voice announced her return with a half dozen menials, and cleaning became a flurry that chased my cousin and maid into our room. "Do you know how the coterie broke into our rooms?" asked Jamarde. "I thought the mahal was supposed to be secure."

"One of the menials said she saw a new cleaner wandering this floor after the coteries left this morning." Rivka extracted the tangled black sash from my fingers. "Among the Kossacans there's a saying that even to clean takes skill, and skill deserves the honor of pay. Do you mind if we use one of the coins to . . ." She tipped her head toward the common room, where the mahal menials chattered as they worked.

"But of course." Estelle pulled the coin from the bag that carried all the items we'd earned during the Quest. "And the cleaning charade is logical for 'the eye sees / what the mind first perceives.'"

Jamarde scrunched her face. "What does that mean?"

"Everyone knew the coteries had left, so no one expected to see anyone but menials, and what is one more menial among many?" I said, holding up my arms as Rivka wrapped the sash around my waist and tied it into a bow in the back. "Using that invisibility, they moved freely, despite security. We see what we expect to see, if given no reason to see otherwise."

My words circled back to me. That might be the solution to navigating Council Hall. If Xander was willing to try.

Xander paced the bedroom as Massard stood in a corner out of his way. Yosi must have had sufficient time to change by now, which meant their departure to the Teardrop was imminent. Yet how could he go? If he met one of the visiting Egdonians or even the wrong Indeli dignitary, they would know him, bandhgala suit or not. But a refusal to participate in this particular task could very well result in a forfeiture of the entire Quest. To forfeit now would be to nullify every reason they were participating. Xander slumped onto a bed. "What am I to do?"

"That would be the question, Your Highness."

"What? No advice?"

For once, Massard's calm confidence cracked. "I offer none because I've become too . . . attached."

Xander stared at Massard, then started to chuckle.

Massard frowned, but truly, to hear Massard's admission, one would think the man had committed murder or high treason.

"Your Highness apparently fails to grasp the gravity of the situation. Anything less than complete and undivided loyalty jeopardizes my ability to protect you."

"Your concern shows I've nothing to be concerned about, and I'm pleased to learn a real beating heart resides beneath that iron exterior of yours." Xander sobered. "Unfortunately, I understand the issue all too well." He plowed his hand through his hair. There must be a solution to this problem. Had to be. Every problem had one. Why couldn't he figure out what it was?

A light tap on the door raised his head, and Yosi entered. It must be time to depart, which meant he must make a decision– one he loathed to make. He rose, feeling the full weight of his twenty-three years twice over. "I fear I have bad news. I cannot attend the next task."

Instead of showing shock or protest, Yosi merely folded her hands. "Of course you can't."

Did she truly feel he'd contributed that little thus far? Admittedly, he hadn't shot well yesterday, and he hadn't helped much with the riddle or at the teahouse. But he had unlocked the puzzle box and–

"I mean as yourself."

He stared at her blankly. "I don't follow."

"Most people see what they expect to see, and your

participation in the Quest is quite unexpected. If we provide them no reason to see more, even someone who knows you will dismiss you as another Quester."

"And how do you propose to do that?"

"Tell me, hasib, have you ever worn your hair long?"

He hadn't, which was how he found himself being fitted with a braided queue of Estelle's hair, clipped from an invisible place where the color almost matched his. Who would have ever guessed they would have need of her variegated hair? Thankfully, Xander had not cut his own hair since arriving in Indel, making it easier to add the queue, and with the application of a gel that darkened the color of both, the addition was imperceptible. Rivka withdrew a cosmetic tray and added several moles along the side of his face, as well as a faded scar.

Throughout the whole process, he kept waiting for questions from the ladies about why he and Massard required disguises, but they never came. Yosi must have found a way to explain the need without disclosing the why. Such discretion was admirable. It was almost a shame she had no desire to enter the politico. Such a trait would be an invaluable asset.

Upon Rivka's presentation of him, Massard grunted. "Impressive."

"I'm glad you think that, because you're next." Rivka motioned for Massard to take his place.

Massard, the man who recoiled from no challenge, retreated. "I think not."

"If you thought Hasib Saunders recognizable, what do you think you are?"

"She's right." Wherever the crown prince's bodyguard was, the crown prince couldn't be far away. Arms folded, Xander relaxed against a wall. There was no way he was missing a moment of this.

As Massard finally sat, Rivka pursed her lips. "It would take too much work to make the scar disappear."

"Since it is hopeless . . ." Massard began to rise.

Rivka tapped him back into place with the end of her cosmetic brush. "Among the Sarmazon, scars are seen as a sign of strength and a source of pride. I propose we follow their example and accentuate the scar." Rivka leaned closer to Massard, mischief crinkling her eyes. "If you will trust me?"

Fixing his eyes on a point other than the woman in front of him, he gave a sharp nod.

Rivka sorted through her tray of cosmetics and paints. "What do you think, sibahs? Dragon, tarantula, or tiger?"

"Dragon," Yosi said immediately.

"Most definitely a dragon," Estelle agreed, with Jamarde nodding her approval.

"Dragon it is." Rivka took up her brush and, within minutes, had recreated a lueng dragon coiling around Massard's neck and spewing flames up his face, the scar central to those flames. When it was said everything was an art in Indel, they meant *everything.*

Last of all, Rivka rubbed three streaks of flaming red into Massard's hair, opposite the scar. Xander whistled. "You should have skipped me. With that, no one will be looking anywhere else."

Massard studied himself in the mirror. "You are an artist."

Rivka fluttered her fingers as if to dispel his compliment. "You are too kind." But her cheeks radiated warmth.

Xander pushed away from the wall. "I appreciate the extra work, sibahs, but it shall be for naught if we don't accomplish that next task soon."

Within a quarter bell, they stood on the steps of the Council Hall. Above the three-story ring that housed the governmental offices jutted the point of the teardrop-shaped theatre, its gilded surface reflecting the afternoon sun. Bright. Magnificent. And every bit as daunting as it had been when his fifteen-year-old self visited with his father on a negotiation trip.

"Ready, hasib?" Yosi's hushed question nudged without forcing. He gave a curt nod.

Their footsteps echoed in the marble hall, the high arches designed to intimidate. Maybe a crowd would have been better instead of the few people they passed–a pair of menials cleaning, three guards standing post, a politico hurrying by on some all-important errand. While more people could increase the possibility of recognition, the emptiness emphasized their presence.

". . . I said no such thing." A loud, angry voice reverberated from farther down the hall. "Now be gone you tatterscamp, before I summon a guard."

A finely dressed man slammed a door in the face of a scrawny boy of nine or ten years wearing neat but worn linens. He crushed the distinctive navy cap of an errand runner in his fist. "But you promised," he croaked to the closed door.

Xander stiffened. Yes, a few thieves worked among the errand runners, but that didn't justify treating them like street muck. After all, there were thieves among politicos and parlies too. Most errand runners were diligent, trustworthy, and hardworking, trying to support their families.

Yosi pressed something into his hand. One of the silver coins. Xander walked toward the boy.

Seeing him approach, the boy scrubbed a sleeve over his face. "May I do an errand for you, hasib? I can find any place and deliver anything, for a modest fee, of course."

"No errand, but I was wondering what he"–Xander nodded toward the door–"promised and did not fulfill."

The boy's gaze darted to the door, but then he straightened. "I don't speak of my hires to other hires." He smashed his cap onto his head. "If you have no business for me, I'd best be on my way."

"Wait."

The boy stopped, skepticism written across his face.

Xander studied him. He held his shoulders back, head high, a posture worthy of a parlie. He might not have much in worldly goods, but he had his dignity, and holding on to that was more important than a single coin, even a silver one. "I don't need an errand, but as you might have noticed, I'm a foreigner, and I could use a guide."

The boy puffed out his chest. "I know this city better than anyone. Where do you need to go?"

Xander stooped forward. "Promise not to laugh?"

"Upon my honor, hasib."

"I need to find the west entrance to the Teardrop." Their tickets didn't specify an entrance, but they were almost to the east one, and the boy would need to feel he had earned his pay. Not to mention it would reinforce the idea that he was a befuddled stranger.

The boy eyed him. "If you are looking for the west entrance, you are about as far away as you can get, hasib."

"Of course I am. It's these halls, I tell you. They all look the same."

The boy thrust a thumb against his chest. "Follow me. I'll get you there."

And he did, utilizing halls Xander didn't even notice until the boy darted down them. Within minutes, they were approaching the west entrance to the Teardrop. "I am much obliged for your help." Xander pressed the coin into the boy's hand.

"Hasib, I can't accept this. It's too much."

"On the contrary, where I come from, knowledge is highly prized, and your knowledge has earned every keshel of that."

The boy bobbed his head, eyes overbright. "You have my gratitude, hasib." He disappeared down one of the discreet halls.

Xander faced the west entrance, its doors carved to depict some of the great performances and oratories of the past. The first production of Tzarmo's *Night Queen* aria. The climactic death scene from *The Fallen Egret,* wherein the greatest prima ballerina of Kossac actually died. The debate between Niclon and Gloud. Each scene a reminder that greatness happened here.

The cavernous interior of the Teardrop only amplified its overwhelming magnificence, its curving design ever threatening to swallow its audience. Built as a theatre in the round, its amphitheatre seating spiraled down to a central circular stage, while balconies curled inward above his head.

Time and age had not softened the intimidation of this place, though the last time he was here, he had sat in one of the upper balconies. His father was giving a speech to the Indeli Council about uniting against the raids by the betweeners living in the disputed borderland between Indel and Egdon. The raids were disrupting trade terribly, trade Egdon needed due to catastrophic storms. His father had been brilliant in his presentation, but the ever-suspicious Council rejected his proposal. The chancellor at that time even implied the betweeners were beneficial, keeping Egdon occupied with other problems than how to annex the borderlands for themselves. The Indelis had no idea what a strain their refusal put on his people, especially over those next two years as they tried to recover from the storms.

Xander pushed away the memories at the approach of a man in formal Council attire, a scarlet-and-gold angarkha over black trousers. The Quest's gold band wrapped around his arm. After introducing himself as Counselor Grebe, he focused on Xander. "Have we met, hasib?"

Had they? Xander searched his memory. "If we have, it is a meeting of which I have no recollection, sri." He shifted the mole-dotted side of his face to the man.

The movement drew the counselor's eyes. "I concur. I see now you only share a great resemblance to someone I have met." He looked again at the group. "Welcome, noble Questers, to the Teardrop, the theatre of theatres, and the hallowed hall of the Council of Indel, governors of Sustainer's justice, where the art of heart and voice mingle." He led them down past the central platform to a series of rooms beneath the stage–prop rooms based on the racks of costumes, set pieces, and the odd assortment of furniture. He stifled a sneeze at the smell of dust, wood, and paint.

The counselor picked up a glass-blown bowl filled with paper-folded animals. "What tasks does Sustainer seek to find you worthy in? Let us discover His will for each of you."

Yosi reached into the bowl, removing a frog. Each of the other ladies followed. Xander stepped forward. *Please, Sustainer, grant Your favor.* He plunged his hand deep into the bowl, closed his fingers around a paper, and retreated so Massard could take one as well. Xander unfolded his paper swan and stared at the two words written there:

Dramatic Recitation

At least he need not sing a song. That would have been disastrous.

The counselor reviewed the papers, noting what each said. "You have one bell to incorporate these six elements into a creative composition, with each performing the task you drew." He waved at the rooms. "You may use whatever you find here, and if you need something specific, ring the bell. Your time starts now." He walked out.

They huddled together to compare notes. In addition to his dramatic recitation, Jamarde and Rivka both received painting, Estelle dancing, Yosi pantomime, and Massard instrumental music. Xander raised an eyebrow at his bodyguard.

"Don't worry about me." Massard rummaged through the instruments.

Estelle looked at Xander. "What we do is determined by you."

"What do you mean?"

"Music, dance, and artistic representation are fluid and flexible, able to be abstracted. Even pantomime can be altered to match words, but dramatic recitation is usually concrete and specific."

Yosi sorted through a stack of scripts. "We need something with a strong voice that the rest of us can portray."

Xander tugged on his collar, the stuffiness of the room closing around him. Oratory had never been his strong suit, and that sounded like the performance rested on his shoulders.

Estelle flipped through some papers. "How about *The Beloved Letters*?"

"Too long." Yosi skimmed a book of monologues. "We don't have enough time to prepare or perform such a lengthy piece. Besides, that's better for a pair of actors. How about 'Telmah's Soliloquy'?"

Jamarde scrunched her face. "Boring."

"Niclon's 'Appeal at Kinah Plain'?"

Estelle shook her head. "Not visual enough. We'd all stand around listening to Saunders speak."

"Then definitely not." Xander's words came out harsher than he intended, and he blew out a breath, trying to release the pressure building inside of him. "We need a story, like a fable or fairy tale, where the narrator is telling the story, not being the story."

Yosi and Estelle locked eyes. "'Wayfarer,'" they said simultaneously.

Rivka clasped her hands. "I love that tale! There's something quite encouraging in how the traveler could never seem to find the right place until the Golden City."

A chill shivered down Xander's spine. How in the Seven Realms could he narrate that? He would feel like a fraud. "I was thinking something more like 'The Seven Golden Grouse' or 'The Shikra and the Mouse.'"

"No, 'The Wayfarer's Tale' is perfect," said Estelle. "Yosi can pantomime the traveler, and we can adapt the three stops for Mascad's music and the painting for Rivka and Jamarde."

"And the thrush's guidance will provide Estelle the perfect opportunity for dance." Yosi extracted a blue-and-orange dress with feathered layers and winglike sleeves from a rack of costumes.

Estelle held it against herself. "It might be too big."

Rivka examined the costume. "It's a simple tuck. I can alter it while you modify the script." She plucked a sewing box off a shelf. "Did you know feathers were most popular fifty years ago during the height of plumiris fashion?"

And on and on the others chattered, plotting the changes to the story, planning the needed sets and props, discussing costume possibilities. Their words blurred together. Because he was to do a "dramatic recitation" at the Teardrop. He who barely made it through a five-minute speech at last year's Winter Solstice Gala. Bands tightened around his chest and spots dotted his vision. He would completely ruin this and–

Heavy hands fell on his shoulders. "Stop. Breathe." Massard's commands broke through the rising tide of panic. "What do you hear?"

Not much, at least initially. The room had fallen eerily quiet, the chattering voices still. His pocket watch ticked off seconds, distant machinery hummed, and boards creaked from someone walking above them.

"What do you see?" asked Massard.

In front of his nose, Massard's shirt bore a few crumbs from Sibah Veli's. A small set of reed pipes poked out of a pocket. The lueng dragon Rivka had created, quite magnificent in detail, drew his attention upward. Beyond Massard's shoulder, the clutter of the prop room—paint buckets, scenery flats, a listing bookshelf—framed four faces lined with concern. For him.

Though Xander had not answered, Massard must have sensed his questions had helped because he retreated.

"If this is too distressing for you," Estelle said, "we can do something else."

Xander shook his head. "I must do a recitation regardless of what you choose, and the story you have selected has all the elements we require. I'll be fine." He hoped.

"Why don't you and Mascad carry up the needed props?" Yosi motioned to a pile of stage pieces. "Jamarde can tell you where they go while Estelle and I rewrite the script. By the time you finish, we should be ready to rehearse."

Xander simply nodded. Doing was better than sitting, and the activity did ease some of the nerves. But the rehearsal that followed was as bad as Xander anticipated. Even though he carefully enunciated every word and paced the pauses, raising and lowering his voice in all the logical places as he had been trained, it simply didn't sound right. Even the ladies couldn't hide their dismay behind their encouraging words. When he'd suggested participating in the Quest, he'd been certain they could reach the finals. Now he would cause them to lose it all. Because he couldn't read a simple six-page story.

When they finished, Yosi shooed the others away to finish preparing their costumes. "I will be there in a few minutes, but I want to help Saunders practice the script one more time. Rivka knows what I need."

The others left, and Yosi perched on some crates across from him. "Let's try again, and this time imagine you're reading this story to someone at home who loves you deeply. Perhaps your fiancé."

Xander stilled. "Fiancé?" What in the Seven Realms was she speaking of?

"You know, your fiancé." When he didn't respond, she hurried on. "The girl you will be marrying when you return home."

"I know what a fiancé is, Yosi. I am confused, not because I'm unfamiliar with the term, but because I don't have one."

That seemed to deepen her befuddlement. "But the bridal egg you showed me–"

"–is for someday. My position will require me to wed, but I do not have a specific bride in mind, and therefore no one to read this script to."

"That would indeed be difficult." The color in her cheeks deepened. "Um. Try selecting a family member instead."

He immediately envisioned Selucreh's mocking face, a sight that had frequently greeted him at past speaking events.

Yosi must have noticed his discomfort, for she added, "I meant someone who would love your performance regardless of quality."

His youngest niece, Ellie, bounced into mind. The mere thought of her always evoked a smile. Her enthusiasm whenever he visited was matched by none.

"Now that looks like the perfect audience," said Yosi. "Read this story to him or her."

He did.

Yosi tilted back, saying nothing.

"That bad?"

"It was an improvement over your stilted reading from a few minutes ago, so keep that person in mind. But you went from sounding like an automaton to a politico reading a speech, exaggerated and overdramatic."

"But maybe I am automaton and you do not know it," Xander intoned.

Yosi laughed. "That only proves my point. You naturally modulate your voice to fit the mood and words when you are conversing, but you overthink it when you read." She drummed her fingers against her knees. "Pardon if this seems forward, but did your father and stepmother love each other?"

A strange change in topic. "Yes, absolutely."

"How could you tell?"

Xander closed his eyes, searching for specific examples. "It was nothing big or showy. The way my father would wink at Mum during some dull party conversation, or how she would listen attentively about his day, no matter how boring."

Yosi propped her chin on her palms. "That sounds wonderful."

"On their good days, it was. When they fought, though, you would think a civil war was beginning." He laughed, or tried to, but a lump in his throat strangled the sound. "Both would tell you their relationship was learned the hard way and in stages. When I arrived, it nearly tore their marriage apart."

"That wasn't your fault."

"But I shouldn't even exist, much less have the position I do." How could he expect an entire kingdom to overlook his roots?

Yosi rested a hand upon the closed script on his lap. "Your father made a wrong choice. There's no denying that. But your father, as powerful as he was, could not create life. That means you exist because Sustainer wanted you to exist."

Her proclamation stole his breath. His birth had been called many things over the years. A mistake. A travesty. A social blunder. A great evil. A great pity. A shameful thing that ought not be mentioned. Never once, however, had he heard anyone–not his father, not his mother, not his stepmum–affirm his birth as from Sustainer's hand, a sovereign act of intention.

"As I recall," she continued, "someone else told me every gear and spring is placed by the inventor to fulfill the role he intends. I'm no inventor, but I've watched Drom enough to know there are no useless parts. Every piece is placed where it is meant to be."

Not a mistake. Not an accident. Not a twist of fate. But he'd thought of himself that way for so long, the idea Sustainer *intended* him to be king from the very beginning–it physically imbalanced him, and he had to steady himself.

Rivka appeared in the doorway, a dress draped over her arm. Yosi rose. "Anyway, the point I was trying to make was that emotions don't need to be affected and grandiose to be visible. Just as you saw your parent's love reflected in small things, so it is with your reading. The key is to speak from the heart, to be authentic. That is what will connect with the listener."

She departed with Rivka, leaving him alone. Simple, authentic, think of Ellie. Put in those terms, this didn't sound quite as daunting. He read through the script again with those thoughts in mind before he was summoned for the makeup he needed. Then they all talked through the script together one last time. Xander would have no career on the stage, but maybe he would not bungle this performance.

With preparation time over, the six of them were escorted onto the stage. Below them in the first row, half obscured in shadow, sat three men and two women. Sweat gathered on his neck beneath the false queue, his body cold despite the hot lights. Did he know any of them? More importantly, did any of them know him?

Counselor Grebe stood. "Welcome, Illuminary. What entertainment do we have the pleasure of today?"

Xander bowed, hands clasped behind his back. "We are presenting a dramatic retelling of 'The Wayfarer's Tale.'" The big space swallowed his words, and the empty balconies glowered down at him. How had his father presented his speech so calmly, so flawlessly, when most of those seats were filled eight years ago?

"Very good. Begin when you're ready."

They scattered. Massard and the girls disappeared behind the curtains of a raised platform. Xander positioned himself behind a podium set to the left, next to a hand crank, and placed the folder with his script on it. The world began to blur, as it did before every speech.

Then a haunting melody rose from behind a curtain and hovered on the air. Where had Massard learned to do that?

A memory came unbidden. He was attending a ceremony with his father at a special school sponsored by the royal family for children deemed deficient. Xander had endured several rude remarks and scoffing comments about the school from a parlie and his family earlier that day, leading his thirteen-year-old self to ask why his father supported it.

"Because I believe Sustainer gave every person a gift," he'd said, "just like Posea the simplewit. Unfortunately, those gifts often go undiscovered because they aren't wrapped in an acceptable package. The world has lost more than it realizes because we determine the value of the gift by the wrapping." His father bore down on him with that penetrating look of his. "Dare to look past the wrapping, Xander–in others and in yourself."

Massard finished his musical prelude, and quiet settled on the theatre.

Xander opened his folder, and a bright blue scrap of paper lay inside. A giant BREATHE filled the middle of it, illuminated with puffy clouds pierced through with a shaft of light. Around the edges were the girls' signatures with a simple *M* in the corner, presumably for Massard.

The central curtain was drawn aside, revealing a plainly dressed Yosi sitting on a stool in a rustic room, ready to act out the words he spoke.

Setting aside the note, Xander breathed as instructed and began to read. "Once it happened, in another time and in another place, that there was a girl who didn't belong. She did her best to blend into the home where she was raised, doing her chores, learning her letters, helping with the farm animals. But her parents had died when she was very young, and those with whom she now lived saw her as nothing more than a nuisance stealing bread from their mouths." The words caught in his throat. This was why he hadn't wanted to do this tale. It felt far too familiar.

Yosi paused her pantomime, waiting for Xander to proceed.

He gripped the edges of the podium and forced himself to continue. "One night, she heard the family plotting to marry her to a cruel man in exchange for a breeding horse. She knew then she could stay no longer. Gathering up her few belongings, she fled into the night, led on by the song of a shama thrush."

Yosi gathered a bag and stepped onto the outer edge of the platform. A lively tune played by an invisible Massard filled the air, and Estelle appeared, the feathered layers of her blue-and-orange dress flaring as she danced around Yosi. Xander quickly stooped and turned the crank. The platform rotated, and Estelle and Yosi matched the pace perfectly, staying ever before the audience as the curtains, embroidered with trees, gardens, and distant villages, passed by behind them.

After they completed one full revolution, they stopped before a second curtained section. Xander turned to his next page. He could do this. It was no different than reading Ellie a bedtime story. "The next day, the wayfarer came across an old woman tending her garden."

The curtain opened to reveal Jamarde painting flowers on a fake stone wall.

"The wayfarer offered to help in exchange for food. The old woman agreed, and the wayfarer labored all day in the garden under the hot sun."

Yosi knelt and pretended to pull weeds while Jarmade added a sun to one corner.

"But when the wayfarer finished, the old woman could provide her only a hard crust of bread and a withered apple, for she was poor and had little to share. The wayfarer realized she could not take anything from the old woman. So after declining the food with a blessing, the wayfarer continued on." The longer Xander read, the more his face reddened, the girls' graceful movements emphasizing his stilted words. "The shama thrush glided ahead of the wayfarer, leading her on. 'Kindness sown reaps kindness,' she trilled, 'for Sustainer notices all.'"

Jamarde pulled the curtain closed, and Xander turned the crank again, thankful for the reprieve as Yosi and Estelle danced a second rotation of the dais.

Xander flipped his page. A green paper greeted him, again signed by his entire coterie. This time the word HOPE nearly filled the page, decorated with curling vines and purple flowers. Such a small word to carry such a weighty meaning. Xander shoved it aside as someone muffled a polite cough.

"After a few days of travel, the young wayfarer reached a small town where a whistle maker lived."

Behind the third curtain sat Massard, working among wood scraps and assorted instruments. Somehow the ladies had made the lueng dragon look like a natural part of his character.

"The whistle maker was looking for someone to apprentice in his trade and to help with his work. He assigned the position to the wayfarer."

Yosi grabbed a broom as Massard played a lively tune, Estelle dancing around them. When they finished, Xander resumed his story.

"She worked hard for several days, cooking, cleaning, and assisting the craftsman. Or she tried to. But she burned food, broke dishes, and gave him the wrong tools. Where he made beautiful music, she created noise."

Yosi blew a whistle, its dissonant pair of notes enough to make anyone cringe.

"Once again the wayfarer packed her belongings, for despite the whistle maker's kindness, it was obvious she had brought more work than help to his home. The thrush assured her that Sustainer did not make every person suited for every job and, once again, led the wayfarer along the dusty road."

Massard pulled his curtain closed, and Xander cranked while Estelle and Yosi traveled another full circuit. But this time the melody drooped, and Yosi's steps lacked the lightness with which she began her journey.

They stopped where Rivka worked at an easel, facing a backdrop of a lake encircled with mountains. The scene he disliked most from the story.

"The wayfarer traveled many more days, working mundane tasks in exchange for food or a place to sleep before moving on to the next town. Was there no place she belonged in this whole realm? It seemed not. Reaching a lake, the wayfarer sat at its edge, intending to wash her tired, dusty feet in its cool waters."

"But before she could remove one shoe, pebbles pelted her back. 'Begone, blemish. Be on your way, tatterscamp.' An artist emerged from behind a tree, scooped up a clod of earth, and threw it at her. 'You are marring the view and ruining my picture.' The wayfarer had little choice but to flee."

Yosi dashed around the corner, Estelle behind her, and Xander had to crank hard to catch up with them. Finally, the platform brought Yosi into view, seated on a rock overlooking a barren wasteland, her face in her hands.

"The thrush found the wayfarer weeping alongside the road. For a long time, the bird sat with her, its song silent. Finally, the wayfarer's tears subsided, and the thrush fluttered up. 'Come, Wayfarer, come, and hold on to hope, for Sustainer does not disdain His own.' So the wayfarer arose once more. She did not know where the path would lead, but it was the path on which Sustainer had placed her. That made it a path that led somewhere."

Xander turned the crank for the last time. It was not by chance he was where he was. Wasn't that what his last words meant? And while he may not know where this path would lead, Sustainer intended it to lead somewhere.

As if to emphasize his thoughts, tucked between the last two pages was a yellow paper with the words *meant to be*, embellished with clockwork gears. Maybe, like the wayfarer, it was time to accept those words.

"The wayfarer continued to travel, visiting every corner of the realm. Days became weeks and weeks became years. She saw mountains and rivers, villages and cities, the thrush leading her ever on. Then one day the thrush came to rest before the gates of a golden city, brilliant and more magnificent than any other the wayfarer had seen."

The final curtain opened, and Estelle sat in front a garden gate. Hardly the glorious gates of the story, but the only one they could find on short notice.

"The wayfarer hung back, insisting she could not enter such a beautiful place. The thrush said, 'But you must, for this is where you belong.' And bringing the wayfarer a beautiful robe to wear, the shama thrush led her into the Golden City, and there the wayfarer stayed forever afterward."

Xander backed away from the podium as Estelle and Yosi danced together in the small space beyond the gate, celebrating the forever afterward. He'd made it through his recitation. Well or poorly was beyond his ability to discern, but at least he had not made any dramatic stumbles as far as he could tell.

They took their bows as Massard played a closing piece, and applause rose from the front row. It wasn't overly enthusiastic, but neither was it politely reserved. Xander gathered up the script, tucking Yosi's notes into his pocket. Did that mean their performance was passable?

Below the stage, they removed the makeup and costumes, then returned upstairs. There seemed to be some heated disagreement ongoing, if the punctuated sounds and sharp gestures from the front row were any sign. If only the offstage lights were brighter. Then again, perhaps it was best they weren't.

Finally, Counselor Grebe ascended the stage. Xander searched for any indication of which way the balance had tipped. Nothing. The Indelis must practice being expressionless.

The counselor extended a pouch. "That was a fine performance, noble Questers. You have shown yourselves worthy." But when Xander took hold of the pouch, the man didn't release it. "Have you visited Indel before, hasib?"

"I did, many years ago."

"But we never met?"

Xander shifted. "I was still a boy my last visit. Perhaps we did and I do not recall it."

"That is probably it." The counselor bent toward Xander and lowered his voice. "For you are very like your father, in carriage, in manner, in speech."

Xander's heart stopped, but his mind instructed him to remain calm. "My father? You were acquainted with him?"

"Yes . . . yes, I believe I was." Then the counselor bowed. "I wish you well with the rest of the Quest."

He departed to meet another coterie, leaving behind an address, a silver coin, some putty, and a tight throat on Xander's part. *You are very like your father.* Could he ask for any higher compliment? All because what he feared had become reality.

The sky had clouded over while we were in the Teardrop, and as we exited the coach for our final task, a sharp northern wind pricked my skin. Then again, the forbidding warehouse before us may have contributed as well. I'd never visited this industrial neighborhood of Kolchan before, and the windowless structure of red sandstone was not making the best first impression. The building wasn't unpleasant to the eye, but the angular shapes of black wrought iron that overlaid the entire exterior weren't inviting either. Yet here we were, at the last preliminary trial. As long as everything went smoothly, we had a real possibility of reaching the finals, unless the other coteries had had a far easier time than we'd had.

"Are you sure we are in the right place?" Jamarde drew closer to me, while Xander and Mascad flanked us. That could be due to either the laborers bustling around us or the ominous setting.

I glanced at the paper I held, trying to ignore a growing ruckus behind us. "Unless you know of another 43 Chordi, this is it."

"It makes a certain amount of sense." Estelle tugged her caplet tighter.

"How so?" asked Xander.

"We have been tested on the intellectual, creative, physical, social, and linguistic arts thus far," she said. "Considering the nature of the Quest, tomorrow's final would entail the spiritual arts. That leaves the art of virtue, and one of the virtues is courage."

Jamarde made a face. "That doesn't mean I must like it."

"That's robbery!" A man's enraged cry pierced through the street noise.

Across the way, a burly man rested against the side of a cart loaded with a half dozen crates, jaw chewing with the laziness of a cow with her cud.

A second man, vibrating with agitation, crushed a paper in his hand. "I need this shipment tonight." Desperation shaded the red haze coloring his words.

"Then pay up." The burly man spat a wad into the street.

"But you promised it wouldn't be more than forty amins." The second man shook the paper. "This says I owe twice that much."

His garments were worn and faded. Did he have that much to give, even if he had known the merchant would increase the cost? It didn't seem likely.

The burly man shrugged. "The cost of business."

Rivka muttered under her breath. "The cost of lining his pocket, he means. Probably promised a rate below expense and is now using a deadline to bleed him dry." Without another word, she marched across the street.

Mascad's face tensed as his eyes darted between Rivka and Xander. He didn't like Rivka approaching the merchant alone any more than I did, but abandoning Xander in a crowd like this wasn't an option.

I glanced at the darkening sky. We were nearly out of time, but we could hardly proceed without Rivka. "We might as well see if we can help."

We wove around the traffic to join Rivka just as she presented a menial's bow to the purchaser. "Good news, hasib! We have discovered a shipment at a bargain price." With a light touch to his elbow, she turned him toward us.

I bit my lip to keep from smiling. The burly man had straightened up, complacency gone as he watched his victim walking away. A victim who was blinking in utter confusion. "Who are–"

Rivka whispered something to him, then raised her voice. "I'm glad I found you in time. It would have been horrible for you to waste your money on this one."

"Impossible!" the burly man shouted. "You're just trying to get a better rate. There is no such shipment."

Mascad stalked forward. "Are you calling me a liar?" He extended a greeting to the purchaser. "If you will follow me, hasib, I will take you to your goods, and we can finish this transaction properly." The three of them walked away from the merchant, who flung curses at them. Rivka could bargain a tiger into giving away its teeth, but when had she become this conniving?

Mascad made brief eye contact with Xander as they passed us. "Skin him." They proceeded on as if we'd never met before.

Xander strolled toward the merchant. "That was a bit of bad luck, wasn't it?"

The burly merchant snorted. "They'll be back."

"Are you sure? The man with the scar doesn't seem like the practical joke type."

The merchant's gaze shifted in the direction the others had gone.

Xander craned his neck toward the crates. "What were you trying to offload on that fellow anyway?"

"What is it to you?"

"Idle curiosity mostly–wait, is that parchment in those crates?" Xander turned to the rest of our group. "Wasn't Oda saying something at breakfast about needing some of that?"

The merchant straightened up, his eyes glinting.

I opened my mouth to agree, then hesitated. *Never make a bid too quickly.* Wasn't that what Rivka always said about bartering? I cocked my head. "Perhaps? I admit I don't always listen well when Avi talks business. All those numbers hurt my head."

"I think Saunders is right, though." Estelle peered at the crate. "Something about a special project. Wouldn't it be fun to surprise him with this?"

Jamarde huffed. "If the price is right. You know how particular he is about spending money."

Estelle's shoulders slumped, and she backed away from the cart. "You're right."

"Besides, we ought to be going." I tugged at Xander's arm. "We're expected elsewhere, you know."

"Of course." Xander dipped his head to the merchant. "Good luck finding a buyer."

We'd ambled no more than six steps when the merchant shouted, "What are you offering?"

Xander glanced back and shook his head. "I'm afraid I wasn't thinking. I haven't much money on me, and–"

"Your bid, hasib."

Xander pulled out the silver coin we collected from the last task. It was worth more than the original price of forty amins, but far less than had been demanded of the purchaser.

The merchant glanced between the coin and the direction Massard and Rivka had disappeared.

"I told you I didn't have much." Xander closed his fingers around the coin. "Good evenfall–"

"Sold. The shipment is yours."

Xander stole a glance at us. I shrugged. "That does seem like a fair price even Avi couldn't argue with."

The transaction was made, and we drove the cart around the corner, where Mascad, Rivka, and the purchaser awaited. Xander presented him the cart with a flourish. "All yours, hasib."

The man's mouth fell open. "You . . . you have my deepest gratitude, hasib." He fumbled with his coin purse.

Rivka covered his hand. "No need for repayment, hasib."

"But–"

"Consider it a gift from Sustainer. Good evenfall." Xander bowed to him and led us back to the warehouse. Our brief excursion had not improved my impression of the building.

Jamarde wrinkled her nose, eyes squinching behind her glasses. "I still don't like it."

"Then perhaps we ought to treat this like a bit of distasteful medicine and finish without delay." Xander strode ahead to the double doors of heavy plank wood.

The rest of us followed, with Mascad bringing up the rear.

"That's odd. There's no handle." Xander raised his fist to knock.

The doors swung silently inward.

Jamarde squeaked, and Xander gave her a crooked grin. "I guess we are expected." He led us into a circular foyer, lit by a single hanging lamp that dispelled few shadows. I rubbed my arms. Was it me or was it cooler here than outside?

"Expected, perhaps, but not very welcoming." Rivka scuffed her toe across the floor, leaving an obvious arc upon the obsidian. "They didn't even bother to sweep."

Leave it to my maid to notice that particular detail.

The doors slammed shut with an echoing thud, and the lamp extinguished, plunging us into darkness. I froze, straining to see. There was only blackness and more blackness. Scuffs and scratches scraped the chilly air. The rest of my coterie shuffled uneasily.

"That was unsettling." Estelle gave a breathless laugh. "Does anyone have a suggestion about what we do next?"

"Connect hands." Mascad's voice came from somewhere behind me. "We don't want to lose each other."

A good suggestion, if I could get my body to follow it. The darkness seemed to have overtaken it. After several thundering heartbeats, I stretched out a hand. Nothing.

How could there be nothing? I had been in the midst of the group when we entered. Someone should be close by. My second hand joined the search. Grunts and murmurs said the others were connecting. Why couldn't I find somebody? Had I become separated from them somehow? Maybe they couldn't find me either. Maybe something else had changed when the lights went out. What if they *couldn't* get to me and I was completely alone and–

Something warm connected with my arm. I jumped.

"All's well." Xander's familiar script curled around me. "I have you now." His hand closed around mine. Firm, solid, comforting.

"Gratitude." The blood pounding in my ears ebbed to a

murmur, and a minute later I linked hands with Jamarde. I wasn't lost. I wasn't alone.

"Now what?" Jamarde's words didn't waver like before, as if she found courage in our touch too.

I closed my eyes, which ached from trying to see in the darkness. Wandering in a dark room without guidance didn't seem prudent. "I suppose we wait." The one thing that would waste the most time, but what other choice did we have?

Jamarde groaned. "Let me guess, the virtue of patience?"

"But for how long?" Xander's grip tightened as if underscoring the tension in his voice.

"'If how long we knew we had / the patience needed–but a tad,'" chided Estelle softly somewhere to my left.

"Among the Ordu tribe of Zantu, they say time is irrelevant." Rivka clicked her tongue at the notion. "I say busy hands speed on time."

Musty dust tickled my nose, making it itch, but I didn't dare release Xander or Jamarde to rub it. "My hands are a little busy, Rivka." I scrubbed my nose against my upper arm, then sneezed anyway.

Jamarde's hand twitched in mine. "Estelle, they say at the Academy you have one of the most beautiful voices. Would you–would you sing us a song?"

"Do you have something in mind?"

"Nothing scary or dark. We have enough of that."

Laughter rippled through our group.

"I think I can manage that." There was a pause, then a voice as clear as a crystal bell rang forth:

"In the wilderness wandered I,
"Weary, scared, alone, and dry.
"The sun burned hot, bleaching the bone
"And turned water to stone.

"Yet from the barren blossoms life;
"The desert made with beauty rife.
"New springs will water all the land,
"Provided by Sustainer's hand."

The room amplified the music, and though I stood in a chilly, dark room, my body warmed as if that scorching sun beat upon me.

"Fainting, how can I now go on?
"Water none comes with the dawn.
"Only endless sand met the eye
"And I must surely die.

Go on. That was what we needed to do. Were we wrong to stand here, waiting for something to happen? Perhaps we were supposed to initiate.

"Upward turn my eyes to the skies;
"To Sustainer my heart cries:
"'Nothing else can I lean upon.
"'Your will ever be done.'"

As Estelle repeated the refrain about the desert blossoming a third time, I shifted uneasily. Could I truly say, "Sustainer's will be done," no matter the outcome of this Quest or even the Strata Exam? My head said yes. My heart said no.

My heart was probably the more truthful of the two.

"Thus I waited, and my help came,
"Diff'rent, yes, than what I name,
"But Sustainer met every need;
"My lack could not impede.

"For from the barren blossoms life;
"The desert made with beauty rife.
"New springs will water all the land,
"Provided by Sustainer's hand."

The last note of Estelle's song faded, yet in the silence that followed, the music lingered, its lyrics challenging us to trust Sustainer even in this moment when we could do nothing.

Doubt splattered across the moment, spoiling the beauty the way water damages an illumination. What if it was Sustainer's will that we fail? What if He decided we didn't deserve success? I squeezed my eyes shut, more out of habit than need. *Please, Effulgence, don't punish the others because of my shortcomings.*

A gasp from Jamarde opened my eyes. An open doorway spilled light into the foyer. Our next step?

Xander resumed the lead as Mascad shepherded us from behind. Once again, the door shut on its own after we'd passed through, but at least this time the lights remained lit. Not that there was much to see. A jumble of wooden crates was stacked before us, with another closed door beyond. Several minutes of examination revealed no way to open it. Of course not. The one task where we needed to hurry was the one task that couldn't be hurried. "If the pattern holds, it will open whenever we prove whatever virtue this room is meant to test."

Rivka carried a box across the room, muttering. "This will never do. Everyone knows you don't store calmar salt near silk. It will eat through the fabric. And who in their right mind stacks parshals next to rubies?"

Beside me, Xander chuckled. I gave a helpless shrug. "Rivka never did like things in disarray."

Mascad reached for a larger box stamped "pottery" that Rivka was trying to lift. She ceded it to him, pointing where she wanted it.

Estelle studied the stack nearest her. "'Order to life, order to mind / showing respect for all humankind.'"

Xander rolled up his sleeves. "Better that than waiting around." We hauled and restacked the boxes in orderly sections under the labels on the walls.

Until Xander whistled at a lidless crate he'd unearthed in the corner. The rest of us clustered around him and gaped. It contained a mound of uncut gems.

"Those aren't real," breathed Jamarde.

"It wouldn't make much sense to send fakes to the best jeweler in Kolchan." Estelle pointed to the label on a lid propped against a nearby wall.

Jamarde picked out a blue gem that glinted with streaks of red and orange as she twisted it in the light–a rare starfire sapphire. One stone was easily worth Avi's annual income. Maybe even a counselor's. With that single stone, we wouldn't have to worry about reaching the finals. Drom's shop would be saved. Estelle could repay him for her training at the Academy. Rivka would have more than enough to start her business as an elite, and Jamarde wouldn't have any worries for the rest of her schooling. Books, clothing, tutoring–she could have it all, maybe with enough remaining to start her teahouse. All from one little gem. It would be easy to hide away, and from that jumble of stones, would anyone even notice it was missing?

Jamarde hissed and flung the stone back into the box. "Close it, close it quickly." She whirled away.

Estelle thrust the lid into place, and Xander slammed the latches shut, jarring me from my trance. The page of my mind warped, images grotesquely distorting, letters elongating, jagged with horror. Had I truly been contemplating stealing? Maybe the legends about the starfire inspiring greed weren't as farfetched as I'd thought. Xander glanced at me grimly. "Don't berate yourself. We were all thinking the same. Mascad, if you would."

His bodyguard placed the crate where it belonged, out of sight behind another stack. We collectively sighed.

The next door swung open. "I hope we're almost done." Jamarde rubbed her arms. "I don't know how much more of this I can handle."

Indeed. The sooner we could leave, the better–and not merely because our time was short. If I never saw the inside of a warehouse like this again, it would be too soon.

The third room was empty and eerily still. Perhaps some sort of loading dock? The large double doors at the far end could easily permit a pair of wagons to pass each other. Not that it mattered. Near them was a table with a row of bowls set upon it. I heaved a sigh of relief. "We must have passed."

Estelle rested a restraining hand on my arm. "That seems too easy, don't you think? Perhaps we ought to exercise caution in proceeding."

I shook her off. "We don't have time for caution." I would show them we need not fear. I strode ahead. All we had to do was take our–

The floor dropped out from under my feet, and I was falling–no, sliding down, down, down, around and around, until I landed with a whomp onto a mattress.

For a moment, I blinked at the thick iron bars separating me from the rest of the stone room. I sat in a cage several feet above the floor.

I was trapped, with no way out.

No, that couldn't be right. This was the Quest. There had to be a way out. I rattled the cage's door, then checked the trapdoor above my head, through which the slide had dropped me. Both locked.

Be still, my heart.

No, I needed to act, not be still. A darkness seeped through me like black ink spilled across a page, swallowing the words of the Scribes, obliterating everything in its path, despite the lamps burning in the room's corners. There was no way out of this. Not without help.

"Hello?" I pressed my face against the chilly bars, searching for any shadow of movement through the open door at the room's far side. Surely the rest of my coterie couldn't be too far away. "Anyone there?"

Silence, cold and impersonal, was my only response.

I gritted my teeth against the burning in my eyes. There was no point in crying over spilled ink, as any sensible person knew. But then, a sensible person would have stayed with her coterie instead of rushing ahead. A sensible person wouldn't be here in the first place, and if she were, she would find a way to clean up her mess.

Good advice. Useless advice.

For there would be no salvaging my mess this time. Any hope of reaching the finals I'd ruined beyond reparation.

When Yosi dropped through the floor, Xander froze. *No, Effulgence, no!* He plunged ahead, caution be hanged. Where had she gone? Was she all right?

Massard tackled him to the floor just as the panel sealed seamlessly back into place.

"Off of me!" Xander fought against his bodyguard.

"I can't let you–"

"You can and you will."

Massard grunted. Stubborn man!

Rivka gingerly poked the spot where Yosi had disappeared. A crease appeared in Massard's forehead. But he couldn't stop Rivka and hold Xander at the same time. "Siv, don't–"

Rivka walked onto the spot, placing all her weight on it. Nothing happened. Not even when she gave a little hop.

Xander slammed a fist against the floor, pain ricocheting up his arm. How were they to help Yosi if they didn't know where she'd gone and couldn't follow?

Massard finally released him. Apparently, Rivka's failure assured him Xander would be safe, except nothing was safe about this place. Nonetheless, he scrambled forward, probing for a hidden latch or lever, some way to reopen the trapdoor. Nothing. He sat back on his heels. "Now what?"

"You could take your prize and go."

An unfamiliar feminine voice turned them all toward the far end of the room. A woman stood next to the table, a bowl in her hands, and a gold band around her arm. Where had she come from? No one else had been around a minute ago, and the empty space furnished no obvious hiding places.

The woman glanced at the darkening skylight above. "If you leave now, you should arrive in time."

"Our coterie is short a member." Xander dusted his hands off as he rose.

"There is nothing in the rules that says the whole coterie must appear, is there?"

Xander had no idea. He glanced at Jamarde, who then looked at Estelle, who in turn stared at her folded hands. "I don't know if that's true."

"We could split up," suggested Massard. "Two of us could go ahead while the others stay. If she speaks truth, we final. If not, we've lost nothing."

As usual, great wisdom resided in Massard's words. "I volunteer to stay behind."

"No." Jamarde blocked their way.

Xander offered her his elbow. "If you would also like to search for your cousin–"

"I don't think *anyone* should go." She folded her arms. "We came this far as a coterie. We ought to final together as a coterie or not at all."

Her words smote him. When had winning become so important that he was willing to abandon the others in the process? The answer struck even harder: when he had started depending on the Quest to make things right rather than trusting Sustainer to provide. "You're right. We all should stay, even if it costs us the Quest."

Rivka, the ever-loyal maid, assented, as did Estelle after a brief hesitation.

"Mascad?"

His bodyguard stared into the distance, his jaw working from side to side. Finally, he nodded. "What good is wisdom without loyalty?"

Xander faced the official. "We thank you for your suggestion, but we have a lost friend to find." He arched his eyebrows. "Do you have advice on how we might find her?"

Her smile crinkled the corners of her eyes. "Indeed, I have, though your chosen path is not an easy one."

"Nonetheless, we remain resolved."

She pointed at a wall, and an invisible door opened soundlessly. "The one you seek is at the heart of this building. Like any heart, a labyrinth protects the treasure it holds from marauders. Tread wisely, and you will find. Tread unwisely, and you may be lost until morn."

"Now there's a cheery thought," Xander muttered to Massard as they proceeded to the doorway.

A narrow flight of stone steps descended before them. They started down them, and once again the door shut behind them, causing the flames of the passageway's scones to flicker. Jamarde shuddered a breath. "I wish that would quit happening. It reminds me of all those ghost stories from the keshel awfuls that Lavidah sneaks into the house."

"An illusion created by a few suggestions and well-hidden levers." Mechanics he itched to have a look at. "You would no doubt find the same tricks magical and enchanting under different circumstances."

"Perhaps." But her tone lacked conviction. Not that he blamed her. The building seemed to contain as many mysteries as Galena's Scroll.

After two flights, they reached a small antechamber with a locked cabinet and plain wood desk. Atop the desk sat a huge ball of twine and five unlit oil lamps. Estelle picked up the twine. "Let me guess. What we need to not get lost until morning?"

"Delightful." Xander lit a lamp with the candle from one of the room's sconces and illuminated the hallway beyond the antechamber. It branched off in three different directions. When the official said "labyrinth," she meant it literally. "This would be faster if we could search more than one path at a time."

"Every ball of twine has two ends," pointed out Massard.

Definitely an idea with the strength of a central shaft, able to withstand the torque of an entire plan. "If someone stays here as an anchor, keeping the rope spooling at an even tension, whoever finds Yosi first can tug three times. Then the anchor can let the other searcher know with the same three tugs."

"What if we run out of rope?" Jamarde asked.

"Hopefully Yosi will be able to hear one of us, and we'll know who should go ahead."

"And if not?"

"We'll fix that cog when it freezes."

Massard and Xander were chosen to be runners, with Estelle and Jamarde acting as their anchors. Rivka volunteered to keep the mess of unwound twine snag-free.

Xander tied an end to his wrist and lit a fresh lamp. But at the first juncture, he halted. Which way ought he go?

I collapsed into the corner of my cage. My hair hung disheveled from trying to use my pins to pick the lock. My muscles quivered from my contortions to wriggle between the bars. My sash and shoes were scattered across the floor below from my attempts to trigger the lever that held my cage aloft. All to no avail. I didn't need a timepiece to tell me that even if we were boarding the coach right now, we wouldn't reach the Fountain Tower soon enough.

And it was all my fault.

I hugged my knees to my chest, resting my forehead on them as silence wrapped around me, undisturbed by anything but my own breathing. Had Lavidah made it? Likely with time to spare. She was driven that way. Strong.

Unlike me. Life had been too easy. I had heard the whispers, the gossip. A spoiled milksop. That was me. Even Jamarde had said nearly as much upon my arrival in Kolchan. No matter how hard I worked to not depend on the advantages given me, it didn't change the outcome–I was soft. Ignorant. Inept. Untried. Unable to pass the simplest test of virtue for a manmade competition.

How would I survive when I faced a real trial?

"Yosi?"

The wispy letters of my name dissipated as quickly as they formed, swallowed whole by the fog enshrouding my mind. Probably because I was imagining things.

"Yosarai Patican!"

The letters turned sharper, more solid, penetrating the cobwebby mist. I lifted my head.

"Yosi, can you hear me?"

Xander. He was somewhere nearby. I tried to respond, but

nothing came out of my parched mouth. I licked my lips and tried again. "Here, I'm here!"

"Keep talking. I'm coming."

"I'm over here, though I have no idea where 'here' is. I do hope you brought a key or a lock pick or some such thing with you."

"For what purpose?" Xander entered my room and stopped.

Tears stung my eyes afresh. I had indeed made a mess of things.

Xander found the lever and flipped it, lowering my cage to the floor. He exaimed the lock, then disappeared back into the hallway for a moment before returning with a key that unlocked my door.

I stepped out, smoothing down my skirt. "Gratitude." I hung my head. "And I'm sorry." I'd lost us the Quest. All our work for nothing. A tear slipped past my barricade.

Xander supplied me my shoes. "What's wrong?"

"Besides getting stuck in a cage because I was in a hurry?" I tried to laugh, but my throat strangled the sound.

"This isn't your fault."

"Don't, Xander. Lies don't become you." I jammed a shoe on my foot, but it crushed my toes oddly.

"Are you saying you intentionally fell through?"

Wrong shoe. I switched them. "I should have been more cautious, like Estelle said."

"Someone else might have gone through anyway."

"I should have found a way out." The second shoe slid on without a problem.

Xander regarded me as he handed me my sash next. "I don't think this was a trial you were supposed to solve."

"We still failed to final because of my impulsiveness." I refused to meet his eyes as I wrapped the fabric around my waist.

"If Jamarde or Rivka had fallen through instead of you, would you be blaming them for our disqualification?"

His question drew me up short. "No, of course not."

"Then why are you blaming yourself?"

I bit my lip, unable to compose a good response that didn't sound outright arrogant. I focused on tying my sash behind my back.

Xander tugged it from my grasp and tied it for me.

I fingered his work–it was as neat as Rivka's. "Where did you learn that?"

"I have a half sister, remember? And Mum–well, I love her dearly, but nothing ever stays properly tied with her. Especially when a major event is about to happen." He slid a loop of twine from his wrist and began winding it into a ball, following it out of the room. "But the point is our success didn't depend solely on you. As Father once told me, the only thing that truly depends on you is your dependency on Sustainer."

I trailed Xander through the narrow hall. His words carried the solidness of truth, but their form seemed far too simplistic. What about all the menials in my father's house? Would they not rely on me after Avi's death? And the upcoming Exam–did not my success rely on me studying well and learning all I could?

"Trust me," said Xander. "It's not as simplistic as it sounds."

"How did you know what I was thinking?"

"Because I thought the same. Remember, many people depend on me too."

"Then how can you say this?"

Xander's shoulders rose and fell. "Because they are ultimately Sustainer's responsibility, not mine. That is why He is called Sustainer, is it not? What do the Writings of the Scribes say? 'With but a breath He sustains all things–'"

"'Bringing light to darkness, order to chaos, and life to the worlds.'" Some of the first Writings every Indeli child learned.

"That means everyone–everything–is dependent on Him, not on me. All I have to do is follow Him, trusting Him to care for the rest, whether through the work He gives me–or through a source separate from me. My obligation is to rely on Sustainer, my job is to obey Him."

Xander spoke those last words with the cadence of a mantra. How often had he repeated those very words as he faced the weight of a kingship he never wanted? Yet he faithfully moved forward, giving up personal dreams and desires because he felt Sustainer had called him to a different role.

Oh, to have that kind of faith! Could I truly believe all that depended on me was my dependency on Sustainer, and He would take care of everything else, all the outcomes and results? Especially in the face of a situation that seemed to tell another tale?

We rounded a corner, bringing us to a small room where the others waited for us.

Jamarde squealed and threw her arms around me. "You're well?"

"All my limbs are intact." I gave her a quick hug back before relinquishing myself to Rivka's fussing.

She tugged my hair back into proper arrangement. "At least your sash is still in order."

Estelle set the ball of twine on a nearby desk. "I don't know about the rest of you, but 'from this place of madness blind / I seek escape and freedom find.'"

"I couldn't have said it better," said Xander, and we murmured our agreement.

We climbed a flight of dimly lit stairs, and once again the door at the top swung open before us unbidden, allowing us entrance into the empty loading area. My gaze shot to the skylight. The clouds were dark charcoal. My mind's eye splattered blue across the scene, like raindrops on a windowpane. We had been so close.

Mascad clasped my shoulder. "Feel no regret, sibah. We lost by choice."

"He's right," remarked Estelle. "We had a chance to send part of the coterie ahead, but we all chose to stay."

"And such loyalty is a virtue of great value due to its rarity." A woman strolled toward us, a Quest band around her arm. She extended a bowl to Jamarde, who took it, eyes wide.

"Sustainer bless you, for your heart has been tried and it has come forth as gold, as much refined gold. And you"–she tipped her head to me–"are rich beyond measure to have such friends." She bowed to us all. "Congratulations on completing the task."

"We thank you, but I fear we're too late." Xander indicated the darkened skylight.

"Have you ever noticed that though punctuality is valued, it is never listed among the virtues?" She gave me a folded paper. "Present this to the gadohen when you arrive."

The tall double doors opened, our coach waiting outside. The woman spoke to the driver and then departed.

I fingered the note from the official, Xander's words echoing in my head once more. *The only thing that depends on you is your dependency on Sustainer.*

New tears sprang to my eyes, this time from gratitude at the vivid picture of that reality. Sustainer did not need my help to accomplish His plan any more than my coterie needed me to escape to complete the task. *Sustainer rules over all, and all will exalt Him in the end.*

I clutched our second chance. "To the Fountain Tower."

May Your will be done.

Lavidah stood on the platform, to the side and back of her fellow Questers. The tasks had been inanely easy, and they'd finished by midday, the first to do so. It must be a sign that this year Sustainer would smile on her. Proof that He knew how much she needed the money from the winner's purse.

Whether proof of blessing or not, arriving first had provided the unseen advantage of watching the other coteries arrive. And when they saw they were not the first, their expressions were an award unto itself.

The sun disappeared behind the horizon. Only two other coteries had completed all tasks correctly thus far, and her cousin's was not among them. As it ought to be. Two foreigners, a mixer, and a menial–they were an insult to Indeli culture and a blasphemy against Sustainer and all the festival represented. At least their failure publicly proved to all their utter incompetence.

The gadohen walked onto the platform, his presence stilling the waiting crowd and sealing the fates of the coteries. Her mouth curved. There would be no last-minute salvation for her cousin this time.

A commotion erupted in the back of the crowd. Lavidah squinted in the torchlight at the irreverent disturbance. Why didn't the priests remove the agitators?

She stilled. It couldn't be. It wasn't possible.

Possible or not, there was her cousin and the rest of her disgraceful group, wending their way to the front. Reaching the platform, they presented the objects collected from the six tasks. But the sun was gone. They would be disqualified, not permitted to continue, and indeed the gadohen dismissed them. There would be no talking her way out of this one.

Her cousin handed the gadohen a slip of paper. After reading it, his head jerked up, and words were exchanged. Her cousin's coterie bowed, collected their items, and ascended to take their place with the other successful Questers. No, this couldn't be. Nonetheless, no one stopped them. What had been on that paper? A bribe? A threat? Surely the gadohen would not succumb to such things, yet what else could it be?

Hisses and murmured threats rippled through the Questers as they walked by. Lavidah pressed her lips together. Though they deserved much worse, it was better to ignore them as inconsequential.

The gadohen stood before the crowd. "Just as the Gatherer and his helpers completed the six tasks laid upon them by the other realms, so the Questers before you have completed theirs. But the journey is not done. The Gatherer, when he claimed our people in exchange for the requested items, found no place to settle. Instead, armies drove the people into a barren wasteland at the heart of the Realms, trapping them in a waterless desert of scorching sun. The people cried out to the Gatherer."

"Give us water, give us water, give us water," responded the crowd.

"As those first people asked, noble Questers, we now ask of you: Give us water." The gadohen lifted a jar, gold outlining the colorful design, glinting in the torchlight.

"Give us water, give us water, give us water," chanted the people.

Lavidah eyed the water jar. So her cousin's coterie had advanced. No matter. Sustainer knew she needed to win this Quest, and the Scribes promised He would provide, just as He had provided for the Gatherer.

This year, she would be the one to give the people water, just like the chosen ones of old.

FINISHING

Finishing well might be one of the most difficult tasks we encounter, because it is the summation of everything that has come before.

For you cannot finish what has never been started, and starting requires courage, hope, vision. Courage to enter the unknown. Hope that what is begun is worth doing. Vision to see what could be before it yet is.

But starting is not enough. Between starting and finishing is the tedious middle. Here the new becomes familiar, and monotony sets in. Only perseverance, discipline, and faithfulness will keep you moving forward.

Then the finish is in sight! O joy! But now new dangers emerge, a temptation to race ahead, to neglect final details. Finishing well requires patience and a refusal to compromise. It requires a steadiness that takes no shortcuts.

Yes, finishing well might be one of the most difficult tasks we encounter, but when we do, we can walk away with our heads held high.

6

"We ought to abstain from the final trial."

Yosi's suggestion rang through their common room at the mahal.

Not compete? The thought clogged the gears of Xander's mind, and he could not force them forward to form any coherent thought worth speaking.

Yosi twisted a bracelet around her wrist. "I know that sounds ludicrous. We have come far and done the unthinkable. It seems foolish not to pursue this opportunity. However, we have already secured a fourth-place purse. Is it worth endangering ourselves for a position we are unlikely to obtain?"

Xander found his voice. "Have you no faith in our skills?"

"It is not our skills I doubt but our competitors' integrity. You heard the threats from the other coteries, and this time they won't be idle."

Estelle gazed at the walls, as if seeing again the slurs scrawled there, though the menials had done an excellent job this afternoon of scrubbing away any evidence of the vandalism. "She's right. The other coteries have discounted us thus far, but now . . . 'The pride of heart, when wounded deep, / awakens wrath that shall not sleep.'"

Keep calm. Don't get frustrated. He relaxed against a wall, adopting a causal stance, as if he didn't care one way or another. "How bad can it become? The rules forbid harming other competitors."

"Rules that can be enforced only when the intent to harm can be proven." Jamarde rubbed a thin scar on the inside of her wrist. "So-called accidents happen all the time."

"As much as I dislike to decline any worthwhile challenge," added Estelle, "I say we celebrate our position as the success it is and withdraw from the remainder of the Quest."

None of the ladies before him were cowards, and yet the fear in the room had thickened tangibly. Had he miscalculated the risk that much? He looked at Massard, who inclined his head in deference. "I concur with the sibahs."

Still, if the threat was that great, would inaction be sufficient to deter their opponents from doing harm anyway? He had no good rebuttals for their concerns, however, and perhaps this might be best, since Jamarde's sister had also advanced. A win on their part would do nothing to ease those strained relationships, and it might even add to the aunt's animosity toward Yosi. He would acquiesce. "In light of our forfeiture, will we be joining the others for the evening's festivities, or will we be requesting a meal here?"

Yosi thought for a moment. "They discovered one bell ago that we advanced, which is not much time to plot our doom. I see no reason not to celebrate our achievement."

As if in response, Jamarde's stomach rumbled and she giggled. "I guess I second that proposal."

With that decided, the six of them proceeded downstairs.

The ballroom was already humming with conversation, punctuated by bursts of laughter. Four couples danced a quadrille to a lively duo comprised of a twelve-stringed manitar and a double obaire. Others lingered along the edges of the room in pairs and trios, accounting for sixteen of the eighteen competitors. The other two were probably in the darkened garden beyond the open, glass-paned doors, and Xander wouldn't blame them. The air was heavy with the lamps' smoke and liberally distributed alcohol. A heaviness that grew thicker as conversations, then music, died as their presence was recognized.

Xander leaned toward Yosi. "Ever feel you're not wanted?"

"Unmistakably."

As if choreographed, the whole group turned their back on them, low conversation and music resuming. Xander drew Yosi and Estelle closer to his side as they circled around the room to a table laden with glasses and drinks, behind which a menial waited. "If that is a sample of warm Indeli hospitality, I think I prefer an icy Egdonian greeting."

A female competitor shoved a glass at Rivka as they passed by her. "Fetch me a drink, siv. Something unique."

Fire burned in Xander's throat. Rivka in her multicolored pavadai sattai could not be mistaken as one of the liveried menials, unless the woman was utterly blind. And there was nothing wrong with the sight of the competitor before them.

Rivka placed a restraining hand on Massard's chest and gave him a wink before taking the glass to the drinks table. She spoke with the server and pointed at several bottles. The server's eyes widened, then he smiled.

"By the way, the rail carriage leaves at midnight." The sharp words drew his attention back to the woman, still blocking their path.

"I beg your pardon?"

She flipped open and closed a fan with impatient boredom. "If you don't like the atmosphere here, no one will stop you from leaving. A rail carriage heads north at midnight."

Rivka returned and extended a glass to the competitor. "To your good health, sibah." She raised a second glass and took a sip.

The competitor huffed and spun away from them. Rivka

nudged them along toward the drinks table, her eyes dancing with mischief.

Yosi arched her eyebrows. "Do I want to know?"

"If there is anything to know, you shall know it soon enough."

The next moment, the woman Rivka had served choked. "Water," she gasped.

Her companion rushed to fetch her some, and Rivka turned. "Pardon me, sibah, you don't want to–"

The woman snatched the goblet from her companion, gulped the water, then spewed it back out, triggering cries of disgust from those nearest. She clutched a hand to her throat. "It burns."

Rivka took another glass from the table with a clear liquid in it. "Try this."

The woman started to knock it from her hand, then seemed to think better of it and downed the contents before collapsing against the wall.

As her companion advanced on them, Massard stepped in front of Rivka.

"What did you put in Elshir's drink?" the other man demanded.

"The same as mine," Rivka answered innocently. "The sibah asked for a unique drink, so I fetched her a Phantom Fire."

Xander choked. He'd had one sip–and only one–of the traditional Mounce drink. His sampling of it earned the respect of the Mounce diplomat, but he would have sworn the burning cocktail of firebrandy and phantom pepper wine left blisters all the way to his stomach.

The woman's companion scowled. "I don't believe you." He confronted the server behind the table. "Menial, what did you make for this siv?"

The server bowed. "Two glasses of Phantom Fire, a traditional Mounce cocktail."

"You're lying. She's one of you."

Rivka held out her glass. "If you are a connoisseur of drinks or know someone who is, please feel free to compare."

The man's gaze skimmed the room, then he summoned another competitor. "Counselor Ahman, can you tell if these are the same concoction?"

The counselor strode toward them, his tread confident and measured, a man who was used to being in control. Like Selucreh. Which was an unfair comparison. This was the same man who caught Jamarde during the opening ceremony and silenced her tricksters. Selucreh would have never done that.

The counselor set his tumbler on a side table and dipped a fingertip into the woman's glass to sample its contents. "Phantom Fire. A bold choice." He tasted Rivka's drink. "Also Phantom Fire. It appears the Quest has brought out the brave and daring among us."

"Yes, it appears it has," the man ground out. "Thank you, sri."

As the counselor nodded and retreated, Rivka sipped at her drink.

The competitor glared at her. "Don't think this absolves anything. The final task lies ahead, and we know how things can happen." He stalked away.

Massard relaxed his stance, and Xander considered Rivka with fresh regard. "Not that she was undeserving, but was it wise to prod a wasp's nest?"

Rivka exchanged her glass for a goblet of clear liquid. "Perhaps not, but since we are not competing further, I figured it could do little harm. After tonight they shall be too consumed with the final hunt to concern themselves with the likes of us."

"I hope you are right." Unfortunately, this group did not

impress him as one to forget an insult, and wounded pride had a way of festering and spewing forth in an unpredictable manner.

Like with Selucreh.

"Nonetheless, perhaps we ought to avoid further confrontation." Massard bowed to Rivka. "Would you do me the honor of a walk in the gardens?" He glanced at Xander. "Unless we ought to stay together?"

"I'm sure we can manage without you."

"Promise me you won't accept any unknown drinks from innocent-looking persons."

Rivka blushed.

Xander clasped a fist to his heart. "Upon my honor. Now go."

Massard and Rivka wandered into the gardens, Yosi tracking them the whole way. Once they were out of sight, she moved toward the drinks table, ordering a Nectar of Paradise. "I'm glad Mascad and Rivka have had this time together. I think it's been healthy for Rivka, giving her some extra incentive to pass her crossover assessment."

Xander requested a Lava Bubbler, before moving aside so Jamarde and Estelle could get their drinks. "I believe Mascad has benefited as well. I appreciate his single-mindedness, but he seems to forget there is more to life than his job." He retreated with Yosi to a quiet corner where they could watch the dancers, the colorful swirl of skirts mesmerizing.

"Will their friendship be a problem? Since he's your . . ." She clamped her lips together.

So she'd determined their relationship. "I foresee no problem on my part. I suspect the biggest obstacle will be the man himself."

He sipped on his Lava Bubbler. Sharp and sweet, but not quite right. Not quite home.

He suddenly wondered how his stepmum was faring, overseeing the preparations for the coronation while eluding questions about his disappearance. Maybe he shouldn't have left like he did. He wasn't the only one grieving his father's death. Moreover, as the next appointed king, he should be dealing with the ever-restless Parliament. His Lava Bubbler flattened into blandness. He ought to return home soon, assassins or no assassins.

"Is something wrong, hasib?"

Xander blinked the world back into focus. Jamarde and Estelle now stood across the room, studying a sculpture, but Yosi remained at his side.

"Homesick, I think, and realizing I'd left a heavy burden upon my stepmum, a burden that is rightfully mine." He almost said more, but cold prickled along his neck. A warning.

Behind him, less than three feet away, stood Lavidah, as cold and brazen as Yosi was innocent and warm. "Really, cousin, if you are going to throw yourself all over this water trog, have the decency of doing it in your rooms. We all know you are a trollop, but goodness, you don't have to flaunt it."

Yosi paled. Fire erupted deep within Xander. To attack Yosi's character in such a way was unconscionable. He ought to–

He ought to remain calm, that was what he ought to do. He was a prince, after all, nearly a king. As his parents often reminded him, being royal meant living according to a higher standard, no matter what those around him did. "Pardon me, Sibah Chiman, but perhaps you ought to have your eyesight examined. For Sibah Patican was not touching me, making your charge impossible."

Lavidah sniffed. "A mouse need not enter by the door to nest in your room."

"Better a mouse than a sand cobra," he countered, "for at least a mouse only seeks to live. A sand cobra seeks to kill."

"Yet the sand cobra has such cunning and beauty, even its victims must stand mesmerized by its presence." Lavidah shimmied closer to him.

Yosi stiffened. "That is true until the shadow of a mountain eagle crosses it. Then even the sand cobra remains still."

A mountain eagle—the royal emblem of Egdon. It would be intriguing to know if she'd chosen the symbol of his position intentionally.

Lavidah's eyes narrowed. "That's true, but even a mountain eagle is not immune to venom, and should the eagle be unlucky enough to snatch the cobra from its victim, it may well feel the bite meant for another."

Did she just threaten him? The veiled meanings, the hidden threats, the double connotations—this kind of wordplay was why he detested court politics. "Such a reaction secures the cobra's destruction. By striking the eagle it sends itself plummeting to its own death."

She lifted her glass. "Then it's best for the eagle and the cobra to avoid each other. If neither interferes with the other, both will live."

"But at what cost?" he asked. "The death of the cobra's innocent victim?"

"That depends." Lavidah's eyes glittered rather snakelike as she downed the remainder of her drink.

"Upon what?"

"Whether the mouse is wise enough to stay out of the cobra's path." She glided away, pausing to toss one last barb over her shoulder. "After all, if the cobra doesn't control the rodent population, who will?"

"Are you all right?"

Concern hung behind Xander's question—which was valid. After all, Lavidah just threatened Egdon's crown prince—soon to be king—and one of the most powerful men in the Seven

Realms. Shaky laughter bubbled out of my mouth. Better that than being paralyzed by fear or dissolving into tears.

Frowning, Xander shielded me from the rest of the room. "Yosarai?"

"If Lavidah knew whom she had just threatened . . ." Tears began to mingle with my laughter, and I dabbed my eyes with a handkerchief. "I beg your pardon, but when I imagined Lavidah's horror if she learned who you are and how she would fawn all over you, assuring you that wasn't what it sounded like . . ." I took a deep, steadying breath. "It was laugh or cry." I looked at my handkerchief. "Or both."

"Are you sure that's all?"

"Lavidah likes to strut."

"You may be underestimating your cousin."

Any vestiges of laughter vanished. "You believe she would follow through?"

Xander fingered the rim of his glass. "I have seen parlies of integrity stoop to bribery when their seat was vulnerable, lifelong friends become mortal enemies over a prized position, and brilliant statesmen resort to flattery and slander to secure the crown's favor. Such driven people can descend to depths once unimaginable to them, and I see that same drive in Sibah Chiman."

Across the room, Lavidah smiled coyly at one of her competitors. She was driven, and some underhanded tricks were normal for her. How far *would* she go? "Then it's good we won't be competing further."

"But will that be enough?"

That was a question for which I had no answer.

A menial meandered by with a tray, collecting glasses. I offered him mine, then noticed a pair of unclaimed tumblers on the side table. I reached to retrieve them for him, but the moment my fingers wrapped around the glasses, a flash overtook me.

I am the drinking glass. Amber liquid swirls inside me. Ice clinks against my crystalline edges, making me shudder. Fingers obscure the world around me. Not that I would see much anyway. It is dark outside. A clock chimes eight bells, mixing with a palm lark's evening call: loop-a-whip-aloo, loop-a-whip-aloo.

"Congratulations on your advancement." The words of the male voice were of a moderate stroke, slightly rounded with a small curl at the end of each one.

My holder says nothing.

Steps shuffle nearer, and the same voice speaks. "A shame about that last coterie though."

"Perhaps." The single word from the man who holds me forms a simple and precise script, but the edges are all blurred, distorted by the hand, hiding any distinguishing traits.

"Two Egdonians, a mixer, and menial? They must have bribed someone."

"Justice will be served in due time."

"How can you know that?"

A finger circles my rim, smearing his script further. "I've heard rumors they are a mask for the Egdonians to assassinate our most esteemed chancellor."

The other man inhales sharply. "Have you notified the authorities?"

"Insufficient evidence. They can't act on hearsay alone."

"But they must be stopped."

"Agreed. We must all do what we can to hinder them, no matter the individual cost."

"I'll let my coterie know. Good evenfall." *Steps walk away.*

"Masterfully handled, sri." A third voice circles us, the strokes of his low words broad and jagged, more a feral scrawl than a true script. "Everything in place?"

"Exactly as you ordered. But will you be?"

"You doubt my skill?"

"There are reasons they say the Quest cannot be rigged."

"Don't worry. I'll be there, receiving the medallion, bravely attempting to save our esteemed chancellor's life from our Egdonian assassin."

"Very good." The second man pads away.

The man holding me chuckles to himself. "Bravely attempting, but failing. A hero too late."

I resurfaced with a gasp, the glasses slipping from my fingers and shattering against the floor.

The menial bent down to collect the shards. "Do not be alarmed, sibah. This happens often."

Assassinations don't happen often–oh, he meant the tumblers. I pressed a hand against my stomach, trying to reorient myself. But an assassination *was* planned for the Ingathering. Not of Xander, like I had assumed. Of Chancellor Serex, by one of the competitors. My gaze darted around the room. Twelve of the other eighteen were male. Would it be possible to identify the speaker? The voice had been quite distorted.

Xander guided me away from the broken glass. "Yosi, what happened?"

"I . . ." My voice faltered. I couldn't tell him. Not here. Not now. Too many eyes, too many ears.

A gong sounded, announcing dinner. Xander's grip on my elbow tightened. "Are you unwell?"

The perfect excuse and a legitimate one, for I did feel unwell. With one word I could escape back to our rooms . . . and lose my best chance to identify the voice. I drew in a breath. I had to attend this dinner. "I'm fine, merely feeling a little weary from our busy day."

He looked at me but said nothing, and we entered the dining room. It was set with four low tables in a square, one team assigned to each table. I sank onto a pillow at the far end of our table, as the rest of my coterie settled to my right, and I stretched my neck to read the nameplate of the abutting table. Valor. That was neither Lavidah's team nor the Whirlwind coterie we defeated at the Fortress. At least I wouldn't be dealing with personal hostility, and perhaps if they started talking, the others would follow.

Once everyone was seated, the menials served the salad course, and I gave a nearby competitor a smile. "The food smells wonderful, doesn't it? I imagine it tastes even better after the busyness of the past two days. There never seemed quite enough time to eat."

He sniffed at me.

So much for pleasantries. I stabbed my salad. Maybe if I could figure out their strategy, I could get them talking. What might that include? Secrecy. Information collecting. Observation. Intimidation. I paused. That might work. I caved my shoulders to make myself look smaller, less threatening. "I've never participated in the Kolchan Quest before, and it is quite daunting. May I inquire how many you have done?"

"Five." His lip curled. "And you don't stand a chance."

The letters of his script squeezed closer together than those in my flash—his voice was higher—and the words tilted upward with the lilt of the northern provinces. That meant he was not my conspirator. "I never expected to reach this far. I don't even know what I would do should we win. You already have plans for the medallion, I suppose."

"Of course I do."

"You do?" asked the woman next to him. "I figured that was something to consider after we won."

The man on her far side shook his head. "Women. Always leaving things to the last minute."

Moderate stroke, script simple and precise. Similar to the conspirator, but was it the same? If only I could have heard him better.

"If that is so, what grand plan have you devised?" she challenged.

"I would book the Teardrop to showcase my musical works exclusively for the next year."

Yonath snorted from Whirlwind's table. "You needed to pre-plan that?"

Yonath's script was as fine and tight as a bowstring, definitely not a match. At least the conversation was spreading.

The composer glared at Yonath. "And what is your lofty ambition should you win the medallion?"

"I don't need to divulge my plans to you."

The man seated at the far end of Valor's table grunted. "You probably don't have any plans to divulge." That man's voice scripted out too long and broad.

My eyes returned to the composer. What possible reason could he have for killing Chancellor Serex?

"If you feel so free, what are your magnificent plans?" challenged Yonath.

"Indel's infrastructure is falling behind the other realms, despite a huge workforce at our fingertips. I would propose a law that would require all menials to provide five years of labor for the country."

All menials? The soup soured in my stomach.

The apprentice counselor seated at Lavidah's left scoffed.

"Such a law would last less than a year, given the outcry from the elites about having their property conscripted. Levies on foreign goods would be far more effective, especially on those from the north."

Another simple and precise script of moderate stroke, though the letters were slightly ragged along the edges. I wished the edges hadn't been blurred in the flash. An apprentice counselor could orchestrate an assassination with greater ease, with more to gain from it. This one also had no love of foreigners.

The man seated next to Yonath, the shooter who attacked Xander at the Fortress, spoke up. "At least he would be accomplishing something, if only for a brief period."

I frowned at the soup placed in front of me. Now that he wasn't growling at Xander, the shooter's script resembled the apprentice counselor's and the composer's. If I couldn't recognize the voice, how would I identify the conspirator?

"All of you are thinking far too small," declared the man sitting near the middle of Whirlwind's table.

Moderate stroke, rounded script, each word curling slightly at the end–the congratulator from the garden? That would eliminate the men from Whirlwind. Swallowing, I forced myself to speak up. "What would you consider a vision grand enough for the medallion, hasib?"

"All foreigners would be deported, their goods confiscated, and mixers reduced to menial status. I'm sure no one would care about the Council conscripting *them*."

The room tilted in such a way that, for a moment, I couldn't tell up from down. Would the Council permit them to enact these awful plans?

I steadied myself. His script did match the congratulator, which meant the conspirator had to be from Valor or Cobra.

A second woman from Valor, the one to whom Rivka had given the Phantom Fire, raised her glass to Whirlwind.

"Admirable plans, though I think it would be easier and more effective to repeal the law permitting a menial to earn elite status. Sustainer has placed each person where they belong; to change that status is a defiance of His will." She fluttered her eyes at Counselor Ahman, seated on Lavidah's right. "What are your plans, sri, if I may be so bold? I suspect you've envisioned something far grander than the rest of us dare to dream."

"I have heard many admirable plans tonight." Despite his quiet voice, firm strokes formed his straightforward script, the precision of each nuance conveying a mastery that quieted all. "But when I win, my focus will be on an even greater threat, one that imperils the security of our entire beloved nation. For in recent days I have become aware of an invisible enemy who has infiltrated every sphere and strata of our society, undermining the very heart of Indeli culture, belief, and way of life." He paused, and everyone waited attentively. "It is the eradication of this scourge to which I have pledged my life, and I will see it done for the protection of all. Winning the medallion would merely smooth our path to victory."

My breath caught. Could the counselor already be aware of those plotting the assassination, or did he speak of a different threat? If only I could be certain. Especially since his script also bore some marked similarities to the conspirator's.

The composer snorted. "If such a threat does exist, that would make a lofty goal indeed, sri. So lofty that I suspect it will be outside even your powerful grasp."

Counselor Ahman hid a smile behind his glass. "Perhaps."

From there conversation continued, but identifying the voice became harder as the evening went on and script overlapped script. I breathed a word of gratitude to Sustainer when dessert was over and we could depart, the first coterie to leave. Reaching our rooms, I sank onto the cushions by the table, a headache squeezing my mind in an ever-tightening grip.

Rivka paced the room. "They were simply trying to intimidate us tonight, weren't they? The Council would never let them do any of those things." I'd never heard Rivka sound so much like a scared child before, even when she *was* scared.

"Except they have before." Estelle wrapped her arms around herself as if chilled, though the room was warm and stuffy. "About five years ago a winner was granted his request for a three-month embargo with Kossac, and two years before that a heavy tax was levied on all non-Indeli craftsmen, which almost ruined Oda before it was repealed."

"So, no matter which of the other coteries wins, someone will be in trouble." Jamarde flopped beside me.

Rivka rubbed her stomach. "Maybe I was rash to give that Phantom Fire."

Bile burned my throat. I had to tell them the rest. "That isn't even the worst part. One of the competitors plans to assassinate Chancellor Serex at the final ceremony–and blame the Egdonians."

Mascad stiffened, and Xander swore. Loudly. Much too loudly. "That would be seen as an act of war!"

"The country is already vulnerable," Mascad said. "We had best inform the authorities. Which competitor was planning this?"

I cradled my head. Why must the room pitch about like an airship caught in a whirlwind? "I don't know."

"You don't know?" Jamarde's voice drove a stake of pain into my head. "How can you not know?"

"I overheard a conversation, but didn't see who was speaking. I tried to identify the voice at dinner, but . . ." I shook my head. Not a good idea. Pain took nausea for a spin about the room. Had I eaten something that didn't agree with me? A haze obscured the last bell.

"Is there any chance they saw you?" Tension radiated off Mascad.

"Set your mind to rest on that account, hasib. I can assure

you with complete confidence they never knew I was there," I managed to say.

At Xander's glance, I gave a single nod in confirmation, but even that miniscule gesture set the room spinning again.

"I can vouch for her invisibility." Xander raised a hand before Mascad asked more. "I was not privy to the conversation, but I was nearby when the incident happened. They did not detect Yosi's presence."

Estelle rubbed her arms again. "So, we have the threat of horrifying laws and an assassination conspiracy. What do we do now?"

I knew the answer. Had known the answer since the flash hit. I'd ignored it, seeking another solution, another possibility. I rose to my feet, and thankfully, my wobbly legs held. Did I have sufficient time to reach our room? "We must win the Quest . . ." I clenched fistfuls of my skirt. Too late. "Right after I get sick." I lunged for a decorative bowl on the side table.

I crumpled the missive in my hand.

One conversation, and the judge had pieced everything together. At least enough to warrant writing the queen. And I would have never suspected, apart from an informant recognizing the letter for what it was. That had been the judge's sole mistake–sending a letter immediately instead of waiting until his return home.

I lit the corner of the letter in the flame of a lamp and placed it on an ashtray. Flames consumed the paper, its warning never to be read by the intended recipient. But the judge was cunning. When he received no response, he would become suspicious.

The flame died, leaving nothing but cinders. How to deal with this latest breach of security? Every possibility included a chance the judge might outmaneuver me. All but one. But as distasteful as that option might be, I had already underestimated him once.

I would not make the same mistake again.

Morning found us wrung out but on our feet, by Sustainer's grace and Rivka's tonic. Jamarde alone did not fall ill, since one dish from the night before had not tasted right to her. The rest of us dealt with varying levels of sickness throughout the night, but it could have been worse. Morning could have seen us bedridden, which was probably the intent of whoever poisoned our food. And I was certain it must have been poisoned, for what were the odds that we alone, in the entire mahal, became ill?

However, Rivka's skills and connections once again served us well, and with Jamarde's help she secured ingredients for a homemade tonic. Though it tasted like sewage, we were dressed, functional, and actually able to eat breakfast by eight bells. Now it was time to join the other coteries in the mahal's foyer for the start of the final trial . . . if we could leave our room. For no matter how much we pushed or shoved, the door refused to open.

"Of all the low tactics!" Jamarde huffed. "They must have done that while we were sleeping."

"Actually, while we were eating." Estelle looked thoughtfully at the table, which held the remains of a breakfast delivered but one bell before.

Xander dragged his hand through his hair. "When does not matter. Escaping does."

Because we still needed to warn Chancellor Serex. Xander and Mascad, despite feeling ill, tried to file a report with the authorities yestereve, but the guards at the gate wouldn't let them leave the mahal "for security reasons." When Xander explained the need to contact the authorities, the guards dutifully wrote down the concern but refused to do more, dismissing the charges as a ploy to eliminate the competition.

Mascad prowled through the suite. "We could break a bedroom window and make a rope to descend, but the sibahs . . ." He eyed the three of us who spent the night sick.

At least the pants beneath my blue anarkali dress would make such a climb easier if it was necessary, but my legs hoped it wouldn't be. I fingered the pearls edging the neckline. *Sustainer, now what? You know we desire to win not for personal glory, but for the saving of a life . . .*

Rivka stacked dishes nearby. She always resorted to cleaning when nervous. Such a menial way of coping, though it probably had more to do with her distaste for messes than her sphere.

I halted, mind racing. "Is there a menial passageway here, by chance?"

Rivka paused in her cleaning. "I haven't seen one, but then again"–her eyes focused on Xander and Mascad's room–"I haven't been everywhere."

Xander swept his arm to the side with a flourish. "Please. Anything to avoid breaking the windows and descending four stories on a bed-cloth rope."

Rivka entered the room, the rest of us clustering in the doorway. *Please, Sustainer. Let there be something here.*

After several moments, she shook her head. "I'm sorry, I don't think there's one here. Unless . . ." She paused by one of the bunk beds.

Mascad bowed, Egdonian style. "If I may?"

He dragged the bed away. The floorboard in the corner was burned with the same marking as the stone in Everstar's park. Rivka pressed down, and a low passageway opened.

"Good thinking, both of you." Xander grabbed a bag containing the objects we'd collected over the past two days. "Now lead the way!"

Rivka ducked into the hole, and we followed her down the steep staircase and through a narrow hall right into the kitchen.

All the menials stared at our appearance. Rivka presented them with a respectful greeting. "Pardon our intrusion. Somehow our door became barricaded, and we needed an alternate exit."

"I told you something was brewing," muttered one menial to another.

"You saw something?" I asked.

The menial hastily bowed. "Yes, I mean, perhaps, sibah."

Rivka laid a hand on the menial's arm. "You are not in trouble, but we would appreciate any information."

"When I delivered breakfast this morning, some Questers loitered in the hallway–from all three coteries."

"Oh, that is bad." Jamarde wrung her hands. "If they are working together . . ."

She didn't need to finish her sentence. Individual antagonism would have been difficult enough. If they were coordinating their efforts, their combined resources would be far more complicated to defeat. Yet with the chancellor's life on the line, what other option did we have?

Another menial held out a covered basket to us. "To help you on the way."

I peeked inside. It was filled with bottles, labeled as various medicinals and tonics, along with bandages, smelling salts, and water flasks.

"We heard what happened after dinner and thought additional . . . incidents might occur."

Tears pricked my eyes as we thanked them and headed toward the entrance.

I expected the main foyer to be empty. With the early

start the others had, they should have left long ago. Instead, they stood in tense knots as far apart from each other as the tight space allowed, as if breathing the same air would enable the others to sniff out their secrets. The leaders of the three coteries were the one exception. They stood around a Quest official, arguing.

"It's obvious they aren't coming. Why delay the rest of us for them?"

"On the contrary, it's obvious they have every intention of participating." The official nodded in our direction. "Illuminary, welcome."

Our competitors glared, and wispy but pointed words floated by from those nearest.

"You said they were–"

"They were. Someone must have missed something." A glare was sent toward Valor.

The kitchen menial was right. The barricade was a concerted effort to hinder us.

The official shifted to the middle of the room. "Welcome, Questers. Now that you have all assembled, we shall begin. Each of you received a coin for every task completed. Since we cannot release you at the same time, order of exit will be determined by bidding, which opens now." He quickened his speech. "Who has one silver coin, one silver coin? Good, good. Who has two? Who has two silver coins? Wonderful. Anyone here have three silver coins?"

I stared at the floor, its inlaid design smearing. It was I who suggested we give the coins away, and it was I who gave away our last coin after yestereve's ceremony to a family with many small and very tired children in obvious need of a hired coach home. Now we had nothing to bid.

"We made the right choice." The bases of Xander's words broadened, adding to them a sense of immovable stability. "Sustainer will supply."

I twined my fingers together. If he could hold on to that, then I could too.

"I have a bid of six silver coins. Do I hear anything different? Six silver, once. Six silver, twice."

"One gold and one silver," called Whirlwind.

Some of the coteries received gold coins for their reward? Perhaps we had not done as well as we thought.

"Two gold and two silver," countered Cobra.

"Two gold and two silver. Do I have–"

"Two gold and three silver!"

The others around me shifted as the bidding continued, and a man appeared at my side–Elder Reuven from the Scriptorium. "The first shall be last, and the last shall be first." He pressed a purse into my hand. "Enjoy your golden harvest."

I poured the contents into my hand. Six gold coins clustered on my palm, one for each silver we'd given away.

"Four gold and two silver. Is there–"

"Five gold," I called. Was I using our coins wisely? Yet it couldn't be coincidence that the money had been given to us in this moment.

The other three coteries stared at us.

I stared at the official.

"Five gold, once."

The leaders from Whirlwind and Cobra merged together. Whispers and sharp hand gestures ensued. What were they plotting?

"Five gold, twice . . ."

Lavidah grabbed the coins Whirlwind extended. "Five gold, one silver!"

I glanced at my coterie. They all nodded. This would not be enough, but we had to try. "Six gold."

"Six gold. Six gold once . . ."

"Six gold and one silver." Lavidah shot me a smug look.

"Six gold and one silver. Does anyone wish to bid more?

Six gold, one silver, once. Six gold, one silver, twice. Six gold, one silver, done. Congratulations, Cobra. You have earned the right to go first." He collected their money. "Sustainer be with you." He waved them through the front doorway.

Lavidah smirked at me as she slipped her hand into the elbow of Counselor Ahman.

Bidding began again, this time for the second departure. With Valor possessing their original six silver coins, and Whirlwind having bartered away two golds to Cobra, we won the second round with three gold coins.

I nearly sprinted down the brick steps toward a waiting coach with covered windows. The sooner we left, the sooner we could overtake Cobra. As I grasped the door handle, Rivka cried out. I spun around. My maid sprawled awkwardly on the stairs, clutching the medicinal basket to her chest. "Rivka, what happened? Are you all right?"

"I'm fine." She struggled to sit as Mascad knelt beside her and glared at the stairs, where a large chunk of brick had been removed. Why hadn't I noticed that when we left? Then Xander picked up a splintered wood sheet, his face grim. It had been painted to match the surrounding brick.

Mascad assisted Rivka to her feet, but when she placed weight on her right foot, she grimaced and would have fallen if it hadn't been for Mascad's grip.

A menacing growl rumbled from him. "You're not fine." He scooped her up, ignoring her protests, and carried her to the coach.

The rest of us settled inside, and as the coach lurched into motion, Mascad pulled out a roll of bandages from the medicinal basket. Rivka reached out her hand. "I can do that."

Instead of surrendering the bandages, Mascad propped her injured foot on his lap and unlaced her sandal. My maid gripped the edge of the seat, her eyes pleading with me to interfere on her behalf. I studied my fingers. The ink stains had nearly faded.

Xander leaned back in his seat. "Don't worry. Mascad is excellent at tending to injuries." Then he rolled his shoulders, as if shaking off the tension of the past few minutes. "That last mishap aside, I believe that went better than we could have hoped."

"How can you say that?" Jamarde's words pitched sharply upward. "Lavidah's coterie has the lead!"

"But we do not know what lies ahead or what we will need," replied Xander. "Yes, they have the lead, but they also have no money. We have walked away with three gold coins, far more than any other team, while retaining second place. That may position us better than all the others in the end."

Would that be true? *Please, Sustainer, let it be so.*

The coach pulled into a stone cavern. Or that was how it sounded, based on the hard echo of the horses' hooves and the coach's wheels.

Rivka adjusted her now-bandaged foot. "Where do you think they're taking us?"

Estelle's light chuckle carried a nervous vibrato. "If you can answer that, you will solve the most guarded secret of the Kolchan Quest. It's said even the chancellor does not know where the final trial occurs."

The rattling-clopping echo filled our silence. Xander's pocket watch ticked off the seconds. Every tick seemed further and further apart. How much longer before we reached our destination?

"All will be well." Once again, Xander's script carried a broadened base that made the words appear unshakeable.

"You can't know that."

He sat straighter. "Yes, I can, for Sustainer rules over all, and therefore all is done according to His plan. His ways are perfect, and what can be better than perfection?"

How could I argue with that? However, Sustainer's perfection did not equal my preference. What if His plan included the unthinkable?

The clopping of hooves slowed. My heartbeat accelerated.

The last trial was about to begin–and our only chance to overtake Cobra.

The tension crystallized in the air as they came to a stop, and Xander practiced the breathing exercises his tutor taught him. *His plan is perfect.* He meant the words when he spoke them, but would he still believe them if this day ended with a declaration of war?

A minute ticked by, then two. Nothing happened. Were they to exit on their own or wait for someone to fetch them? Another coach rattled toward them and stopped nearby, followed by low voices. On their own, then. Xander reached for the door. It opened.

A priest beckoned them out. "A thousand pardons for the delay, noble Questers. Your patience is a virtue to you."

A virtue perhaps, but a detriment as well, for a second priest already ushered Valor, the coterie who arrived after them, into a narrow tunnel on the far side of the natural cavern. A third coach stood nearby, presumably Cobra's.

Had the priest delayed on purpose? No ripple of guilt disturbed his placid face. Nonetheless, encouraging deliberate slowness was a cog that would fit well into Cobra's scheming.

He shouldered the pack of objects, while Rivka handed the basket of medicinals to Estelle before Massard helped her to alight. She listed to one side, supported by Massard, but at least she could put some weight on her foot.

"If you will follow me." The priest shuffled toward the tunnel at the pace of a seaslug. More and more, this bore the mark of intention rather than coincidence. What could they do, though, but follow along and hope they could regain the time lost?

They bypassed three barred stairwells before the priest unlocked the gate of a fourth. "May Sustainer go before you, guard behind you, hover over you, uphold under you, providing all you need."

The steep stairs would force them to walk single file. Xander glanced at Massard, who was informing Rivka he would be carrying her down. "Take the rear." Then he began the descent.

After about a dozen steps down, a loud boom and clank reverberated against the stone. Jamarde yelped. "What was that?"

"I believe we were just locked in," Massard said dryly.

Xander glanced back. "Stay close." A useless warning, but something needed to be said to get them moving again.

"How far down do you suppose this goes?" Yosi asked.

"No idea."

"At least we won't get lost." Leave it to Rivka to be practical. "I wonder if Emori remembered to dust the grooves in the stair-step clock at home. It loses time dreadfully when they're dirty." And completely random.

Estelle chuckled. "'To lose time and one's way, / both shall discourage and dismay.' It would be horrid to fail the trial due to a wrong turn."

The stairway curved, and the space widened. "I think the end is near."

With a mixture of dread and excitement, Xander descended the final stairs into a square room. He'd conjured up many possible scenarios: a cantankerous priest-turned-trickster, a complex contraption to draw water, a series of physical obstacles to reach the water jars. None of his imaginings had prepared him for the colorful bas-relief mural that covered the walls, floor to ceiling, depicting a surreal landscape.

A monkey, looking very cold, sat on the snowy roof of a

bakery, its windows golden with light and hot rolls displayed. It overlooked a hill over which dozens of black-spotted puppies poured in pursuit of a pair of rabbits. A pink horse lay in a meadow, a rainbow pouring forth from the horn on its forehead. The rainbow arched over a dark chasm, which contained a skeleton clutching a corroded knife and was surrounded by rats and snakes, before ending at a black pot filled with . . . Xander examined it more closely. Gold coins? Why would anyone put that in a cauldron? But was that any odder than the nearby painted meadow, which boasted an unattached archway through which could be seen a forest and a winged being of fire? And so the mural went, strange and stranger.

But as Massard put Rivka down, it was Jamarde who pointed out the strangest thing of all. "Where's the exit?"

Xander scanned the room. The stairwell from which they'd just emerged was the sole opening.

"Please tell me we aren't trapped." Her words sped up like a mechanism wound too tight. "Tell me there's a way out."

Xander clasped her shoulders. "Jamarde." He tried to infuse her name with the same confident tenderness his father had used with him when he panicked over a speech or social gathering. "We are not trapped."

She focused on him, questions in her eyes.

"The Quest is meant to test, not to trap. That means an exit is here."

"Then how do we find it?"

That was the heart of the matter. How to find what had been well-concealed. For they weren't here by mistake. They had been led here. Which meant they were here intentionally, for a reason.

Just as you are crown prince for a reason? The unexpected thought unbalanced him for a moment.

"I don't know about how, but Saunders is right. We will find it." Yosi drew their attention to a banner unfurled over one part of the mural, inscribed with a quote from the original Ingathering story. "As that says, 'Sustainer has provided all you need.'"

"And what we need is some sort of locking mechanism." Xander closed his eyes since the picture distracted his thinking.

Because it was a distraction? What if the key lay not in the mural but elsewhere? His eyes flew open . . . and landed on a circular groove on the floor. Xander knelt beside it. Etched words filled the circle with shallow holes beside each word. The words themselves seemed to have no correlation, except they were all nouns. Flowers intertwined with the names of prophets, inventions intersected with foods, locations overlapped common household objects, all arranged in an intricate design. More than beautiful, however, it was also practical. "A circle lock. We insert levers into the proper holes and turn the plate until a door opens."

"But how many holes and which ones? And from where do we get the levers?" asked Jamarde.

"One thing at a time, as Oda would say," Estelle said. "First, what do we use as levers? Determining the right holes does no good without them."

Yosi gazed at the banner on the wall. "'Sustainer has provided all you need . . .'"

Xander stopped. *Has* provided. As in, they already possessed. "The objects from the tasks!" Xander shrugged off the bag. They helped him spread out the objects they'd acquired over the past two days. The trio of eating utensils were the obvious choice, their handles the perfect size for the holes.

"That also tells us how many," Estelle noted. "Now all we need to know is which ones."

They tried a couple of combinations, but nothing worked.

Yosi fingered the fork. "Why eating utensils? Why not give us levers or cranks or shafts? 'Sustainer has provided all . . .'" Her eyes widened. "'In this way Eshom spoke to those with him:

"Sustainer has provided all you needed, supplying His good gifts for the tasks ahead." Thus, the elchan were bestowed.'"

Six elchan, six tasks, six objects–that couldn't be coincidence. Xander closed his eyes, tugging the next words from memory. "'To Posea, the simplewit of Egdon, was given the ability to eat the very words of Sustainer and know the flavor of the future . . .'"

"The food diviner." Jamarde knelt along the edge of the circle, shoving up her glasses. "We look for words related to food. That still gives us six options: pottage, seacrackers, lemon, cocoberry custard, spretzeletti, and spiny kale."

"It's more than food. The words had a taste," Yosi said. "Taste comes in four types: sweet, sour, salty, and bitter. The only sour one is the lemon." She tried the utensils in the hole by "lemon." The fork and spoon were too small, but the knife slid in with a click. "Of course, you need a knife to eat a lemon."

"So, following that logic . . ." Jamarde pushed the spoon into the hole by the cocoberry custard. Like with the knife, a click suggested a correct match.

That left a fork and four choices: seacrackers, spiny kale, pottage, and spretzeletti. It also left two tastes: salty and bitter.

"We can ignore pottage," Yosi said, "as it is rather bland and eaten with a spoon. But both the kale and the spretzeletti are eaten with a fork, one bitter and the other salty. Which one is the right one?"

"The simplest way to know is experimentation." Xander inserted the fork into the hole next to the spretzeletti. When nothing happened, he tried the hole by the spiny kale. A click announced success.

With all three utensils in place, he tried to move the lock. It refused to budge. What had they missed?

"What if . . ." Rivka placed a finger into the hole beside the seacrackers. There was click. "We needed all four tastes, and seacrackers are eaten with the most common utensil of all." She turned the dial with her inserted finger. A door in the mural swung open.

A low rumble of fast-moving water met their ears. Xander walked onto a stone peninsula jutting into a lake and surveyed the surrounding cavern. The well-lit room was not huge as far as caverns go. Many at home were more spacious. Still, it was sizable. Six peninsulas, including the one he stood upon, were evenly dispersed throughout the room, each beside a tunnel that allowed the water to flow out of the cavern.

He inhaled a sharp breath. This was no ordinary underground lake. This was *the* spring that fed the six Aiyn rivers and the origin of the miracle that the Ingathering and final trial referenced. Xander gripped the top rail of an iron fence along the edge of the peninsula. Massard released a low whistle. "Is that what I think it is?"

"If you are thinking that is Ayin Chi, the Spring of Life, then yes, it is." Awe filled Yosi's voice.

"They let us in here?" Rivka whispered.

"It appears that way." Estelle pointed across the cavern, where Cobra huddled around a contraption on a metal island–one of six floating on the surface of the lake, surrounded by colorful lily pad-like rafts.

"What are we to do now?" asked Jamarde.

Xander shook himself. They had a job to do, or Egdon would face consequences harsher than being barred from the sacred places of Indel.

Parked beside their peninsula was a skondola fashioned like a gondola boat, its cable spiraling upward around the entire circumference of the cavern before stopping at a suspended platform with a clear box on it. The object inside looked like a water jar. But the cable wasn't moving, and even if it was, the skondala wouldn't have gone anywhere. Its roller mechanism had been disengaged.

Cobra whooped; a waterwheel attached to their island

was turning. The pieces clicked in his mind as clear as one of Drom's diagrams. Align the lily pads into a bridge to the island and start the waterwheel to create steam to power the skondola, which would transport them to the suspended platform with the water jar. "It can be done."

"What can?"

Xander explained the process, and when he finished, the others gaped at him. "What?"

"'What is plain to the wise / others' minds could never devise.'" Estelle smiled at him. "Oda would be proud of you."

Voices echoed from their left, where Valor marched across to their island.

Massard blocked Xander's view. "Focus on the problem, not the competition."

That meant deducing how to reach their own island. Too far apart to jump, the colored lily pads had to be aligned somehow. Perhaps someone needed to swim to them.

"Don't even think about it. The bottom of Ayin Chi has never been found"–Yosi gestured at the bubbling center–"and the spring creates powerful currents that would sweep us away into one of the rivers." She waved at the archways.

Estelle joined them at the open tip of the peninsula. "If the first puzzle was based on the first elchan, is this based on the second?"

A solid suggestion. Which one, then, was second? He never could keep them straight.

Yosi closed her eyes, her fingers caressing the air, as if reading by touch rather than by sight. "'To Kayapo, the cripple-legged boy of Sarmazon, was given the ability to hear the song from which all things were built and bring back all into harmonious alignment, healing both body and soul.'"

"The song healer."

"Alignment is what we need, but how?" asked Jamarde.

Estelle pulled out the bowl from their pack. "With sound."

Kneeling, she filled the bowl with water to the first line and pinged the edge.

The third, seventh, and twelfth platforms moved toward center. They paused there a moment, gears whirling, then returned to their former positions.

Estelle filled the bowl to the second line. A similar thing happened, with platforms two and five moving this time. At the third line, three other platforms moved, including the one nearest them. That one latched into place, while the other two retreated. Estelle drained the water back to the second line, and this time the second platform latched onto the first platform.

"Brilliant," Xander breathed.

Piece by piece, she built the walkway, random notes meshing into a melody. Even here the Indelis couldn't resist creating beauty, although true randomness would have been more effective and challenging. Estelle dipped her bowl into the lake to refill it. A screech rang out. She startled. The bowl plunked into the water.

"No!" Estelle dove for it.

Xander dove for her.

I gasped as Estelle lunged for the bowl. Xander grabbed her arm before she plunged into the lake. She made a wild swipe, splashing water. "The bowl–"

"Is beyond retrieval and not worth your life." He pulled her away from the edge, and she slumped onto the ground. Safe.

Too bad the same couldn't be said for the bowl. I glared at the coterie circling above in their skondola. A woman saluted us. This had to be Lavidah's doing. She hadn't played fair for years, and there was no reason to expect her to do so now. But such an underhanded trick wouldn't stop us. Not this time.

"What do we do now?" asked Rivka.

"There is nothing we can do." Estelle's script, usually elegant and fluid, turned uniformly rigid so it resembled typewriter print more than a handwritten script.

Xander crossed his arms. "I refuse to believe that."

She sighed. "That's reality. Sometimes bad things happen, and there is nothing you can do about it."

But if we didn't figure out how to overcome this bad thing, even worse things would come. Even as we dallied, Whirlwind strolled down their peninsula. "Yes, our bowl is gone, with no way to retrieve it. But just because we cannot change the past, there is no need to admit defeat in the present."

Cheers echoed across the waters. Valor's waterwheel began turning. Estelle glanced over at them. "When the future has been determined, is it worth fighting for?"

I'd never seen her this dejected.

Xander crouched beside her, forcing her to look at him. "Yes, because time belongs to Sustainer, and if He has brought us here at this time, it is for a purpose."

"Then what do we do?" Under different circumstances, Estelle's words might have been a challenge, but a violet strand of yearning threaded among them; she was simply looking for hope.

A fragment of Estelle's song whispered in my ear: *Thus I waited, and my help came; diff'rent, yes, than what I name.* I knelt beside Xander. "Does it have to be a bowl? Or will a human voice work as well?"

"It seemed activated by the specific note"—he rubbed his chin—"so, in theory, voice would work."

I laid a hand on Estelle's arm. "Don't you have perfect pitch? Can you replicate the bowl's notes?"

Her glazed expression faded. "I'll try."

She started singing, her voice even more clear and perfect than the bowl. She worked through the notes already played, gaining strength as they melded into a beautiful melody. The other platforms locked into place until one was left. Without hesitation, Estelle's voice soared up into a final note the bowl would have never produced.

The final part of the walkway locked into place. Second test completed.

But four more awaited us, if one object was needed per test. Tests we weren't completing nearly fast enough. Cobra huddled around a water jar on one of the suspended platforms. Valor circled the cavern in their skondola, while Whirlwind poked at machinery on another island halfway across the cavern.

"What is next?" Jamarde followed me to the island of machinery.

"'To Quarmis, the one of Mounce who had neither hearing nor speech, was given the ability to taste good and evil and to recognize the difference between right and wrong,'" I quoted.

"I was going to say the waterwheel, but that works too." Xander inspected the nearest contraption. Beside seven levers were seven small bowls with various powders. "Spices."

Perfectly logical since the third elchan was truth taster. Which lever were we to use, however? Maybe we should test them at random.

Jamarde pulled down the first lever. A red light flashed, something clanked, and a timer started ticking down. "Uh-oh."

Xander tugged on the other levers, but they refused to budge. "Locked. We won't be able to do more until the timer is out."

Jamarde paled. "I thought it might be faster . . ." She hung her head. "I mean, it worked with the first puzzle. I'm sorry."

I touched her shoulder. "If you hadn't done it, I would have. Meanwhile, let's figure out the puzzle." I withdrew the spice jar from the bag. "I suspect this is the one we need."

Estelle examined the jar. "Levers one and four are wrong– not the right color. Beyond that . . ."

"I've spent a fair amount of time in the kitchens. Let me try." Rivka limped over and sniffed the jar's spice, then the bowls by the levers. "Not two, five, or six."

"That leaves three or seven."

A clank sounded. Whirlwind's waterwheel was now functioning.

Jamarde twisted her hands together. "The clue was truth taster, was it not?"

Of course. Jamarde had been identifying the finer flavors of food the whole competition. I held out the jar to her. "I suspect you can identify a match easier than the rest of us."

Jamarde hesitated, then tested the spices once, then a second time. "Seven?"

Estelle glanced between our waterwheel and Whirlwind's. "I don't mean to be contrary, but theirs appears to be lever three."

"On the other hand," said Xander, "nothing says the machines are identical."

The timer dinged. Everyone looked at Jamarde.

I offered the jar to her again. "You have the most sensitive palate of anyone I know. Trust it."

Jamarde hesitantly took another sample, paused, then pulled lever seven.

A green light flashed and the wheel began turning. We burst into cheers.

I hugged my cousin. "You did it!"

We turned to our other contraption, whose numerous pipes were twisted around each other to form the head of a maned moonbear. Tracking the path of a particular pipe would be impossible, at least by sight. Xander flipped various latches at the pipes' bases as steam puffed.

I stepped to his side. "The next elchan is word breather. 'To Zibar, the ancient one of Zantou, was given the ability to smell the meaning of any word, even those hitherto unknown to him.'"

"Then we need the incense. With it we can sniff the pipes to know which latches to open and close, so the steam exits those pipes." He pointed to a pair that went up to a box connected to the cable.

I reached for the bag to retrieve the incense when Mascad barreled toward us. "Cover!"

Xander dropped to the ground, yanking me down beside him. The metal bruised my knees and elbows. Then Mascad dropped his full bulk on top of us, expelling what little breath I had left.

A shrieking crunch reverberated throughout the cavern. I wanted to cover my ears to block out the metallic noise, but my hands were pinned beneath me. A thunk shook the whole platform, followed by something plopping into the water. Then stillness.

I struggled to catch my breath. Did the quiet mean we were safe? Maybe more trouble was being prepared.

"A thousand pardons!" Raucous laughter burst out above us.

Xander squirmed beside me. "You can let us up now, Mascad."

His bodyguard slowly rose, revealing the boiler. Half of the moonbear's head was mangled beyond recognition.

"Oh no!" I scrambled up to examine the damage. "What do we do now?"

"Give thanks that wasn't your skull, sibah," remarked Mascad.

I swallowed hard. He was right. If whatever had struck the pipes had struck any one of us . . . I shuddered.

Xander inspected the boiler. "I don't think anything was damaged beyond function. Let's test that theory, shall we?" He poured some incense into a slot.

The pungent scent filled the air. After a few minutes of

experimentation, the cable above our heads began moving. We collectively released a breath of relief and returned to our skondola.

I pulled out the mirror. "'To Kalani of Waibean, who was great with child, was given the ability to see inside and grasp the heart of a matter." My voice warbled. The whole purpose of a heart seer sounded so simple, so straightforward. Yet with every passing year, understanding my elchan seemed to grow more complicated.

Xander squeezed my hand. "That's quite a gift."

A gift. Not a burden. If only I could remember that.

Mascad extended his hand. "If I may?"

I gave him the mirror.

He climbed into a precarious position on the end of the skondola and extended the mirror above his head. Two twists and the reflected light found a hidden prism. The light split into a rainbow. With a clank, the roller mechanism dropped, engaging with the cable. Jamarde clapped her hands as we began to move. "Almost there, and look!" She pointed. "We're not far behind!"

A skondola hung beside a narrow ledge, where Lavidah's coterie exited through a broad archway. The other two huddled around their water jars on the suspended platforms.

If Cobra had taken this long to finish, what awaited us?

Our skondola glided to a stop beside a suspended platform. In the center, a glass box encased a lidded jar of chestnut clay. Plain and unimpressive. It was nothing like I expected, for the jar used during the final ceremony radiated with vibrant color, embossed with gold and often studded with precious gems.

Swallowing away my disappointment, I recalled the next section of the Writings. "'To Renata, the sightless one of Kossac, was given the ability to feel the textures of speech and mold all languages to her tongue.'"

Estelle removed our last item from the bag. "The elchan of

speech sculptor, which explains the putty, but from where do we get the words?"

We examined the area, but the platform's planks were plain-sawn and unpainted, the rail of basic design.

"Maybe we are to make the putty into a word?" suggested Jamarde.

"But into which word? In which language?"

I shook my head. "Our instructions said Sustainer would provide all we needed. Therefore, what we need must be here somewhere."

"But the only thing here is the jar and its case," said Xander.

Perhaps the jar itself contained a clue? Crouching, I rested my hand on the glass for a closer look.

A series of slashes and dots was imposed on my sight, and then, stroke by stroke, they were mirrored.

I jerked backward with a gasp.

"Yosi? Is there a problem?"

"I . . ." Another flash? Except there was no sense of otherness, of being something else. Rather, it felt like when I read, hearing the writer's thought-voice and glimpsing what they were seeing as they wrote. I bent forward. Some light scratches marred the glass. "Putty please."

The others were asking questions, but I hardly heard them as I flattened the putty over the area I'd touched, then peeled it off. The scratches imprinted slashes and dots into the putty. A Sarmazon dialect. One I'd read but never actually heard pronounced. "Can anyone here read Equazale?"

Everyone fell silent. Finally, Mascad extended a hand. "Allow me." He produced a series of clicks and gliding tones that somehow emulated the written script, all with the fluidity of a native speaker. When he finished, there was a ding.

"There must be more." I ran my fingertips over the glass. Nothing. I moved to the next panel. More etchings, this time in Mouncite.

"I can handle that." Estelle read the sentence, and another ding, one note higher, rang.

The next sentence, written in Kossacan, I handed to Jamarde, since my tutoring had revealed she had better pronunciation than anyone else I knew. That gave us a third ding, still ascending in pitch.

But the fourth script I'd never seen–and I had seen many over the course of my illumination studies. "It appears to be an ancient runic language, similar to Egdonian, but that's all I know for sure."

"It's the ancient royal script of Egdon." Tension stretched out Xander's script long and thin. It would require the tiniest nib I had to replicate it on paper. And no wonder. It was said only Egdonian royalty and a few close advisers to the throne were ever taught it.

Jamarde brightened. "You work in the Egdonian court. Can you read it?"

Xander cleared his throat. "I can."

Estelle glanced at Xander. Apparently, she realized no mere court inventor would be privy to such information. Xander read the script flawlessly, and with a fourth ding, the glass retracted. The jar was ours.

Rivka traced the curve of the handle with reverence. "I never thought we'd succeed."

Neither did I, if I was honest. I glanced at the ledge. "What are the chances we can overtake Cobra?"

"We still have three gold coins," said Xander. "Perhaps we can furnish our driver with extra incentive."

Estelle nodded. "'Gold can bend the rigid heart / and cause leaden feet to dart.'"

I gathered the jar in my arms. Odd. Somehow I thought it would be heavier. At least that meant carrying it would be easy. We returned to our skondola. Mascad used the mirror to release the latch, and soon we coasted to a stop behind

Cobra's skondola. The archway led to another narrow stairway, winding upward.

Xander once again led, and we followed, the water jar cradled in my arms. But though success should be pushing me onward, the more I climbed, the heavier my feet grew. My eyelids too. I yawned. Why was the air hazy? And the smoke smelled wrong, too saccharine. Had someone improperly filled the lamps? Maybe they had used the wrong oil.

"Can we take a rest? I am *so* tired." Jamarde's speech slurred, as if to emphasize her exhaustion.

"We should . . . keep going." A yawn broke up Estelle's words. "But my feet feel quite leaden."

"Mine too." I stumbled. Something in the back of my mind blared a warning, but it was muted, far away, and my chin hit my chest, my eyes unable to focus. Why was the scent familiar?

I stumbled to my knees, cracking my shin against stone. I set the water jar on a step before I dropped it. Just a minute. That was all I needed. Long enough to regather my strength. I rested against the cool stone, my head too heavy to hold up any longer.

Xander yelled my name.

I should respond, let him know I was all right. My tongue refused to form the words. So sleepy.

The alarm broke through. Sleeping powder. The kind that made me sick. Very sick.

I fought back to awareness, but it was too late.

Darkness pulled me under.

Lavidah had won.

Xander's body refused to synchronize. Left foot. Right foot. Left foot. Up the stairs. It shouldn't be that hard. But twice his toe caught, as if he had no more coordination than a tot on his first airship voyage.

Something scraped behind him.

Xander turned just as Yosi laid her head upon a step, water jar beside her. Behind her, Rivka, Jamarde, and Estelle rested on the stairs. What were they doing? This was no time for a nap, as wonderful as that sounded. He called Yosi's name as Massard struggled past their prone forms, his face covered in a handkerchief. He grabbed the basket Estelle had been carrying and half dragged Xander up the stairs. He muttered two words. Seeping power? No, sleeping powder.

Xander snatched out his handkerchief and pressed it to his mouth and nose as he stumbled after Massard. Would this stairway never end? Then they burst into the cavern where they had begun. He slumped against a wall and gulped down clean air.

Massard supplied a bottle. "Smell this."

Xander took a deep whiff, then grimaced. The entire inside of his nose burned, but his mind's fog was gone.

"I said smell, not snort." Massard returned the bottle to the basket at his feet. The one the menials had packed. Sustainer reward them for their foresight.

"We need to get the sibahs." The more they inhaled, the longer they would sleep. Xander looked around. "Hello, anyone else here?" Despite three coaches standing ready, no drivers appeared, nor any Quest officials or priests. They were on their own to rescue the others.

Massard poured water on a length of cloth. "Wrap this around your face." He did the same for himself. They retrieved the others, one by one. Thankfully, they were nearer the top than he'd first thought. Even so, after two trips, he had to sniff more salts to clear his own head.

Once everyone was in the cavern, Massard returned for the water jar. Xander waved the bottle under Yosi's nose, then Jamarde's. Coach drivers wandered into the cavern, looking unsteady on their feet, though their odor suggested their unsteadiness was due to something they'd ingested, not inhaled. Xander moved on to Rivka and Estelle as Massard placed the water jar beside them. A moment later, Whirlwind exited the stairwell at a run, Valor in pursuit. Xander gritted his teeth. All twelve Questers had their faces covered; they had known about the sleeping powder.

"Focus," Massard rumbled.

Xander passed the bottle under Yosi's nose again. She was the first to be carried out, so she should have inhaled the least. Which meant she should have awakened first. Yet she slumbered on, almost deeper than before.

Jamarde stretched and yawned. "Wha–what happened?"

"Someone put sleeping powder in the lanterns."

Estelle was blinking her eyes open. "What did you say about sleeping powder?"

As Xander explained the situation to Estelle, he kept an eye on Yosi, still sleeping deeply.

Rivka scrubbed her face and sipped the water Massard provided. "What happened?" Her eyes widened when they landed on Yosi. She scrambled for the basket. "Is there any lakotun and gingermint in here? And we need a bowl of boiling water. Now!"

They looked at her in confusion.

"Sleeping powder extremely sickens Yosarai. The last time she was given some, it nearly killed her." She snatched bottle after bottle from the basket.

That was all Xander needed to hear. He strode over to the coach, donning his full imperial bearing. "I need a bowl of boiling water–immediately!"

The driver slouched on his seat. "I'm not supposed to interfere–"

Xander yanked the man down from his perch. "Perhaps I

didn't make myself clear. I need that water now or someone is going to die."

The man's gaze skittered to Rivka, who was pounding herbs with a rock. "Yes, hasib. Right away." He lurched down a side tunnel.

Please, Sustainer, let him hurry. Xander paced the cavern. Soon a priest appeared, a bowl and steaming kettle in hand, face lined with concern. He knelt beside Rivka, and after a rushed exchange, they worked together, mixing more powders and leaves.

Massard guided Estelle and Jamarde over to him, giving the other two room to work. Jamarde's eyes glistened. "I should have remembered. I knew, but I had forgotten. If anything happens to her . . ."

Xander put an arm around her shoulders. "She'll be fine." He hoped.

Rivka poured hot water over the medicinals as the priest propped Yosi up. The bowl was held under her nose, forcing her to inhale the steam.

Jamarde scrubbed a handkerchief over the spotted lens of her spectacles, her movements jerky, angry. "This is Lavie's doing. I just know it."

"Your sister?"

"She knows about Yosi's reaction to sleeping powder. She's trying to do more than win the Quest. She's trying to eliminate Yosi from the Exam. She knows Yosi will remove her from the top five."

Xander's stomach churned as if Selucreh had once again stuffed his mouth with rotten lakeweed and clamped it shut, forcing him to swallow the vile sliminess. By participating in the Quest, he had sought to protect Yosarai from her aunt. Yet in paying attention to the noisy threat, he may well have missed the silent–and more deadly–one.

Estelle rested a hand on his arm. "This is not your fault, hasib."

A well-meant sentiment from one with more compassion–or less understanding–than he. The taste of rotten lakeweed grew stronger. "Except it is."

"You gave her the sleeping powder?"

"Of course not."

"Then you made others do it for you?"

"Never!"

"Ah, you must have the elchan of food diviner and tasted this beforehand."

Perhaps she had not quite shaken the sleeping powder herself?

Estelle softened her voice. "Hasib, 'if not corrupt in act / nor negligent in fact, / then let no guilt attack.'"

"But she participated because of my insistence!"

"I've not had the pleasure to know Yosarai long. However, she doesn't present herself as one to be coerced."

Jamarde uttered a short laugh. "Never."

Xander clenched his jaw, wanting to argue but unable to find an appropriate response.

Estelle focused on Yosi, beside whom they strained steeped water into a cup. "I do not understand why this happened, especially when much seems to depend on haste. But if you try to shoulder responsibilities meant for Sustainer alone, you will exhaust yourself trying to be One whom you were never meant to be."

Because a crown could be worn by only one at a time, as his father would say. Xander forced himself to take several slow breaths. Responsible or not, he could do nothing to change the scene before him. *Please, Effulgence. You came to bring life into the world. Please now give life to Yosi.*

Then he watched. And waited.

Wake, sleep. Sleep, wake.

The two desires tugged me in opposite directions, and my head paid the price. What started as a dull throb intensified to a full storm of piercing lightning strikes. I moaned. Sleeping would be better. It didn't hurt as much.

"Please wake up. Please."

Rivka's pleading tiptoed through the pain. Couldn't she see I wasn't feeling well today? She ought to let me sleep.

The scent of mint and other spices tickled my nose. Their pastel green and cooling blue swirls soothed all they touched, while a strand of yellow lured me toward wakefulness.

"Now is not the time to sleep, sibah." A commanding, masculine script broke through. Why had Rivka let a strange man into my bedchamber? Such a breach of etiquette could not go unaddressed. Reprimand ready on my lips, I forced my eyes open. Once, twice . . . finally on the third try, they stayed open, grey rock greeting me instead of my bed's canopy. Where was I?

I closed my eyes and opened them again.

The Quest. The cavern.

The sleeping powder.

I struggled to sit, sending the world into a spin.

The unfamiliar man, who wore priest robes, brought a cup to my lips. Tepid, minty water steadied the world again. "Slower is better, sibah."

No, it wasn't. We needed to reach the Fountain Tower before Lavidah and her coterie so we could warn the chancellor. "I'm fine. Much better." The lie was bitter but necessary. Now to get onto my feet without collapsing.

Xander extended a hand, which I accepted. "Fine or not, you need not rush. The other coteries left a while ago."

His words slammed into me, and I swayed. We were too late. How would we warn Chancellor Serex now?

The priest patted my shoulder. "Do not fret, sibah. Sustainer often regards our first as His last and our last as His first. Trust He will provide." He ambled past the others, who had surrounded us, relief on their faces.

Of course, he didn't understand, didn't know what was at risk.

"Breathe, Yosi," Xander instructed. "The day is not done, so hope remains."

"But what can we do? No one will listen to us."

"No one?" Estelle cocked her head. "'They would hear us not / for our message was not for them.' Could we intercept the chancellor as he leaves the palace for the Fountain Tower?"

Such a simple solution. An obvious one, in many ways. Why had we not considered that before?

"If that's our plan, we had better hurry," said Jamarde. "Noon bells must be near, and that's when the chancellor's appearance at the Tower is scheduled."

Rivka packed up the basket while Xander approached the driver. "We need to reach the Chancellor's Palace as quickly as possible."

The driver reclined against the coach, arms crossed. "I drive you here. I drive you to the Tower. Those are my orders."

Xander tensed. Leaning heavily on Estelle, I shuffled to the coach. If only my head wouldn't throb with such fierceness. "We're not asking you to disobey orders. We simply wish to detour past the Chancellor's Palace on the way."

"An order is an order. I do what I'm paid to do. No more, no less."

"Of course, you ought to be compensated for your trouble." I withdrew two of our gold coins. "Will this be sufficient?"

The man straightened up, eyes glinting. "I suppose that will do, as long as you make it quick."

"If you make it quick getting us there, I might have one more of those with your name on it."

"I hear and obey, sibah." With unexpected agility, he leapt up onto the driver's seat. "Let us be off."

"Indeed," muttered Xander as he helped me into the coach. "Why is it that, with people, money is the best lubricant?"

We all had barely sat when the coach jerked into motion. I grabbed Xander and bit back a groan. Must my head pound like a hundred tabla drums struck in time with each other? At least the coachman was hastening as promised.

Rivka pressed a leaf into my hand. "Chew this. It will ease the pain."

I did as instructed, and by the time the coach stopped, the orchestra of drums had been reduced to a small ensemble.

"You can stay here while we speak to the chancellor," Xander whispered.

A generous offer, but one I could not take. "I overheard the threat. I need to be there."

We alighted, and Xander strode toward the closed gate. The guards on duty stiffened into high alert. Surely that was a good sign, for they wouldn't be this intense if the chancellor had left for the Tower, would they?

Xander's stride didn't even hitch. "We need to see the chancellor."

The guard, a dalem, sneered. "No one is permitted in the palace without an appointment."

"We don't want in the palace. We want to see Chancellor Serex. Has he already left for the Fountain Tower?"

"That information is not for the general public's knowledge."

"Cogs and bolts, man, I'm not asking for a detailed itinerary of his movements! We simply want to know if he is still here."

"I am not permitted to tell you, and even if I were, I

wouldn't reveal that information to a foreign lava slug. Now you're leaving. The how is your decision." The guard aimed a gun at Xander's chest.

Mascad started forward, but Xander held out a restraining hand. "We'll leave, but–"

"Mikah!" Estelle hailed an older soldier walking beyond the gate, the slightest of limps evident in his gait.

"Sibah Estelle?" He turned toward us, revealing the rainbow of cords on his shoulder. Not just an alef, but an alef sri–the highest and most honored of all soldiers. Drom had connections all over the city, but an alef sri? And one who was part of the chancellor's guard at that.

"Oda made his grandson a small army of mechanical soldiers," Estelle said before meeting the alef sri at the gate. "Has the chancellor left for the Festival?"

"About a quarter bell ago."

Jamarde moaned. "We're too late. Again."

Alef Mikah's eyes flickered to the rest of us, then the coach, which bore the Quest's crest of a water jar, out of whose top spouted six streams of water. "What is this about?"

I rubbed my temples, those drummers in my head inviting a few more of their friends to participate. "Someone plans to assassinate Chancellor Serex during the ceremony today and blame the Egdonians."

Xander slid a supportive arm around my waist. "As you can imagine, the success of such a plot would be devastating."

Mikah worked his jaw. "Who made such a claim?"

Estelle inclined her head. "All we know is one of the conspirators is participating as a Quester."

"Dalem," Mikah barked, "ready my horse immediately."

"Alef Sri, I beg your pardon, but you don't actually believe them?" The guard spat the last word.

Alef Mikah arched an eyebrow at his subordinate. "They are here instead of at the Fountain Tower, forfeiting their chance to win the Quest. Why do that for a lie? But maybe you're right and they are lying. Are you willing to risk our esteemed chancellor's life upon that belief?"

The guard flattened his lips.

"I thought not." He turned back to us. "We don't want to alert the conspirators. Proceed to the Tower and fulfill your duties as Questers. I will ride ahead and warn the chancellor myself."

Estelle bowed deeply. "Thank you, Mikah."

A quarter bell later, the coach delivered us to a walled courtyard of limestone–probably the kodesh complex along the Fountain Tower's western edge. I clutched the water jar, despite both Jamarde and Estelle volunteering to carry it. It gave me something to focus on besides my aching body. At least Rivka's leaves finally banished the drummers from my head.

A priest met us. "Welcome, Illuminary. Follow me." He led us through a maze of covered archways into a small garden with a bubbling fountain at its center. "I will inform the others of your arrival. Please wait here."

More waiting? There didn't seem to be any possible reason to delay us further. The other three coteries must have arrived long ago, sealing our loss. I swayed on my feet, the sun beating down on my head.

Xander guided me to a shaded bench on the far side of the fountain. I sank onto it, setting the water jar at my feet. The others gathered around.

"You should drink something too." Rivka produced a water flask from the folds of her dress. Leave it to my maid to remember such a thing before we left the coach.

"Gratitude," I murmured. As I reached for it, my headache flared, unbalancing me. My foot jerked out. The jar tipped over. With a gasp, I swiped for it. My fingertips brushed clay but grasped only air. The water–

The jar hit its side, and the lid popped free of the mouth. But the anticipated gush never came.

The jar that was supposed to pour forth water at the coming ceremony was empty.

I stared into its bone-dry depths. That was why it had been light. There was no water and never had been. How could we present an empty jar to the priests?

Jamarde took the flask from Rivka.

I snagged her wrist. "What are you doing?"

"Providing water like we are supposed to." When I didn't loosen my grip, she huffed. "Obviously we were supposed to fill the jar at Ayin Chi."

Rivka frowned. "But that wasn't in our instructions."

"Maybe not directly, but like Eshom the Gatherer, we were supposed to provide water for the people."

Reasonable words. Logically sound. Why, then, did the action seem so wrong?

Xander peered into the jar as if needing to confirm it was empty. "That seems rather deceptive."

"We weren't told where to get the water. Only that we're responsible for it."

"'A responsibility done is a responsibility filled / whether over, under, around or through.'" Estelle tapped the flask. "But that won't be enough to fill the jar."

"There is plenty more to be had." Jamarde pointed at the fountain.

Still, I couldn't bring myself to loosen my grip on my cousin's wrist. "If we have already lost the Quest–"

"Maybe we haven't. Maybe the other coteries thought their jars were full too. Don't you see?" Jamarde pushed the jar closer with her foot. "It wasn't any accident you tipped the jar. Sustainer has opened the way for us to win the Quest and warn Chancellor Serex."

Estelle fingered the jar's lid that she'd retrieved. "But Mikah said he would–"

"What if something prevented him from reaching the chancellor? Sustainer has provided us a new opportunity to win. Don't we have the responsibility to take it?"

I nibbled my lower lip. It was our responsibility . . . or was it? I covered the jar's mouth with my free hand. "We can't."

"It's not hard to fill a jar."

"I mean, we shouldn't, because it's not our responsibility. 'Sustainer brought forth water and provided streams to water the land.' Sustainer provided the water. Not the Gatherer's helpers. Not Eshom. Sustainer. Neither, then, ought it depend on us." I sought out Xander's eyes. "For, as a wise man told me once, all that depends on us is our dependency on Sustainer."

Jamarde flung her arm once more at the fountain. "Maybe this *is* Sustainer's way of providing."

"Jamarde." Xander's tone was quiet but firm. "While Sustainer does provide us good gifts to use, reliance on those gifts is not the same as reliance on Him."

"Fine. I won't put any water in the jar." Jamarde thrust the uncapped flask into my hand, her face harder than I'd ever seen it. "Choose wisely, cousin, because it could mean the difference between life and death."

I flinched. Not here. Not now. Not the first flash from Ima's book. Having anyone's life depend on me was hard enough, but for that life to be the chancellor's . . .

This was more than a decision with far-reaching implications. This could have national–indeed, international–implications. Because the only way we could know Chancellor Serex had been warned was to do it ourselves.

Yet if all that depended on me was my dependence on Sustainer, wasn't even this His responsibility? *Please, Effulgence, let this be the right decision.* I poured out the water.

It hit the ground with a splash.

I handed the empty flask back to Jamarde. "Too often I have relied on my resources and the resources of my father to provide, and the results rarely turned out as well as hoped for." My eyes flicked from Estelle to Rivka to Xander and back to Jamarde, each of whom had been hurt by my self-reliant problem-solving. "If we need water, then Sustainer will provide it. If we need to win the Quest, Sustainer will orchestrate that. If we need an audience with Chancellor Serex, Sustainer will arrange that. He does not need our conniving or meager resources to accomplish any of it. Just our trust that He will provide, as He did for Eshom and his helpers." I replaced the water jar's lid.

A priest appeared from an archway. How much had he heard? Not that it truly mattered. The decision had been made. He bowed. "This way, if you please."

I cradled the empty jar in my arms and walked ahead, trying to feign confidence. As I passed Jamarde, she breathed, "Sustainer, have mercy."

Have mercy indeed.

The priest led us into a circular room, sunlight bouncing off glass mosaics that covered its entirety. "Illuminary."

The other three coteries were already assembled. I clutched our empty jar to my chest. Had I made the right choice?

The gadohen arose from a central chair. His vibrant ceremonial robes glimmered in the light that poured through the skylights. "Let one Quester from each coterie present their jar."

Lavidah knelt before the gadohen, setting her jar before her. The Questers from the other two coteries mimicked her actions, presumably in order of arrival.

Hesitantly, I knelt at the end of the line.

The gadohen opened the jars of the other teams. Each jar was brimful of water.

As he stepped before me, I tried not to shake. I was the

one who insisted we leave the jar empty, so I would bear the consequences alone. The priest lifted the lid and stared into our empty jar. Snickers rippled through the other coteries. My stomach sank.

"Sibah, your water jar is empty." The gadohen's voice was strangely devoid of emotion, a letter with no illumination.

"Yes, gadohen."

"Did you spill your water?"

"No, gadohen. The jar was empty when we retrieved it."

"Why did you not fill it?"

"Because that would be doing Sustainer's will by my strength. For Eshom the Gatherer said, 'This day, Sustainer will provide the water you need.'"

The priest inhaled a sharp breath. "And provide He will." His voice sounded hoarse. "Illuminary, follow me."

Picking up the jar, he guided us into an adjourning room, windowless, plain, and barely large enough to hold us all. The sole piece of furniture was a cabinet made of wood almost black with age. The gadohen locked the door behind us, set the jar in the middle of the room, and retrieved from the cabinet an alabaster bottle, half the size of the flask Jamarde had wielded in the courtyard.

"Please kneel."

Not daring to glance at each other, we did as he said. I was directly before the jar.

"Blessing upon blessing, honor upon honor, glory upon glory–these be Yours, O Sustainer of all, in ever-increasing measure. For in Your mercy, You have washed away our wrongdoing. In Your mercy, You have shown us how things ought to be." He opened the bottle and started pouring water into our jar.

And he poured.

And poured.

And poured.

The bottle could not have held even a quarter of the clay jar's volume. Still, the water kept coming until it overflowed. The chestnut clay transformed. Intricate designs in vibrant colors and outlined in precious metals depicted Ayin Chi. A jar fit for the Ingathering finale.

A design near the jar's neck caught my eye. It looked like a stairway on which four women reclined while two non-Indeli men ran for the top. That almost looked like . . . but that was impossible!

The overflowing water soaked through my skirt, and as it wetted my knees, I was snatched into otherness. Grey mists. Black shadows. Shards of painful light. They mixed together in chaotic swirls without any discernable pattern. I closed my eyes to block out the disorder and stretched out a hand to steady myself. It connected with something soft . . . skin? Then a despairing grief so deep, so endless, swallowed me whole.

Despised. Unwanted. Destined to wander, ever and ever. A means to be used and thrown away. I wouldn't want me; why would anyone else? I don't deserve to live, but I want to live. No hope, but hope won't die. Endless, ever endless. Just keep moving, maybe then it won't hurt so much . . .

I pulled back. The grief ebbed away, and the thoughts faded, taking the feminine script with it. One whose form, beyond the jagged edges of grief, seemed familiar. But whose was it? Maybe if I experienced it again, I could figure it out. I reached forward.

A gloved hand grabbed my wrist in a steel grasp. Black slashing letters, almost illegible in their lack of control, spilled into my mind with an arrogant voice.

Destroy as they destroyed. Every slight. Every hurt. Every wound. With interest. Two, three–no, seven–times over. Steal as they stole what was rightfully mine. Take it back. The guilty will not go unpunished! I. Will. Rule.

I wrenched away, and blissfully, the anger and voice vanished with the physical connection. I needed to get out of here, wherever here was. The sooner, the better. But how? Just sitting here was getting me nowhere. But neither did I know how to move through this place.

Finally, my hand tentatively stretched out. This time, it slid into something–a substance thicker than air, thinner than water, and as comfortingly warm as a blanket on a cold autumn's eve. As for the emotion–the only description that came even remotely close was love. Except love, in its comparative smallness, was an insult to this, far too limited to encompass the vast complexity that went far beyond a single emotion. Grief and anger blended with joy and tenderness, among others. Indeed, it was so far beyond emotions it could not be called an emotion at all. Then the most beautiful, most perfect script I'd ever seen flowed around me, even more glorious than that contained within the Writings' original scrolls.

Though darkness comes, I am with you. Always.

Then the sensation retreated. I expected to feel bereft, but while the otherness had withdrawn, it did not leave, staying as promised. *Though darkness comes, I am with you. Always.*

The sense of elsewhere faded, and the sound of a bottle being stopped up drew me back to the moment. The gadohen relocked the alabaster bottle inside the cabinet, murmuring to himself, "Sustainer's ways are indeed mysterious." He turned to us. "For the first time in two decades, the final trial has been completed correctly. Well done, Illuminary. You have lived up to your name. Now, let us celebrate what Sustainer has provided."

I blinked, not sure his words could mean what I thought they did.

We had won?

Cheated again. Lavidah struggled to maintain a composed expression while she internally screamed at her cousin every derogatory and degrading name she knew–including a few she shouldn't. There was no way that coterie should have won. They were the last to arrive, looking less than respectable at that, while her team had arrived first, their jar full of the water pulled from Ayin Chi itself. The people had called for water. Their group had delivered.

As they traipsed through a tunnel to the Fountain Tower for the final ceremony, her fury built. They had done everything right and still lost. Not that Ima would believe her. It would be her fault her dreamer cousin won. It would be her lack that caused her to lose. Never mind her coterie included five other people. The full weight of failure would be placed on her shoulders, her every fault enumerated in detail as proof.

Lavidah swallowed back the bile. She had endured other reprimands from her mother, and she would endure this one. Unlike her weakling sister, this would make her stronger. Uncrushable. Unconquerable. She would triumph in the end–or it could well be the end of her.

Counselor Ahman, who was escorting her, patted her hand. "Do not worry, sibah. Those foreigners think they have won, but the day is not through, and Sustainer is just. All will be made right."

They exited the Tower and walked onto the platform circling the base, now set with tables. Ahman walked to the edge, and flagging an errand runner, he pulled out an envelope and a gold coin. "Deliver this to the address written upon it. After the man there reads it, he will ask you a question. No matter what he asks, tell him, 'two.' If you return to me in a quarter bell, I will provide a second coin. Don't think to deceive me. I will know, and if you do, I'll . . ." He whispered something in the boy's ear.

The boy paled and scurried off after a quick bow.

Lavidah scrutinized the counselor, waiting for some kind of explanation.

He obliged her. "Like others, I had plans for winning, and in my ardor, I acted hastily. A slight course correction was needed." The counselor led her to one of the tables reserved for losing Questers. "Such is the hazard of being a leader. Sometimes you must take bold steps to secure what is best. That's what separates a good leader from a great one. A good leader takes bold steps despite the risk of failure. A great one does whatever is necessary to guarantee those bold steps succeed."

Whatever is necessary. The counselor's words repeated in her mind as she watched her cousin paraded up the ramp spiraling around the Tower. She had taken some bold actions in the past, but the Quest had proven that wasn't enough. If she wanted to replace her cousin in the top five of the Exam–and with the loss of the winner's purse she needed that position more than ever–she had to do whatever she must to make it happen.

Whatever was necessary. No matter the cost.

Never in his wildest dreams had Xander imagined standing atop the Fountain Tower. He was a foreigner, an outsider. Not a part of the kodesh. Not an Indeli. Not even an open member of Tipheret. The midlevel platform he'd stood on the day they'd visited with Drom was as high as he thought he would ever climb, and he had been fine with that. How much different would it truly be to stand on the top?

Apparently, quite different.

Kolchan shimmered in the midday sunshine, its white stone almost blinding, a gleaming pearl among rich golds, bronzes, and rubies of the surrounding countryside. Below him, the circular lawn was packed with people, a dizzying mass of undulating color divided by the six stone channels stretching from tower to wall. Somewhere among all those people was a man–or woman–bent on murder.

"Breathe," whispered Yosi. "It's quite beneficial to one's well-being, or so I hear."

"Is that right? I was under the impression it was overrated."

That evoked a soft chuckle from her, and his own body relaxed at the sound. An assassin was out there, but it wasn't his job to save the chancellor anymore that it had been to save Yosi. Nonetheless, in Sustainer's providence, He had placed them here, at this time. Therefore, Xander would remain vigilant to however Sustainer might wish to use him.

The gadohen motioned for them to sit on the cushioned bench that edged a circular platform. Xander settled between Estelle and Yosi, facing toward Kolchan, Massard behind him. Between the two of them, they should be able to see the entire area and identify any trouble before it happened. In theory, at least.

The gadohen lifted high the transformed water jar and walked the aisle between the bench and outer wall of the tower.

The crowd began chanting, "Give us water, give us water, give us water."

People had spoken of a wall of sound, but he'd discounted it as a metaphor until this moment. The Tower, which had seemed immovable, vibrated beneath him.

The gadohen climbed the three steps onto the central platform. The crowd quieted. "Sustainer has heard your cry, and from His bounty has provided through the hands of His faithful servants."

Estelle tilted his direction. "Do you see Alef Mikah?"

Xander scanned the area. The guard was nowhere in sight, but maybe the alef sri waited with the chancellor? There were simply too many unknowns, and unknowns meant assuming the worst until they knew otherwise.

Behind him, the gadohen cried out, "Praise Sustainer for sustaining our lives!"

"We praise You, Sustainer, for sustaining our lives," echoed the crowd.

Indeed, Sustainer had sustained his life, as the multiple failed attempts on his own life proved. Could those experiences now help him identify an Egdonian assassin? He searched for a place from which an attack could be launched.

The gadohen resumed the Ingathering story from where he'd ended yestereve. "When the people cried out to Eshom the Gatherer for water, he cried out to Sustainer, and Sustainer brought him and his helpers to this plateau. Placing the six around the hill, the Gatherer commanded them to make a hole by removing seven handfuls of dirt, while thanking Sustainer for the miracle that was about to occur."

A miracle was what he needed, for no logical place existed in this open forum for an Egdonian killer. Unlike Mounce or Sarmazon, Egdonians preferred long-range weapons to avoid hand-to-hand combat, but if the position was too far away, the shot became more chance than calculation. And Egdonians hated the unpredictability of chance. Moreover, an easy escape was a must, as an Egdonian would be easily apprehended in this crowd.

"At the Gatherer's prayer, water sprang from the earth. At first, it was a trickle."

Water pinged against metal. On either side of him, it flowed through a channel, the mere width of his fingertip, across the floor, and into a trough along the rim of the Tower.

"But soon more water poured forth, filling the holes. Puddles became pools, pools overflowed into streams."

At a click, water gushed forth and raced down the chute circling the tower. Xander bent forward for a better view. The hidden doors he'd oiled with Drom opened, adding more water to the flow. At the bottom, the water surged into the six channels, splashing those nearest, eliciting shrieks of delight.

"The streams became rivers, which spread throughout the land, sating the thirsty ground, driving back the armies trapping them in the wilderness. Along the rivers' edges, all sorts of plants sprang forth, ripe for harvesting."

Priests and menials began circulating among the crowds, laden with baskets of food, which they handed out. Did anyone reject the gift? Such a disturbance could indicate someone who didn't belong.

"The people ate their fill that day, and in the days that followed, they harvested a crop they did not plant, one abundant enough to carry them through the winter rains. To this day, our land flourishes, filled with abundance by Sustainer's hand and His gift of the Six Ayin."

"We praise You, Sustainer, for sustaining our lives," called out the crowd again.

"Indeed, we praise Him. We give thanks for His provision, and to these, His servants, for their faithful service. Receive your reward, most favored ones."

If a disturbance occurred, he'd missed it. Maybe Massard was having better success. Xander reclined back as six menials presented each of them a covered basket. Tantalizing aromas tickled his curiosity as well as his nose. Was that mahi he smelled? He hadn't had any of that delicacy since leaving Egdon. His fingers itched to lift the lid.

Then Chancellor Serex entered, flanked by two bodyguards.

Tall, serious, and commanding respect without threatening. Upon first impression, the Indeli politico had chosen their newest chancellor well. He wore no crown, being a chancellor and not a king, but a gold collar and cuffs symbolized his position as servant of Sustainer and the people of Sustainer.

Not all past chancellors remembered that role. But even his ceremonial jama, whose brilliant autumnal colors reflected the festivity of the occasion without excessive extravagance, spoke of a man of sense, practicality, and stability, though he could not be more than a year or two older than Xander. Despite the chancellor's age, his dark eyes reflected the sorrows of someone a decade older. Was that what ruling a country did to a person? Yet all those sorrows looked old, his face lacking the lines of current anxiety, his shoulders relaxed. Either Alef Mikah had contacted him and the threat had been eliminated–or he knew nothing of the threat.

Behind the chancellor were an aide and a menial who carried a pillow with six medallions upon it. Two more guards followed. No alef sri, though. As the gadohen greeted the chancellor, Xander scanned the area again. Nothing out of the ordinary.

Estelle groaned softly. "He didn't make it."

"What do you mean?"

"Mikah is not with him. He would be here if he had made it."

That meant the chancellor remained unaware of the plot against him. Xander glanced at Massard behind him as the chancellor presented Estelle her medallion. His bodyguard shook his head.

A light cough brought Xander's head around. Chancellor Serex stood before him, medallion in hand. "Thank you for your faithful service, noble Quester. As a token of our gratitude, we award you this medallion and a pledge to fulfill one heart's desire, as far as it is within our power and the laws of Sustainer." He slipped the ribbon over Xander's head.

"Please, Sri Gadol, I must speak to you."

The gadohen frowned at him, but holy ceremony or not, the man's life might be in danger. "It is of utmost importance–"

The aide snorted. "What could be more important than this ceremony? Please continue, Sri Gadol." He inserted himself between Xander and the chancellor, motioning to Yosi.

Xander ground his teeth, started to rise. The chancellor leaned around his aide and mouthed, *Soon.* He proceeded to repeat the same thanks to Yosi and slipped a medallion around her neck.

Xander fidgeted in his seat. Dare he interrupt one of the holiest Indeli celebrations in fear that soon would not be soon enough? He gripped the basket in his lap as he fought to control his breathing, to think clearly instead of letting emotion drive him. *Please, Effulgence, guide me. Show me what I'm missing, what I should do.*

"Come, noble Questers, let us feast, for today is a day of celebration." The gadohen motioned them to shift toward the platform, tucking their legs under them. The chancellor, his entourage, and the gadohen settled on the platform itself to eat, menials bringing forth extra platters of food. Should he speak again, or wait for the chancellor?

Mimicking the others, Xander overturned his basket's lid on his lap like a tray, then took the folded napkin and spread it across the lid. Yellow flowers were embroidered along the edge. Egdonian water roses. How had they known? He glanced at the others' napkins. Yosi's bore a traditional river lotus while Estelle's was edged with a rainbow iris, a flower native to Mounce. If the food was as personal as the decoration, could that truly have been mahi he smelled earlier?

A shadow passed over his head. Odd. The sky arched above in an unblemished dome of blue. No clouds, nothing but a . . .

Shikra?

The hairs pricked along his neck. Shikras were a common

enough sight in the area. There had been one circling the tower the day he'd visited with Drom. Yet these golden-red feathers glinted wrong. Not merely iridescent, but metallic.

"Now, hasib." The chancellor, seated across the platform, shook out his own napkin, as if they were simply having a normal teatime conversation. "There was something urgent you wished to tell me?"

Here was his chance. "Indeed, Sri Gadol, I must warn you that . . ."

The shikra circled by again, and a light flickered beneath the backlit wings, as if it carried fire in its talons rather than the standard prey.

Suddenly, the pieces clicked into place. This shikra was no living bird. It was an automaton, carrying an explosive. The perfect weapon for an unseen Egdonian assassin who wanted easy access to the Tower without worrying about the mob below.

Heat poured through his body. He had left his country and hidden himself among a foreign people, many of whom scorned him, to avoid being assassinated. Now he was to be killed in an assassination meant for another? Maybe he should be more worried about the life of the chancellor, but at the moment, determination not to be an unintentional casualty dominated.

He leapt to his feet as an object plummeted from the shikra. "Massard, gun!"

Massard whipped out the weapon, and the chancellor's bodyguards started toward him. Massard tossed the pistol to Xander. He would get one shot and only one shot. *Sustainer, use me.*

He focused on the falling object. Steadied his breathing. Almost in range . . .

"Cover!" And he fired the pistol.

Chaos erupted.

A gunshot. A shattering. A puff of light. Xander tackled by two guards, Mascad straining against the two others. Powder scattering across the rooftop–gunpowder. Little fires sprang up and were stomped out. The sunfire shikra, if that was what it was, circled back to the city, disappearing.

Xander surrendered the pistol, not fighting the guards as they restrained him.

"Stop!" I bolted to my feet. "You're hurting him!" This wasn't how protecting the chancellor was supposed to end.

"He pulled a weapon on our most esteemed chancellor." A guard sneered at me, as if I were nothing more than a simplewit schoolgirl.

"He pulled a gun to *save* him." I whirled toward the chancellor, who was being helped up by his aide. "Sri Gadol, this man is not your enemy. If not for his quick thinking and skill, we would all be injured, if not dead–"

Chancellor Serex held up his hand. "Peace, sibah. Some may accuse me of poor eyesight, but I saw what he did as well as you." He flicked his hand at his bodyguards. "Release them."

His aide shadowed him. "Pardon my forwardness, Sri Gadol, but is that wise?"

The broad, jagged script suggested by the aide's raspy voice formed an almost feral scrawl in my mind. Unique. But familiar. Where had I encountered it before? I'd never been introduced to the man. I would have remembered his long, snout-like nose and his lean body's hunched posture, reminiscent of a hunting wolf. Even his achkan jacket used a jagged twill weave as if it were made of silvery fur.

The chancellor inclined his head toward him. "Explain yourself, Zev."

"These men, these foreigners, did not save you. Why would they? They are not of us, but from that barbaric people of the north." The aide's eyes remained on Xander.

"Despite that, they did save me. All of us. Despite their nationality or loyalty." Thick ice encased the chancellor's script, dense enough to solidify steaming water.

"A ruse, Sri Gadol. They couldn't have responded so quickly if they hadn't known this would happen. That could have been an ordinary shikra or one trained to scatter flower petals. Yet they knew otherwise, and how would that be possible unless they were involved?"

The aide's words were persuasive. Logical, reasonable. And from the shifting expression on the chancellor's face, working.

"They knew because of me," I blurted.

The chancellor's eyebrows rose. "You're claiming to be a traitor, a part of this plot?"

"No, of course not, Sri Gadol." Why had I opened my mouth? Simplewit fool. I was only making things worse and–

Be still. Sustainer rules over all.

Chancellor Serex pressed fingers to his temples, as if he had a headache. "Explain."

Be still.

I couldn't do this alone. *Give me the right words, Sustainer.* I exhaled slowly. All I must do was depend on Sustainer and let Him handle the rest. "Yestereve, prior to dinner, I overheard a conversation wherein a competitor spoke of plans for assassination."

"Then why weren't we informed of this earlier?" The aide flung the jagged words at me, their points sharpened to draw blood. "Why wasn't that competitor arrested?"

A strange calm blunted the force of his accusations, and I met his glare evenly without shaking. "I could not identify which Quester was the conspirator, and when we notified the authorities, we were dismissed as trying to interfere with the Quest and eliminate the competition."

"Moreover, at risk of forfeiting the Quest, they came to the palace today to warn you, Sri Gadol." Mikah appeared at the top of the ramp, two more guards behind him, all winded. Mikah climbed the stairs to the platform and bowed, hands clasped behind his back. "However, you had already departed for the festival. I left to warn you myself, but when I arrived, I was barred from approaching since you ordered no one was to contact you until after the feast."

Chancellor Serex's brow furrowed. "I left no such orders."

One of the men with Mikah spoke up. "Hasib Zev told us otherwise, Sri Gadol."

The aide retreated, bowing his head and opening his arms wide. "I was seeing to your welfare, Sri Gadol. You never have a chance to enjoy a day uninterrupted, and you did ask that today be free from political maneuvering. I acted exactly as you ordered."

Exactly as you ordered. Those words, that script–the third voice from the flash. "You–you were in the garden!" I said. "You were the one conspiring with the Quester to assassinate the chancellor."

A snarl curled the aide's lip. "That is preposterous."

"Is it?" Mikah rested a hand on his gun. "What time did the conversation occur, sibah?"

My bubble of calm began to implode, for I could not know how far in the past a flash occurred unless . . . The clock had been chiming. I drew in a quick breath. Sustainer had already provided all I needed. "About eight bells."

Mikah's jaw tightened as he narrowed his eyes on the chancellor's aide. "I'll have to recheck the record, but I believe Hasib Zev left the Palace before eight bells and returned shortly thereafter."

The chancellor shifted, as if he physically weighed the different possibilities against each other.

Zev bristled. "I have served you faithfully for the past five years, and if this conspiracy had succeeded, I would have been in as much danger as you! You cannot be considering that I would participate in such a plot."

"Of course not." A sly smile crept over the chancellor's face. "As you noted, I asked for this day to be free of political maneuvering. Guards, take him into custody. I will attend to this matter after the ceremony."

Two of the guards hauled the man away, thrashing and howling protests. The chancellor turned to the gadohen. "Let us continue the celebration."

The priest faced the murmuring crowd, motioning for quiet. "Sustainer is good."

"May He be praised forever," responded the crowd.

"This day, Sustainer has not only reminded us of what He has provided in the past, but He has preserved our esteemed chancellor's life from the hand of his enemies. Therefore, let the celebration continue!"

A cheer went up, and their feasting resumed.

The festival continued as if nothing unusual had happened. But even so, fresh worry slithered in. What if another attempt was made on the chancellor's life? I ate my meal without tasting much, conversation blurring into an undecipherable smear. I scanned the crowd, then the sky, then the crowd again. But all was well, and at last, the final blessing was pronounced, and the chancellor left, still very much alive, Sustainer be praised.

We followed the gadohen down to the base of the Tower, where we were swamped with people congratulating us on our success.

"Yosi!" My father waved his hand above the crowd as he elbowed–politely, of course–his way forward.

My heart leapt. I pushed my way toward him, not so politely.

"Avi!" He wrapped me in his embrace, the scent of ink and paper and wood polish enveloping me. The smell of home. I rested my head against his chest.

"I'm exceedingly proud of you, my little illuminary." He kissed the top of my head. "I can tell we have much to talk about."

"Indeed we do." Grinning, I tilted my head back to look at him. But instead of meeting my gaze, his eyes were focused on something behind me. Xander perhaps? Or maybe Jamarde, who stood alone, hugging herself, neither her mother nor her sister in sight. "Is something amiss?"

Someone tapped me on the shoulder. A priest stood behind me. "I beg your pardon, sibah, but you are needed." He extended a hand toward an open door in the Tower.

I began to protest.

"We will meet later, Yosi." Avi squeezed my hands. "Go, with my love."

"I love you too, Avi." I reluctantly rejoined the rest of my coterie, now all inside the Tower, in the room with the pool. Had it truly been less than a month since Drom brought us here to sketch? Back then, winning the Quest seemed but a dream, full of magic and longing and untouchable desire. Now I stood in the same place, living the impossible, and I wanted nothing more than to rush back outside and retreat someplace quiet with Avi and pretend these few days had never happened.

As we waited, the other coteries were escorted inside, presented their finalist purses, and released from the Quest. Most of the coteries ignored us, though a couple of the competitors offered us genuine congratulations, including Yonath. Cobra was the last to enter. Counselor Ahman gave us a nod and a simple, "Well done," before going on his way. Lavidah collected her purse and veered toward us. She bowed in respect, but as she straightened, her eyes met mine. Black rage mingled with unmitigated hatred. Walking past me, she spoke in a low voice meant for my ears alone. “This isn’t over, cousin.”

Then Alef Mikah approached. “Esteemed sibahs, honored hasibs, it has been a long and trying day, but if we may presume on your patience a while longer, we would like to resolve some of the day’s more unsettling events before evenfall.”

Estelle bowed, somehow looking as if we were merely discussing which china to use for an upcoming dinner party. “But of course. We are at your disposal.”

How could she be so calm and composed? Just the thought of discussing earlier events with the chancellor sent my stomach tumbling. Surely, if any deserved the right to enter the world of the politico, it was Estelle.

Alef Mikah escorted us through another tunnel to a waiting coach, which bore us to the famed Judgment Hall. Here the most important matters of state were conducted, as well as trials for any crimes against the politico. My report from a school tour here three years ago had been filled with words like *massive, stately, imposing,* and *intimidating.* All understating the Hall’s impact. The marble room, with its soaring ceiling and broad girth, emphasized the smallness of any who entered. *Breathe, Yosi.* Though we weren’t the ones on trial this evenfall, the long walk over the scarlet runner between massive alabaster pillars did little to soothe frayed nerves.

Alef Mikah gave us a sympathetic smile as we stopped before the gold-and-gem-encrusted chair upon its imposing dais. “Peace. All will be well.”

Chancellor Serex entered from behind the chair, his Ingathering jama replaced by a regal, gold-embroidered sherwani. The knee-length jacket of deep purple over white trousers made his stature seem even more imposing. I bowed with the others, hands clasped behind my back. After he settled on the chair, he studied us one by one, his presence both commanding and weighted with deep weariness. He did not want to be here anymore than I did.

He began to question us about the assassination attempt, working methodically through the events of the day. I did most of the talking since I'd "overheard" the plot. I kept things as simple as possible, describing only what could have been witnessed in person.

Hiding my elchan's role proved easier than expected. Although the chancellor questioned me thoroughly, his attention was divided. His gaze kept checking a side door as if he expected someone's arrival. "And this other conspirator–do you think you could identify his voice?"

I dipped my head. "I'm afraid not, Sri Gadol. I tried to do so at yestereve's dinner, but though I could eliminate those who were not the conspirator, I could not conclude who was."

His eyes flickered toward the doors once again. "Provide a list to Alef Mikah of whom you determined was not involved so we can investigate the others. On our end, we will pressure Zev to reveal with whom he met." The chancellor shifted to Xander. "Now I have a question for you, hasib."

Xander calmly met the chancellor's gaze. "And what question might that be, Sri Gadol?"

"Why was your man carrying a gun?"

I froze. *Your man.* Two simple words, but ones that showed the chancellor had deduced there was far more to Xander than had been said. Would Xander reveal his identity here, to this man who was his true equal? Such a revelation could strengthen the relationship between our countries or weaken it.

But Xander's expression and posture never altered. "I have no doubt that you have heard of the danger to any connected with Egdon's royal family due to the many recent assassination attempts."

"And you have such a connection?"

"I have. Thus, my man was charged with my safety, and as

you well know, he would be a poor guardian indeed if he failed to carry a weapon at all times."

The chancellor leaned back in his chair, steepling his fingers. "I suppose my country and I owe you and yours a great debt."

Xander held his tongue, making no move to exploit the implied offer.

"Perhaps someday I will find a way to repay you."

"I have no doubt that you will, as Sustainer sees fit."

Then the side door opened, and Counselor Ahman entered, seemingly agitated.

Chancellor Serex frowned. "Where is the prisoner, Ahman?"

"I regret to inform you, Sri Gadol, the prisoner is . . . dead."

Dead? The room wavered. How could that be? It had been less than three bells.

The chancellor sat upright. "Clarify."

"The traitor Zev now faces the judgment seat of Sustainer, Sri Gadol. Whether he was sent there by his own hand or by that of an overzealous guard, or even by the Spectre, remains unknown. But I have begun an investigation and will not rest until the matter is satisfactorily resolved."

"Knowing you, Ahman, you will do exactly that, but I need you to remain alert." The chancellor rubbed his forehead. "Therefore, I order you to sleep at least six hours a day while the investigation is pending. As for the rest of you, I see no reason to detain you further. Please provide Alef Mikah those names, sibah, and then you may return to the Quest mahal to celebrate this momentous occasion. Without disruption this time." He gave us a wry smile, then exited the room, the guards and Ahman close on his heels.

After I gave Mikah the names of those I believed were not involved, one more short ride took us back to the mahal, which seemed eerily quiet since the other coteries had dispersed to their homes.

Before we could ascend to our suite, a menial greeted us.

"If it pleases you, esteemed sibahs and honored hasibs, we have readied a light evening repast for you in the dining room."

"I wouldn't mind something," I confessed. "I was too nervous to eat much earlier."

Estelle breathed a sigh of relief. "I thought I was the only one."

"You looked so composed."

"A skill learned in self-defense. It is never helpful to let your enemies see how much they unnerve you."

Xander spoke up. "Then I suggest we do as the chancellor said and celebrate." He escorted Estelle and me, while Mascad accompanied Rivka and Jamarde.

As we entered the banquet hall, a soft thundering greeted us. Menials lined both walls, drumming hands against thighs. Between them lay a banquet fit for the chancellor himself.

Tears welled up. This day, as surreal as it had been, truly had happened. Not only did we saved the chancellor's life, but we also won the Kolchan Quest. Somehow, impossibly, our odd team of menials, mixers, and foreigners had bested the best, defeating born and bred Indeli elites and politicos, some of whom had long trained to win this event. My hand grasped the medallion that still hung around my neck, real for the first time all day. "We did it, didn't we? We won the Quest."

Xander's grin stretched wide. "That we did. By Sustainer's grace, through His provision, we won."

From that moment on, the evening acquired an ethereal glow as we sat at the table, laughing and talking, reliving the highlights of the Quest and dreaming about the future.

Anything seemed possible.

A season of beauty. A season of death. A season of the pure and fresh. A season of the bitter and sharp. A time of rest and a time of scarcity. Such are the extremes this season evokes–depending on one's preparation.

For the well-provisioned, in a warm home away from howling winds and biting cold, these days provide a much-needed change from the intense labors of the other seasons. It is a time to pause, to reevaluate, to plan, to learn something new, to do tasks long neglected. Winter, for the one prepared, is a season of refreshment.

But to the one who ignores its coming, winter is a scourge wielded by the specter of death. The sting of anxiety, the chill of fear, the bite of want drives ever onward, survival dependent on not stopping. Even night brings no rest, only cursing and despair.

Yes, winter approaches. All must pass through it. None can escape it.

Are you ready?

7

Xander surveyed the shop that had become a haven during his time of need. It had been a place to grieve, a place to heal.

Though those two processes were nowhere near complete, he could breathe again and think again. Which meant the time to leave had come. Certainty of that resonated within his bones. He'd drawn too much attention from winning the Quest and the subsequent foiling of the chancellor's assassination, now over a week ago. The latest letter from his stepmum only confirmed his decision. She didn't say it outright, but Parliament was growing restless with his prolonged absence, and they were positing the monarchy was an unnecessary expenditure.

Xander cinched his bag tight, his sketchpad and a few pieces of the wedding egg stowed inside. What he was taking would never account for what he was leaving behind. For despite knowing his position here was temporary, he'd become attached to this place, these people. Nonetheless, he left richer for the experience, and hopefully Drom would forgive him for his gift, stashed in the pages of the ledger–all his wages plus a little extra.

As if summoned by the thought, Drom wobbled into the shop with that strange, yet now familiar, gait. "All packed?" No hint of a stutter marked his words today. Drom was comfortable with him at last.

"I am." Xander swung the bag over his shoulder and tried to soak in the warmth of the shop. But this wasn't goodbye. Somehow he'd find a way to visit. "I don't suppose you would consider moving to Egdon, would you?" He kept his voice light, but his heart meant it with all seriousness.

"Perhaps, someday. After I've completed my work here."

That wasn't the answer he expected.

Drom hobbled closer, and Xander knelt down to eye level.

"Sustainer makes no spare parts or misshapen pieces. As every gear is shaped precisely for the automaton, so is each person." Drom pressed something into Xander's hand, then bowed. "Safe travels, Your Highness." Then he disappeared into his back room, leaving Xander slack-jawed.

His gaze dropped to the object in his hand. It was a pocket watch, its gold casing bearing on one side the royal seal of Egdon, complete with a detailed mountain eagle, and the words *Lean into your shape* inscribed on the other. How had Drom known? He flipped open the lid. A transparent clock face revealed the inner workings, each miniature piece unique and brightly colored so they continually formed new patterns, like a kaleidoscope. It was mesmerizing.

"In case you were wondering, I didn't tell him."

Yosi's quiet voice jarred him from his trance, and he rose, carefully pocketing Drom's gift. "I never suspected otherwise. Drom has a unique knack for understanding the inner workings of whatever he handles. He probably knew the day we met, the moment he took my hand."

Yosi nodded. "You noticed too."

"It's hard to miss, watching him work." Xander skirted the table so he was on the same side as Yosi. She wore a floral anarkali, which brought out the pink in her face. "Have you been crying?"

"I do not know the standard practices of Egdon, but here it is not uncustomary to shed a few tears at the departure of a dear friend, and both Rivka and I shall miss the presence of Hasib Mascad." She descended the stairs.

"Only Hasib Mascad?" He trailed after her.

She busied herself with closing the door. "How does one determine which tears are shed for which friend, hasib?"

"Then you do consider me a friend."

One corner of her mouth quirked up. "I suppose I do."

"Good." He helped her into the coach waiting to take him to the rail station. "For I only invite friends to visit."

"Visit?"

"I was hoping you and your father would do me the honor of being my guests at the palace during Winter Solstice."

Silence met his invitation.

Did he say something wrong? Maybe he had read too much into her friendliness. "Of course, if you already have other plans–"

"I would be delighted to come. As long as Avi agrees, of course."

"Then I'll have a formal invitation sent as soon as I'm home. Though I do have one condition," he added.

"Oh?"

"You must bring Rivka with you."

Yosi's eyes twinkled. "I wouldn't have it any other way. It would be cruel to keep dear friends apart any longer than necessary, after all."

"My sentiments exactly."

Quiet settled on the coach. Beyond the window, the passing street paraded its colorful pageantry one last time, unmarred by the cool, cloud-filtered light. It was indeed beautiful here, and yet how he missed the vast stretches of water, the rugged cliffs, the unadorned homes of stone. He wouldn't miss the place of Indel as much as certain people.

"What will be the first thing you do upon arriving home?" Yosi asked.

"Depends if snow has fallen. If not, return home to a thorough interrogation by Mum."

"Sounds terrifying." She feigned a mock shudder. "And if the snow has fallen?"

"You promise not to tell?"

She solemnly raised a hand in a vow of silence.

"I'll throw a snowball at Massard. If I'm lucky, I shall hit him with it. More likely he'll sense it and dodge it. Either way, I will have to endure a lecture on proper royal behavior."

"Which you'll deserve."

"But it will be worth it, especially if I do manage to land a strike."

She laughed.

"I suppose you don't see much snow here."

"Not much," she said. "Maybe once every four or five years. Our winters are mostly brown and grey."

"We don't have much deviation either with ours being white and grey. In fact, you may find it quite drab after the novelty of snow has faded. We don't have your flair for beauty."

Yosi shook her head. "After all this time, you still haven't learned the first principle of art, have you? Beauty can be found anywhere. Sometimes you must look hard to find it, but it will be there, somewhere."

"Then I shall look forward to you helping me find it come Solstice."

The coach stopped, and the door opened to Massard, Rivka a few paces behind him. He was glad he had convinced his bodyguard to take this last bell to be with her. He would resume his duty soon enough.

Yosi accepted Massard's extended hand and exited the coach. "Thank you, Massard." Her inflection emphasized the last syllable of his name.

His bodyguard glared at him.

Xander shrugged. "It doesn't matter much at this point, does it? And she would discover the truth come Solstice anyway."

His bodyguard glanced sideways at Rivka. Xander suppressed a smirk. He'd keep Massard in suspense a little longer as to whether Yosi's maid would be accompanying her.

The rail released a big puff of steam and whistled a five-note warning. Massard sprang into action, overseeing luggage before Xander could do it himself. Soon that extra camaraderie Xander had enjoyed with Massard over the past few weeks would be gone. Although it existed only in public as a façade, he would miss that interaction. Sometimes being royal was quite lonesome.

Impulsively, he turned to Yosi. "Before I leave, would you address me by my given name?"

Her eyes widened. "Pardon?"

"I've had to use an assumed name the last few weeks. When you visit, protocol will require you to use my title. But at this moment, I no longer need to hide my identity, as I'll soon be gone, nor do I need to resume my duties yet. So I have the chance to be just myself." Be himself? That had to sound more halfcocked to her than it did to him.

But then she spoke. "Names are important, and I would be pleased to use yours . . . Xander."

Not Saunders. Not Your Highness. Not Prince Xander. Just Xander. An equal. A friend. "Thank you." He reached for her hand. He'd intended to squeeze it to convey his gratitude, but he found himself bestowing a kiss on her knuckles instead as the train whistled its final warning. "Until Winter Solstice."

He snatched up his handbag and boarded the rail, Massard in his shadow, the familiar mantle of responsibility and authority settling into place. Yet somehow, it didn't feel as heavy or awkward as when he shed it at the beginning of this trip.

It was time to discover Sustainer's purpose in giving him a throne.

The problem of necessary evil was that it was so . . . necessary.

I peeled off the gloves soiled beyond recovery. They would need to be burned as soon as I returned to my rented suite. Another problem with necessary evil. It tended to be messy. Which was why I preferred others to handle such things. But that was not a luxury I could afford this time, and survival required one to perform distasteful chores upon occasion.

I mounted the borrowed horse tethered at the far end of the moonlit field. As unpleasant as the night's work had been, it mingled with the sweetness of a job correctly executed. A problem had been solved, and the judge's suspicions would no longer be an issue.

My horse settled into an easy canter down the country road, the night birds extending their congratulations even as a keening wail arose in the distance.

Two days after Xander's departure, I stood once again on the station platform, Rivka in my shadow and cold air nipping at my cheeks. Winter had not officially arrived, but it wouldn't be long now. I bounced on my toes, though not from the cold. My fur-lined cape kept me warm. I hadn't seen Avi since the Ingathering, now almost a fortnight ago, and I was eager to tell him about Xander's invitation. I braved the cold weather and arranged for the driver to take a long, meandering route through Kolchan back to my aunt's home. I had packed hot tea to enjoy along the way. Surely that would provide sufficient time to persuade Avi to travel to Egdon during Solstice.

I glanced at Rivka. Watching her and Massard separate had been difficult. Perhaps I should persuade her to stay with Massard in Egdon rather returning to Indel with me. I'd miss her, but she planned to leave as soon as she passed her crossover assessment and I completed the Exam. Avi, romantic as he was, wouldn't mind, not once he saw them together.

The opening notes of "Duyah March" whistled through the air, announcing the rail's arrival at the station with pomp. With a blast of steam, the rail rolled to a dignified stop. Stairs were lowered, chains unfastened. People descended, luggage was unloaded and claimed. I bounced on my toes again. Where was Avi? He was usually one of the first off. Had I mistaken the time? I dug for his latest letter.

"Sibah Patican."

I startled at the formal address as our head steward, Meltzar, materialized from the direction of the menial cars. That was odd. Avi always arranged for the menials to ride with him. "Hab Meltzar, Sustainer's peace to you. Where is Avi, may I ask?"

Meltzar presented me with a deep bow, hands clasped behind his back, the bow usually reserved for the politico. My stomach clenched. Meltzar never breached etiquette. Ever. Not even when we asked him to.

I tugged my cape tighter around me, yet that was more to give my hands something to do than anything else, for I no longer felt the sting of the air or the warmth of the fur. It was as if I stood outside the scene altogether, seeing, hearing, but not experiencing what was occurring. As if I weren't really here.

"If the sibah would follow me, I bring news best shared in a place of privacy."

The rail station blurred, then was replaced by an empty waiting room, as if someone had changed pictures in a magic lantern show. The fire blazing at the far end emitted no more heat than one in a photograph.

My usually stoic steward knelt before me, bowing his face to the floor in a gesture of highest deference, and when he lifted his face, the man who showed less emotion than anyone I knew had tears tracking down his cheeks.

I waited for something in me to respond to the sight with compassion or concern or worry or even fear. Instead, nothing. A blank page had replaced my heart. Even that failed to raise an alarm it should have.

"Sibah, I have no good way to tell you this." Meltzar lifted his face heavenward. "Oh, Sustainer, why have You brought such tragedy upon one so young and sweet?"

Rivka hovered at my elbow. This was too far-fetched to be real. A dramatic moment in some tale where a tragedy was about to befall the heroine. It wasn't really occurring. Not to me.

"What has happened, Meltzar?" That sounded like my voice, yet it came from somewhere too far away to have emanated from my throat. "Has Avi been hurt in an accident? Taken abed with illness?"

He shook his head. "No, sibah. Your father . . ." He hesitated, then in a second breach of protocol, clasped my hands in his.

Warm. Solid.

Real.

"Your father is dead."

GLOSSARY

CHARACTERS

Ahman - a leading politico (counselor) and advisor to Chancellor Serex

Ayah - menial child born on Patican estate

Bahrain - historical king in Indeli history

Bane - unwanted suitor of Yosi

Caleph Patican - Yosi's father and a wealthy judge of Cashirsa Province

Demaus - friend of the royal Egdonian family

Dowser - Patican family dog

Drom Hadas - a reclusive inventor and automaton maker from Mounce, who is said to be the best in the Seven Realms

Ebon - butler in the Chiman household

Ellie Torris - Xander's youngest niece, daughter of Patra

Elshir - Quester with the Valor coterie

Emori - menial in the Patican household

Epolene Torris - queen of Egdon and Xander's stepmum

Eshom the Gatherer - a deliverer from ancient Indeli history who gathered the Indeli people from the other six Realms

Estelle Assah - a Mouncite-Indeli (mixer) student at the Academy and part of Yosi's class; Drom's niece

the Gaddans - a wealthy family

Gloud - a politico that engaged in a famous debate at the Teardrop Theatre

Grebe (Counselor) - a politico serving as a Quest official at the Teardrop Threatre

Grebe (Hasib) - a member of Yosi's class at the Academy and the son of a counselor

Hezzy - menial in the Patican household

Iris Tombay - the leading fashionista of Kolchan

Jamarde Chiman - Yosi's cousin, younger sister of Lavidah and daughter of Mirina Chiman

Jasmene Patican - Yosi's late mother; considered one of Indel's greatest artists

Kalani - one of the Gatherer's elchan-gifted helpers; from Waibean, she was great with child and was given the ability to see inside and grasp the heart of a matter (heart seer)

Kayapo - one of the Gatherer's elchan-gifted helpers; a cripple-legged boy from Sarmazon, given the ability to hear the song from which all things were built and bring all into harmonious alignment, healing both body and soul (song healer)

Kells - Indel's best illuminator

Kimchi - a female kitchen menial in the Patican household

Lascar - a male menial in the Patican household, married to Muri

Lavidah (Lavie) Chiman - Yosi's cousin, the older sister of Jamarde, and daughter of Mirina Chiman

Lev - an apprentice counselor and part of Lavidah's coterie (Cobra)

Mascad - Massard's alias

Massard - Xander's bodyguard

Meltzar - head steward of the Patican family

Mesoni - a famous Indeli military leader, who worked up from the rank of dalem to the rank of alef

Mikah - an older soldier of the rank alef sri and a senior member of the chancellor's guard

Mirina Chiman - Yosi's widowed maternal aunt, mother of Lavidah and Jamarde, a teacher at the Academy

Muri - a female menial in the Patican household, married to Lascar

Naviv Dov - one of the Scribes

Nehi - a rail menial

Niclon - a politico that engaged in a famous debate at the Teardrop; also the author of the famous speech, "Appeal at Kinah Plain"

Nidhi - daughter of a family who once served a cruel elite; now menials in the Patican household

Patra Torris - Xander's half sister and princess of Egdon

Pom - a rail menial

Posea - one of the Gatherer's elchan-gifted helpers; a simplewit from Egdon who was given the ability to eat the very words of Sustainer and know the flavor of the future (food diviner)

Quarmis - one of the Gatherer's elchan-gifted helpers; a deaf-and-mute man from Mounce who was given the ability to taste good and evil and to recognize the difference between right and wrong (truth taster)

Renata - one of the Gatherer's elchan-gifted helpers; a blind girl from Kossac who was given the ability to feel the textures of speech and mold all languages to her tongue (speech sculptor)

Resha - a member of Lavidah's coterie (Cobra)

Reuven - a senior member (elder) of the Kolchan kodesh

Rion Torris - the late king of Egdon; Xander's father

Rivka - Yosi's maid

Saunders - Xander's alias

Selucreh Torris - Xander's older half brother

Serex - the chancellor of Indel

the Spectre - an elusive Egdonian assassin

Veli - the owner of Indel's most exclusive teahouse

Xander Torris – the crown prince of Egdon; the late king's illegitimate son

Yonath – the best archer at the Academy and a member of the Whirlwind coterie

Yordan – a coach driver (menial) for the Chiman household

Yosarai (Yosi) Patican – a wealthy elite student who dreams of becoming an illuminator; the daughter of Judge Caleph and Jasmene Patican

Zev – the chancellor's personal aide

Zibbah – a menial cook for the Chiman household

Zibar – one of the Gatherer's elchan-gifted helpers; the ancient one from Zantou who was given the ability to smell the meaning of any word, even those hitherto unknown to him (word breather)

Locations

Academy of the Seven Arts – also known as the Academy; an expensive, prestigious school for elites in Kolchan; said to train only the best of the best

Aiyn Chi – also known as the Spring of Life; a fresh-water spring located under Kolchan from which flow the six Aiyn rivers and the source of the water that turned Indel's wilderness into a habitable land

Arboretum Capital – public gardens found in Kolchan, said to be unrivaled for its beauty anywhere in the Seven Realms

Banyans – a middle-stratum neighborhood of Kolchan where Massard and Xander stay

borderlands – a mountainous strip of land located between Indel and Egdon, whose ownership is disputed

Cashirsa Province – a province of Indel; Yosi's home province

Chancellor's Palace – the private residence of Indel's chancellor

Chordi – a street in an industrial neighborhood in Kolchan

Council Hall – a three-story, circular building housing the offices for the counselors and where governmental matters are handled; also houses the Teardrop Theatre

Duyah - the province where Kolchan is located

Egdon - one of the Seven Realm, located north of Indel, and home to Xander

Everstar Tower - a monument at a famous battlefield, whose beacon shines day and night, ever lit in memoriam of those who lost their lives there

Fortress Duyah - military training facility in Kolchan

Fountain Tower - a tower on the outskirts of Kolchan where the Ingathering Festival occurs

Hallel - one of the six Aiyn rivers

Hypoyan Stoa - an open-air market in Egdon

Indel - one of the Seven Realms and home to Yosi

Inner Sanctum - a chapel within the Sanctum where the daily rituals are held by the kodesh

Judgment Hall - a formal governmental hall where the most important matters of state are conducted, as well as trials for any crimes against the politico

Kolchan - the capital of Indel

Kossac - one of the Seven Realms, located northwest of Indel; known for its ice forests

Lower Market - a neighborhood in Kolchan made up of small shops and outdoor vendors

Lubzen Gallery - a prestigious art gallery in Kolchan

mahal - a walled mansion usually found within a city

Memorial Hall - a building attached to the Everstar Tower containing the history of the site

Mounce - one of the Seven Realms, located northeast of Indel

Musician's Forum - an open-air park where street performers entertain

Ora Peak - one of the mountains of Egdon

Sanctum - worship complex of the kodesh

Sarmazon - one of the Seven Realms, located southwest of Indel

Scriptorium Grande – museum in Kolchan where the original Writings of the Scribes are stored; also called the Scriptorium or, poetically, the House of Books

Seven Realms – the seven countries comprising this world: Indel, Egdon, Mounce, Waibean, Zantou, Sarmazon, and Kossac

Sibah Veli's – Kolchan's most famous and exclusive teahouse

Teardrop Theatre – a prestigious theatre shaped like a teardrop, located in the middle of Council Hall, used for both political and theatrical events

Thalassa – the geothermic lake that surrounds the islands that make up most of Egdon

Waibean – one of the Seven Realms, located southeast of Indel, known for its crystal caves

Werec – the village nearest the Patican estate

Zantu – one of the Seven Realms, located south of Indel

Clothing & Fashion

achkan – a knee-length jacket worn by men

anarkali – a long, full-skirted dress worn with leggings underneath

angarkha – a formal robe with long sleeves

bandhgala – a suit for men comprised of fitted pants and a jacket with a high, stand-up collar

jama – a long coat reaching to the ankles

kurta – a collarless tunic

lehenga – a skirt and top usually worn with a wrap

luanchari – a blouse stitched to a long, full skirt and worn with a sash

pavadai sattai – a cone skirt and blouse commonly worn by female menials

sari – a woman's garment made of one continuous piece of fabric wrapped around the waist and draped over the shoulder

sherwani - a formal, button-down jacket for men, usually knee-length, with a stand-up collar

Religious Terms

Effulgence - Sustainer-Made-Visible, according to the Tipheret sect

elchan - spiritual/supernatural gifts, first given to the helpers of Eshom the Gatherer and categorized into six groups: food diviner, song healer, truth taster, word breather, heart seer, and speech sculptor

Fates - an Egdonian concept for what controls one's destiny, an impersonal deity

gadohen - the highest ranking priest of the kodesh

heart seer - an elchan gifting of the ability to see inside and grasp the heart of a matter

Ingathering - a religious festival celebrating the creation of Indel as a country

kodesh - the religious sphere of Indel, primarily comprised of priests

seeker - a non-Indeli who is curious about the Indeli religion, especially the Tipheret sect

Sustainer - Indel's God

Tipheret - a religious sect that believes Sustainer's Illumination has already arrived in the form of Effulgence

the Writings of the Scribes - Indel's holy Scriptures

Time, Currency & Celebrations

amin - a type of currency

bell - one hour

birthfest - birthday

coteries – the teams of six participating in the Quest
evenfall – evening, sunset
half bell – 30 minutes or halfway through an hour
Ingathering – a religious festival celebrating the creation of Indel as a country
keshel – a coin worth a very small amount
mornrise – morning, sunrise
noonpast – the time after noon (afternoon)
quarter bell – 15 minutes (based on the chiming of a clock at quarter hours)
Quest – a competition that takes place during the Ingathering Festival involving several tests over a three-day period as a reenactment of the original events of the Ingathering
Shabbah – the weekly day of rest
Winter Solstice – a midwinter festival celebrated by all Seven Realms
yestereve – yesterday evening

Titles, Nicknames, & People

alef – the highest military rank
alef sri – the highest and most honored of military rankings
avi – father
betweeners – those living in the disputed borderland between Indel and Egdon
blighter – a person who is regarded with contempt; one whose presence mars something
chancellor – the ruler of Indel as the appointed head of the Council
Council – the ruling body of Indel
dalem – military rank lower than letad
dodah – aunt
Egdonian – a person from Egdon (also the language)

Eghead – a derogatory term for an Egdonian

elder – a title for a senior ranking member of the kodesh

elite – one of the spheres of Indel; seen as higher than menial and lower than politico; a freeman/gentry class

hab – a masculine title of respect for a person belonging to the menial sphere

hasib – a masculine title of respect for a person belonging to the elite sphere

hasib gadol – a masculine title of respect for an elite in a position of high authority, such as a teacher or the head of a household

illuminary – a person who brings light into the darkness and makes the unseen visible

illuminator – a person who creates illuminated manuscripts

ima – mother

Indeli – a person from Indel (also the language)

indenture – a person who offers years of service in exchange for money, often to pay off sizable debts, common in Egdon and Mounce

Kossacan – a person from Kossac (also the language)

letad – a military rank, higher than dalem, lower than alef

menial – the lowest sphere in Indeli society; servant class

mixer – a derogatory term for one who is not full-blooded Indeli

Mouncite – a person from Mounce (also the language)

oda – uncle

Parliament – the ruling body of Egdon along with the royal family

parlies – members of Egdon's Parliament

politico – the highest ranking sphere of Indel, a nobility class primarily comprised of politicians

sibah – a feminine title of respect for a person belonging to the elite sphere

sibah gadolah – a feminine title of respect for an elite in a position of authority, such as a teacher or the head of a household

siv – a feminine title of respect for person belonging to the menial sphere

sphere – one of four classes in Indeli society: menial, elite, kodesh, politico

sri – a term of respect for a politico or an elite of outstanding merit

stratum (pl. strata) – the societal rankings within the spheres, often based on the type of work one does

streeter – an orphan who lives on the streets

tatterscamp – a derogatory term for a person of low class believed to be untrustworthy

water trog – a derogatory term for Egdonians implying they are contemptible and socially inferior

Other

crossover assessment – a test for a menial to become an elite

Exam – formally known as the Strata Exam; a test taken by all Indeli elites to determine what kind of jobs they are suited for and who qualifies for advancement to the politico sphere

flash – description for one aspect of Yosi's elchan gift, where touching an object allows her to experience something in the past from that object's point of view

keshel awfuls – cheap publications of sensationalized stories, including ghost stories

leadstick – a drawing/writing utensil

rails – trains

scarriage – a steam-powered automobile

scope – telescope

the Scroll of Galena – also known as Galena's Scroll; a legendary scroll reputed to contain the inner workings of all things, required by Egdon in exchange for the Indeli people living within their borders

the Seven Arts – the seven areas of skill every Indeli strives to excel at, including the Art of Creativity (emblem: paintbrush), the Art of Social Graces (emblem: teacup), the Art of Tongue (emblem: pen), the Art of Mind (emblem: scroll), the Art of Body (emblem: sword), the Art of Virtue (emblem: open hand), and the Art of Faith (emblem: flame)

skondola – sky gondola; cable car

thought-voice – the "thinking" voice of a person Yosi "hears" when reading words with her fingers via her elchan gifting

Acknowledgments

Writing an acknowledgments page is a daunting process. As a writer, I spend the vast majority of my working time alone, with only a pen, notebook, my imagination, and God to keep me company. That makes it easy to overlook the invisible network of people that enables me to do that work, and the last thing I want to do is forget any of those who have made this work possible. So, praying that I miss none of those crucial supporters, I would like to pull back the curtain to thank those who have given so much help behind the scenes:

First, thank you, book lover, for taking a chance on this novel. Story is meant to be shared, so without you, penning these whimsical imaginings would be pointless. Therefore, I want you to know that I appreciate you for giving me some of your precious time. I pray that you have found it to be time well spent.

Next, I'm indebted to the team from Enclave/Oasis who took a great risk to turn this manuscript into a book. I do not love logistics, and it is wonderful to have a skilled group of people willing to help with things like editing, proofing, formatting, cover design, printing, marketing, and a dozen other details. So, a round of applause to Steve and Lisa Laube,

Lindsay Franklin, Sara Ella, and all the others who invested in this book!

But Enclave wouldn't have had a manuscript worth the risk if it weren't for the fabulous authors in my critique group, especially Sharon Hinck, Beth Goddard, Cathy McCrumb, Angela Bell, and Michelle Griep. They voluntarily spent many hours slogging through early drafts and rewrites of this story. Without their brainstorming, encouragement, and insights, this novel probably would be languishing in a file on my computer. Three cheers for writing friends!

I also must acknowledge another group who will probably be surprised to find themselves listed here, the members of the small Bible study I teach: Elaine, Neal, Bob, David, Arlene, Freddie, Jim, Barbara, Tatianne, Angela, and Tabitha. They would say they contributed nothing to this book. However, their prayers and encouragement, coupled with their special superpower of keeping me grounded while keeping me on my toes, has carried me through many a tough spot. They also push me to continue learning and digging into Scripture, which I believe has been essential to my growth as a Christian writer. My hat is off to them all.

And I must spotlight two people already listed, who have gone above and beyond, and without whom I would have been lost: Sharon Hinck and Angela Bell.

Sharon Hinck has been a mentor, friend, cheerleader, encourager, and listening ear extraordinaire. Why she decided to invite a newbie into her critique group many years ago is beyond me, but her friendship has borne blessing upon blessing upon blessing since then. A five-finger friend I hope to cherish for many more years to come.

As for Angela Bell, I prayed as a teenager for a close friend who would get me, with whom I could share the ups and downs of life. God answered that prayer with Angela. Our biweekly chats have kept me afloat through the rough seas of writing and life. Her quirky humor has brought light into many dark moments and sparked laughter so that tears didn't overwhelm. Her quiet prodding has gently nudged me back onto the right path many a time and reminds me to focus on God. A gem of a person worth more than a thousand starfire sapphires.

To these two amazing ladies, a big bouquet of roses is due.

No doubt if this were a speech at the Oscars, the orchestra would be playing, telling me it is time to quit, but I cannot, not yet, not without recognizing my parents, Jim and Barbara Schroeder. Not every writer enjoys the support of their family, so I count myself blessed beyond measure to have such unwavering champions. My parents are my biggest supporters and my greatest cheerleaders, and Dad is my best brainstormer. They are the patrons who have provided me the space and freedom to pursue this art. Without them, this story would have been never written. Without their love, I would have never pursued this dream. Words are simply insufficient to express my love and gratitude. These two will always have front row seats in my heart.

But most of all, if there is anything good or right or true or noble or beautiful or admirable in this book, all credit belongs to my Lord, Jesus Christ. I cannot recount how often I despaired over this story, aggravated by that internal critic berating me to "grow up" and "be realistic." Nor can I number the times I sat down to write, looked at the page, and thought, "I have nothing. I'm completely empty." Yet my Lord graciously came beside me day after day, week after week, silencing the critic, stilling my fears, providing words and ideas, building a story I never expected. (Obviously, for my simple stand-alone novel somehow became a trilogy!)

To You, O Lord, I bow and return this gift.

May it be pleasing to You.

About the Author

Chawna Schroeder is a Minnesotan writer who enjoys snow, chai tea, and playing "what if?"—even if that game occasionally gets her into trouble. She also loves stretching both her imagination and her faith to their limits and helping others do the same. As a result, her writing explores the wonder of God, His multifaceted nature, and the potential of a life lived with Him. This means both learning boundaries He created for our protection as well as demolishing the human boxes that restrict both God and people.

When she isn't reading or writing, a variety of other activities fill her "free" time: practicing piano, preparing Bible study lessons, studying the biblical languages, or working on one of her handwork projects while enjoying a movie.

Chawna's other books include *Beast,* a coming-of-age fairy tale, and *The Vault Between Spaces*, a fantasy with a Cold-War vibe. You can connect with Chawna through her website (www.chawnaschroeder.com) or Facebook (www.facebook.com/ChawnaSchroederAuthor/).

ALSO FROM CHAWNA SCHROEDER

The Vault Between Spaces

In a prison no one escapes, Oriel's defiance may spark the resistance against an unstoppable evil.

www.enclavepublishing.com

ALSO FROM CHAWNA SCHROEDER

BEAST

A powerful tale of truth and transformation
for anyone who has faced the monster within.

www.enclavepublishing.com